NIGHT OF KNIVES

NIGHT OF KNIVES

A NOVEL OF THE MALAZAN EMPIRE

Ian C. Esslemont

A Tom Doherty Associates Book

New York

NIGHT OF KNIVES: A NOVEL OF THE MALAZAN EMPIRE

Copyright © 2005 by Ian Cameron Esslemont

Introduction copyright © 2005 by Steven Erikson

Maps © Neil Gower

Previously published in the UK in 2005 by PS Publishing LLP and in 2007 by Bantam Press, a division of Transworld Publishers.

A Tor Book
Published by Tom Doherty Associates, LLC
175 Fifth Avenue
New York, NY 10010

www.tor-forge.com

Tor® is a registered trademark of Tom Doherty Associates, LLC.

Library of Congress Cataloging-in-Publication Data

Esslemont, Ian C. (Ian Cameron)
    Night of knives : a novel of the Malazan Empire / Ian C. Esslemont.—1st U.S. ed.
        p. cm.
    "A Tom Doherty Associates book."
    ISBN-13: 978-0-7653-2371-2 (trade pbk.)
    ISBN-10: 0-7653-2371-0 (trade pbk.)
    ISBN-13: 978-0-7653-2369-9 (hardcover)
    ISBN-10: 0-7653-2369-9 (hardcover)
    I. Title.
PS3605.S684N54 2009
813'.6—dc22
                                                            2009001517

First U.S. Edition: May 2009

Printed in the United States of America

0 9 8 7 6 5 4 3 2 1

This novel is dedicated to
Steve
who made the world real

ACKNOWLEDGEMENTS

This work's long journey from conception to print has been full of aid from many unexpected directions. It grew out of a collaboration of many years' standing with Steven Erikson that continues to be rich and rewarding, creatively and in friendship. To him must go my greatest thanks for our partnership in creating the world of Malaz. I would also like to thank Simon Taylor for his generosity of spirit, William Thompson for his encouragement and editing skills, my agent, John Jarrold, and Gerri Brightwell for her long-standing support and insightful comments. And finally, extraordinary thanks to Peter Crowther for taking a chance on an unknown.

INTRODUCTION

THE WORLD OF MALAZ WAS BORN IN 1982, AND FROM THAT moment onward that world's history slowly took shape. On summer archaeological digs and winters spent in Victoria, B.C., in the midst of degrees in Creative Writing, in Winnipeg and on Saltspring Island – wherever Ian (Cam) Esslemont and I crossed paths for any length of time. We were co-writers on a number of feature film scripts, and it was clear that our individual creativities were complementary, and during our breaks from writing we gamed in the world of Malaz.

When the notion of writing fiction set in that world was first approached, it seemed obvious that we would divvy up the vast history we had fashioned over the years. And so we did. Since the publication of *Gardens of the Moon*, I have heard from and read of fans wanting to know about the old empire, the empire of the Emperor, Kellanved, and his cohort, Dancer. And time and again I was asked: will you ever write of those early times in the empire's history? Or, will you write about The Crimson Guard? And I have always been firm in my reply: no. The reason should now be obvious.

This is a huge imaginary world, too big for a single writer to manage in a lifetime. But two writers . . . that's different. The dedication in *Gardens of the Moon* was to Ian C. Esslemont. *Worlds to conquer, worlds to share.* I do not think I could have made my desire, and intent, more clear. Granted, it has taken a while for this, Cam's first work set in Malaz, to arrive. Our life journeys diverged for a time, and other demands occupied

Cam – family, postgraduate studies and so on. But I always had faith, was always aware that a surprise and a treat were on their way, and this novel, *Night of Knives*, marks the first instalment of this, the shared world that we had both envisioned years ago.

Night of Knives is not fan fiction. We shaped the world of Malaz through dialogue; our gaming was novelistic and with themes that were, more often than not, brutally tragic. At other times there was comedy, usually of the droll variety. We duelled each other on understatement and absurdity, and we made it a point to confound the genre's overused tropes. The spirit of that has infused every one of my novels set in the Malazan world. And it infuses Ian Esslemont's writing in the same imaginary world. That being said, the novel in your hands possesses its own style, its own voice. The entire story takes place in the span of a single day and night, and it is exquisite. Readers of my own work will recognize the world, its atmosphere, its darkness; they will see the characters in *Night of Knives* as simply more players woven into the same tangled tapestry, they will see the story as one more blood-stained piece of imagined history. And there's so much more to come.

To this day, we continue to work on the Malazan world's history, poring over its details, confirming the sequence of events, discussing the themes, subtext, and ensuring the consistency of cross-over characters. We hammer away at the timeline and the fates of countless characters, many of whom no one else has met yet. And we discuss deviousness, and as the readers of the *Malazan Book of the Fallen* know, deviousness abounds.

From the beginning of the Malazan series, I was writing to an audience of one – Cam. And he has reciprocated. Thus, the dialogue continues; only now there are others, and they are listening in. Finally, to both sides of the conversation.

We hope it proves entertaining.

Steven Erikson
Winnipeg, Canada, 2004

NIGHT OF KNIVES

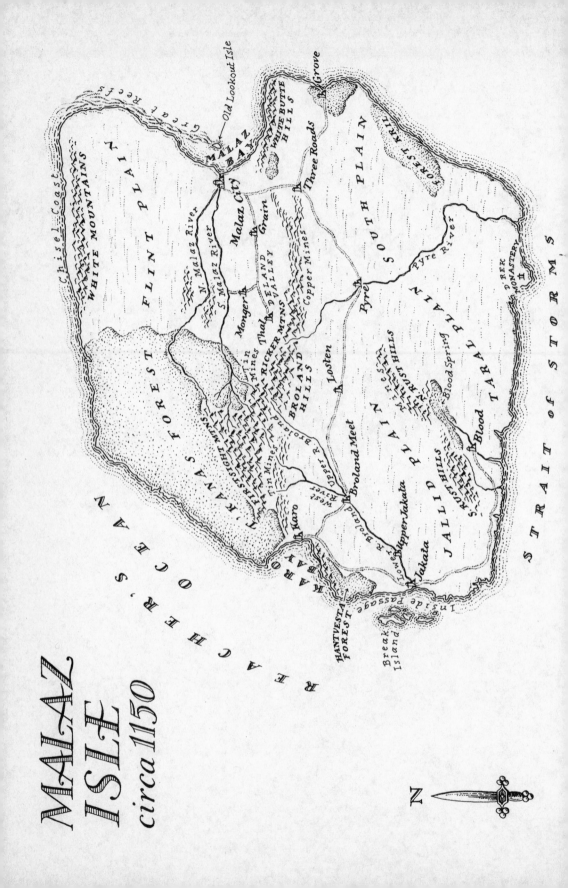

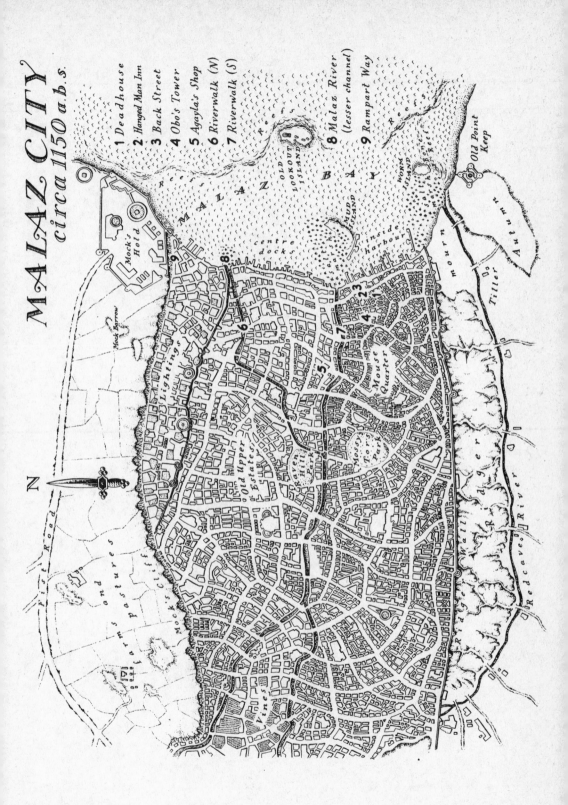

MALAZ CITY
circa 1150 a.b.s.

1 Deadhouse
2 Hanged Man Inn
3 Back Street
4 Obo's Tower
5 Agayla's Shop
6 Riverwalk (N)
7 Riverwalk (S)
8 Malaz River
  (lesser channel)
9 Rampart Way

N

MALAZ BAY

Reefs
Reefs
Reefs
Reefs

OLD LOOKOUT ISLAND
MUD ISLAND
WORM ISLAND
Walsh Rock

centre docks
Insside harbour

Mock's Hold

Mock Barrow

Lightings

Old Upper Estate

Craen Hill Park

Mossy Tops Park

Mouse Quarter

Mock's Cliff

Vines

Farms and pastures

Fisher Road

Old Point Keep

mourn

Tiller Autumn

Ridge Watch

Redcaveo River

DRAMATIS PERSONAE

THE MALAZANS
Emperor Kellanved, absent ruler of the Malazan Empire
Dancer, Master-Assassin and bodyguard to Kellanved
Surly, Mistress of the Imperial assassin corps, the Claw
Tayschrenn, Imperial High Mage
Temper, a Malazan soldier
Corinn, a mage, member of the Bridgeburner Brigade
Ash, an ex-officer of the Bridgeburner Brigade
Seal, a one-time Malazan army healer
Dassem Ultor, Champion and 'First Sword' of the Empire
Chase, an officer of the garrison at Mock's Hold
Hattar, bodyguard to Tayschrenn
Ferrule, member of Dassem's bodyguard, the Sword
Possum, an imperial assassin, Claw

INHABITANTS OF MALAZ ISLE
Coop, proprietor of the Hanged Man Inn
Anji, servitor at the Hanged Man Inn
Kiska, a youth hoping to enter Imperial service
Lubben, gatekeeper at Mock's Hold
Fisherman, a mage of Malaz Isle
Agayla, spice dealer and mage of Malaz Isle
Trenech, regular at the Hanged Man Inn
Faro Balkat, regular at the Hanged Man Inn
Obo, a mage of Malaz Isle

OTHERS

Edgewalker, elder inhabitant of the Shadow Realm
Jhedel, a prisoner of the Shadow Realm
Oleg Vikat, a scholar of the Warrens
Surgen Ress, last Holy City champion
Pralt, a leader of the shadow cult
Jhenna, Jaghut guardian of the Dead House

PROLOGUE

Sea of Storms south of Malaz Isle
Season of Osserc
1154th Year of Burn's Sleep
96th Year of the Malazan Empire
Last Year of Emperor Kellanved's Reign

THE TWO-MASTED RAIDER *RHENI'S DREAM* RACED NORTH-east under full straining sails. Captain Murl gripped the stern railing and watched the storm close upon his ship. Pushed to its limit, the hull groaned ominously while the ropes skirled high notes Murl had never heard.

The storm had swelled like a wall of night out of the south, a solid front of billowing black clouds over wind-lashed waves. But it was not the storm that worried Captain Murl, no matter how unnatural its rising; *Rheni's Dream* had broached the highest seas known to Jakatan pilots, from the northern Sea of Kalt to the driving trade winds of the Reach south of Stratem. No, what sank fingers of dread into his heart were the azure flashes glinting like shards of ice amid the waves at the base of the churning cloud-front. No one told of seeing them this close. None who returned.

Riders, Murl and his fellow pilots called them. Sea-demons and Stormriders to others. Beings of sea and ice who claimed

1

this narrow cut as their own and suffered no trespass. Only his Jakatan forbears knew the proper offerings to bribe the swiftest passage south of Malaz Isle. Why then did the Riders pursue? What could entice them this far north?

Murl turned his back to the punishing wind. His cousin, Lack-eye, fought to control the helm, his legs splayed, arms quivering at the tiller's broad wheel. As the ship canted forward into a trough, Murl tightened his grip against the fall and booming impact. 'Did we forget any of the offerings?' he shouted over the roar of the wind.

Gaze fixed ahead to the bows, Lack-eye shook his head. 'None,' he called. 'We've tried 'em all.' He glared over his shoulder with a pale blue eye. 'All save the last.'

Murl flinched away. He drew himself amidships hand over hand along the guide ropes. Already the deck lay treacherous beneath a sheet of ice. Wind-driven rime as sharp as needles raised blood on his neck and hands. *All save the last.* But that rite he'd never enact. Why, in Chem's cold embrace – every soul on the *Rheni* was blood-kin to him! Murl remembered the one time he'd witnessed that rite: the poor lad's black-haired head bobbing atop the waves, pale arms clawing desperately at the water. He shuddered from the cold and something worse. No, that he could not bring himself to do.

Murl crouched next to a slim figure lashed to the mainmast, slumped as if asleep. With a hand numb from the freezing salt-spume, he reached out to caress a pale cheek. *Ah Rheni dear, I'm so sorry. It was just too much for you. Who could possibly hope to soothe a storm such as this?*

Ice crackled next to Murl as his first mate, Hoggen, thumped against the mast and wrapped an arm about it. 'Shall I break out the weapons?'

Murl choked down a maniacal urge to laugh. He peered keenly at Hoggen to see if the man were serious. Sadly, it appeared he was. Frost shone white in his beard and his eyes were flat and dull. It was as if the fellow were already dead. Murl groaned within. 'Go ahead, if you must.' He squinted up to the mast top. A shape straddled the crossbar there, at mast and spur. Something glinted over his trousers, shirt, and arms: a layer of entombing ice. 'And get young Mole down from there.'

'The lad won't answer. I think the cold's done for him.'

Murl closed his eyes against the spray, hugged the mast.

'We're slowing,' Hoggen observed in a toneless voice.

Murl barely heard him through the wind. He could feel his soaked clothes draining the life warmth from him. He shuddered uncontrollably. 'Ice at the sails. They'll tear soon.'

'Have to hammer it. Knock it off.'

'Try all you like.'

Coughing hoarsely, Hoggen laboured to pull away from the mast. Murl held to. It was fitting, he decided, that he should meet his end here, with Rheni, on the ship he'd named in her honour. Why, he was virtually surrounded by family; even loyal plodding Hoggen was related by marriage. Murl glanced down. How he ached to stroke the long black hair that shivered and jingled now like a fistful of icicles.

'Rider hard a-port!' came a shout. Dazed, Murl was surprised that a crewman remained aware enough to raise the hail. He swung his gaze there, squinting through spume spraying high above the gunwales.

Waves twice the height of the masts rolled past, foaming with ice and rime. Then Murl saw it, a dazzling sapphire figure breaching the surface: helmed, armoured, a tall lance of jagged ice couched at the hip. Its mount seemed half beast and half roiling wave. He fancied it turned a dark inscrutable gaze his way through cheekguards of frozen scale. Then, just as suddenly, the Rider dived, returning to the churning sea. Murl was reminded of blue gamen whales leaping before the prow. Another broached the surface further out. Then another. They rode the waves abreast of *Rheni's Dream* yet seemed oblivious to it. Were they men or the ancient Jaghut race, as some claimed? He watched feeling oddly detached, as if this were all happening to someone else.

A crewman, Larl, steadied himself at the railing and raised a crossbow at the nearest Rider. The quarrel shot wildly astray. Murl shook his head – what was the use? They were dead already. There was nothing they could do. Then, remembering the sternchaser scorpion, he tore himself from the mast and lurched sternward. Lack-eye still stood rigid at the wheel, arms wide, staring ahead. Murl wrapped one numbed arm around the pedestalled weapon and seized the crank. The iron bit at his flesh as if red-hot, tearing patches of skin from his palm as he fought the mechanism.

'What do they want?' Murl called to Lack-eye. Tears froze in his eyes, blinding him. The scorpion wouldn't budge. He pulled his hand free of the searing iron. Blood froze like tatters of red cloth. Lack-eye did not respond; did not even turn. Throwing himself to the wheel, Murl thrust an arm through the spokes.

Lack-eye would never answer again. Standing rigid at the wheel of *Rheni's Dream*, the helmsman stared straight ahead into the gathering night, his one remaining eye white with frost. His shirt and trousers clattered in the wind, frozen as hard as sheets of wood.

Horrified, Murl stared, and in Lack-eye's indifferent gaze, directed ahead to unknown distances, he had his answer. The Riders cared nothing for them. They were here for another reason, answering some inhuman summons, heaving themselves northward, an invading army throwing its might against the one thing that had confined them so long to this narrow passage: the island of Malaz.

The ship groaned like a tortured beast. Its prow heaved, ice-heavy, submerging beneath a wave. The blow shocked

4

Murl from his grip at the wheel. When the spray cleared Lack-eye remained alone to pilot the frozen tomb northwards. Sails fell, stiff, and shattered to the decks. Ice layered the masts and decking, binding the ship like a dark heart within a frozen crag that rushed on groaning and swelling.

Still the storm coursed northward like a horizon-spanning tidal bore. From its gloom emerged a flotilla of emerald mountains etched by deep crevasses, the snow at their peaks gleaming in the last light.

Like unstoppable siege engines constructed to humble continents, they surged onward. At their flanks the Riders lunged forward, lances raised, pointing north.

A PATH WITHIN SHADOW

A FEEBLE WIND MOANED OVER A VAST PLAIN OF HARDPAN sands scattered with black volcanic rocks where dust-devils danced and wandered. They raised ochre plumes then faded to nothing only to suddenly swirl into existence elsewhere. Across the plain, all directions stretching to a featureless horizon, identical, monotonous, a figure hitched a cripple's slow limp.

Like a playful follower, a whirlwind lurched upon the figure, engulfing it in a swirling winding-sheet of umber dust. The figure walked on without flinching, without raising a hand or turning its head. The dust-dervish spun on and away, scudding an aimless spiral route. The figure tramped a straight path, its twisted right leg gouging the sand with every step.

It wore the tattered remains of what might have once been thick cloth over armour of leather and scale. Its naked arms hung desiccated and cured to little more than leather-clad bones. Within a bronze and verdigrised helm, its face disclosed only empty pits, nose a gaping cavern, lips dried and withdrawn from caried teeth. A rust-bitten sword hung across its back.

Far in the distance a dark smudge appeared, but the figure continued its laboured march, on and on under a sky that remained hazy and dim, where shapes resembling birds swept

7

high into the clouds. Only once did the figure halt. Glancing to one side, it stood for a moment, motionless. Far off, the horizon had altered. A pale silver light glowed over darkest blue like the mirage of distant mountains. The figure stared, then moved on.

The distant smudge became a mound, and the mound a menhir. The figure limped directly to the foot of a blade of granite twice its height and stopped. It waited, facing the menhir while the dust-devils criss-crossed the plain. Vertical striations gouged the stone like the claw marks of some ferocious beast. Spiralling down and around the stone wound silver hair-fine symbols. Stiffly, the figure knelt to peer more closely, not at the glyphs but at a shape of brown and mahogany hunched at the menhir's base.

The hump shifted, raised a hairless head of chitinous scales. Almond eyes of burning gold nictitated to life. A broad chest of angular plates swelled with breath.

'Still with us after all, Jhedel,' observed the crouched figure. Its voice was the dry breath of the tomb. It straightened.

'Nice to see you too, Edgewalker.'

Edgewalker half turned away, examined the plain through empty sockets, staring out to the silver and blue bruising.

Jhedel rolled its head, grunted. It stretched out one leg of armoured plates and lethal horned spurs, flexed its broad shoulders. It tensed and heaved to rise, but failed. Its arms disappeared behind its back, sunk up to the wrists in the naked granite of the menhir.

'What brings you round?'

Edgewalker turned back. 'Has anything passed by, Jhedel?'

Jhedel's yellow fangs flashed in what might have been quiet humour. 'Wind. Dust. Time.'

'I ask because something's coming. I can sense it. Have you . . .'

The amber eyes narrowed. 'You know this small circle is my world now. Have you come to taunt?'

'You know I am bound just as tightly.'

Jhedel looked Edgewalker up and down. 'Not from where I'm sitting. Poor Edgewalker. Moaning his enslavement. Yet here you were long before the ones I slew to take the Throne. And here you remain after those who bound me in turn are long gone and forgotten. I've heard things about you ... rumours.'

'The power I sense is new,' Edgewalker said, as if the other had not spoken at all.

'Something new?'

'Very possibly.'

Jhedel frowned as if unsure what to make of new. 'Testing the Realm?'

'Yes. What do you make of it?'

Raising his head, Jhedel sniffed the air through slit nostrils. 'Something with a heart of ice and something else ... something sly, hidden, like a blurry reflection.'

'Eyeing the Throne I think.'

Jhedel snorted. 'Not likely. Not after all this time.'

'A Conjunction approaches. I am for the House. There might be an attempt upon it. Who knows – perhaps you will be released.'

'*Released?*' Jhedel snapped. 'I will show you my release.' He drew his legs up under his haunches, strained upwards; his clawed feet sank into the dust. His shoulders shook. The chitinous plates of his arms creaked and groaned.

For a time nothing seemed to happen. Edgewalker watched, silent. Dust drifted from the chiselled sides of the menhir. It appeared to vibrate. A burst of silver light atop the monolith dazzled Edgewalker. It spun like lightning down the coil of silver glyphs, flashing, gathering speed and size as it descended until Edgewalker averted his face from its searing fire.

9

Jhedel gave a mad cackle. 'Here it comes,' he shouted over the waterfall roar of swelling, coalescing power.

The ball of power smashed into Jhedel, who shrieked. The land buckled. Edgewalker was thrown from his feet. Dust and sand eddied lazily in the weak wind. When it cleared, Jhedel lay motionless, sprawled at the menhir's base. Smoke drifted from the slits of his eyes and slack jaws.

Edgewalker's fleshless face remained fixed. He was silent for a time, then he rose to a crouch. 'Jhedel? Can you hear me! Jhedel?'

Jhedel groaned.

'Do you remember?'

Prone, the creature nodded thoughtfully. 'Yes. That is my name. Jhedel.' He shrugged in the dust.

'Do you remember who bound you?'

'Whoever they were, they are long gone now.'

'I remember them. They were—'

'Don't tell me!' Jhedel kicked himself upright. 'I want to remember. It gives me something to do. Wait . . . I remember something . . .' He thrashed his legs away from Edgewalker, hissed out a breath: 'A rumour about you!'

Edgewalker took a few limping steps from the menhir.

After a moment Jhedel called, 'Come back. Please. Release me. It's within your power. I know it is!'

Edgewalker did not reply. He walked on.

'Release me, damn you! You must! . . *Damn you!*'

Jhedel wrenched savagely on his arms. Dust flew like a scarf from the menhir. Through the dust the glyphs glowed like finest filigree heated to burning.

'I will destroy you!' Jhedel bellowed. 'You and all those who've come after! Everyone!'

It twisted again, screamed out its rage and pain. As the ground lurched Edgewalker tottered. He glanced back to the menhir. Something flailed and heaved amid a cloud of kicked up dirt at its base. A plume of dust climbed into the sky.

Edgewalker continued on. He was late, and time and the celestial dance of realms waited for no one. Not even entities as insane and potent as the one pinned behind him. When they conversed during more lucid moments, it could remember its full name, Jhe' Delekaaran, and that it had once commanded this entire realm as King. Liege to the Que'tezani, inhabitants of the most distant regions of Shadow. And mad though he may be, Jhedel was right in one thing: it had been long since the Throne last held an occupant. With the coming of each conjunction, this absence worried Edgewalker. But this time what intrigued him most was something so rare he'd almost failed to recognize it . . . the coiled potential for change.

CHAPTER ONE

PORTENTS AND ARRIVALS

OUT AMID THE CHOPPING WAVES OF THE STRAIT OF WINDS, the sails of an approaching message cutter burned bloody carmine in the day's last light. Temper set his spear against the battlement wall of Mock's Hold and looked out over the edge of the stone crenel. A hundred fathoms below, the cliff swept down into froth and a roll of breakers. He glanced over his shoulder to the grey barrel wall of the inner keep: its slit windows shone gold. Shadows moved within.

He muttered into the wind, 'Trapped between Hood and the damned Abyss.'

What could there possibly be for an Imperial official – a woman, an Imperial Fist – at this backwater post? He nearly jumped the first ship out when she'd arrived on the island three days ago. But he'd managed to drown that urge in the dark ale at Coop's Hanged Man Inn. None of this, he told himself, over and over, had anything more to do with him.

He stretched and winced. The surprisingly chill evening had revived the twinge of an old back injury: a javelin thrust many years past. A Seven City skirmisher had ruined the best hauberk he'd ever owned, as well as come damned close to killing him. The wound had never healed right. Perhaps it was time again to see that young army medicer, Seal. He scratched his chin and wondered whether it was bad luck to recall death's brush when the sun was lowering. He'd ask Corinn if he saw her.

Just three days ago he'd stood with hundreds of others at the harbour wall to watch the Imperial official disembark. Cries of surprise had run up and down the streets as first light revealed the blue-black sails and equally dark-tarred hull of a Malazan man-of-war anchored in the bay. Only too well did men and women of the city remember their last visitors: elements of the Third Army rendezvousing with recruits and enforcing the Imperial Regent's new edict against magery. The riots that followed engulfed a quarter of the town in flames.

News of the ship's arrival had drawn Temper up the narrow staircase at Coop's. Finished shaving, he'd tossed a towel over his shoulder and ambled down to Front Way. He squinted between warehouses to the harbour and the bay beyond. Anji, Coop's serving-girl and sometime mistress, came labouring up the Way carrying twin buckets of water. She lowered them to the cobbles, pushed her long brown hair from her flushed face and scowled in the harbour's direction. 'Gods, what is it now?'

Temper frowned. 'A man-of-war. Front-line vessel. Built for naval engagements, convoy escort, blockades. Not your usual troop transport or merchant scow.' *And what in the name of Togg's teats was it doing here?*

'Must be on its way south to Korel,' said Anji. A hand shading her eyes, she turned her gaze to him. 'You know, the war and all that.'

Temper hawked up a wad of phlegm and spat to one side. No one would order a man-of-war down to Korel all on its lonesome. And – from what he'd heard – Hood knew it would take more than one warship to turn the tide down south.

Skiffs bobbed into view out from the wharf. Long sweeps powered them across to the enormous vessel. Temper guessed the garrison commander, Pell, of honorary Sub-Fist rank himself, might be floundering seasick in one of them. He took a deep breath of the chill morning air. 'Guess I'll have a look.'

Anji again pushed back her long hair. 'Why bother? For certain it means more of our blood spilled.' She hefted the buckets. 'As if we haven't paid enough.'

The harbour view proved no more enlightening. At the warehouse district, Temper overheard whispers that the vessel must hold a new garrison commander, or that the Hold was being re-activated as command base for a new campaign against Korel. But he also heard the opposite: that the vessel carried Imperial Command from Korel, in full retreat. One old fisherman voiced the opinion that it might be the Emperor himself, returned. Men and women raised their hands in signs against evil and edged away. The fisherman lent Temper a wink.

Boxed cargo appeared at the vessel's high side and the crew lowered it into skiffs that rocked along its skirts like water bugs around a basking sea beast. Rumour of retreat from Korel was of interest. Word from the south was one of ferocious local resistance, casualty rates high enough for official denial, and almost no advances made since the initial landings half a decade ago.

At other campaigns on continents far away Temper had travelled on ships identical to this. All carried the emblem on this one's sails, the upright three-clawed sceptre gripping the Imperial orb. He'd witnessed port assaults during which these orbs glowed like pale suns, blasting walls and mole defences into rubble. During deep-sea engagements the orbs boiled

15

waves, burst hulls into flame, and lashed summoned sea-demons.

Perhaps this vessel had returned from warfare at such a front. Korel was reputedly a series of archipelagos in which naval forces would make or break any campaign. That would explain its appearance here.

The first of the skiffs returned to the military wharf beneath Mock's Hold. They carried personnel only. Dark and richly cloaked figures stepped onto floating docks. Temper's eyes narrowed as he watched the men and women, hoods over heads, file from sight among the defences. He did not like the look of this – not at all. These figures were all too familiar in their dark leather boots and gloves. With a sick feeling in his gut, Temper remembered another garrison where vessels such as this could be found: at Unta across the strait; the Imperial capital.

The fisherman had lifted his chin towards the wharf. 'Y'see? I was right.' And he cackled hoarsely, then hacked into his fist.

Now, as he shivered in the cold evening air, Temper remembered watching that man-of-war and wondering: were they here for him? Had they tracked him three thousand leagues? If so, they were making quite a show of it. And that was, all things considered, careless.

Up on the battlements, the bell ending the day and Temper's watch rang brassy and deep from Mock's Tower. On its pike at Temper's side, Mock's Vane, the winged demon-shaped weathervane, shook and hummed as if caught in a steady gale. Temper frowned at the old relic; the winds were calm this evening.

Moments later he heard his superior, Lieutenant Chase, come tramping up the rampart steps. He sighed at the heavy measured pace. One of these days someone was going to have to take the young pup aside and explain that he wasn't marching up and down the parade ground anymore. Still, being as green as a spring shoot also meant being punctual – *and the long afternoon does dry a man's throat.*

Chase stopped directly behind. Temper ignored him. He listened to the surf, watched a lithe message cutter swoop like a gull across the whitecaps dangerously windward of the reefs at Old Lookout Isle. Wind-talent drove that navigation. That or a fiend-driven helmsman in an unholy rush to meet Hood.

A sword point dug into the small of his back. 'Turn for recognition, soldier.'

'Recognition? Chase, sometimes I wish we'd never met.' Temper turned and planted his elbows on the gritty limestone crenel.

Chase sheathed his sword and straightened to proper parade ground angle. Tall feathers of some colourful bird fluttered at the peak of his iron helm. The brass and copper gilding on the breastplate of his cuirass gleamed, freshly polished. The youth's leather boots alone looked to be worth more than Temper made in a year, and he looked down at his own patched open sandals, ragged cloth wrapping his legs, and the threadbare black and gold surcoat of a Malazan garrison regular.

'Start acting the part of a real guard, old man,' Chase warned. 'At least while the official's here. D'rek's mysteries, man. I might've been – what is it? – *one of her own.*' He glanced up to the keep. 'They would've handed you your heart as a warning.'

Temper stiffened at *her own.* Where had the lad picked that up? It'd been a long time since he last heard that old term for the Imperial security cadre, the Claws. Of course an Imperial Fist would have a detachment of Claws – for protection, intelligence gathering, and darker, unsavoury tasks. Sidelong, he studied the lieutenant and wondered: had that been a probe? But the youth's clear brown eyes and smooth cheeks behind his helmet's face-guards appeared no more capable of deceit than a clear grassland stream. Temper recovered, bit down on his paranoia, and thanked the twin gods of luck that Chase had missed it.

He spat onto the crumbling limestone blocks. 'First of all, lad, I heard you coming. And no one ever hears *them*. And second, when they do come,' Temper tapped a finger to his flattened nose, 'you can always tell by the stench.'

Chase snorted his disbelief. 'Gods, greybeard. I've heard talk of all the damned action you must've seen, but don't pretend those Claws don't curdle your blood.'

Temper ground his teeth together and quelled an urge to cuff the youth. But what could this pup know of things that turned the stomachs of even hardened veterans? Temper knew the Seven City campaigns; he'd been there when they took Ubaryd. They'd reached the Palace at night. The marble halls had been deserted but for the corpses of functionaries and guards too slow to flee the Emperor's smashing of the Falah'd's power. Upstairs they found the private chambers and the Holy One herself tied by silk ropes to a chair. Three Claws stood about her, knives out. Blood gleamed wetly on the blades and dripped from the moist bonds at the Falah'd's wrists and ankles, pooled on the coral marble. He and Point had held back, unsure, but Dassem surged ahead and thrust aside the Claw standing before the woman. Her head snapped up, long curls flying back, and though her eyes had been gouged out and her mouth hung open, tongueless, blood streaming down her chin, she seemed to address Dassem directly. The Claws, two men and a woman, eyed each other. One backed away, raised his bloodied knife at what he saw in Dassem's gaze. The Falah'd's lips moved silently, mouthing some message or a plea. The female Claw's eyes widened in sudden understanding and she opened her own mouth to shout, but too late. It happened so quickly it was as if Dassem had merely shrugged. The Falah'd's head spun away. Blood jetted from her torso. The head toppled to the marble flagging. Its long black curls tangled in blood as it rolled.

Though Temper couldn't be sure, it seemed the words she mouthed had been *free me*. Thus the end of the last Holy Falah'd of Ubaryd.

Temper rubbed the sickle moon scar that curved down his left temple to his chin and breathed deeply to calm himself. He forced himself to think of what Chase must see when looking at him: a broken-down veteran too incompetent or sodden to have passed corporal's rank in a lifetime of soldiering. This was, after all, exactly the role he'd created for himself. He said, low and level, 'They only disgust me.'

Chase stared, unsettled by the emotion in Temper's voice, then scowled at the implied criticism of the Imperial Throne. He pointed to a corner barbican. 'You're relieved, old man.'

Off-duty, Temper hung his spear, surcoat, and regulation boiled-leather hauberk in the barracks armoury. He adjusted the rag swathings at his legs, then rewound the leather straps of his military sandals over them.

He searched for his single extravagance, a lined and brushed felt cloak from Falar. It was in the guardroom wadded up on a bench under Larkin's wide ass. Seeing that, Temper almost turned and walked away. Larkin knew full well when the shift ended and had sat on the cloak as a challenge. Temper had no choice but to respond.

Larkin was holding court around a table, the other guards crowded close, shoulder to shoulder over the unvarnished slats where enamelled tiles – the Bones – lay arrayed in midplay. None paid the game any attention for Larkin was nearing the climax of yet another of his drawn-out stories.

Temper leaned against the squared timber that stood for the

doorjamb, crossing his arms. Here was Larkin, only a month back from the Genabackan front, rotated out to garrison duty on a leg wound, and Temper believed he could already recite every one of the man's engagements.

'It was in Black Dog Forest,' he drawled, dragging out the tale – clearly one of his favourites. The guards nodded, waiting, knowing what was to come, yet still savouring the anticipation.

'The Crimson Guard . . .'

The troops, young and impatient with a garrison posting so far from any action, eyed one another. Some shook their heads in awe. Even Temper had to admit he felt it – a shiver of recognition and dread at the name. The mercenary company sworn to destroy the Empire. The force that had handed Malaz its first major defeat by repulsing the invasion of Stratem, and which now opposed the Empire on four continents.

'Who'd you see?' asked one guard, Cullen, island born, who claimed to have pirated off the Stratem coast in his youth. Larkin nodded, as did Temper. It was a good question, one asked by those who knew enough to ask.

Larkin cleared his throat, eased back into his story: 'Was a general advance; a push to prise them out of the forest and open a road south to the Rhivi Plain. The commander, a Sub-Fist nobleman out of Dal Hon, had us in three columns to stretch them thin – superior numbers you see. The Guard was fleshed out by local recruits, Genabackan tribals called Barghast, townsmen, militia, foresters and other such trash. Daytime was fine, an easy campaign. For five days we advanced while they melted before us. So much for the invincible Guard! Of course a few Barghast and woodsmen potshot at us over stream crossings and uneven ground, but they ran away like cowards whenever we counterattacked. Then came the sixth night . . .'

Temper could only shake his head at the staggering stupidity of an advance by columns into unsecured deep forest. Of course they were allowed to advance. Of course the Guard, outnumbered, avoided any direct engagement. And finally, once the columns were isolated, far enough apart to prevent any hope of possible reinforcement, the attack had come.

The guards nodded their outrage at this shameful strategy and Temper wanted to shout: don't listen to the damned fool! But he was a minority of one. Though a pompous ass, Larkin was popular, had seen recent action in distant lands and enjoyed being the centre of attention. Temper knew that the younger guards didn't like or understand his silence, and that because of it some even doubted he had any experience to speak of. Any complaint from him would be dismissed as sour grumbling.

'They attacked at night like plain thieves,' Larkin spat, disgusted by such underhanded tactics.

Temper stopped himself from laughing out loud – well did he remember similar moonlit engagements, but with the Malazans themselves the attackers!

'Was utter chaos. Screaming Barghast leaping out of the darkness. They were behind us, in front of us, circling our flanks. We were totally surrounded. There was nowhere to go. I joined a knot of men at a tall boulder lit by the light of brush fires. Together we held a perimeter, wounded at our rear. We repulsed three Barghast assaults.'

Larkin coughed into his fist, scowled, then fell silent. Temper gave him a hard look. Was it the horror, the memory of lost friends? Then why so eager to drag out the yarn every other night?

'I saw three Guardsmen in the distance, through the undergrowth. I didn't recognize any of them. Then Halfdan jogged past. I knew him by his size – half indeed!'

The guards chuckled at this cue. 'Once served under Skinner, they say,' added Cullen.

Larkin nodded.

'Then another Guardsman came out of the night. I'll never forget the way he stepped from the darkness . . . like some fiend out of Hood's own Paths. His surcoat shone in the flames like fresh blood. Lazar it was, with his visored helm and black shield. We fought, but it was no use . . .' Larkin slapped his game leg and shook his head.

Temper threw himself from the room. He cooled the back of his neck against the damp stone wall. Fener's bones! The lying bastard. Fought Lazar! Temper himself had never faced the Guard but Dassem had clashed with them for decades – and that alone was enough to give anyone pause regarding their prowess. Dassem never spoke of those engagements. It was said the Avowed were unstoppable, but Dassem had slain every one who had challenged him: Shirdar, Keal, Bartok. Only Skinner, they say, had come away alive from their clash.

Laughter brought Temper's attention around. The carved tiles of the Bones clacked against wood. He took a long breath, stepped back inside.

'Larkin. You're on my cloak.'

Larkin looked up, tapped a tile against the table. He hooked one beefy arm over the shoulder rest, gestured to the table where the tiles lay like a confused map of flagged paths. The paint of their symbols were chipped, the tiles soiled by generations of soldiers' grimy fingers.

'I'm playing,' he grunted, and lowered his head.

'Just raise your fat ass so I can get my cloak.'

Larkin didn't answer. Two of the guards shrugged, pursed their lips and glanced their apologies to Temper. Larkin set his tile down by pressing it in place with the end of one thick finger. Temper strode foreword and plucked it from the table. Five sets of eyes followed Temper's hand then swung back to Larkin.

Larkin let out his own version of a long-suffering sigh. 'Don't you know it's bad luck to disrupt a game?'

Their eyes met. It was clear that the fool meant to put him, the only other veteran here, in his place. He'd been avoiding the man for just this very reason: questions of where he'd fought and with whom were the last he wanted to answer. He'd been doing his best to stay anonymous, but this was too much to stomach. He couldn't have this ass lording it over him like a barracks bully.

'Give me the damn piece,' Larkin said, and he edged himself back from the table. 'Or I'll have to take it from you, old-timer.'

The guards lost their half-smiles, dropped their amused glances. One blew out a breath as if already regretting what was about to happen. Temper thrust out his hand, the tile in his open palm. 'Take it.' A part of him, the part Temper hadn't heard in a year, urged the man on. *Try it*, the voice urged, smooth and edged at the same time. *Just try it.*

Larkin's eyes, small and hidden in his wide face, shifted about the room as if wondering what was going on, just who was joking whom. This clearly wasn't going the way he'd imagined. But then he shrugged his round shoulders, and in the way his lips drew down, confident and bored, Temper saw the reaction of a man far too full of himself to listen to anyone.

Shaking his head as if at the senile antics of the aged, Larkin reached for the tile, but Temper snatched his wide wrist and squeezed. The tile clattered to the table.

Larkin jerked as if bit by a serpent. His lips clenched in surprise and pain. The guards caught their breath. Larkin tried yanking back his arm. It didn't move.

Temper smiled then at Larkin, and the man must've read something in that grin because his free hand went to the dirk at his waist. The short-bladed knife shot up from the table and Temper's other hand snapped out and clasped that wrist with a slap.

Larkin's laboured breathing filled the room. The blade

twisted relentlessly to one side, edged its way toward his fore-arm. Panting, face red with effort, he lunged to his feet, the bench slamming backwards. The blade kissed his forearm, began sawing back and forth just up from the wrist. All the while Temper trapped the man's eyes with his. Blood welled up, dripped to the table with quiet pats.

By his wrists, Temper heaved Larkin close, whispered into his ear: 'Lazar would've sliced you open like a pig.'

Hands and arms clasped around Temper. They yanked, urged. The guards shouted but Temper wasn't listening. Larkin threw back his head and roared. Then Temper released him and he stumbled backwards onto the flagged stone floor and sat cradling his arm. The guards pulled Temper into the hall where they whispered their amazement, watching him warily. One slipped a truncheon back into its mounting on the wall.

After a few minutes one came out with Temper's rolled cloak. He heard them whisper how they'd never seen anything like it, but was preoccupied by the awful consequences of what he'd just done. Standing over the table, he'd seen droplets of blood spatter the Bones.

Soldier, Maiden, King, and the rune of the Obelisk. For damn sure that meant a boat full of bad luck about to cross his bow.

As far as Kiska could tell the crew of the message cutter acted as expected during docking: stowing gear, securing the ship against the first chill storm of Osserc's Rule blowing over the island from the south. But details gave them away. Where were the chiding, the complaints, the banter of a crew at port? The eagerness to be ashore? And not one malingered. The hand supposedly doing just that – loitering at the gangway – scanned the wharf with the lazy indifference of a lookout. And she should recognize the pose; she had trained herself in the same posture.

Flat on the deck of the next ship opposite the pier, Kiska rested her chin in one gloved fist and quietly watched. The slightest drizzle was sifting down, slicking hair to her face, but she didn't stir. The men were just killing time: re-coiling ropes, strapping down dunnage. Waiting. Waiting on one person, one action. That meant all worked for the same individual.

Odd. An Imperial message cutter crewed by sailors all of whom appeared to be guards for whoever had commissioned the ship. Kiska had grown up clambering over these wharves. To her such an arrangement smelled of clout, of influence great enough to procure one of these vessels – an accomplishment in itself – topped by the authority to replace the regular crew with his or her own private staff.

The question was what to do about the discovery? She looked to the mottled seaward wall of Mock's Hold rearing above the harbour. Report it to the Claws? Why should she go to them after they'd made it so clear they had no use for her?

She recalled how she'd felt when dawn, just a few days before, had revealed the Imperial warship *Inexorable* anchored in the harbour. It had seemed the most important day of her life, an unlooked-for, and unhoped-for, second chance. But already she felt as if she'd aged a lifetime. No longer the girl who climbed over the tall stone walls enclosing the military wharf; that sneaked up onto the flat roof of a government warehouse to watch the docks. Had she lost something that child possessed? Or gained? A knowledge seared into everyone at some point in their life.

That morning she had watched while the first skiff returned from the ship burdened by seven hooded figures. Imperial officers from the capital, she was sure. From where else could they have come but Unta, across the straits? They clambered to the dock and drew off their travelling cloaks, folding them over arms and shoulders. At first she'd been disappointed: there were merchants in Malaz who dressed more richly than this: plain silk shirts, broad sashes, loose pantaloons. Yet one shorter figure failed to shed its cloak. That one gestured and Kiska thrilled to see the other six spread out. Bodyguards!

Who was this? A new garrison commander? Or an Imperial inspector dispatched from the capital to take Pell to task? If so, gods pity the Sub-Fist for what the officer would find in Mock's Hold: chickens cackling in the bailey, pigs rooting in the cracked and empty reservoir. Kiska eased herself to her haunches as the party took the main route inland, up a gently rising hillside. She vaulted from roof to roof and balanced on the lip of a wall to reach an overlook which the party ought to pass beneath. Gulls exploded from her path, squalled their outrage.

She'd find out. She would present herself to the representative. Offer her services. Perhaps she'd gain a commission. An Imperial official such as this would certainly see that talents such as Kiska's were wasted on this wretched island.

Up the narrow walled road the party approached. Kiska eased herself forward to watch. The first two, a slim man and a heavier woman, walked nonchalantly, hands clasped behind their backs. Kiska spied no weapons. What sort of bodyguards could these be? Aides, perhaps, or clerks. Nobles out for a walk among the rustics. This last thought raised a sour taste in her throat. The shorter figure appeared; hood so large as to hang past the face, hands hidden in long sleeves. Kiska strained to discern some detail from the loose, brushing folds of the cloak – black was it? Or darkest carmine night?

Something yanked her belt from behind, pulling her from her perch. She spun, lips open to yell, but a gloved hand pressed itself to her mouth. She stared up into hazel eyes in a man's face, angular, dark with bluish tones, the tight curls of his hair gleaming in the dawning light. Napan, Kiska realized.

'Who are you?' he asked. Kiska did not recognize him from those who'd disembarked. In fact, she had never seen the man before – and she would have known if one such as this lived on the island.

The hand withdrew. Kiska cleared her throat, swallowed hard. Stunning eyes devoid of expression seemed to look right through her. Eyes like glass.

'I . . . I live here.'

'Yes. And?'

Kiska swallowed again. 'I . . .' Her gaze caught a brooch on the man's left breast, a silver bird's claw gripping a seed pearl. A Claw! Imperial intelligence officers, mages, enforcers of the Emperor's will. This was a greater discovery than she'd imagined. No mere inspection, this. Only the highest-ranking officers rated Claw bodyguards. This visitor might even be an Imperial Fist. 'I meant no harm!' she gasped, and damned herself for sounding so . . . so inexperienced.

The Claw's lips tightened in what Kiska took to be distaste. 'I know you didn't,' and he stepped away. Soundless, she marvelled, even on a broken tiled roof spotted with bird droppings. Then she started, remembering. 'Wait! Sir!'

At the wall's ledge he paused. 'Yes?'

'Please. I want, that is, could I meet him or her – this official?'

The man's hands twitched like wings then settled on the sash at his waist. 'Why?'

Kiska stopped herself from clasping her hands together, took a deep breath. 'I want to be hired. I want a chance. Please. I have talent, really, I do. You'll see. All I need is a chance.'

The Claw's hands slid from his sash, clasped themselves at his back. He gave a one-sided smile that didn't make him look at all amused. 'So. You have *talent*, have you?'

Kiska's heart lurched. She faltered, but stammered on, 'Yes. Yes, I do.'

The Claw shrugged. 'This is a matter for the local commander. A Sub-Fist Pell, I believe. Take it up with him.'

'Yes, I have, but he—'

The man stepped noiselessly off the wall and disappeared. Kiska lunged to the edge. Nothing. A good three man-height's fall to a cobbled road, empty. Kiska's blood surged. She hugged herself, thrilled at the encounter. Amazing. The blunt mottled walls of Mock's Hold beckoned above and she raised her fist.

She'd take it up all right. As high as she could! How could they possibly refuse her?

Crossing the inner bailey of Mock's Hold, Temper shook out his cloak and pulled it over his shoulders. The courtyard was empty. All non-essential personnel had been cleared from the Hold. The guard complement either stood their posts or slept in the barracks. Everyone had been pulling double shifts since the nameless Imperial 'High Official' had arrived. She and her entourage had taken over the top three storeys of the inner keep, evicting the garrison commander, Pell, who now slept in the armoury drinking even more than his usual.

Why the visit? Temper had heard twenty opinions. Talk at the Hanged Man ran to the view that command at Unta was thinking about finally closing down the garrison and abandoning the island to the fishermen, the cliff rookeries, and the seal colony south at Benaress Rocks. In the meantime no extra shifts had been assigned his way. Seniority of age did carry some privileges. He smiled, anticipating an evening sampling Coop's Old Malazan Dark.

At the fortified gatehouse, Lubben, the gatekeeper, limped out of the darkness within. His huge iron ring of keys rattled at his side. The hunch of his back appeared worse than usual, and his one good eye gleamed as he scanned the yard. Temper was about to ask what calamity had shaken him from his usual post snoring by the guardhouse brazier, when a flick of his hand warned him away.

'Gate's closed for the night, soldier.'

'*Soldier?* What's the matter, Lubben? Gone blind from drink?'

Lubben jerked a thumb to the dark corridor at his rear, mouthed something Temper couldn't hear.

'What in the Enchantress's unsleeping eyes is going—' Temper broke off as someone else stepped soundlessly from the shadows. An Imperial Claw in an ankle-length black cloak, hood up. Lubben grimaced, offered Temper a small helpless shrug of apology. The Claw's hood revealed only the lower half of a lined and lean face tattooed with cabalistic characters. Symbols that looked to Temper like the angular script of those who delve the Warren of Rashan, the Path of Darkness. The Claw turned to Lubben.

'Trouble, gatekeeper?'

Lubben bowed deeply. 'No, sir. No trouble at all.'

The hood swung to Temper, who immediately jerked his head down. Perhaps he was being too careful, but the Claw might interpret the act as deference. He'd seen in the past how deference pleased them.

'What do you want, soldier?'

Temper squeezed his belt in both hands until his fingers numbed. Staring at the courtyard flagstones – two broken, four chipped – he began, cautiously. 'Well, sir, I'm pretty much retired from service y'know, and I've a room of my own in town. I was only called up on account of the visit. Extra guards, y'see.'

'Gatekeeper. Do you vouch for this man?'

Lubben flashed Temper a wink. 'Oh, aye, sir. 'Tis as the man says.'

'I see.'

The Claw stepped close. Temper raised his head, but kept his gaze averted. Sidelong, he watched the Claw examine him. The last time he'd stood this close to one of these assassins had been a year ago and that time they'd been trying to kill him.

He'd been prepared then, ready for the fight. All he felt now was shocked amazement at actually having run into one of the official's escorts. Were they out patrolling as Chase suggested? Why this night?

'You're a veteran. Where are your campaign badges?'

'I don't wear them, sir.'

'Ashamed?'

'No, sir. Just consider myself retired.'

'In a hurry to leave Imperial service?'

'No, sir. I've just worked hard for my pension.' Temper took a breath, then hurried on: 'I'm building a boat you see. She's the prettiest thing you'd ever—'

A hand rose from within the cloak to wave silence. 'Very well. Gatekeeper, allow the man to pass.'

'Aye, sir.'

At the far end of the entrance tunnel, Lubben lifted his ring of keys and unlocked the small thieves' door in the main gate. Temper stepped through. Lubben poked his head out after him and grinned lop-sided, 'You never told me you were building yourself a pretty little boat.'

'Kiss Hood, you sawed-off hunchback.'

Laughing silently, Lubben answered with a gesture that needed no words then slammed the door. The lock rattled shut.

Temper started down Rampart Way's steep slope. A staircase cut from the very stone of the cliff, it switched back four times as it descended the promontory's side. Every foot of it lay within range of the Hold's townward springalds and catapults. Above, a cloud front rolled in over the island, massing up from the Sea of Storms. The night looked to be shaping into one to avoid. Island superstition had it that the Stormriders themselves were responsible for the worst of the icy seasonal maelstroms that came raging out of the south.

The cliff rose as a knife-edge demarking the port city of Malaz's northern border. Hugging its base was the Lightings, the rich estate district, taking what security it could from the shadow of the Hold above. South and west the city curved in a jumble of crooked lanes around the river and the marshy shore of Malaz Bay. Inland, modest hills rolled into the distance. Wood smoke drifted low over slate and flint roofs. A few lanterns glowed here and there. A weak drizzle drifted in behind the cloud front, obscuring Temper's view of the harbour. Droplets brushed his neck like cold spit.

Of late the harbour served mainly as a military transit point, yet still retained some trade, a portion of which was even legitimate. All in all it was a lean shadow of what it had been. Deserted houses faced sagging warehouses and tottering, wave-eroded piers. Once home port to a piratical navy, then a thalassocracy, then an empire, the city now seemed crowded more by ghosts than people. It had given the empire its name, but had lost all tactical and strategic value, save as a staging point as the empire's borders swept on to distant seas.

For a time, the Korelan invasion changed that, of course, and the residents had reawakened to renewed promise for the isle. But the campaign had since proven a disaster, an abyss of men and resources best left alone. The city, the island, now carried the haunted feel of a derelict. And thinking of that, Temper realized why this pimple on the backside of the empire should now receive the first message cutter he'd seen here: it was a missive for the official. The machinery of Imperial governance had returned, if ever so briefly, to where it had begun.

At the last switch back, Temper squinted up into the thin rain. Through a gap in the low clouds, Mock's Hold appeared as if it was riding a choppy sea, overbalanced, about to capsize.

Temper rubbed a palm over his close-cropped hair to wipe away the rain and continued on. He wondered if this were a night for spirits even stronger than Coop's Old Malazan Dark.

*

Stretched out on cold ship planks, the memory of those grand dreams so alive just days ago made Kiska once again feel the heat of shame at her cheeks and throat. How childish she'd been! What a fool! Most of all she recalled her idiotic shock, her befuddled, dumb surprise when at the entrance to the Hold another bodyguard – a Claw, no doubt – took her aside by her arm – by her arm! – like a child.

Play elsewhere. We won't be needing your services.

Recounting it over and over was almost enough to make her slam her fist against the decking. But she recovered and bit her lip instead, tasting salty blood on her tongue.

How could they? This was her territory! She'd grown up poking into every building and warehouse in the city. She'd memorized every twist and dead end of the narrow walled ways. Pell had even told her that if he could award commissions he'd have attached her to the garrison as intelligence officer. There was nothing on the island she couldn't steal, had she been so inclined.

Problem was there wasn't a damn thing on the island worth stealing. So she busied herself keeping an eye on the petty thieves and thugs: Spender's outfit that ran the waterfront; the Jakatan pirates who preyed from time to time on coastal shipping. Anyone going to and from the harbour.

She'd simply been brushed aside. Maybe that was what hurt the most. Because it was needless and ill-considered; because she'd actually hoped they might have . . . she stopped herself from thinking through all that again. She couldn't bear to remember her naïve hopes, the things she'd bragged to people. They were indeed Imperial Claws. And escorting what indeed was an Imperial Fist. One of perhaps only a hundred administrators, governors, even generals of the armies.

Kiska clenched her teeth till they hurt. So what if she hadn't graduated from one of those fancy officer schools at Unta, Li Heng, or Tali? So what if she had no access to any Warren magic? She was good enough to get the job done without it. Aunt Agayla had always said she had a natural talent for the work. As good as any intelligence officer, or so Kiska believed.

This official's visit was a Gods-sent second chance, not to be missed, after last year's stop-over of troop transports. Then, while resupplying, the army had enforced the Regent's new edict against magery, and it all had spiralled out of control. Agayla had locked her away, saying it was for her protection, just when her talents and local knowledge could have been of most use. It had been the perfect opportunity for her to prove her value, to catch the attention of someone in authority that would recognize her worth. She had sworn then that she'd never again allow the woman to interfere with her chances to get off the island. Though, as the flames spread and the riots ended in indiscriminate slaughter, she grudgingly allowed that Agayla might well have saved her life. Nevertheless, while everyone else on the island wished the soldiers good riddance, hurrying them on their way with obscenities and curses, Kiska had watched the huge ungainly transports lumber from the bay with a feeling of desolation. At that moment she believed she'd never get off this gaol of an island, despite her talent.

And it was this talent that allowed her to spot the oddity of activity on this message cutter, even if she had to admit that she'd only come down to the harbour to sulk. She'd smelled the action immediately. This *must* bear on the presence of the official. Just a simple message? Why all the secrecy? And how strange that no message – or messenger – had yet to leave the ship. What were they all waiting *for*? Icy droplets tickled Kiska's back but she refused so much as a twitch. The cutter had almost rammed its mooring in its haste to make the harbour and now they just sit—

Ah! Movement. One at a time four of the crew came down the gangway to the pier which stood slightly lower than the ship's deck. They wore sealskin ponchos and kept their arms hidden beneath the wide leather folds. They took up positions around the bottom of the rope-railed walk. Kiska assumed that under the ponchos each man held a cocked crossbow, possibly of Claw design: screw-tension, bowless. A similar weapon was strapped to her right side, bought with all the money Kiska possessed in the world from a trader who'd had no idea how the unfamiliar mechanism worked.

After squinting into the thickening drizzle and eyeing the stacked cargo, one of the men signalled the ship. He wore a plainsman's fur cap and boasted the long curled moustache of the Seti tribes. Shaking his head and spitting on the planking, his disgust at the crowded dock, the poor visibility, was obvious even from Kiska's distant vantage.

A fifth man came down the gangway, medium height, slim. He wore a dark cloth cloak – hooded – leather gloves and boots. He stopped and glanced about. The gusting wind billowed the cowl and Kiska glimpsed a painfully narrow face, mahogany and smooth, with a startling glimmer of shining scalp.

The Seti guard flicked his hand again, signalling. The three others tightened around the man. Kiska recognized a variation of the sign language developed by the marine commando squads and later appropriated by just about every other Imperial corps, Claws included. One she had yet to find a teacher for.

They started up the pier. The drifting rain closed between, the five men blurring into a background of siege-walls and the gloom of an overcast evening. Yet she did not jump up to pursue. Remembering her teaching, she suspected others might remain behind with orders to follow at a distance.

It was her style to allow a quarry plenty of breathing space, especially if they believed themselves free of surveillance. She liked to think she had an instinct for her target's route, as she always had even as a child blindfolded during street games of hide-and-seek. She liked to joke that she just followed what spoor was left. As it was, she almost yelped in surprise when a grey-garbed man stepped out from a dozen or so weather-stained barrels in front of her. Jerking down out of sight, Kiska watched. She'd been about to let herself over the ship's side. Where in the Queen's Mysteries had he come from? While she chewed her lip, the man peeked around the barrel, then continued on with an almost jaunty air, hands clasped behind his back, a bounce to his stride.

Another bodyguard? No one else had left the ship. She was certain of it. A rendezvous? Then why keep back? She decided to rely upon Agayla's advice that anyone, until proven otherwise, could be an enemy.

She waited while he walked on, then slipped down to the dock. Assuming the fellow, whoever he was, wouldn't lose the man from the ship, she'd follow him. At the guard hut she looked back to the barrels, realizing what had bothered her about the fellow's sudden appearance. She'd given all the cargo a good search earlier. The pocket between those barrels had been empty, inaccessible without entering her line of sight.

That left only one option – one that was beyond her, but one this fellow obviously freely employed. The stink of Warren magic cautioned her. Perhaps she should report this after all. But to whom? The Claws had taken command of the Hold in the name of some unknown official. The thought of meekly submitting a report to the Claw she'd already met, or one of his brethren, made her throat burn. Damn them to the Queen's own eternal mazes. She'd tag along for a while and see what turned up.

At the bottom of Cormorant Road, Temper spotted old Rengel fussing at the shutters of a ground-floor window, a pipe clasped in his teeth. The old man was grumbling to himself, as usual.

The road lay empty save for the retired marine and sail-maker, which surprised Temper, seeing as it wasn't yet the first bell of the night.

'Evening.'

Rengel turned. 'Hey? Evening?' He forced the words through his teeth. Squinting, he nodded sourly, then returned to the shutter. 'That it is. And an evil one. Surprised to see you about. Thought you'd know better.'

Temper smiled. Rengel's conversation was either mawkishly nostalgic or blackly cynical, depending upon whether you found him drunk or sober. Temper judged him to be lightly soused at present, but the night was young. He inspected the low clouds coursing overhead.

'Doesn't look all that bad.'

'Hey? Bad?' Rengel look up, grimaced. 'Not the blasted weather, you damned fool.' He pulled at the shutter. 'Blasted, rusted, Togg damned-to-Hood . . .'

Temper stepped up. 'Let's have a look.'

Rengel gave way, puffing furiously on his pipe. 'Where is it you hail from anyway, lad?'

Studying the shutter's latch, Temper smiled. When was the last time someone had called him lad? 'Itko Kan, more or less. Why?'

Temper heard Rengel snort behind him. 'If you'd been born here, you'd stay put tonight, believe me. You'd know. The riots an' killin' and such this year prophesied it. Maybe even summoned it. A Shadow Moon. The souls of the dead come out under a Shadow Moon. Them and worse.'

Temper worked the shutter free, swung it shut. 'Shadow Moon? Heard of it. But I'm new here.'

'They're rare, thank the Gods.' Rengel stepped close. Rustleaf, rendered glue, sweat and gin assaulted Temper's nose. The old man swayed slightly, as if in a crosswind, and exhaled a great breath of smoke. 'I was off island the last one, serving on the *Stormdriver*. But the one afore, I was just a lad, near fifty years ago. The pits of the shadows open up. Damned souls escape and new ones get caught. Devils run amok through the streets. I heard 'em. They howl like they're after your soul.' He jabbed the pipe-stem against Temper's chest. 'And avoid anyone touched. They'll be snatched sure as I'm standing here.'

Touched. Common slang for anyone who knew the Warrens. The skills to access them could be taught, but it was much more common for someone to just be born with it – the *Talent.* No doubt in the old days people suspected of such taint did disappear on strange nights; in Temper's opinion they were most likely dragged away by a superstitious mob to be burned or hanged. He gave Rengel a serious nod that the old man returned profoundly.

A woman shouted above. 'Rengel!'

The widow Teal glared down over the slim railing of a second storey window. Temper smiled a greeting, but was always struck by her similarity to a fat vulture draped in a black shawl. She disappeared and the shutters banged closed.

Rengel clamped down on his pipe, grumbling under his breath. Temper rapped the shutter's stained wood slats. 'Solid as rock, I'd say. And I plan to be inside all night as well, so don't fret. I'll be testing the brew at the Hanged Man.'

The old man's brows quivered with interest. 'What's that? Testing, heh?' He grinned, puffing more smoke. 'Well, don't be too hasty in making a decision.'

Temper laughed. 'Gods, no. Likely take till the morning.'

At the door, Rengel hesitated, urged Temper close with a crook of a finger. He growled in an undertone, 'What d'you know of the *Return*?'

Temper shook his head, perplexed.

Impatient, or maybe disgusted, the old man waved him off. 'Stay indoors, friend. Fiends and worse will rule this night.'

Temper backed away, unsure what to make of his warning.

Rengel tapped the door, pointed to something – a mark chalked on the wood – then yanked it shut. The door's rattle echoed down the narrow lane.

The sign of Coop's Hanged Man Inn was just that: a painting of a hanged man, arms bound behind his back, his head bent at a sickening angle. Rain, falling freely, now brushed past in gusts. Temper's cloak hung heavy and cold from his shoulders. He heard the surf rolling into the pilings just a few streets down, while the bay glistened in the distance like an extension of the rain.

The clouds still held some of the day's light, but the gloom obscured anything a stone's toss away. The evening was developing into a night to chill the bones and numb the spirit. He looked forward to slipping into his regular seat just within distance of the inn's massive fireplace. He also hoped Corinn would stop by so he could ask her about Shadow Moons and this prophesy business . . . though it'd been nearly a week since he'd last seen her and, truth be told, he worried whether he'd ever see her again. He'd reached a few conclusions of his own. *Return* stank of the cult that worshipped Kellanved, the man who along with his partner, Dancer, had founded and built the Imperium. They'd been missing for years. Some thought both dead, others that they'd vanished into some kind of thaumaturgic seclusion.

Opposite the Hanged Man, across the wet cobbles, hunched the low stone wall of what was reportedly the oldest building in the city. It was an abandoned stone house, too far gone to repair. Temper had never paid it much attention, except that now old man Rengel's tale called to mind another local superstition: that the house predated the town, and that its ruined walls and abandoned rooms had always been haunted.

Rumour also held that it was there Kellanved and Dancer, along with others including Dassem and the current Regent,

Surly, had lived and plotted everything that followed. Eyeing it now, on a dark wet night, with the black limbs of dead trees outlined around it, and the bare and tumulus-looking grounds, it did appear sinister. The locals preferred the pretence it didn't exist, but whenever they had to mention it, they called it the Deadhouse. Personally, he couldn't believe any sane person could have lived there – which meant Kellanved and Dancer could very well have once stared out of its empty gaping windows. He shrugged and turned away. Sure it was haunted. To his mind, the entire Empire was haunted, one way or another.

Two men stood in the rain out in front of the Hanged Man, backs pressed against the windowless walls. They hung close enough to either side of the entrance for Temper to hear the droplets pattering off their leather cloaks. He'd felt their eyes on him as he approached. Now near they ignored him.

'Bastard night for a watch,' Temper grinned to the one on the right.

The man's eyes flickered to him, looking him up and down, then squinted back into the rain. 'We're waiting on a friend.'

Temper paused at the steps down to the front entrance. Everyone knew the Hanged Man was a veteran's bar, so there was little need for these two to pretend they weren't keeping an eye out for friends inside. He almost called them on it but didn't; they looked new. Maybe they just didn't know the drill. Feeling old, he thumped down the steps.

Coop's Inn was the other oldest building in the town of Malaz, or so Coop avowed. True or not, the building did stand much lower than the street, and its outer walls were large hand-hewn limestone blocks – the same sort as lay in nameless ruins all over the island. The inn's common room was so far beneath street level that the steep stairwell leading to it was eerily like a ship's companionway down to the lowest hold. Rainwater had poured down the worn steps and pooled at the threshold. Temper's cloak dripped into the puddle as he shook the moisture from his head. He took hold of the oak door's iron handle and, with the other hand, reached up to the chiselled scars that crossed as faintly as spider's webbing along the low lintel. He believed everyone had their own personal superstitions, soldiers and sailors more than most. This was one of his. He thought of it as an acknowledgement of the forgotten folk who'd raised the stones in the first place. A sort of blessing – given or received, he wasn't sure – and as a gesture towards his own continued safety. After all, he did live upstairs. Or rather he lived at ground level. His arrow-slit of a window stood barely an arm's span above a rat-run between the inn and Seal's whitewashed brick and timber house behind.

The Hanged Man's common room was large and wide, the ceiling beams low enough to touch or, if one weren't attentive, seriously damage one's head on. They'd brought more than one drunk's evening to an abrupt and painful end. Fat stone pillars stood in a double row down the chamber's centre as if marking a path from the entrance to the crackling, rowboat-sized fireplace directly opposite. Long oak tables stretched to either side of this central walk, shadowed in differing distance to the fire. The stone walls were stark, unrelieved but for the occasional miniature vaulted recess, each now dimly illumined by a lamp. Most of the room's light, however, came from bronze oil lanterns hung from crusted iron hooks set deep into the pillars and the walls. The huge fireplace lit the far end of the room with flickering amber light, dispelling the chill air of the chamber and adding, sullenly, to the illumination.

There was enough smoke to fog the room, but it was warm and dry at least. Temper loosened his cloak. To either side men talked, laughed, and drank. A much larger crowd than usual, and younger, more rowdy. Anji passed, a brownstone jug on one hip, refilling mugs. She gave Temper a harried nod, already weary. He smiled back, but she'd passed on. Poor gal, she'd been spoiled by the regular crowd of quiet old duffers who'd nurse a tumbler of liqueur for two or three bells each. Tonight she was more than earning her keep.

As Temper passed between the long tables he felt the weight of numerous eyes and paused, but no one returned his gaze. Instead, they stared at their cups or the gouged tabletop, murmuring to one another as if they hoped he would just move on like any unwelcome guest. Unusual behaviour from men who appeared hard and ragged enough to have been emptied out of a prison ship, or culled from the press gangs that fed the Empire's constant need to replenish the oars of the Navy. Temper crossed to his regular seat, sensing the odd charged tension in the air.

Passing the last tables, he glimpsed a crowd of mangy looking fellows dressed in threadbare tunics and cloaks who struck him as nothing more than destitute street-sweepings. These men sat alongside others who suggested the cut of military service with their scars and heavier builds. An unusual crowd for Coop's. But the old man, Rengel, had warned him to anticipate a night of strangeness.

Someone had taken his regular bench along the rear wall. Considering how crowded the room was, Temper half-expected it, but couldn't avoid feeling irritated. Couldn't Coop have kept it for him? What did he pay rent to the damn brewer for anyway? That tiny cell upstairs? The wretched food?

The man occupying his seat wore a leather vest over a padded linen shirt that hung in tatters down over the bench and leggings of iron-studded leather. Oiled leather wristlets half-covered forearms that bore a skein of scar tissue: puckered remnants of scoured flesh, thin pale crescents of bladed edge, and the angry pink mottling of healed burns. Head low to the table, he spoke to a companion shrouded in shadow.

For a moment Temper hesitated. He considered addressing the man. Not that he expected to retrieve his seat, but to

41

challenge him enough to better glimpse his features. The fellow's face remained averted. Stiffly so, it seemed to Temper. Intangibly, the space between the two momentarily seemed to contract. Coop materialized, stepping through a rear narrow door. He scanned the room, hands tucked behind his leather apron. He waved towards a sole empty table and Temper ambled over; he'd just stood a half-day watch and was damned if he would stay on his feet a moment longer.

Coop sat with him. 'Sorry about that, Temp.' He raised a decanter of peach brandy.

Temper nodded. 'Quite the crowd,' he offered, but Coop simply poured. He shrugged and raised the tumbler for a toast.

'To the Empire,' said Coop, raising his own glass.

'To the bottom of the sea,' returned Temper, and downed the shot.

Sucking his teeth, Coop pushed his seat back against the rear wall to better view the room. 'Yes, a different bunch. But it's just the one night y'know.'

'A Shadow Moon.'

Coop looked up. 'Yeah, that's it. First I'd heard of it though.' He pulled a rag from behind his apron and used it to wipe his glistening forehead then his retreating, curled red hair.

Temper slid a forearm onto the table, inclined his head to the room. 'Rough looking . . .'

Coop waved the suggestion aside. 'A quiet bunch, considering all the young bloods. Nothing broken yet except the seals from two casks of stout.' He chuckled knowingly.

Temper sighed. In his eyes Coop's main failing was his unflinching optimism. Coop's steady supply of it would have made him suspect simple-mindedness had he not known otherwise. Perhaps, he thought, Coop was inclined to be hopeful, given all the coin passing his way.

He considered dropping in on Seal later. Gods knew the young army medicer could probably use the company tonight.

42

But the lad was likely already up to his elbows in his own medicine chest. Then he thought of something better and gestured Coop closer. 'Haven't seen Corinn around, have you?'

The brewer cracked a broad smile and would've nudged Temper if his scowl didn't promise a beating for it. His grin fell as he considered the question. 'No, can't say as I have. Sorry, Temp.'

With a shrug, Temper sat back. 'Thought she would've at least said goodbye.'

'Same old Temp, always thinking the worst. I'll have a mug of Dark sent your way.' Standing, he slapped Temper's shoulder.

Temper waved Coop off and turned his chair to lean against the wall. Of the immediate tables, all crowded, only a couple of familiar faces stood out. They belonged to the two other men who rented rooms from Coop: Faro Balkat, a frail, dried old stick who swallowed Paralt water like it wasn't the poison it was, and who rarely knew whether it was day or night; and Trenech. He was a giant of a fellow, as broad and seemingly bright as a bhederin, who did occasional bouncing and guard work for Coop in exchange for free beer.

Though Coop had dismissed his sour predictions, and Temper didn't want to admit it, he was afraid that maybe he'd seen the last of Corinn – that despite a tongue sharper than a Talian dagger. He'd met her . . . what . . . less than a month ago? And in that time he'd surprised himself by how much he'd come to look forward to hearing her recount legendary campaigns over wine. He tried to remember their last conversation: had he said something worse than his usual stupid hints? Too crass a joke regarding a couple of old warhorses stabling together for warmth? Though they were both veterans and saw the world through the same cynical eyes, she treated him as if the mere pike-pusher he pretended to be. Maybe he was just daydreaming, but was it possible she saw more than that?

Anji pushed through the servant's door beside the table, slamming down a pewter mug of Malazan Dark as she passed. He offered her a wave; she rolled her eyes at the way the evening was shaping up. As she passed a nearby table a fellow grabbed at her ass. She swung round and dumped a tall mug of ale over his lap and had to be stopped from breaking the mug across his skull. From all around came hoots and cheers of delight.

The outburst brought round the gaze of the fellow who'd claimed Temper's seat. The burns on his forearms extended to his face, and in a flash Temper recognized the source: Imperial alchemical munitions. An incendiary, most likely.

The toughs quieted under the man's glare and this surprised Temper. Among the soldiers he'd known, such a look would have provoked a tossed stool or mug or whatever lay close to hand. He watched sidelong as the fellow turned back to his companions. The man gestured broadly, as if imitating a sword cut, and a tattoo flashed briefly beneath the short sleeve of his tunic. An arched bridge, a background of licking flames: the emblem of the Bridgeburners.

Temper felt as if those flames had scorched his own heart. Halfway across the chamber sat a man he may have met in earlier days – a different life. The urge to flee made his arms twitch. He forced his head down, as if studying the depths of his drink. The odds were they'd never actually run into each other; he knew that. More, the Bridgeburner probably wouldn't even notice him, and this would be nothing more than another heart-stopping brush with his past. He forced himself to take another drink. The warm Malazan Dark coated his throat. He almost laughed aloud at his nerves. Gods, man! A bare year out of action and behaving like a skittish colt!

Barely raising his head, he viewed the smoky room. It was a chilly, rainy night; his favourite seat was occupied; his past grinned like a death's head from the neighbouring table, and once more Corinn had stood him up after, of late, spending most evenings with him swapping tales and maybe getting a certain look in her eyes at the last. All in all, the evening called for a dignified retreat. A bottle of his homeland's red wine waited tucked beneath his pallet for just such an ill-starred evening.

Standing, he pushed back his chair. He felt as if every eye in the chamber were crawling over his back. He pulled open the servant's door, ducked, and stepped into an antechamber that Coop had sketchily adapted to a storage room by the addition of a few shelves. The room was dark, cold, and cramped. Temper could touch both walls without stretching either arm. In the wall was a portal barely wide enough for his shoulders, though they were broader than most. It opened out onto circular stairs that led up to the kitchen and the rented rooms, as well as down to the lower cellars.

He started up the steps, feeling at his back the steady draught of cold air that welled constantly out of the building's depths. He wondered at the puzzle of a Bridgeburner being here on the island. Now that he was on his way to his room, he felt an urge to sit down with the man and spin yarns of the old days. But the stories of the wanderings of retired or discharged veterans usually proved sad or unremarkable. He could imagine the fate of such a soldier outside the Bridgeburner squads: no posting would have been desirable. Even the role of marine would have been confining and frustrating. Direct dismissal from service was preferable. And following that, aimless drifting and befuddlement at civilian life.

Temper could sympathize: when his own place in the ranks had been taken from him he'd experienced something much the same. He'd even presented himself with false papers to the local garrison in order to return to the only life he'd ever felt was his own.

Yet there was more to this puzzle than just the one man. Passing the kitchens, Temper waved to Sallil, the cook, who nodded back, then returned to fanning himself at the rear door's steep steps that led up into the alley. In the dark of the stairwell, Temper felt his way to the upper rooms, some rented by Anji and a few of her friends for occasional whoring, and one occupied by Coop himself. In the narrow hall it occurred to him that once before he'd seen a ragged gang of men such as the crowd below. They'd disembarked from a galley hailing from the island's other settlement, Jakata, that had berthed overnight at the public wharves.

Outside his door, he paused, the puzzle solved. Jakatan-registered vessels enjoyed one of the rare charters that allowed 'interception' of non-Imperial shipping off the coasts of Quon Tali. In short, the long tradition of piracy survived in Jakata. This man, an ex-Bridgeburner, would find himself quite at home among such a lawless bunch.

They must have put in for the coming storm; no wonder they had posted two men to keep an eye out. There were probably merchant cartels represented here whose shipping had been *liberated* by these very same men.

Temper took out the keys he kept on a leather thong around his neck. He was reasonably sure he'd threaded together the how and why of the crowd downstairs. Now he could drink his wine and pay them no further mind. What remained to be seen was whether anything would come of this Shadow Moon nonsense.

CHAPTER TWO

ASSIGNATIONS

THE FISHERMAN SET DOWN THE RIND OF BREAD AND LEFT his bowl of soup steaming on the table. He went to the window where a rag of cloth fluttered in a frigid south wind. From beside the fire, his wife turned towards him. 'What is it, Toben?'

He pushed aside the rag, stared to the south for a moment. When he turned back to her, his eyes were downcast. 'I've got to go out, love.'

'Now?' She lowered the sweater she was mending to her lap.

'Aye.'

'There's no fish to be caught by the light of *this* moon.'

'True enough – it draws other things.'

'You've never had to go out any of the other times.'

'No.' He came to her, gently drew the sweater from her hands. 'Things aren't as they were before. They're all out of balance.'

She raised a hand; he took it and she grasped tightly. 'Don't go out,' she whispered, fierce. 'Please don't. I dread it.'

He bowed to kiss her eyes, each sightless, each staring. 'Sorry, my chick. I must.'

'Then you know you go with my love.'

'Yes, dear one.'

The fisherman drew on the sweater. He shovelled embers from the hearth into a brazier, then filled a short clay pipe and lit it with an ember from the fire.

'Good-night, love.' He smiled. 'Sing for me, won't you?'

She raised a hand. 'You know I do. Come back quickly.'

'I will. Soon as I can.'

She turned her head to listen to the door, heard the wind moaning through the rocks, the ocean heaving itself against the shore with slow, insistent pressure. The door latched shut. She lowered her head and folded her hands in her lap.

The wind blew steady and chill. Clouds raced overhead – the leading banners of a solid front filling the entire south horizon. Beneath the silver eye of the newly risen moon nothing moved among the shacks perched on the barren southern shore of Malaz Isle except the fisherman picking his way down to the wave-pounded shingle. In the lashing wind his brazier flamed like a beacon. For a moment he stopped to listen; he thought he heard the hint of a hound's bay caught on the wind. Squinting towards the south he grimaced: along the dark horizon of cloud and sea blue-green lights flashed like mast-fire. Lights that sailors claimed lured men to their doom.

He found the surf had risen almost within reach of his beached skiff. He set the brazier into an iron stand at the middle thwart, put his shoulder to the bow, then jerked away as if stung: scaled ice covered the wood like a second skin. He mouthed a curse and laid a hand against the wood. The ice melted, beading to condensation over the age-polished wood and steaming into vapour the wind snatched away. Singing low under his breath, the fisherman shoved against the prow. The skiff skimmed over the stones and he pushed on, wading into the surf up to his thighs, then clambered in.

While he pulled on the thick wood oars, he chanted a song that was old when men and women first set foot upon the island. The humped, time-worn bedrock hills shrank into the distance as if the raging wind itself had swept the island away.

With one oar he turned the skiff amid the waves, then turned around to face the stern, bow to the south. Between the skiff and Malaz, now a dark distant line at the north horizon, the sea rose in slow heavy swells as smooth as the island's ancient hills. Hail lashed white-capped waves all around, yet none touched the fisherman's grey hair as it tossed in the wind. Deep ocean surge, tall as any vessel, bore down on him, ice-webbed, frost and spume-topped. But they rolled under his bow as gently as a meadow slope while he crooned to the wind.

Out of the south the storm-front advanced, thickening into a solid line of churning clouds. Driven snow and sleet melted to rain that dissipated long before reaching the skiff. Lightning crackled amid the clouds while beneath emerald and deepest blue flashed like wave-buoyed gemstones. The fisherman saw none of this; facing north, teeth clamped down on his pipe, he droned his chant while the wind snatched the words away.

Kiska soon lost track of the fellow who had popped up so suddenly before her at the wharves. Again, she smelled the Warrens in that, and hoped the possibility of a tail never occurred to him. If it had, he'd be right behind her now, waiting, watching from a path in the Rashan Warren of Darkness or perhaps even Hood's own demesnes, the Paths of the Dead. Though on a night like this accessing either of those seemed imprudent, even to her.

The trail of her target and his guards led her inland through the warehouse district, continuing on into the poorest quarters of rag shops, bone renderers, money lenders, and tanneries. If her quarry kept on in this direction he would soon confront an even fouler neighbourhood, the Mouse – the filthiest, lowest, and most disease-infested locale in the city.

At the first muddy lane bridged by plank walkways, her mark's trail turned abruptly northward. Kiska was not surprised by the sudden change in direction; she imagined their disgust at the redolent sewage and rotting kitchen refuse awash in stagnant water that percolated from a nearby marsh. She could have pursued them easily enough through the maze of alleys, especially now, as many of the ways were nothing more than glutinous paths through the blackened wreckage left by last summer's riots. But it was mainly because she'd grown up in this quarter, spent her life clawing out of it, that she was reluctant, always, to enter its ways again.

The trail led on up a gentle grade leading to the wealthy merchant centre. It crossed market lanes and angled more or less straight north, up cobbled arcades past shop fronts, closed and shuttered now against the coming night. Through the cloth merchant district it continued on, climbing hills northwest into the Lightings, the old estate quarter. Most of the manor houses stood vacant behind tall gates. Now they served merely as provincial retreats for the aristocratic families that had transferred their interests north, across the Strait of Winds, to the Imperial court at Unta.

The evening had cooled rapidly. A frigid wind from the south, out of the Sea of Storms, gusted down from the isle's meagre headlands. The cloud cover remained unbroken, sweeping northward like driven smoke. Her heavy cloak billowed, snagging as she kept to the ivy-choked iron fences that lined the district's boulevards. One edge of it remained tight against her side, however: the right side, held straight by the crossbow stock disguised inside her cloak.

Kiska paused in the shadow of an ancient pillar, a plinth for the marble statue of a Nacht, the fanged and winged creature once said to have inhabited the island. The streets were deserted. The last souls she'd seen, other than glimpses of her target and escort, were a few stragglers. Hunched under shawls and scarves, they'd hurried home as night lowered.

Tonight. This night of all possible nights. Shadow Moon; All Souls' Fest; the Night of Shadows. Its titles seemed endless. Kiska had grown up hearing all the old legends, tales so imaginative and fabulous she rolled her eyes whenever her mother dragged them out. That was until a few days ago, when she'd overheard that by some arcane and unspecified means a Shadow Moon was predicted for tonight. Since then she'd eavesdropped on talk that lingered around gruesome stories of monstrous hounds, vengeful shades, and that local haunt, the Deadhouse. Any mention of those precincts brought wardings and whispered hints of even darker legends; tales of fiends so malevolent to have once inhabited it, as if borrowing something of its ancient brooding essence – Kellanved, Dancer, Surly, and the dark heart of the Empire to come.

From the stories she'd overheard, it seemed to her that everyone had an ancestor or relative who'd disappeared during a Shadow Moon. As good a night as any, she figured cynically, to run out on a harridan wife or ne'er-do-well husband.

Right now her own mother was no doubt barricaded in her room, eyes clenched shut, mouthing prayers to Chem – the old local sea cult – for the safety of her and her own. If she'd spoken to her within the last few days, she probably would have attempted to keep her indoors this night, just as Agayla had done during the riots of the Regent's new laws. But she'd grown up ignoring her mother's prohibitions on almost everything, so why heed them now? Especially when this was the first Shadow Moon in her lifetime.

Those she followed walked the deserted lanes boldly. For them tonight held no dangers. If they knew of the legends – which was doubtful – they would probably view it as nothing more than a quaint local custom during which souls, monsters, and fiends purportedly took to the streets. Her home's back-water superstition shamed Kiska. Yet what if she did break off the surveillance? Run to hide in a sacred precinct or temple? If she abandoned the pursuit now she could already imagine the Claw commander's sneer. After all, what more could one expect of local talent?

Ahead in the distance, flattened by the overcast gloom, her quarry and guards continued to climb the cobbled street. Ground fog rose now, swirling in the wind, as her target rounded a corner and vanished. Kiska kept behind cover. For all she knew they could be waiting just ahead. She could walk right past them and not know until cold iron slid between her ribs. Or, more likely, a knotted silk rope snapped about her neck like a noose.

Kiska tightened her cloak, tried to shake off her dread like the rain from its oiled weave. She would simply have to proceed under the assumption she'd yet to be spotted. Her nerves would rattle to pieces otherwise.

The corner revealed a carriage way, twin gullies pressed into the stones by centuries of wheels. The party had disappeared. Down the way, between tall walls, stood a massive gateway of carved wooden doors. Kiska knew what lay beyond. The E'Karial family manor. Smallish, compared to some of the town's grander estates, but comfortable, or so it had looked from the outside on her nocturnal wanderings. It was also long abandoned. If this were a meeting, Kiska imagined its partici-pants couldn't have planned a more isolated location. Of course, it could also be that some massively ill-informed scion of the E'Karial family had arrived to inspect their inheritance.

She took several slow breaths, then crossed the carriage way to the mouth of the lane opposite, where ivy hung so thick she could hardly see through it. At each step her back prickled under imagined dagger-points. But the ivy-choked walls swallowed her without incident. She jogged to another alley, this one plain mud, that she knew led to a postern gate behind the estate. Edging around the pooled rainwater and fighting the thorny brush that snagged at her cloak, she nearly missed the recessed entry hidden in the shadows.

She knelt at the moss-covered door, rearranged her cloak, and listened. Raindrops pattered from leaf-tips, the wind rustled overhead through branches and, no more than a distant murmur, the ever-present surf punished the island's shores. The door stank of rot while the arched recess retained the must of long-damp humus. She didn't plan to open the door, of course. One glance was enough to tell *anyone* that was no longer possible: a portion of the wall's weight had settled onto the frame. If she pushed on the rotted planks she'd probably tumble right through into the rear garden. This was simply a lower profile for listening than poking her head over the wall.

She heard no one and gave it long enough: fifty heart-beats. Most likely they were inside the estate. Time to try the wall. She stepped out of the recess and appraised the blocks and the vines that smothered their rough surface. No problem. For cover, she climbed up to where three aruscus trees rose as a clump within the compound. Head and shoulders above the top, she studied the landscaped garden. It looked even worse than the last time she'd seen it. Raised beds now held only dead stalks and weeds. A central tiled patio shone dully under the cover of dead leaves. And there, side by side on a marble bench so white it glowed in the night, two men sat. Kiska froze.

She'd heard nothing because neither spoke. Both looked to the southern sky. For all she could tell they were quietly study-ing the clouds. The one on her right was the man she'd followed, hood back, shaved scalp dark as rich loam, a long queue draped forward over one shoulder. The other was an old man, ghostly pale, white-haired, thin shoulders hunched like folded wings, his head tilted at an angle. They sat like that, statues almost, and time stretched. Couldn't they move, speak, or do something? She wondered how long she could hang there on the wall, toes jammed against a crack.

Presently, after what seemed a full bell's time, but was only one hundred and fifty heartbeats, silver light broke through the night as the moon shone through a cloud break. The old man threw back his head, barked a harsh laugh. He sounded vindicated. The man from the message cutter answered, his tone grudging, non-committal; he still studied the night sky. Kiska strained to catch their words, but the branches soughed and rattled overhead.

After a few more exchanges, the old man clutched the other's arm and snarled something. The second rose, brushed the hand from his cloak. He spoke softly to the older man who remained unresponsive then he walked away to the front of the grounds. The old man remained seated, head sunk as if he were a seer searching for patterns among the cracked tiles and leaves swirling around them. Kiska eased herself back down the wall.

What had she just witnessed? Nothing more than a simple meeting between estranged relations, or two who once were friends? Clandestine, yes, but that alone was no crime. The rendezvous had an aspect of ritual about it, an observance of some sort. The old man might be a shunned relation. Perhaps she'd stumbled onto some business the E'Karial family wanted kept hidden, a skeleton in the garden, so to speak. She should make inquiries. Collecting leverage was, after all, part of the job.

From somewhere far off, in the town, a dog howled at the now brightened moon. The call's ferocity chilled Kiska, reminding her of the demon hounds that figured so prominently in Shadow Moon legends. If that damned baying kept up all night, as it probably would, she could imagine tomorrow's tales down in the market, stories of narrow escapes and terrifying visitations of huge supernatural beasts. People would believe what they wished to.

She was about to push her way back through the wet leaves

to the alley mouth when a noise from behind the wall brought her around: tiles clattering. She hesitated, wondered if she'd imagined it, then jumped back up for a second look. The bench was vacant, but next to it knelt the intruder from the wharf, the man who'd so earlier surprised her. He straightened up from a bundle at his feet and disappeared into nothingness as though the shadows had wrapped themselves around him. Kiska stared, awed. Warren magic. It took her a few moments before she recognized what he'd left behind crumpled on the patio: the old man, lying face down.

Kiska dropped and spun, pressed her back into the vines on the wall. Droplets showered her. Had he seen her? Was she next? She pulled out her long knife. Hilted for parrying, it was the heaviest weapon she carried other than the crossbow, which she now swivelled from her hip to cover the alley. An adept, that was plain. But which Warren? His disappearance resembled Rashan's blotting darkness, only somehow different. And that scared her the most. An awful thought struck: what if this man were a Claw? He seemed skilled enough. Terror gripped her: the arrival of an unknown high official, Claw bodyguards, a covert visit . . . had she stumbled onto the Imperial Regent's housecleaning? If so, she was finished. What was the old saying? Claws only travelled on business! She almost laughed aloud but instead took comfort from the feel of her glove wrapped tight around the knife grip.

Time passed and eventually, though with an odd reluctance, Kiska had to admit that she wasn't about to be murdered. She might as well discover as much as she could of what had happened here. She sheathed her gauche and jumped once more onto the wall. The old man's body still lay behind the bench. No one was about. Moonlight played raggedly over the ruined gardens. A second howl burst out of the night causing her to flinch. Gods! It sounded as if the blasted beast was right at her shoulder!

Who kept animals like that? Kiska decided that before dawn she'd knife that dog if someone else didn't get to it first. Cautious, she lowered herself down into the enclosed yard.

The old man was thrust twice through the back. She wondered if this piece of work was by order of her target. Had he offered the old man a proposition? One that could not be turned down? Perhaps he was unaware of the murder. The Claws, or someone else, might think this meeting should never have occurred. She nudged the body over and began rifling through its clothes.

She slipped her hand inside the tunic, still warm with blood. The man snatched her wrist and his eyes snapped open. Automatically, she yanked out her gauche and shoved it into the man's chest, leaning her full weight onto the blow. It was a mortal thrust, she was certain of it, but still he stared and held his grip. A death rictus? Horribly, he smiled and opened his mouth. A stream of blood welled out, blackening his chin. Steady, unnatural pressure pulled her close. The bloodied lips turned down reprovingly.

'But I *am* dead, you see,' he whispered wetly, 'and the Shadow Moon is risen.'

Facing a horror she'd been warned of but never actually believed, Kiska's training – sketchy, only informal – crumbled and she screamed.

Temper was wrestling with the corroded lock on his door when someone murmured his name from down the hall. He jerked up from examining the stubborn lockplate. Corinn waved from behind a door barely opened. He straightened, would have shouted hello, but something in her tight expression silenced him. She waved again, impatient, and he ambled down the hall. At the door he grinned, tried to look in past her. It was the room Anji and a few other girls used for their whoring. He arched one brow. 'Well, I thought you'd never—'

'Just get in here, damn you,' she hissed, pulling open the door and yanking him in.

Despite the woman's obvious anger, Temper felt himself grinning idiotically. They stood close in the cramped closet of a room. Her tongue, sharp as a Darujhistan rapier, cut everyone who dared come close. But here, nearly touching her, Temper was suddenly very aware of the depths of her deep brown eyes, and the filigree detail in the black tattooing that ran from the tip of her nose to her forehead.

He sometimes fancied catching interest in those eyes, sidelong, hidden, but tonight concern tightened them. He'd daydreamed of just such an encounter, usually when drink softened his judgement or loneliness emptied his chest and he desired someone to talk to. But now he felt awkward and self-conscious while she looked straight at him and shook her head.

'You just had to show up tonight, didn't you.'

For an instant, Temper felt like a wayward husband finally dragging himself home after a three-day binge. He laughed, pointed back to his room. 'Corinn – I live here. Where else am I supposed to go?'

'The barracks! You're supposed to have stayed. Why didn't you just . . . Oh, never mind.' She waved for silence. 'Listen to me. We've only a minute. What I'm going to say and do, I'm doing to save your life. Understand?'

Standing so close, he caught the dusky hint of her scent – perfume of some unknown flower? Foreign spices? Incense? She was half-Napan, someone had once said: half as dark. He blinked, swallowed. Here he was, an old warhorse long out to pasture, yet flaring its nostrils at a passing mare.

'Saving my life? Corinn, I'm hitting the sack and a bottle of Kanese red. That is, unless you've something else in mind . . .'

Her eyes flashed with anger. 'You damned idiot. I'm trying to save your worthless hide.' She raised a fist, opened it palm up. A small badge lay there on the pale lined flesh, metal

57

painted and enamelled in the sigil of a stone arch over a field of flames. The badge of the Bridgeburners, the very regiment of the man downstairs, once of the Third Army. An army that Dassem, with Temper at his side, had led in Falar and the Seven Cities.

All he could think was: *so it is the smell of smoke that surrounds her*. A dusky scent that took on a lethal edge in the face of that small badge. 'Aw, no,' he groaned, 'Hood, no. Why? What do you want?'

Footsteps sounded from the hall. Corinn leaned close. 'I want you to do as I say because I know who you are. I recognized you. I was at Y'Ghatan. I saw the Sword broken. I know.' She took his arm, her hand warm and hard through his shirt. 'Stand aside tonight and it will remain our secret. Just . . . stand aside.'

The door swung open behind him. He turned. The man with the burn scars stood in the hall, two of the men he'd sat with behind him, crossbows levelled. The man eyed Corinn who answered his gaze with a short nod. 'He's unarmed,' she told them.

All Temper could think of were her words: *I know who you are*. Did that mean she'd been sent? Been watching him? He was stunned, as if everything he'd hidden from this last year now crashed upon him like an undermined wall.

The man's gaze was deceptively bland. 'My name is Ash,' he said, his voice soft. 'Sergeant Ash. You, on the other hand, are my prisoner.'

They sat him at a rear booth beside Coop, opposite Trenech and old Faro Balkat. The old man appeared asleep, sagging against the wall, eyes staring sightlessly. A drop of saliva hung from purple-stained lips. Oddly, Trenech was gently propping him up with one huge hand. Temper glared at Coop, who appeared more confused than worried, then turned to watch

58

Ash. He claimed to be a sergeant but was probably an officer. In the centre of the room he conferred with Corinn and a few others.

'What will they do?' Coop whispered.

'I don't know.' At first Temper thought they'd come for him, that they'd finally reached his name on the long list Surly kept of her enemies. But now he wondered.

'What happened?' he asked Coop.

Out came a cloth and the brewer wiped his glistening jowls and forehead. 'I blame myself,' he stuttered. 'I can't believe it. They made me send away all the staff. How could I have fallen for that?'

'For what, man. What?'

Coop blinked at him. 'Thieves, of course. A pack of damned thieves!'

Temper choked down a laugh. He turned away, tried to catch Corinn's eye. 'No, Coop. I think it's something more than that.'

Corinn met his gaze, but her face remained flat, as if she didn't know him. He gave the ghost of a nod in response and looked away – straight into Trenech's eyes. The hulking fellow stared at him, or rather through him. Sweat beaded his brow. His right hand clenched the table in a white-knuckled grip.

Temper had spoken with the fellow only a few times. He thought him slow-witted, like an infant in a giant's body. Was he terrified by all this, or mindlessly enraged? Temper imagined he ought to say something reassuring but didn't know what.

Turning his head slightly, he studied the men. The majority, some thirty or so, sat gathered towards the door, voices low as they whispered among themselves. Closer, in the flickering light of the fireplace, Ash, Corinn, and a dozen others sat together at two tables. Of these, Temper guessed the average age to be around the mid-thirties. They adjusted the straps of their armour and weapon belts. Some smoked short clay pipes. None spoke. Temper identified three Wickan tribesmen, moustached, wearing studded boiled-leather hauberks with mailed sleeves; two dark Dal Honese, one with the raised cuts of facial scarification on his cheeks, the other's right eye a pale milky orb; one Napan, short and thick-set like a stump, his bluish-toned skin faded to a silty green; two dusky men from Seven Cities in mail shirts under long surcoats that they adjusted and belted snug; and the rest probably Quon Talian, in army-standard Malazan hauberks, one with rows of blued steel lozenges riveted over the leather. Every one of them possessed a crossbow, either at his back, on the table, or at the bench beside him. Short swords hung sheathed at belts and shoulder harness. Veterans, and probably all Bridgeburners as well.

The others were the street-sweepings and thugs Temper had identified earlier. Many carried curved short swords sheathed pommel-forward, Jakatan style, while on others Temper identified plain Talian long knives, curved Dal Honese daggers, and on two, long double-edged Untan duelling swords. They wore a mishmash of armour, the heaviest of which amounted to nothing more than boiled-leather vests or padded long shirtings.

Some pulled at their leathers, obviously uncomfortable in them. Temper looked away in disgust: city toughs, not a veteran among them. What could Ash hope to accomplish with these? And Corinn? Head down, she spoke with the sergeant. Temper eyed her hard, hoping to raise her head by the heat of his gaze. He knew she was a mage, but was she really a Bridgeburner cadre mage? He thought they'd all died during the campaigns of Seven Cities and Genabackis.

He sighed, rubbed his eyes. All the gods above and below. Seven Cities. Y'Ghatan. He could almost smell the desert's faint cinnamon scent, feel the punishing heat. That day, that betrayal – returned like a stab to the chest, and he shuddered.

He remembered how the dust had risen in choking clouds that scoured his throat and blinded vision; the hordes of robed Seven City defenders. He saw Dassem, unbelievably thrust through, supported by Hilt. He recalled the glimpses he'd caught of Dassem stumbling, holding his chest. He'd said something to Temper, some joke or farewell lost amid the screams and clash of battle.

Temper unclenched his jaws and eased his tension in a long slow exhalation. So now both he and Corinn knew of each other. What was it she wanted from him? Perhaps nothing. Perhaps this was just a warning that he should keep his head down and not interfere or she'd reveal who he was. Like she said, maybe she was just trying to save his sorry ass. Leaning forward, he tried to catch her eye across the room.

A dog's howl cut through the stone walls like the concussion of Moranth munitions. It rose and fell, deep, resounding, the most savage and lustful call Temper had ever heard. Corinn flinched as if bitten, snapped a panicked glance to Temper, then turned away. The young toughs peered about, their eyes wide. The veterans' hands twitched towards their crossbows.

From the corner of his eye, Temper caught a sly, disturbingly cretinous smile grow on Trenech's fat lips. Temper swallowed to wet his own suddenly dry mouth. Here he sat, prisoner to a gang of ruthless criminals or deserters – betrayed by a woman, beside a fool, a mindless drooling wreck, and a moron the size of a bhederin – on the most locally dreaded night of this generation. Could things possibly get any worse?

Faro Balkat's eyelids flickered open, revealing orbs rolled back to whites. As calmly as if ordering another drink he announced into the silence: 'The Shadow Moon is risen.'

Kiska wondered if she was hallucinating, for she suddenly found herself lying at the narrow bottom of a deep defile. Streamers of cloud threaded across a ribbon of sky high above.

Wind tossed hot dust in her face, soughing down the curves of the canyon. She rubbed her eyes. What had happened? Barked laughter jerked her to her feet.

A man slid down the side of the canyon using his hands and feet, digging his elbows to slow his descent. At the bottom he fell, tumbling, robes flapping around pale shins. It was the dead old man. He lurched to his feet, closed on her. Kiska ran. He yelled a word and she stopped, legs numb. He came around to stand before her, grinning like one of the Nacht statues in the gardens and alleys of Malaz. Kiska could still move her arms so she punched him across the mouth and he fell back in surprise. With that she was free and she ran on around the curve of the canyon.

Two sinuous turns later the channel ended in a cul-de-sac of stone layered like folded cloth. Snarling, Kiska threw herself at it. She scrabbled and grabbed for hand and footholds. After she had climbed only an arm's length the rotten layers crumbled beneath her like brittle old leather, and she slid down, scraping her side and chin. She lay gasping in the dust.

'Nothing's as easy as it seems, is it? Would that I had kept that in mind.'

Kiska yelped and lunged to her feet, drawing her knife.

The old man sneered, brushed dirt from his robes. 'I'm dead. Remember?'

Kiska didn't allow the point of her blade to waver. 'Where are we? What's going on?'

The man's wide crazed grin returned. He opened his arms, looked about. 'Magnificent, isn't it? This place?'

'What have you done to me?'

'A place,' the old man continued, 'whose existence has been theorized for the last millennia. A place whose characteristics I deduced from ancient sources. A place – a *Realm* – that, should it belong to anyone, belongs to me. *My* realm which I should rule, suzerain. The Path of *Shadow*.'

The man's a gibbering lunatic. 'Send me back. I don't want to be here. I want to be back home, on Malaz.'

He raised one crooked finger. 'Ah. But you are, you see. You're still on your wretched little isle. And at the same time, you are here. Two realms overlapping. Two places at once. What is called a Convergence.'

'I don't give a shit what it's called. Send me back!'

The man's lips moved but his words were obliterated by the bellow of a beast that echoed through the maze of canyons surrounding them. Shards of stone clattered down around them. The hairs of Kiska's arms and neck stood on end. *That was no dog . . .*

The man darted his gaze to the sides of the canyon, his face falling. 'Less time than I'd hoped.'

The blade quivered in Kiska's hand. She wanted to run, to scream, to plead for help. 'Time for what? What's—'

The man silenced her with a wave. 'Listen to me. My name is Oleg. Many years ago a man came to me. He claimed to be interested in the arcanum of my research. We worked together. We shared knowledge. His prowess and grasp of Warren manipulation astounded me. I, who admit no peer in such mastery. He—'

The old man jammed the heels of both hands to his eyes then let out a wordless scream of rage. 'He betrayed me! He stole my work and left me for dead!' His fists slipped down to his mouth. 'A life's work,' he moaned, staring at some scene. 'Gone. Obliterated. Wrenched from me like a limb. My sight. My power of speech.'

'Send me back, Oleg,' Kiska whispered. 'Please.'

Throwing his face up to the sky, he yelled, 'You . . . will . . . not . . . succeed!'

Kiska stared, stunned by the extravagance of his madness.

Ignoring her dagger, he took her by the shoulders, stared with eyes like pits in which things writhed. 'That man was

Kellanved, Emperor of Malaz. He returns tonight to this island. The Claws and their mistress no doubt think he returns to reclaim the throne, but all who believe such things are fools. He returns to attempt to re-enter the Deadhouse. They are after another, far greater prize. He and Dancer.'

Oleg's hands were hot on Kiska's shoulders. She struggled but he held with a grip like a beast. For some reason she could not bring herself to use the weapon in her hand – perhaps because she did not want to know just how useless it was.

Oleg continued, his eyes white all around. 'Should they succeed, this realm where we stand, Shadow Realm, will be theirs! Long ago Kellanved and Dancer entered that cursed *place* you call the Deadhouse and there discovered a strange thing. Strange discoveries that have taken him a hundred years to understand.'

He ducked his head with a grimace. 'That and my work, of course. But now they are ready. They must be stopped. Tell – tell the man I met – the blind fool! Tell him that now *I* have entered Shadow, I have seen it all. I was right!'

Kiska twisted herself free, backed away. 'But how can I?'

Oleg opened his mouth but a dog's howl, titanic, penetrating, swallowed up his words. Kiska snapped a look behind her, expecting to see the beast about to close its jaws around her neck. She saw instead that what stood behind her now was not a steep cul-de-sac, but two sinuous paths forking off at a wind-sculpted rock shaped like a tree. She turned back to Oleg.

'What's happening?'

Oleg pulled his hands through his wild hair. 'The strain of deflecting them is exhausting.' He spoke as if he were alone. 'Not much longer now.'

His eyes focused on Kiska. 'Tell him – that man – transubstantiation must be the time of striking. Entombment is the way to end one such as him! Tell him Kellanved plans to lose all in order to gain everything. I can foresee now that his victory will be sealed by his defeat. Tell him such is what I say.'

'What in the Queen's wisdom is that supposed to mean?'

Oleg shuddered convulsively. 'He must not succeed! The Throne is mine! Our time is finished.'

'But wait, I—'

Kiska's vision blurred, the landscape darkened. She staggered, fell. A moist wind brushed her face and distant surf pulsed like a slow heartbeat. Oleg's corpse lay at her feet amid the shards of broken tiles. She pressed hands to an aching head. What had happened? Had anything? She knelt on her haunches beside the corpse, touched the blood soaking its clothes. Wet and tacky still. What had all that been? Some kind of a spell, an illusion? A madman's insane gibberish?

'Damn you,' she whispered to the now inanimate husk. 'What have you done to me?'

She glanced around. How long had she stood entranced? Broken clouds rolled overhead and patches of rain swept down, fiercely cold. Every now and again the stars shone through, but faintly, as if cowed by the fat silver moon that squatted just above the horizon. She turned away from it, shaken by the old man's words.

Should she wait out the rest of the night in the brush next to the estate wall, or run to tell someone what she'd heard? But who? Mock's Hold and the Claws? Hardly. According to Oleg they were one of the powers contending this night. One group among many in a field far more crowded than even they knew. And right now she wasn't sure she wanted to just blindly approach them. Where then? Sub-Fist Pell? He'd handed over all authority to the Claws without even lifting his fat ass from his chair! No, there was only one person on the island who could possibly make any sense out of all this: her aunt Agayla. She'd know what to do. But still . . .

She studied the body. It looked obscenely flat, as if deflated by the loss of blood and secrets. Maybe all that talk was just the last reflexive outpouring of a madman. A lunatic schemer to the end. Comforting, that thought. Yes, that was it, most likely. Anything else . . . well, it was all too outrageous.

She turned her sight towards the inland hills. Low patches of cloud hugged them. The storm appeared to promise nothing more than a series of flitting shadows and numbing rain. Shivering and worn out, Kiska pulled at her wet clothes and pushed her flattened hair back behind her ears. It was just the sort of dreary night that always depressed her. She wondered how much time had passed and whether she might catch a glimpse of her quarry – the man Oleg had demanded she approach – between here and Agayla's. It might yet be possible. And what if she did manage to find him again? What should she do? Walk up to him and tell him she had a message from a ghost?

She turned away and grunted at what she saw behind her. There stood the fellow in the dull grey cloak, his head cocked, studying her. He stepped forward. Up close he was rather shorter than she'd thought. She slipped her right hand into her cloak, onto the crossbow's grip. He raised his closed hands before him, a shoulder's width apart. She saw nothing between them, but recognized a garrotist's stance.

'Who are you?' she called softly. She resisted the urge to raise a hand to her throat. He advanced, silent. She stepped backwards, considered her options: how far to the wall? What cover was there? Just how fast could this fellow be?

The marble bench and Oleg's corpse passed on her left as she retreated. 'Who are you!' she shouted, damning any pretence to secrecy now. He smiled a tight predatory grin and kept advancing. What made the assassin so cocky?

Raising his arms up higher than his head, as if he could just walk up and throttle her, he stepped over Oleg's corpse. Or rather, stepped through it. His foot disappeared. She snapped up the crossbow and fired, but the bolt shot right through what was just an image evaporating into shadows.

A self-damning 'Shit' was all she managed before wire closed around her neck from behind. Ice-cold pain knifed though her flesh. She couldn't breathe. She wanted to scream, plead, cry, anything. But nothing could escape her throat.

The assassin leaned close, his chin on her shoulder. 'I was going to pass you by,' he breathed into her ear. 'But you persisted. None of this concerns you. You were mere clutter. Now I send you to my master.'

She felt the fists to either side of her neck tense for a final yank. She arched her back, flailed her arms, kicked, but nothing shook him.

Then something swam into view before her like a fish rising from lightless depths. A body and face took form – Oleg. The shade pointed past her shoulder and its lips moved. The wind sighed words in a guttural language. A cry and an eruption burst beside her. She spun in darkness, limbs flying wildly. From close by screaming filled the air, and Kiska felt herself slammed into the wet loamy ground.

She opened her eyes slowly. Her clothes felt hot and damp. She was sick with dizziness; her ears rang and throbbed. Had she passed out? No, the roaring echo of thunder still reverberated while steam rose from her cloak. She lay in the north planting bed of the E'Karial estate, alive, unhurt even, or so it appeared. Raising herself onto all fours, she hoisted herself upright, wobbled, groggy, then pushed her way through the brittle stalks and grasses onto the patio.

The marble bench lay on its side. Beside it a hole in the tiles steamed in the misty rain. A true lightning stroke? Or magery? The corpse lay where it had. Of the assassin nothing could be seen.

She cursed, or tried to. A cross between a cough and a croak was all she could manage. She slapped at the heated fabric of her cloak. How could she have survived that? Pushing back her hair, she staggered to the overturned bench. It was too heavy for her to lift so she simply slumped onto one carved marble leg. Her fingers traced the gash across her throat. Hissing a breath, she yanked her hand away and studied the glove. Blood showed dark, wet and glistening in the moonlight. Maybe she hadn't survived.

That struck her as hilarious. She laughed, then gasped at the pain. Hood's breath! It hurt just to swallow. Perhaps that was a good sign. After all, did shades feel pain?

She took a long slow breath, felt the air scrape like a wire brush down the raw flesh of her throat. This was definitely news to take to Agayla. The cover of the Shadow Moon was being used to settle old scores. She'd have to get going. Someone was bound to investigate. This was an aristocratic district, after all.

Slowly, her hearing returned. She thought she caught distant sounds: the baying of a hound. Yes, fierce bellowing. And, from far away, shrill cries that could have been screams. Her own hurts faded as it occurred to her: perhaps this night everyone might be too busy to care.

After Faro spoke Sergeant Ash glanced to Temper's booth. His gaze, hooded, merely flicked to one of his men, then returned to the parchment he was studying with Corinn and a few others. That man, another Bridgeburner veteran Temper figured, pushed himself up from his table and strode across the common room, his tread loud in the silence.

'Shut the old man up.'

He wore a hauberk of iron lozenges riveted into boiled leather, and a bare pot helm of blackened steel. The tip of his nose had long ago been sheared off. A thin moustache hung down past his chin. He appeared bored, as if he didn't care much either way, and in this case Temper could tell that appearances weren't deceiving. He would slit Faro's throat if he spoke again. Beside him, Coop gaped up, mute with shock. Trenech stared blankly. The man's hand closed on the horn grip of a dagger shoved into his belt.

'We'll keep him quiet,' Temper said, quickly.

The man hesitated, looked them over, then grunted and sauntered away. Coop stared. 'My God! You don't think he'd have—'

'Shut up, Coop.'

Coop flinched, hurt. Temper squinted sidelong at Ash and the others gathered around the far table. They were studying something – a map?

The howling rose again, further away this time. The men looked about, at the walls, each other. To Temper the tension in the room seemed as thick as the hanging curtains of smoke. Faro stirred again, as if dreaming uneasily. Gently, Trenech clenched the old man's shoulder and Faro murmured something: garbled nonsense, or another language. Trenech seemed to understand. He squeezed again, nodded.

Temper's attention was pulled away by benches scraping and boots stamping the stone floor. The men were readying to leave. Ash stood by the door giving orders to five men. Sergeants, Temper decided. With twelve veterans and another thirty or so hired swords, they had a force of some forty men. Plus Corinn; a true cadre mage would be invaluable. Yet what could they hope to achieve? A limited tactical goal? But what could that be on this island? All he could come up with was the Hold, but that made no sense. Nothing worth anyone's life would be found *there*. Unless it wasn't something they were after, but someone . . . the visiting official. Assassination? But no one took forty armed men on an assassination attempt. That left . . . kidnapping? Temper shook his head. Ludicrous!

Ash, followed by Corinn, approached their booth. Standing close, the man concentrated on adjusting his armoured leather gauntlets. 'You have my word you'll see the dawn if you sit here and make no trouble.' He glanced up. 'Understand?'

Only Temper nodded. Coop squeezed his cloth in both hands and Trenech stared past Ash at Corinn. He looked as if he were about to ask her a question.

'Very well,' and he stalked away. Corinn lingered, sent Temper a hard do-as-he-says look. He simply eyed her, uncertain how to respond. She gave a last quizzical glance at Faro as if she were studying him for the first time.

Temper watched as the squads filed out. The brazier flames jumped in the gusts of damp air blowing from the door. Corinn hung back until nearly all had exited. Their eyes met across the smoky room. She gave a small apologetic shrug then left. Four men remained. All looked to be mere hired swords, street refuse as far as Temper could discern. Two more guards were likely outside and would be spelled as the night progressed. The four sat at a table roughly halfway between the front door and the rear booth. Out came a set of bones. For a time all that could be heard was the wind outside, the snap and crackle of flames, the tossed knuckle bones clicking, and the guards' low talk. Temper studied the men. What were his chances? Could he count on Coop? On Trenech?

He'd seen the hulking fellow break up fights for Coop. He'd just tuck a drunk under each arm and toss them out. But hired swords? He glanced over at Trenech and nearly swore aloud; the fool was dozing! Mouth open and wet, eyes closed, he breathed long and deep; his broad chest rose and fell like a blacksmith's bellows. Temper glared irritation. Everyone seemed mad this night.

The guards laughed, leaned back. One, the youngest, rose from the table and swaggered to the booth. The skinny lad wore a long leather hauberk, slit at its sides, that his legs kicked as he walked. His thick curly black hair stuck out from an undersized helm. He hooked his thumbs into his belt and sneered down at them. Just a youth, Temper reflected sourly, the faintest blond down pale on his upper lip. But his kind were dangerous, with too much to prove to themselves.

'Where's the good stuff, innkeeper?' Coop stared, eyes wide. The youth scowled, shifted a hand to the knife at his belt. 'Don't fool with me or I'll use this.'

Temper nudged Coop who started as if jerked from a dream. 'The pantry,' he gasped, 'through that door. Glass bottles.'

The youth went to the door, opened it, and returned carrying a brown bottle. He paused at their booth. 'You storing ice in the kitchen, old man?'

His brow furrowed with puzzlement, Coop shook his head. Scowling, the guard returned to his table.

'What is it?' Temper whispered to Coop.

'Moranth distilled spirits.'

Temper stared back at the innkeeper. 'Gods, man. That's pure alcohol. How long have you been hiding that?'

Coop lowered his eyes. 'Sorry, Temp. I use it to fortify the liqueurs.'

'They'll be blind in a few hours, but I can't wait that long.'

Coop opened his mouth but one of the guards shouted, 'Quiet back there, damn your eyes! No whisperin'.' Coop snapped his mouth shut. Temper half sat up, but decided against blindly charging in and eased himself back down. He'd wait and watch a few minutes more.

While they played their game of bones the guards tossed back shots of the spirits, gasping as it seared their throats. Temper silently cursed them for amateur fools, the most useless hands out of a bad lot. Of course there was no way Ash would've spared good men for this duty; he needed everyone he could muster for whatever lay ahead. Fists clenched on the table, Temper could stand the inaction no longer and called out to them across the room: 'You don't really expect Ash to come back, do you?'

71

Coop gaped at him.

All four guards turned, their eyes glistening through the brazier's hanging smoke.

'Shut your Hood-cursed mouth.'

'Been paid already have you?'

The youngest jerked up from the table. Another pulled him down, growled, 'Shut that mouth or I'll pin your tongue to your jaw.'

Temper grimaced into the haze. He was almost disappointed he hadn't goaded them into action. At least then it would all be over, one way or another. Waiting was not his strength. Fifty more heartbeats and he'd charge them. That bottle would do well as a weapon. He had to get moving; he wasn't even sure where Ash and his gang were headed.

Coop's boot nudged his. Temper glanced over. The innkeeper, pale-faced and goggle-eyed, stared down at the floor. Temper followed his gaze. Fog, like the advancing lip of a tide, covered the stone floor in a layer no thicker than a thumb's width. It was welling up from behind the small pantry door. *That dark stairwell down into cold cellars no one ever enters.* Soliel's Mercy! Never mind the storm outside: what was gathering right here around them now?

Faro suddenly jerked upright, making Coop yelp. His eyes, clear and aware, made Temper glance away; they opened onto depths far greater than those of any cellar. Faro murmured to Trenech, *'Shtol eg'nah lemal.'*

It was a language Temper had never heard before, though it reminded him somewhat of Old Talian. But Trenech understood. His eyes snapped to the front of the room.

The young guard jumped to his feet. 'Shut that old—'

A hound's roar tore through the air of the common room, exploding from just outside the door. The guards froze, glanced to the door then each other. Their eyes gleamed wide in the firelight. A scream sounded then, a man's cry of utter horror and hopelessness, ending in sobs even as the guards erupted from their chairs. Weapons scraped from sheaths and the guards whispered among themselves, then the oldest of them edged to the door. His free hand hovered at the latch.

'Bell?' he called. 'Bell? You there?'

The latch ground as he opened it. He pulled the door towards him and looked out. A cold wind blew in, whipped flames and sent the clouds of smoke and fog swirling. Temper heard rain hissing down.

The guard shouted up the stairwell. 'Bell? Theo?'

A sigh from across the table brought Temper's attention around. Faro murmured to Trenech, 'Soon, my friend. Very soon.' The man now spoke thickly accented Talian.

Trenech nodded. They ignored Temper and Coop, who sat, eyes bulging, the rag pressed into his mouth.

From across the room, the youth came snarling to the table, his knife out. His pale face glistened with sweat. He waved the knife first at Trenech, then Temper, but when they didn't flinch he turned his attention to Faro. To get at him he'd have to reach in past Trenech, and Temper could see he was unwilling. The knife shook in his hand. He quivered with nerves, frustration and fear. This, knew Temper, was the moment a man could snap.

'You shut him up or by the Gods I'll kill the bastard. I will!'

Temper nodded. Trenech and Faro acted as if no one had spoken.

'Eli!' the older guard called. 'Eli, get back over here, damn you!'

Hunching, the youth edged away, his boots scraping the floor. The door was eased closed and the four conferred. It sounded to Temper as if they were arguing over just who would go outside to check on their companions.

The low fire in the massive hearth guttered then, and went

out. No one said a word. The braziers and low torches now supplied the only light, dim and smoky-yellow. The fire hadn't been blown out or smothered. Rather it seemed to Temper as if the flames had been sucked back down into the very stone itself. A damp cold bit at his ankles. There was sorcery gathering as of a slow summoning, an upwelling like the pressure behind a geyser. Temper had felt its like on a hundred battlefields; soon it would burst.

Low under his breath, Temper hissed to Faro, 'Stop it. No sense making things worse.'

The old man blinked his rheumy eyes as if he were fluttering on his own knife-edge. '*Things*,' he announced, 'will become *much* worse if you do not leave this place at once.'

Temper gaped and pushed himself back from the table. What was the old man up to?

Eli had heard. 'That's damn well it!' he shouted, and came marching across the room.

Temper shot an appeal for help to the other three guards. They looked on with lazy indifference. None moved to help.

Eli waved the knife. 'Get out of the damned booth.'

Faro didn't even seem aware of the threat. He stared off into space.

'Come on,' said Temper, trying to sound reasonable, 'the old man's booze-addled.'

The blade swung to him. 'You,' breathed Eli, his eyes dilated, 'can shut the Abyss up.'

Temper said nothing. At first he'd been hopeful, seeing that no veteran had remained behind. Now he wished one was here. Any veteran of Imperial engagements, marine or otherwise, would smell the danger, the oddness, the charged atmosphere. It reeked of the Warrens; of sorcery. And all any poor foot soldier could do in the face of that was run for cover.

Faro broke the stalemate. He announced, unbidden, 'You have all been warned.'

Eli lunged into the booth but Trenech's hand grabbed his arm. He gave a sharp twist and Temper heard the snap of bones, then Coop's scream. Trenech released the arm and Eli straightened, gaping at the ragged end of bone poking out from the meat of his forearm. He threw his head back and loosed a shriek that ended when Trenech chopped a hand across his throat. A lash of hot blood droplets whipped across the booth as he toppled backwards.

Coop screamed again but Temper clamped a hand over the brewer's mouth. He held himself motionless, staring into Faro's glazed eyes.

A stunned pause, then the trample of boots as the three remaining guards rushed Trenech. Curses, a hoarse yell, a crash as a body slammed into one of the heavy oak tables. Then silence. It had lasted barely an instant.

Coop struggled in Temper's grip then froze. Faro was staring across the table. His lips climbed into a satisfied smile. Temper released Coop, who lay his head on the table, whimpering.

'Leave now,' Faro said. 'Shadow – and Others – come. The Heralds announce. We must be ready.'

Temper swallowed, nodded. Coop took breath to speak but Temper covered his mouth again and edged out of the booth, dragging the man after him. Trenech stood with his back to the room, blocking the front entrance like a granite obelisk.

Temper pulled Coop to the back door but across the floor lay all the guards, dead, crushed by blunt blows. The brewer took one look at the mangled bodies and fainted dead away.

CHAPTER THREE

HOUNDS OF SHADOW

THE SINGLE TINY VESSEL STRUGGLED LOST ON AN OCEAN OF storm. Above, lightning lashed through a solid roof of cloud. The brazier at the boat's mid-thwart glowed, a single beacon of orange against the night. The fisherman rowed, driving the skiff's prow into the heaving waves. All around hail and driven rain tore the slate-grey waters, yet no spray touched the boat to hiss in the brazier or flatten the fisherman's blowing hair. Bronze torcs gleamed at his tanned wrists and the bulk of his wool sweater hid the strength of his arms. Overhead, the roiling clouds seemed to shudder with each sweep of his oars, and every flex of his broad back. He chanted louder now, teeth clamped onto the stem of his pipe, keening into the raging wind:

> 'Was summer I went a rowin' with my glowing bride
> We laughed and tarried 'mid the silken pools.
> Prettier than the lily blossom is my love,
> She moves with grace upon the sheen.
> Her eyes are deeper than the sea,
> Her heart is warmer than all the cold, cold, sea.'

Out amid the waves, riders broached the surface. Their opalescent armour shone silver and sapphire. They leant back then heaved jagged ice-lances. The gleaming weapons darted across the waves. As they entered the eye of calm surrounding the skiff, they burst into mist.

From the distant south, parting a curtain of driving sleet as it came, reared a crag of deepest aquamarine and hoarfrost silver. It advanced upon the skiff with the irresistible majesty of a glacier, but the fisherman heaved upon his oars. In front of him the brazier glowed like a crimson sun. Pennants of vapour shot from the iceberg's leading face. Shards calved away, throwing up clouds of spray.

At the iceberg's skirts the waves churned into a boiling froth as it drove on towards the skiff. But before it came close it sank down, sucked into the depths. The remaining emerald slick of sizzling water disappeared under a slurried web of ice.

New figures now broached the ice-mulched sea. Deepest indigo, their scaled helms revealed only darkness within. Instead of a long lance of barbed ice, each bore short blunt wands of amethyst and olivine. These they levelled at the distant skiff. From their tips cyan lightning leaped, splitting the air, only to dissipate into nothing before the skiff's prow. One by one the figures dived, wands held high.

For a time the skiff was alone on the waves, rising and falling like a piece of flotsam as the fisherman rowed on. But soon more shapes appeared, pale, opalescent, diving in circles around the skiff. Then, from out of the fog, came another ice mountain. Driving sleet tore into the waves all around, but still the fisherman heaved on the oars, back hunched, pipe jutting from between his teeth. He chanted . . .

'Her heart is warmer than all the cold, cold sea.'

*

Kiska jogged down Riverwalk. To one side the Malaz River flowed dark and gelid within its stone banks. Her leather slippers padded silently on the wet cobbles. She'd seen nothing of her target since leaving the Lightings. A low swirling ground-fog obscured the distance and brushed cold fingers across her face and shoulders. Black clouds rushed overhead; it was as if the stars themselves were snuffed out. Only the moon, low on the horizon, cast a tattered pallid glow over the glistening streets. Kiska hoped to check on her quarry closer to the centre of town, yet she'd seen nothing of him thus far. Had he and his bodyguards come this way? Perhaps some errand had taken him elsewhere. But where else could he have gone?

She felt as if she were the last living soul on the island and she shuddered at the thought. On Stone Bridge she paused to glance up and down the river front. Thin rain, more like hanging vapour, softened the distances. Nothing moved – yet things seemed to be moving. She glanced back, squinted. Shadows. Shadows that flickered like soot-fouled flames.

As she watched, the wave of shadows came sweeping down the hillside. It engulfed the riverfront shacks on their stilts and swept on, swallowing the water like a wash of treacle. In a few heartbeats it would pass right over where she stood. Too late, she urged her legs to move. She was still on the bridge when it enveloped her. She ran blind, wiping at her eyes. As the cobbles of the bridge fell from under her feet she yelled and stumbled into ice-cold water.

At first she thought she had fallen into the river, then realized it was only a surface flow – a thin sheen over wet sand. She straightened, gasping for air, her heart hammering. Now that the shadows had dissolved the night brightened. Kiska saw that she stood among tall sand dunes, silver in the moonlight.

She was no longer in Malaz – she knew that – though she had a suspicion of where she might be. The sky was an angry pewter, streaked by high clouds that rippled as she watched. Steep dunes surrounded her like tall waves. She climbed one and turned to marvel at her new surroundings. Smooth, almost sensual, curved hills of sand stretched in every direction. The region resembled the place Oleg had just taken her – the Warren of Shadow.

One detail was jarring, however: the source of the silver-green glow that dominated one horizon. A glacier. Kiska had never seen one with her own eyes, but it resembled the descriptions she'd heard from travellers – a mountain of glowing ice, they'd called it. She'd discounted the stories herself, thought them exaggerated by booze-addled memories. But here was proof. Kiska reflected sourly on just how small her island was, just how bounded her own experience must be. She tried to imagine the crushing weight of all that ice, its dimensions. Just how far away was it? The rolling landscape gave no clue. She brushed the wet sand from her clothes and shivered in the cold wind.

A breathless voice spoke behind her: 'I'd forgotten just how impressive it is at first sight.'

She spun, knives out, only to jump back and yelp her surprise.

Whatever it was, it was dead. Or rather, it was a corpse. Desiccated flesh, empty eye sockets, grinning yellowed teeth. Rags of clothing hung from its angular frame – what was once a thick layered cloak over age-worn leather and bronze armour. The hilt of a sword in a corroded scabbard jutted behind one shoulder. Cold horror stole over Kiska.

'You're from Malaz?' the corpse asked in archaic Talian.

'Yes,' she stammered, 'Malaz. Malaz Island.'

Its head, seemingly welded to its helm of corroded bronze, nodded slowly. 'An island now, is it? I have walked that land many times.'

'Who are you? Where am I?'

'I am called Edgewalker. I walk the borders of Kurald Emurlahn. What you call Shadow. And this is part of that realm.'

Kiska pointed a knife to the far mountain of ice. 'Then what is that?'

'Something that belongs here no more than you.'

'Oh.' Kiska lowered her arm, shivered. 'Well, I didn't ask to come here.'

'You were swept up by a Changing, a shadow storm. They will be frequent. I suggest you stay indoors.'

'Indoors?' Kiska barked a laugh. '*Where?*' Then she clamped her mouth shut. 'You mean . . . you will send me back?'

'Yes. I will. You do not belong here.'

'Then I suppose I should give you my thanks.' Kiska pushed back her hair, eyed the dunes. Was this really Malaz? Then she remembered. 'Do you know a man named Oleg?'

'No. I know of no one by that name.'

'What of a ruler? If this is Shadow then does it have a throne?'

Edgewalker remained silent for a time, long enough for Kiska to lean closer. Had he died?

But at last he asked, 'What of it?'

'I was told someone would attempt to take it this night.'

'Countless have tried. All have failed. Even those who succeeded for a time. Myself included, after a fashion. Now I walk its boundaries forever. And I fared better than most.'

Bizarrely, Kiska felt disappointed by the acknowledgement. She'd half-suspected, half-hoped, that Oleg had been insane. Now she tried to recall more of his babbling.

A low moaning raised the hairs at her neck. The creature raised one sinewy arm like the twisted branch of an oak and pointed back across the stream. Gold rings glinted on his withered fingers. 'A Hound has found your scent. Run while you can, child.'

She needed no more convincing, yet she suddenly remembered. 'What is entombment? What is that?'

'The price of failure. Eternal enslavement to Shadow House.'

The baying returned, closer now, echoing from the distant wall of glittering ice. 'You haven't much time,' said the being, its voice no more than the scratching of leaves. 'Go to Obo's tower. Beg his protection.'

'Obo's tower? But that's an empty ruin. Obo's just a myth.'

'No doubt so were certain Hounds a mere hour ago.'

Kiska blinked her surprise. 'But what of you? Will you be safe?'

The brittle flesh of the being's neck creaked as it cocked its head to regard her through empty sockets. 'The Hounds and I are akin. Slaves to Shadow in our own ways. But I thank you for your concern. Now you must go.'

The creature raised a clawed hand in farewell and at that the world darkened. All around shadows writhed like black wings. For an instant she thought she heard a chorus of whispers in a confusing multitude of languages. Then the shadows whipped away, and she recognized where she stood: Riverwalk, south of Malaz River.

Immediately, a howl tore through the night so loud that Kiska jumped as if the Hound was beside her, ready to close its jaws. She took off at a run, not daring to glance behind. Ahead, a mere few blocks, the jagged top of Obo's ruined tower thrust into the clouds like a broken dagger. Another bellow, loud as a thunderclap, and she stumbled. Screams rose around her, torn from the throats of terrified citizens locked in their houses. She raced around a corner and over an open square, then dived the low stone wall of the tower grounds. Amongst the leaves and tossed garbage of the abandoned yard she lay trembling, straining to listen.

But she heard nothing, only the surf, strangely distant, and the rush of wind. Slowly, she brought her breath under control, stilled her pulse. Something kicked through the fallen branches and she suppressed a yelp. She raised her head a fraction: a thin foot in leather sandals. She looked up. An old man in tattered brown woollen robes, hefting a tree limb as a staff. He was bald but for strands of long wild white hair in a fringe over his ears.

He glowered down the length of a long hooked nose. 'What's this?' he muttered, as if he'd stepped on a cow turd.

Kiska blinked up at him. Who was this doddering oldster? Surely not Obo, the malevolent ogre of legend. 'Who in the Queen's wisdom are you?' she asked warily, and climbed to her feet, watching the man all the while.

'Who am I?' the fellow squawked. 'Who am I? Some gutter-snipe invades my home and questions me?'

'*Your* home?'

'Yes, *my* home.' The old man swept his staff up at the tower and Kiska saw that it now rose massive and undamaged into a night sky gleaming with stars but free of any moon. She peered around – the familiar hillsides ran down to the sea while to the north the cliffs rose like a wall – yet no city surrounded them. Not one building marred a field of wind-swept marsh grasses and nodding cattails.

'Where are we?'

The old man jabbed her arm with the staff. 'Are you dense? My tower.'

'*You're* Obo?'

The old man screwed up his mouth in anger and raised his staff.

Kiska snatched it from his hands and threw it to one side.

The old man gaped at her. 'Why you . . .! That was my stick!'

Kiska tensed, waiting for a blast of magery or a flesh-rotting curse. Instead, the old man turned sharply around and marched up the stone steps to the tower's only door.

'Wait! Hey you – wait!'

The door slammed. Kiska ran up the stairs and beat her fists on the wood. 'Open up. What am I to do?'

A slit no larger than the palm of a hand opened. 'You can go away.'

'But there's a hound out here! You can't leave me outside . . .'

One watery eye squinted past her. 'It's gone away. Now you go away.'

Kiska waved one hand to the marsh. 'Go where? There's nothing *out* there!'

The old man – Kiska couldn't bring herself to identify him as *the* Obo – a legendary name of dread as a sorcerer from ages past. Another favourite of the blood-splashed stories her mother used to tell. He snarled his exasperation. 'Not *here*. You don't belong *here*. You go back to where *you* came from.'

She nodded. 'Good. Yes. That's what I want.'

'Then go away and stop bothering me.' The portal slammed shut.

She backed down the stairs. 'Okay. I will!' she shouted, 'No thanks to you.'

At the low wall she paused and listened. For what, she wasn't certain. A hound's call, she supposed. But there was only the wind hissing through the tall grass and the churning of the surf. Lights caught her eye and she turned, staring to the far southern sky. Blue-green flashes played like banners painted in the night. Kiska shivered, remembering legends that the lights were reflections of the Stormriders, rising to drag ships down into their icy sunken realm. Tales she used to laugh at. But now . . . now she didn't know what to think. She wiped her hands at the thighs of her sodden pants and blew on them. What had the old man meant, '*go back to where you came from*'? How? What was she to do?

In the gloom she could make out slabs of standing stones, a structure of some sort surrounded by a copse of stunted trees and low mounds. It appeared to stand right on the spot where, in Malaz City . . . Kiska's breath caught and she backed away. *Burn preserve my soul.* It stood right where the Deadhouse would stand, or had stood. Only now it was a tomb.

She hugged herself as she shuddered. It wasn't so much the cold as the shock of recognition. This really was her home, or would be. She felt suddenly very insignificant, even foolish. All her life she'd been so sure things never changed here. She wondered whether she could trust what this fellow hinted – that she would somehow return to the city. But then, what choice did she have?

If she did succeed in returning, Kiska vowed she would head straight to Agayla's. If anyone knew what was going on – and what to do – it would be her. Never mind all this insane mumbling of the Return, the Deadhouse, and Shadow. What a tale she had for her aunt!

She took a deep steadying breath, stepped over the wall, and immediately lost her balance. The stars wheeled overhead until clouds like dark cloths flew across her vision, blotting them out. Now the moon glowed behind the clouds like the eye of giants from long ago. Ribbons of fog drifted over her. Wincing, she stood, rubbed at a bruised elbow. Turning, she glanced up to the shattered walls of Obo's tower: a ruin once more. She was back in Malaz – the Malaz *she* knew. He'd done it; or perhaps he'd done nothing and simply walking out of the Tower's grounds had returned her. Who knew how any of this worked? Perhaps Agayla could explain. In any case, she was back and had to get to her aunt's as quickly as possible. That meant braving the streets again. She automatically slipped into the cover of a nearby wall.

Yet, she glanced back to Obo's shattered tower. Maybe she could hide in the grounds till dawn. After all, who was she kidding? She now knew she was outclassed. Who would blame her? Kiska almost growled her frustration. Agayla *must* know what was going on. She had to talk to her.

A bellow erupted from the distance. Kiska flinched – *Gods below!* – and bolted from the shelter of the wall and down the narrow street.

The night's second bell rang out tonelessly as Kiska reached Agayla's rooms. Her aunt lived alone behind her shop on Reach Lane, a street so narrow its second-storey balconies butted each other overhead and occulted the moonlight.

Kiska leaned her weight onto the door and hammered her fist on its solid timbers: planks from a shipwreck, Agayla once told her. Kiska's blows hardly raised a quiver. She stepped back, rain-sodden and exhausted. Woven garlands of ivy and twists of herbs hung over the lintel and down both jambs. When had that been done? Under its small gable, the door's panels had been washed in dark tarry swathes as if a handful of leaves had been ground over them. She caught a sharp peppery scent. Too tired to wonder, she pressed herself to the wood. She whispered, 'Auntie? It's me. Open up. Please open. Please.'

'Hello? Who's there begging and scratching at my door? What lost soul?'

'It's me! Open up.'

'Me? Oho! Any shade will have to do better than that to cross my threshold. Go and pester someone else.'

'Auntie! Please! There are *things* out here! Let me in!'

With a rattle, the door swung inward. Agayla stood at the narrow threshold, a candle in one hand that cast her sharp features into stark shadow and light. 'I know there are, dear. That's why you shouldn't be out.'

Kiska stumbled in, slammed the door. Panting, chilled to the bone, she pressed her back to it, threw home the bolt.

Agayla shook her head as if Kiska had been out playing in the mud.

Still breathless, Kiska pointed to the door. 'Don't just stand there! There are monsters out there. Ghosts! Demons! I saw them. I was almost killed.'

Agayla's lips tightened. 'Everyone knows that, dear. And everyone else has the sense to stay indoors.' Her long skirts rustling, she retreated into her shop, adding over her shoulder, 'Everyone except you it seems. Now come on, we might as well get you cleaned up.'

Kiska could only gape at her back. How do you like that? All she'd been through and not even one word of what? Sympathy? Curiosity? Not even a *How nice to see you*?

While Agayla wrapped her in blankets and rubbed her hair dry, Kiska poured out everything she'd encountered – the men from the message cutter, the meeting, Oleg's murder, the Shadow Realm, and the hound. Or almost everything. She held back her meeting with the ancient Shadow creature, Edgewalker. And Obo; no sense in making things sound even more unbelievable than they were.

Throughout, Agayla said nothing. Letting her talk herself quiet, Kiska guessed. After she stammered to a halt, Agayla put a hand under her chin and raised her face. She winced.

'Is that all?' she asked, pushing damp strands of Kiska's hair back behind her ear.

All? But Kiska nodded.

Lips pursed, Agayla shook out her skirts and stood. 'I'll get some medicine for that neck wound.' She went to the front, disappearing among the rows of standing shelves, each studded by tiny drawers containing a seemingly infinite variety of herbs.

Kiska drowsed in the heat of the thick blanket and the blaze of the fire that burned in a small hearth in the rear wall. Shadows flickered over her as Agayla moved about the shop front. Kiska heard the shush of drawers opening and the clatter of glass jars. Above her head wire baskets hung from the rafters in clusters as thick as fruit. Dried roots, leaves, and entire plants reached down like catching hands. Banks of wall cabinets rose to the ceiling, holding hundreds of slim drawers labelled by slips of yellow vellum. Over the years, Kiska had peeked into almost every cubby-hole, sniffing and studying the dried peppers, powdered blossoms, roots, bulbs, leaves and stems pickled in vinegar and spirits – all manner of bizarre fluids – in bottles, casks, decanters, vials, wax-sealed ivory tusks and even horns, the size of some which made her wonder what sort of animal they could have come from.

Now the mélange of scents seeped over her, stronger then ever. For the first time since stepping onto the docks, Kiska eased the pent-up tension from her limbs and allowed herself to relax.

Agayla returned carrying a tray loaded with a large bowl and folded cloths. Her skirts brushed the floor. She'd pushed up the sleeves of her blouse over her forearms and tied back her long black hair. Setting down the tray, she lifted a kettle from the fire and poured steaming water into the bowl. Petals floated on the surface and powders swirled in its basin.

Imperious, Agayla pushed back Kiska's forehead and began cleaning her neck as if she were a mud-spattered toddler. Kiska winced again.

'Now,' began Agayla, 'what you've been babbling on about is very confused, but I think I can summarize: it looks like you've stuck your nose where it doesn't belong and nearly had it bitten off. And rightfully so.'

'*Auntie!*'

'Shush, dear. Listen to me. That assassin was right. None of what's going on concerns you. As for Oleg, he should never have spoken to you. Frankly, I am very disappointed by his lack of judgement.'

Kiska pushed Agayla's hand away. 'You know who he is – was?'

Agayla raised Kiska's chin. 'Yes. I know who he was, long ago.'

Kiska struggled to stand but Agayla pressed her back. 'Then what about—'

'Sit down!' she commanded, then, more softly, 'Please, sit.'

Startled into silence, Kiska eased herself back down. Agayla had always possessed a high-handed manner, but rarely had Kiska experienced it raised against her.

Agayla sighed and wiped her own brow. 'I'm sorry. This is a trying night for all of us. I—' She silenced herself, listening. Slowly, she turned to the front.

Kiska listened too. The scratch and scrabble of claws on stone, unnaturally loud. Then bull-like panting, snuffling, right at the door. A moment of silence, shattered by blood-freezing baying. Kiska clapped her hands to her ears. Agayla shot to her feet, both hands raised. Then the call diminished as the beast loped off into the distance.

Kiska tried to swallow. *Burn the Preserver*, had that been the one that had followed her? Had it been after her scent? She looked to Agayla. Her face had gone pale. Her raised hands shook. Kiska couldn't believe her eyes; this woman, who seemed to fear nothing, was terrified.

Kiska reached out to a surprisingly chill forearm, whispered, 'Tell me, Agayla. What's going on?'

Blinking, as if returning from somewhere far off, Agayla pursed her lips. She studied Kiska, then managed a tight smile. 'Very well. I will tell you a story – but only if you promise to follow my advice. Promise?'

Kiska hesitated. She wouldn't try to hold her to something she couldn't possibly keep, would she? Agayla had always been stern, but never unreasonable. And she always seemed so well informed about everything. To discover such secrets . . . Kiska nodded.

'Good.' Agayla pushed Kiska's head back, resumed dabbing at the wound. Now it stung and she flinched. 'You know the legends about the Emperor: Dancer, his partner and bodyguard; Surly, creator of the Claws and now Imperial Regent; Dassem, the Sword of the Empire; Tayschrenn and all the others. Well, now I'm going to give you a version that should never be repeated.' Agayla pinched Kiska's chin between thumb and forefinger and gave her a warning look. Kiska nodded again.

'Good. The Sword of the Empire was broken just this year far to the north at Seven Cities. You heard?'

'Rumours came with the army.'

'Well, the breaking of the Sword leaves Surly next in line for succession. Dassem, and the two others of the Sword who survived the battle, died that night. Some say Surly had a hand – or a Claw – in that breaking and in those deaths, but that is neither here nor there.

'Perhaps you didn't know that lately Kellanved and Dancer have been seen less and less. I've heard they've become engrossed in their own arcane research. The Imperial generals, governors and Fists have been complaining to Surly that Kellanved neglects his duties. No doubt her Claws fan the flames of discontent while eliminating their competition, the Talons. Many say that Kellanved and Dancer are dead, consumed in an experiment into the nature of the Warrens that went awry. Oleg believed he knew the truth of that. In any event, a prophecy arose that Kellanved would return here to Malaz Island where everything began so long ago. And behold, a few years later comes a Shadow Moon to Malaz. So, various parties and interests have gathered together in the rather tight confines of this small island, gambling that the future of the Imperium will take a radical turn this very night. As if things weren't dangerous enough with a Shadow Moon . . . and all the rest.'

Agayla squeezed the cloth over the basin. Kiska straightened. 'That's pretty much what Oleg said, that *he* was coming.' But she remembered more – Oleg snarling that *he* would claim the

Realm. But what did the Deadhouse have to do with Shadow? What on earth did the old man mean?

It all sounded so foolish now. Transubstantiation, entombment – though Edgewalker had recognized it. *And who and what was he anyway?* And that riddle of Oleg's. Pure foolishness: 'His victory would be sealed by his defeat.'

Kiska glanced sharply at her aunt: 'And all the rest?'

'Oleg Vikat,' Agayla continued, preparing a white cloth dressing. 'A one-time acolyte of Hood and a theurgical scholar. Claims to have discovered a foundational understanding of the Warrens, and even beyond.' She sighed. 'Mad, perhaps. But the Imperial High Mage himself, Tayschrenn, acknowledged a certain bizarre logic haunting the thicket of his theories. The man has been in hiding these past decades.' She shook her head again. 'To think he feared death from the knives of the Claws.'

'The man in grey. Wasn't he a Claw, sent to silence Oleg?'

Agayla got to her feet to wrap the dressing around Kiska's neck. She folded it tight from behind. 'No, dear. That was a cultist. A worshipper of the Warren of Shadow. Assassins all. They are here as well, gathered for their worship and blood rites under the Shadow Moon.'

Kiska touched at the rough cloth of the dressing. When she swallowed it felt almost too tight. 'Yes . . . he said he'd send me to his Master. But what of the other things? The shadows shifting, the other sights?'

Her aunt's shrug told her that she considered the full explanation beyond even her knowledge. 'You saw these things simply because on this one night of all nights every portal, every gateway, every fault between Warrens, all open a crack. Every ghost, revenant or god can touch the world, however tenuously. So far you have been unusually lucky in your encounters, given what you *may* have run into, which is why—' She stopped herself, dried her hands. 'Well, we can talk of that later.' She sat at Kiska's side, took her hands in a surprisingly strong grip. 'You see? There is too much here for any one person to get hold of. This is a night for long-awaited vengeance and desperate throws. A rare chance for the settling of old scores when the walls between this world and others weaken . . . when shadows slip through. Dawn will come – and it will – no matter what occurs tonight. It will, no matter who lives or dies. Tomorrow there will still be a need for spices and herbs, and for nosey non-commissioned intelligence agents who know the town. Even fat old Sub-Fist Pell will probably still command the garrison. Life goes on, you see?'

Kiska pulled her hands free. 'I know what you're getting at. But I can't just sit here. Not again. Not after the riots.'

Agayla's mouth thinned. 'I probably saved your life, child.'

'I'm not a child. I won't stay locked up tonight – or forever. I can't. I'd go insane. In any case, I'm involved. I have a message to deliver.'

Snorting lightly, Agayla waved that aside. 'The insane predictions of a selfish, power-hungry fool.'

It did sound ridiculous – but that ancient creature, Edgewalker, accepted it. She regarded Agayla narrowly. How much did she really know of her? She called her *Auntie* yet no blood tie lay between them. Sometimes it seemed that half the people on the island called her that. During the enforcement of the Regent's edict against magery, Agayla had done her best to keep her indoors, though she'd managed to be out for most of the unrest. Only for the worst, the wholesale rounding up of anyone suspected of Talent, had she kept her locked upstairs.

What a night that had been! Crying, pleading with the woman, trying to force the windows but finding them somehow impervious to her hammering. Having to content herself with merely watching and listening from the small upper window. Who could've guessed that fires could be so loud? The roar of the flames, the crackling and tornado of burning winds. The reek of scorched flesh; the screams. Men and women charging back and forth in the darkened streets. And the blasts – magery! Later that night she had spied from the top of the stairs, while at the door Agayla faced down a mob of rioting soldiery. Its leader had barked at her, 'You're under arrest, you damned witch.' His grey surcoat and cloak appeared dark, so fresh were they from their dyeing. An Imperial Marine recruit.

Agayla had merely crossed her arms. Kiska had imagined her hard reproving stare. A look that seemed able to melt stone. The soldier had hurriedly raised a hand against the evil-eye and drawn his sword.

'Curse me, will you—' he snarled.

Another soldier pushed this one aside. He too wore marine greys, though these hung loose, frayed and discoloured. Kiska caught the flash of silver regimental and campaign bars at his breast. An Imperial veteran.

'There are plenty of wax-witches and sellers of love potions elsewhere,' Agayla told this one. 'You aren't going to harass me, are you, sergeant?'

This soldier drew off his gauntlets and slapped them against his cloak. Rust-red dust puffed from the cloth. Ochre dust! The very sands of Seven Cities still caked to the man's cloak? The veteran and Agayla eyed one another. After a moment he spat to one side, muttered, 'We've five cadre mages with us if push comes to shove, you know.'

'Go ahead and summon them. But think of your mission here, sergeant. Is it to train these men, or to lose them?'

The solder snorted at that, said under his breath, 'Train my ass.' He inclined his helmeted head to Agayla, waved to the troop of soldiers. 'Get a move on, you worthless camel shits.'

The one who'd been shoved aside raised his sword. 'But Aragan, this is one of 'em . And they say she's—' He eased up close to the sergeant, whispered something.

93

Kiska thought she heard the word *rich*. The veteran snatched the man's sword from his grip and hit the flat of the blade across his shoulder. The man yelped and ducked from sight.

The sergeant shouted after him, 'I said get a move on! Damn your worthless hides.' He turned on Agayla, pointing. 'You,' the fellow ordered, 'keep that damned door shut or I'll come back here and drag you out by the hair.'

Agayla inclined her head in kind. 'Yes, sergeant. I shall.'

When Agayla came back upstairs, Kiska told her that she would never forgive her for locking her inside during the most exciting day she'd ever known. Agayla had merely cocked one brow. '*Exciting?*'

Now, here she was, once more in Agayla's chambers, on another similar night. Yet again she had delivered herself into the protection – and judgement – of this woman.

Kiska cleared her throat. 'This is what I've been wishing for all my life. Please. Let me *do* something.' She stared to one side, not daring to catch Agayla's eye, afraid she sounded like a spoiled child. In the air above the basin of water she saw vapour curling. Vapour?

Agayla remained silent.

'Auntie . . . what is that?'

Agayla peered down. She went still, then whispered, 'Dear Gods.'

What moments before had been a basin of hot water was now a frozen hemisphere of ice steaming next to the fire. Kiska said softly, 'What's going on?'

Her face rigid, Agayla rose. The fabric of her skirts whispered as she crossed to an old desk piled with scrolled correspondence. 'Very well,' she said brusquely. 'I have to admit that I would prefer to keep you here against your will.' She glanced over her shoulder. 'But then you would never forgive me, would you?'

Kiska merely nodded, fighting a smile and the urge to throw herself at the woman's feet.

Agayla sniffed, plucked a scroll from a cubby-hole. 'Yes. All these years wishing for action, marooned in this forgotten corner of the Empire, and now you have it, and more than you or I expected, I should think.' She scratched a message on a yellow sheet. 'If you must do something or never forgive yourself – or me – then I will give you something to do.' She rolled the parchment, sealed it with a drop from a candle, and pressed a ring into the wax.

'Well?' She waved Kiska over. 'Come here. Now, take this to the man you call your target. Do what he says after he's read it. Hmmm?'

Kiska tucked the scroll inside her shirts. 'Yes, Auntie. Thank you so much. But who is he? Where will he be?'

Agayla waved the questions aside. 'He wouldn't appreciate me telling you. But if anyone can take care of you this night, he can. You'll find him somewhere between here and Mock's Hold. And girl, if he gets to the Hold before you reach him, don't go in there. Promise!'

'Yes, Auntie. I promise.' She hugged Agayla round the neck, inhaled her scent of spices.

'Now, child,' she warned, pulling away, 'you might not thank me later. I'd rather you stayed. But somehow you've become entangled in all this, so I must not interfere.'

Kiska nodded, adjusted her shirt, pocketed vest and cloak. She touched gingerly at the dressing over her neck and found that the pain had gone.

Agayla took one of her hands. Kiska glanced up and was surprised by how the woman studied her, her eyes warm, but with a touch of hardness. 'There are things out there that would crush you without a thought. If you should meet one of those beasts, just stand still as if it were any normal wild animal.' Agayla took a slow breath. 'It should ignore you.'

Now that she was free to head out under that moon, Kiska paused. That bellowing. The scouring of those claws on cobblestones. Fear crept back. She ventured, her voice faint, 'Yes, Auntie.'

'Good. Now, before you go, I'll prepare some things for you to take,' and she led the way to the front.

Temper shouldered Coop on his back while Coop's boots dragged behind, scoring twin trails through the mud. One of the brewer's beefy arms was slung stiffly across one side of Temper's neck. The other Temper trapped in his left hand, one of Sallil's largest cooking knives gripped in his right. Coop was a heavy man but Temper ignored the weight, concentrating instead on watching Back Street, and stepping carefully through the trash-littered alley. Moonlight shone down, rippling and shifting as the clouds roiled above. The way ahead appeared empty.

Knees bent, he shuffled farther down the alley. Coop's wide body brushed against the walls to either side until he stepped into the street. He stopped at the first door on his right: Seal's residence.

'Seal,' he called, trying to sound hushed. 'Seal. Open—'

A howl thundered through the town, seeming to erupt from every alley mouth and street. Temper lost his footing and nearly dropped Coop.

'To Hood with this.'

Grunting with effort, Temper cocked one foot and kicked. The door crashed open, the jamb splintering. He threw himself in, dropped Coop, then stood the door back up against the frame. Embers glowed in a stone hearth along one wall, but other than this the only source of illumination was moonlight streaming in through the broken doorway. He saw a chair and kicked it over to wedge against the door.

'Don't move!' a voice ordered from behind and above.

Facing the door he froze, raised his arms to either side. 'It's me, Seal, Temper.'

'Turn around!'

Temper turned, squinting. In the dark, he could just make out Seal standing at the top of the stairs, wearing a nightshirt. He was holding something – a huge arbalest that was balanced on the second-storey railing.

'It's me, dammit!' Temper growled.

Seal didn't move. 'Yes, I can see that. You've got a knife. Cut yourself.'

'What?'

'Cut yourself. On your hand where I can see it.'

'I don't have time—'

Seal levelled the crossbow. 'Do it.'

Coop groaned from where lay, stirred sluggishly.

Temper clenched his teeth then pressed the kitchen knife's keen edge into the flesh at the base of his thumb. Blood welled, running down his hand and forearm. He held up his lacerated thumb. 'See?'

Seal grunted, took a few steps down the stairs, the crossbow still aimed. Closer, Temper saw that the weapon was an ancient cranequin-loading siege arbalest. One of the Empire's heaviest, ugliest, one-man missile weapons. Seal could barely hold it upright and steadied himself against the banister. Temper fought an urge to jump aside in case it triggered accidentally. If it did, he and the door would have damned big holes in them.

'Careful . . .' he breathed, his stomach clenched.

Seal appeared surprised, then glanced down at the weapon and lowered it. 'Sorry.'

It wasn't even loaded. Temper let out a breath, shook his head. He should've noticed that.

Seal dropped the arbalest on a table and knelt beside Coop. 'Hurt?'

'No,' Temper laughed. 'Just scared into a dead faint.'

Crossing to the hearth, Seal touched a sliver of wood to the embers and lit a lamp. 'What happened?'

Temper surveyed the street through the propped door. 'Let him tell you when he comes around; I don't have the time.' He turned. 'You still have my gear?'

Seal nodded. The long and loose kinked curls of his black hair spilled forward over his face. He motioned to the rear. 'In the storeroom.'

'Right.' Temper stepped over Coop.

'Wait, dammit.' Seal waved helplessly to Coop. 'Help me get him onto a bench.' With a sigh, Temper pulled aside a table. He grabbed the unconscious man under the shoulders while Seal took his feet. Together they swung him up onto one of several benches that lined the walls of the room. Waving Temper aside, Seal began unknotting Coop's apron.

Temper lit another oil lamp. 'Why the cut?'

Seal was bent over Coop's head, examining his eyes. 'What?'

Temper held up his blood-smeared thumb. 'My hand. Why'd you make me cut my hand?'

Seal raised his head, smiled. 'Ghosts don't bleed, Temper.'

'That damned arbalest wouldn't be much use against a shade.'

Seal shrugged his thin shoulders. 'Well, I couldn't load it anyway.'

'Fener's tusks, Seal. You've got to get yourself squared away.' As he reached the storeroom door Temper thought he heard a woman's voice call down to Seal, and the medicer's soothing reply.

In the storeroom, behind a travel-chest, he found the bundle of possessions he dared not keep in his room. It was wrapped in canvas, as long as his length of reach. He set it onto a chest and began unbuckling the two leather belts holding it together. Tossing back the oiled hide, he pulled out two belted and sheathed swords. These went over each shoulder, the blades hanging at his back. Short, blunt fighting daggers went beside each hip.

He groped behind the travel chest again and pulled out another bundle, head-sized. Holding it up in one hand, he peeled aside the soft leather. A helmet stared back at him. It was of blackened steel with a mail coif hanging like tattered lace all around, and an articulated lobster-tail neck guard. The T-shaped vision slit and closing cheek guards fixed on him like a ghost from the past: the severed head of his alter-ego. His breath caught; for so long he'd dared not even look at it. He found his armoured gauntlets still stuffed into the padded space within. The stink of sweat, oil, and, he supposed, blood, was prominent. He could almost hear the clash and wails of battle. He shook his head free of the clinging wisps of memory and tucked the helm under an arm. Picking up the oil-lamp, he snorted at the quilted muslin shirt and leather vest he wore. He'd look like a blundering fool strutting around in his bare padded shirt, armed to the teeth and crowned with a helmet!

Downstairs Coop lay moaning, a wet cloth covering his face. Seal crouched at the hearth of mortared stone, feeding a growing fire. A black pot steeped over the flames.

'What kind of poison you boiling up?' Temper dropped the helmet onto the table.

Seal turned. His gaze shifted from Temper's weapons to the helmet on the table. His answer died on his lips. Still eyeing it, he shook himself. 'Just some barley soup. I'm hungry.'

Temper felt his own eyes drawn the same direction. The helmet looked like a grisly trophy. He cleared his throat. 'Ah, Seal, you wouldn't happen to have any armour around, would you?'

Poking the embers, Seal snorted. 'You're not actually heading out there again, are you?'

Temper bristled. 'Yes.'

'Whatever it is, it can't be that important, Temp.'

'I don't even know if it is. But I've got to find out.'

Seal raised an arm, pointed to an iron-bound chest against the far wall. 'My great-uncle's. From the Grist-Khemst border wars. Long time ago. All I've got.'

Temper unlatched and opened the chest. 'Togg's teeth,' he breathed. Inside was a jumble of bundles, sacks, bits and remnants of armour: swatches of mail, grieves, boiled-leather vambraces set with steel rings. From amongst this tangle he lifted a cuirass and skirtings that looked long enough to hang to his knees. It consisted of a front and back with shoulder and side strapping, and coarse scaled sleeves. A leather underpad, almost as thick as his thumb and softened by years of use, supported a layered and patched hodgepodge of mail, bone swathing, studs and horizontal steel, ribbed down the front and back. Interlocking iron rings were sewn from the waist down and over the slit leather skirting. He hefted it, whistling. Whoever humped this over a battlefield must've been a bull of a man.

Temper examined the straps. 'Hadn't they heard of using the point up there?'

'It was all hack-and-slash in the north back then.'

He nodded, thinking back to all he'd heard of the generations of internecine warfare between the Gristan minor nobles and their confusion of principates, protectorates, baronies, and freeholds. He'd joined up long after the Emperor had pocketed them like so many paltry coins.

He caught Seal's eye. 'Can I use this?'

He waved a help-yourself.

Temper pulled off his weapon belts and began readying the cuirass. While he worked, Coop groaned, then pulled the wet cloth from his face and raised his head. He blinked at Temper. 'What happened? What're you doing?'

'I'm going after those thieves, Coop.' Temper raised the undershirting, began wriggling into it.

'Thieves? But, Trenech ... he, and then he ...' Coop groaned again, shut his eyes. 'Burn preserve us.'

Seal cocked a brow, mouthed, *'Thieves?'*

Temper shrugged. He was struggling with the side-buckles, and for a minute Seal just watched. Then he crossed the room, pushed Temper's hands away and began expertly fitting the leather straps. Temper watched his deft fingers.

'You've done this before,' he joked.

Seal glanced up, his mouth tight, then returned to his work. The anger in his eyes startled Temper. 'Usually I undo the armour. And usually the soldier is lying down, spitting blood and absent a limb or two.'

Temper swallowed at the bitter tone, but said nothing while Seal sized the cuirass as best he could. Finished, Seal slapped him on the back and said acidly, 'There you are. Fit for the Iron Legion now.'

'Thanks,' Temper said, not caring if Seal took offence because he meant it. Yet, in his peculiar way, Seal had both praised and damned: for while the Iron Legion had been an elite heavy infantry regiment, it had been annihilated during Kellanved's invasion of the once independent kingdom of Unta.

Whatever Seal had seen or been through during his career as medicer for the Malazan Army, it must've been soul-destroying to have left such scorn in one still so young. When Temper had first arrived, he'd met the young scholar at the Hanged Man and often they'd talked. But while Seal seemed eager for the company, he also seemed impatient, damning everything Temper had to say. The young man had also picked up an addiction to the stupefying D'bayan poppy during his travels with the army. The habit disgusted Temper. Eventually they'd argued and Seal ceased coming around. Temper had counted on Seal being conscious tonight, but more than half-expected to find him insensate instead, embalmed in a cloud of choking jaundiced smoke, grinning idiotically while the town went to Hood around him.

Seal retreated to the table, but shied away from the helmet. He smiled suddenly and laughed. 'I suppose tomorrow they'll be clamouring for my services. Fluttering rich Dowagers with vapours to calm and nervous disorders to diagnose.' His gaze passed over Temper quickly, rested on Coop. 'Don't let anything happen to you because you couldn't afford me.' He gave a sour, self-deprecating smile.

Temper tucked the helmet under his arm. 'Sorry about the door.'

Eyes closed, Seal shrugged. 'I guess it'll be open from now on. Come around and show me what's left of you.'

Temper hefted the door to one side. 'Will do.' He gave a salute – the old Imperial fist to chest. 'Thanks for the armour, and stay off that damned smoke.'

Sighing his distaste, Seal answered the salute.

Temper jogged up Back Street, heading for the Old Stone Bridge close to the swampy mouth of the Malaz River. Three blocks from the Hanged Man he came to a darker pool of wet on the cobbles around a pile of viscera. He stopped, listening. The night was still. The surf moaned, strangely muted, while the wind whispered and gusted. The surrounding streets showed no other sign of violence. Crouched on his haunches, he looked more closely. Human innards, steam rising in the damp air. Was this all that remained of Bell, late guard at the Hanged Man? Was it a hound's work? It looked more like the attack of a predatory cat such as the catamounts of the Seti Plains, or the snow leopard of the Fenn Ranges of northern Quon Tali. Still, that damned baying sounded as if it reverberated from a beast the size of a bhederin.

He stood, eyed the frowning cliff face and Mock Hold, perched above like a dark thunderhead. No lights shone, no fires burned along its walls. It was as if the fortress was as lifeless as a crypt. Yet Temper felt certain he'd find the answers to tonight's mysteries concealed within its halls. At least he hoped to; he had no idea where else to look. He jogged on, heading across the centre of town.

On Agayla's doorstep, Kiska had waited, enclosed in a hug that seemed to go on forever. Letting go, Agayla had eventually stood back, hands still tight on Kiska's while she stared out into the darkness. For one terrified moment Kiska had thought she would forbid her to leave. She revisited her haunted vision of wasting away on the tiny island, walking in circles round and round its narrow shores. But the instant 'Burn watch over you' had passed the old woman's lips, Kiska's thoughts were free to fly ahead into the night. She waved goodbye, but her mind already was on Cutter's Strait – the main north–south concourse dividing the old town from the new.

Now, crouched deep in the shadow of a chimney, her toes curled around the edges of wet roof tiles and her back to the warm brick, she looked out over the deserted streets. From here the town seemed dead – every window shuttered, cloth hung to disguise any sign of life. The moon leered down like a mocking eye.

She gripped the crossbow across her knees, trying to squeeze reassurance from its weight and resilience. Tonight, just a mere few turnings into the streets, and she no longer knew where she was. The experience had shaken her to her very core. It was as if she had suddenly found herself in another town. She had no idea which direction to take or how to get back. Yet the streets possessed an eerie familiarity. This looked to be near where she'd run during the riots that erupted in response to the Regent's ban against sorcery.

It had been the first night of the protest, before simple crowd dispersal had degenerated into outright looting, arson and extortion; before Agayla locked her away. She'd watched from the rooftops while unseasoned soldiers ran wild, drunk with their newfound power, behaving like wharf-front thugs. The few veterans seemed unable – or unwilling – to contain them.

She'd turned away, sickened, carefully tracking a rooftop path from the worst of the crash of shop-fronts and roaring fires, when a shout pulled her attention down into the confines of a dark alleyway. Three soldiers baited an old man, grey-haired, whip-lean. A fisherman by the look of his thread-bare shirt and oiled trousers. Laughing, they punched and kicked him while he retreated up the alley. The sight enraged her, and without thinking she'd pried loose the largest roof tile she could find and heaved it down amid the soldiers.

One man fell immediately, dropped by the heavy ceramic. His friends shouted their astonishment and ran from the alley. The old man staggered back. Kiska ran to a roof corner over a grated window and let herself down. From there, holding fast to the window bars, she set her feet atop a fence, then lowered herself to the garbage-strewn pavement.

The soldier lay stunned, perhaps even dead. His friends had vanished. She searched for the old man but found no sign of him. He must have stumbled off while she was climbing down. Shaking her head she turned to go, but discovered that the other two soldiers had not fled as far as she'd expected. They now blocked the only way out – unless she attempted to climb again. And she didn't believe they'd give her time for that.

A step scraped the stones behind her and she spun to put her back to the wall. It was the fallen soldier, now standing. Blood smeared one side of his face, his leather helmet askew. Fury glistened in his dark staring eyes.

Kiska's hands flew to her knives but the soldier clamped her arms to her sides in a crushing bear hug.

'C'mon boys!' he yelled, laughing. He pushed his blood-slick face against hers, searching for her mouth. He whispered huskily, 'What a great trade we've made.' He wrenched her wrists together and clasped them in one hand. His other hand squeezed at her chest, tore at the lacing of her shirt beneath her vest. His friends shouted encouragement, while from all around came the roar of the mobs on the streets.

Kiska froze as the full horror of her position suddenly struck home. How could she have done this to herself? She almost opened her mouth to plead, then remembered Agayla's training. Her arms pinned, she lifted her head back as far as she could, then head-butted the soldier with all her strength. He bellowed, released her and staggered away. She blinked back tears. Stars dazzled her sight.

'Bitch,' he snarled, from somewhere close. His voice was barely audible over the surrounding shouts and screams of fighting. Kiska caught the grating of steel clearing a scabbard. She shook her head, blinked back tears and lashed out back-handed with the pommel of one dagger. She caught the man across the wounded side of his head and he fell without a sound.

From the mouth of the alley one of his friends shouted, 'Goddamned whore!' Moving fast, he closed on her, arms wide to stop her should she try to run past.

She watched his approach, marvelling. Did he really think she'd just try to run away? Couldn't the fool see how things had turned? That it was he and his friend who ought to run? She shrank away as if terrified and the fellow immediately stepped in close. She kicked him in the groin. He doubled over while his breath exploded from him in a whoosh. She reversed her dagger and smacked him across the temple and he toppled.

Kiska raised her eyes to the remaining soldier. He stood still, silhouetted from behind at the alley mouth by the glow of torches. Exhilarated, panting, Kiska invited him in with a wave. *Come and get some.* He ran off like a startled rabbit.

She sat down heavily in the filth of the alley. The noise of the riot seemed to recede, along with its orange and yellow glow.

Her limbs shook and she bent over, heaving up her stomach. She wiped her arm across her mouth. Burn's consuming embrace! That had been far too close to be worth it – and worth what, anyway? Saving an old man from a kicking? She sat for a time, sick and angry with herself, then stood. She sheathed her daggers and pulled herself up the fence. She vowed then that would be the last time she ever stuck her neck out for anyone.

Yet here she was, out in the night while her flesh crawled with dread. The town seemed to be changing before her eyes. Shadows moved. Unfamiliar streets and buildings shimmered into view only to waver, dissipate and reappear elsewhere. Even the night sounds seemed distorted. Where was the surf? Kiska had grown up in this port and couldn't think of a single day empty of the sea's steady pulse. Now it had vanished. On any other day or night she knew exactly where she stood just by smelling the air and listening to the voice of the waves. But everything was all twisted around and backwards. She couldn't even be sure in which direction lay Mock's Hold. Like that night just months ago, this was more than she'd bargained on. That night it had been an attack on her body; tonight she felt much more than mere flesh was at stake. She hated herself for it, but felt she ought to hide here like a rain-damp stray till dawn. Not even the possibility of a hound sniffing at her trail would impel her to move on.

Blinking, wiping away the icy mist on her face, she watched thin clouds flit and roil over the town like angry harrying birds. One roof-hugging tatter of vapour, opalescent silver, darted suddenly between buildings just to her right. As it arced down it took on a semblance of a giant lunging hound, its forepaws outstretched. An instant later an ear-splitting howl shook the walls and sent her jumping as sharply as if a dagger had plunged into her back.

She screamed, her voice melding with those of people locked

into their homes beneath her, and she scrambled away, running from roof to roof, oblivious of the rain-slick tiles.

She leapt down onto second-floor balconies, balancing on their rickety stick railings, and threw herself across lanes to ledges and gables opposite. She scampered up clay tiles, the sound of their fall clattering below, over shake-roofed breeze-ways above alleys, and across flat brick and stone-roofed government buildings. From a featureless gable of one building, she jumped over the gap of a lane to land onto a temple dedicated to Fener. Her gloved hand caught a boar's head gutter funnel. Grunting, she pulled herself up onto the walkway behind and knelt, hands on knees, drawing air deep into her burning lungs.

Surely it couldn't follow her here. Not into sacred precincts. Certainly now she must be safe. She raised her head to peer over the stone lip. Shadows swirled like wind-swept veils. She looked away, dizzy, pushed back her hair. Probably nothing had been after her, but who would wait to find out?

A man stepped out from an open archway. A priest of Fener, complete with boar's tusk tattoos curling across his cheeks. He smiled as he saw her. 'So this is our fearsome invader.'

Kiska backed away around the walkway.

'Wait! Stay!'

She heard him coming after her and stepped up and out onto another boar's head finial, where the wind tugged at her wet clothes.

'Fener's blood, child. Don't!'

She pushed off with her legs as strongly as she could. Her outstretched hands slapped against the ledge of the building opposite. One knee cracked into the stone facings and she almost lost her grip at the shooting pain. She heaved herself up, thanked the gods for the crammed cheek-by-jowl housing of the city, as well as the cheapness of her fellow Malazans, too tight-pursed to pull it all down and start over again.

Prostrate on the rain-slick roof, Kiska saw that the priest still watched her, his face wrinkled with concern. She dragged herself to her feet, then waved.

The old man cupped his hands at his mouth, yelled through the gusting wind: *'I'll send a prayer after you!'*

She waved one hand in thanks, and limped on despite the burning of her knee.

The final expanse of roof to cross stopped her. Sucking in gulps of cold night air, she stood at the very lip of a third-storey gable, overlooking the stretch of copses and hilly meadow littered by the ruins everyone called Mossy Tors.

She studied the rooftops behind her. What a fool she'd been! To imagine she'd be safe anywhere out of doors! *Gods above.* Here was high sorcery such as she'd never dreamed to see. It was like stories of great Imperial engagements, when the Malazan mage cadre smashed the Protectress of Heng; the breaking of the legendary island defences of Kartool; the siege of the Holy Cities; or the massed battles far overseas on the Genabakan continent.

As the fear gradually drained away and her heart slowed, she brought her respiration back under control. Dread eased into excitement, a rush such as she'd never known. Her limbs tingled and clenched for action; she felt potent, competent. She could smell the power out there, and she wanted it for herself.

Kiska studied the thinly forested commons. Perhaps her flight hadn't been as blind as she'd thought. Something was out there, among the trees. She lay down on her stomach alongside the gable. She watched for a time, motionless. Ragged moonlight shone down through the wood; aruscus trunks glowed in the monochrome light as if aflame.

Then movement . . . what she'd thought to be shadows of branches shifting in the uneven wind resolved themselves into shapes flitting from cover to cover. Grey-clad figures, ghost-like, crawled and darted as they closed on the largest of the moss-covered stone mounds. Through the branches of twin tall cedars a flash glimmered then disappeared – what might have been the faintest reflection of moonlight on polished metal.

Well, these cultists had been following her target earlier, so why not now? After all, how many others could be stupid enough to be out on a night like this, other than herself? Kiska turned to find a route down.

After running across a lane and pushing through thick brush, Kiska edged from tree to tree. Near the middle of the green she stumbled across a body. Whoever this grey – Shadow cultist, she corrected herself – had been, she couldn't have been much older than herself. Her body slumped to one side, propped up at the base of a lone leafless oak. Kiska knelt to inspect the corpse. The robes were fine-spun linen and from their disarray she guessed the body had been searched. She'd been killed quickly, professionally, by the single thrust of a large weapon from the front. Blood pooled on the girl's lap, blackening the knotted tree roots beneath her.

Gloves on, Kiska took a handful of the long sandy hair and lifted the head. No one she recognized. But that didn't mean much if the society was as secret as Agayla claimed. For all Kiska knew, the woman could've come all the way from the Free Confederacies said to lie far to the south of Genabackis.

Letting the head loll forward, Kiska glimpsed a discolouration on the woman's chest. The thin tunic beneath the robes had been torn open. She carefully peeled back the fold of cloth. A tattoo rode high on the woman's chest: the likeness of a severed bird's foot. A bird of prey, perhaps a falcon or a hawk. Kiska studied the mark, wondering about its significance. Agayla had mentioned *Talons*, old rivals to the Claws, but it was the first she'd heard of them. A pocket of wind-driven rain pattered down and droplets fell from her hair. They struck the tattoo and its colours blurred. Fascinated, Kiska rubbed two fingers across the sigil. It smeared into a mess of pigments.

She sat back on her haunches. Well, well. Some sort of recognition sign? A pass? Why a bird's foot? The Claws came to mind, but she knew the sign of the Claws and this wasn't it. Yet another mystery in a night virtually raining mysteries. She'd file this one away for later investigation; it had delayed her long enough.

The oak the body lay under rose from a hollow between two low stone walls, so buried in damp blankets of moss as to appear no more than twin and parallel lumps. The cultist might have been guarding this route because it led to a hillock of blocks that, if memory served, should lie along one side of the main formation. Studying the woods, Kiska realized that the unnerving shadow-shifting had ceased. The night was still now. Either the phenomena came and went, or this area was somehow unaffected. Alternately crouching and crawling, she reached a wall that she thought ought to offer a view of the main ruins. She leaned against it, gathered herself, checked her crossbow, then peeked over the top.

She spotted the one she sought almost instantly. He sat against a stone, legs straight out before him, arms crossed, his hood pulled back. His queue of long black hair hung forward over one shoulder. Raising a dark and lean face towards the night sky, he scowled, not liking what he saw. His four body-guards occupied positions around him: two hunched behind blocks, two standing edge-on against pillars of vine and moss-encrusted stone. Further out, encircling the ancient mound, waited cloaked shapes as motionless as the rocks. Fifty at least. They'd harried her target here, that much was plain. And now they waited – but for what?

Though she wore gloves, Kiska rubbed a hand on her thigh as if to wipe sweat from her palm. No doubt they meant to send the man to their master, just as they'd tried with her. Yet they appeared to be waiting for someone or something . . . some sign. She damned her luck. Here she was in sight of her quarry, yet he remained as unreachable as if she'd never found him. Damn Fate and the feckless Twins – they played havoc tonight!

The bodyguard with the long tribesman's moustache and fur cap approached her man, gestured to the north – Mock's Hold? He nodded, stood, brushed at his loose pants. He pulled his cloak tightly about himself. The guards fell in about him.

Some of the cultists stirred, closing on the outcrop. Kiska counted fifteen. She wanted to hail a warning, but surely the man must know. Then she glanced back over the encirclement and froze. Three extraordinarily tall and thin cultists in ash-pale robes now stood to one side. Where in the Queen's Mysteries had they come from? It was as if they'd *stepped out of the night*.

One raised a gloved hand in a negligent gesture and the cultists charged in.

Kiska dashed to new cover to keep her quarry in sight. He and his guards maintained a steady and tight retreat. Cultists darted in, knives flashed, robes twisted and flew, and the man and his companions kept backing off, leaving dead behind. The three commanders, or priests, followed at a distance, observing. Kiska moved parallel to the fight, catching glimpses through the trees: the guards duelling, disengaging, ever edging backwards around her target. Their skill amazed her.

A larger knot of cultists coordinated an attack from all sides. Each guard was engaged by more than one man and Kiska's heart went to her throat. This was the man Agayla had sent her to find! This was the man Oleg said must act tonight! Here he was, about to be butchered by these assassins and there was nothing she could do about it. She was too late! Kiska fairly screamed her frustration.

While she watched, two of the guards fell and the cultists streamed in on her man. He snapped a hand-gesture and a brilliant flash blinded Kiska. Thunder rolled over her as she blinked and rubbed her eyes. She glanced back. Where a struggling knot of some ten figures had writhed and fought, now only three stood: the man and his two remaining body-guards. He now faced the three tall cultists. They halted.

The one at the centre raised a hand like a man parting cobwebs blocking his path.

The lesser cultists waited, weapons bared.

Though not a *talent*, Kiska knew herself to have a feel for such things, and though she stood some hundred yards off, she could feel the forces gathering between the two men. It was like being deep within a ship's hull, knowing that dark incomprehensible forces churned scarce inches from you, forces that could smash you into non-existence in an instant. She held her breath, waiting for the slightest motion to release the power building between them.

Then a hand in a rough leather gauntlet clamped itself over her mouth, and an arm wrapped around her waist and lifted her away from the stones.

Kiska dropped the crossbow, flailed and kicked her legs. All the while she slowly drew her slimmest knife with her right hand. As the dagger cleared its sheath her head was given a savage wrench. Sparks burst upon her vision and searing currents lanced down her spine.

'Drop it, lass,' a low voice growled, 'or I'll snap your neck like a twig.'

Numb, Kiska let the dagger drop to the ground.

The man slung her over his shoulder, limp, her heart flutter-ing, hiked back down between the parallel ridges, past the dead cultist that Kiska concluded he must have killed. She damned herself for not suspecting the murderer might still be hanging about. And now she was being carried farther and farther from the ruins. She strained to listen for sounds of battle but heard nothing. Once her captor entered thicker woods, two other men rose and joined him. They were either soldiers or plain ruffians. It was hard to tell, though they did carry themselves with the discipline of veterans. One faced her, pulled a black cloth from his belt, while the one holding her removed his hand from her mouth.

'Quiet,' he warned.

A gag was snapped over her mouth before she could recover and the cloth, a bag, was tossed over her head. She did try to yell then, stupidly late, and fought while they tied her wrists in front, followed by her ankles.

She was again hefted over a shoulder and hauled like a sack while the man jogged through the woods. She stopped struggling then and burned instead at the indignity of it.

She'd been wrong about one thing. Someone else *was* stupid enough to be out this night. And she'd become so engrossed in watching the battle she'd completely dropped her guard.

Disgusted, she decided she deserved whatever was to come.

After a fair march she was carried into a room and dumped into a chair, which left her hip smarting. People – men – moved about, muttering. Hands patted her down, found her throwing spikes and daggers. But the search was rushed, missing one throwing knife secreted in a flap of her cloak's collar. Impatient hands prodded up her sleeves, turned her arms this way then that, pulled open her jerkin, her padded vest, and tore the string ties at the neck of her linen undershirt. Had she not been gagged, Kiska would've laughed as she knew exactly what they searched for: tattoos – the real article or fake – of either the severed bird's foot or a claw.

Finding neither, the hands pushed her clothing closed again. She heard a male voice, close: 'Damned fools.' The hood was yanked off, then the gag. Kiska blinked, shook her hair from her eyes. She scowled up at a sinewy, broad-shouldered man whose weathered face bore a startling pattern of burn scars from lye or boiling oil.

He stepped back, glanced to a table where the man who'd first grabbed her sat with his feet up on a chair. Kiska recognized him by his leather hauberk with its iron lozenges riveted in rows and his plain blackened iron helmet. A thin moustache hung down past his chin and scar tissue made a knob of his nose. The man shrugged. 'Nab someone, you said. I had one of them grey-robes but she was too much trouble. Grabbed this one after that. She was eyeing the fight.'

They were at an inn. Kiska recognized it: the Southern Crescent. Men stood about, either watching her indifferently or scanning the street from windows and the door. She counted about forty.

The scarred man turned to her. 'All right. What's your story? Who do you work for?'

'Who do you work for?'

The man slapped her. It felt as if a slab of iron had been smacked across her chin. She blinked back tears, shook her head, stunned more by the casual brutality of the act than the pain.

His eyes remained chillingly flat, merely judging the effectiveness of his blow. Then something caught his attention behind her and he grunted, turning away. A woman walked out from behind Kiska. Short, dark, a thread-fine tattooing of lines and spirals running from her hair line to the tip of her nose, she raised Kiska's chin in a gesture eerily similar to that of Agayla's. Kiska had seen the woman around. Carla? Catin?

Studying her, the woman pursed her full lips, nodded as if identifying her in turn. Kiska was shaken to see regret follow the recognition – she wouldn't live through this; she'd been sentenced the moment the hood left her head.

The woman was turning away when her gaze stopped at Kiska's chest. She extended a hand and Kiska felt her fingertips tap Agayla's flattened scrolled letter. Kiska stared into the woman's eyes, silently pleading. The woman met her stare,

114

sympathetic but pitying too, as if Kiska was already dead. She approached the scarred man at the table.

'She's local talent,' she said, her voice low. 'Independent. Reports to Pell only.'

The man shrugged as if he no longer cared. With one finger he traced a curve on a parchment spread across the table. 'We'll just go around. Ignore that crowd.'

'What if we run into them again?'

The man looked up, stared in his bland manner. 'Your job is to see that we don't.'

The bindings cut into Kiska's wrists. She ached to speak in her defence, to beg, stall ... anything ... but the words bunched in her throat, constricted by the intuition that if she spoke they'd just kill her to be done with it. So she remained silent, listening instead. What was this gang of brigands up to? Looting under cover of tonight's chaos? If so, what did the cultists have to do with it? Had they clashed?

The woman glanced at her again, took a breath, and leaned close to whisper something to the scarred man. He smiled in reply, his lips merely tightening over his teeth, utterly empty of humour. 'You going soft on us?' he answered, without looking up.

Adjusting her vest, the woman offered Kiska a slight shrug to convey she'd done all she could. Though it was her life the man had just dispensed with, Kiska forced herself to respond in kind – a small nod. Fear no longer clenched her throat. She wanted to cry. Grotesquely enough, what stopped her was something she'd never have suspected: pride.

The parchment crackled crisply as the man rolled it up. Handing it to one of his followers, he beckoned the others to him. Kiska tensed, her breath shallowing; they were readying to leave and she wouldn't be going with them.

The scarred man spoke to four of his men, one of whom was the man who'd snatched her. They were all older, more hardened and at more ease than the others. Kiska knew she wasn't being discussed; her fate had been decided.

A young man at a front window yelped, then jumped away from the wall. 'A Hood-spawned ghost! A shade! At the door!'

The scarred commander and his squad broke into motion without orders or comment, confirming to Kiska that they were a team of veterans, perhaps part of a unit of Imperial marines.

The one with the lozenge armour drew two curved swords and went to the door. With a sharp blow of his elbow he shoved aside the young hiresword who had been standing guard. Just back from the door two veterans knelt, crossbows levelled. The remaining soldier, along with the commander and the woman, positioned themselves behind. All of them waited, tense, focused upon the door. In her chair far to the back near stairs down to a lower room, Kiska watched as well. Oddly, she too had felt something at the door: a nagging pull like faint scratching.

One of the others, a hiresword Kiska supposed, crept away from the side door he'd been guarding, past Kiska, until he was close to the commander. 'What is it?' he whispered.

Glaring savagely, the commander waved him back to his post.

The veteran by the door crouched, looked back to the woman who nodded. Grinning like a fool, he yanked the door open.

It swung inward, revealing an empty street of gleaming rain-slick cobbles and, barely visible through the mist and shadows, Mossy Tors Commons across the way. The man poked his head out only to suddenly flinch back and scramble away.

Light flickered over the door's solid recessed panels in a restless curving design of shadow and phosphorescence. The woman pushed forward, studied the restless glow. After a few seconds she backed away.

116

'Well?' demanded the commander.

The woman clenched and unclenched her hands as if she wished to do something with them but dared not. 'It's a Hood-damned invitation. A summons. We've got to go. Now!'

'That's fine with me.' He motioned his men away from the door, flashed a hand signal.

'We're movin' out!' bellowed the soldier in lozenge armour. Those covering the windows and at the tables blinked at him. Their gazes shifted to the street front. 'That's right my pretties,' he said, as cheerily as if facing a summer's day. 'Back into the teeth of it!'

Kiska stared at him. Was he mad?

The sergeant – Kiska decided he must be – set his fists at his belted hips and regarded the room as if he smelled something distasteful. 'Get your—'

A howl as brassy as the largest temple bell tore through the night. The timbers of the wall and floor vibrated, so loud and close did it sound. Kiska flinched violently, causing her chair to jump and almost canter over with her. The men froze, eyes round. Only the commander and the woman seemed un-affected. 'Shut the blasted door!' he snarled.

The sergeant moved to obey, but gripped the door only to stare out, immobile. 'Hood's own demons,' he gasped in awe.

From where she sat, Kiska couldn't see the street. Instead, all she saw was one young hiresword at a window as he screamed and gagged, vomiting while the commander drew his blade. With all his strength the sergeant hurled the door shut then leapt aside. 'Ready crossbows!' he yelled, and the men scrambled to raise their weapons.

At that instant the door burst inward in splinters that flew apart like shards of glass. A hound thrust its head and shoulders through the doorway. It was larger than Kiska had ever imagined: the size of a mule, its shaggy coat dappled light tan and grey. It swung its massive head from side to side as if to study everyone, first through one brown eye, then a pale-grey eye. A fusillade of quarrels met it only to slam into the jambs or skitter from its flesh. It shoved forward, its muscular shoulders bunching. The jambs to either side shattered.

The room erupted in cries. Furniture crashed, the hound's snarls and coughs burst like explosions. Its hot moist breath filled the room. Men slashed at the creature, but to no effect Kiska could discern. Most just tried to flee out of the windows or hide under the tables. Tipping her chair, she threw herself to the floor just in time to see the commander running upstairs. The woman had vanished already. A few feet away the sergeant grabbed one screaming hiresword by his hauberk and threw him fully at the hound, then leapt through a shuttered window. Kiska reached up and back and snatched the knife from behind her neck. She sawed furiously at the rope around her ankles and thanked the twin gods of chance that her hands had merely been bound at the wrists.

Rolling under a table at a booth, she watched while the beast barged about the room, slashing left and right, knocking men spinning as it lunged and snapped. Catching one man by his waist, it tossed him away like a bone. Blood spattered the plaster walls, the tarred timbers, splashed up its massive paws as they thudded across the straw-covered floorboards. Growling like a fall of gravelled stones it stalked the room, stepping over toppled tables, ducking its bloodied muzzle into booths. The hot rank blast of its breath reached Kiska as it neared her.

From where she lay frozen, Kiska could see that three men remained upright. One was hunched inside an opposite booth, his breath coming in short, rasping gasps. He stared at the beast the way someone might watch on-rushing doom. By the door the second wept uncontrollably, fumbling with his cross-bow. The last was a veteran, jammed into one corner, a short sword levelled before him.

The growling stopped and the room became silent. Flat and motionless, Kiska watched while one blood-soaked paw stopped before her booth. Its claws tore splinters from the hardwood floor. She found she couldn't move, couldn't breathe to scream even had she wanted to. A spicy desert odour seemed to fill the air. Kiska pictured its huge muzzle above her, lowering. She squeezed her eyes shut and wrapped her arms about her head.

Close by someone coughed and the beast swung away. Wood crashed, snapping, then Kiska heard the wet crunch of bones. Peeking out, Kiska saw the hound raise its glistening wet muzzle from one body to regard the man fumbling to cock his crossbow. Sensing its attention, he stilled. Looking up his eyes became huge. The hound lunged forward, took one arm in its jaws and shook the man savagely. With a dull, wet tear his body flung free, whirling in the air for a moment before smacking hard against a pillar.

The second man – a youth – wept in terror. With a sudden dash he threw himself to the floorboards where he knelt, head down, as the hound snarled. Then opening his arms wide he screamed, 'Kellanved! Protect me! I invoke your name!'

Now Kiska remembered her bindings and sawed frantically. Her ankles came free. Hardly knowing what she was doing, she reversed the blade to hack feverishly at the rope between her wrists.

Across the room came the scraping of claws as the hound leapt forward like a sprung catapult. It closed its jaws over the man's head and clamped down. Bone crunched. Blood and mulched flesh flew from the hound's maw. Tossing its head, the hound flicked the man's headless torso away. It rolled to a stop close to Kiska's booth, blood jetting across the floor. Kiska fought down the surge of bile at her throat.

Into the silence following, the veteran drawled, 'Well, I guess the old man wasn't listening.' He tossed aside his sword to stand empty-handed.

The hound turned to regard him. Kiska also stared, fascinated by the man's calm. From a pouch at his side he drew a round object about the size of a large fruit, dark green and shiny. His gaze caught Kiska's and he nodded her to the rear stairwell.

He held up the object to the hound and pointed. 'It's just you and me now, boy.'

Kiska's breath caught. She'd heard stories . . . she dived down the short stairs to the lower room, rolled, came up running. In the dark she slammed against a table, stood gagging for air. Barely able to straighten up, she glanced around and caught a shaft of moonlight near one wall illuminating a servant's staircase.

From the room above pounded a man's scream of pure rage and hate. Kiska staggered to the stairs, kicked open the bolted door at the end of a dry-goods larder, and ran straight out only to trip and smash down onto a gravel drive, wrenching her shoulder and cracking one knee. As she lay half conscious an explosion of light and heat punched a gasp of pain from her gut. A burst of flame blinded her, shards of wood tearing overhead, larger flaming pieces crashing down all around. She heard a long bray of pain that faded as the hound fled. Headed for the water perhaps.

Dead to any injury now, as if her nerves had burst beneath their strain, Kiska pushed herself upright and limped down the alley. Even had she broken her back, she knew she'd have dragged herself away from the horror of that slaughterhouse. Behind her what was left of the inn flared brightly into the night, lighting her path down the alley through burning timber and debris.

A wordless cry stopped Temper. It echoed from among a maze of alleyways to his right. A young woman, shrieking as if her soul itself were at stake. He froze, scanning among the dark openings. From the shadows ran a girl in dark clothing, her long black hair blowing about her face.

She saw him and hesitated, then called, 'Please, help me. Please.'

He waved her forwards. 'Damn, child, are you wounded? Where's your home? Is it near?'

She threw herself onto him, a mere bundle of bones in his arms. She sobbed something, terrified.

He squinted past her into the darkness. 'What is it?' One of her hands clasped his arm while she buried her face at his shoulder. He pulled at her. 'Child? What?'

Stinging pain pierced his neck. The girl's arm writhed around it like a vice. Her legs twisted and kicked, crossing themselves behind his back. Temper staggered from side to side in the lane, pushed at her shoulders to force her head from his neck. 'What in cursed Rikkter's name?'

The girl threw back her head. Eyes as black as night regarded him. She smiled slyly, revealing needle-sharp teeth. Temper snapped a hand to her neck just under her jaw and held her there.

She smiled even more widely at him over his hand. 'You're not going to turn me out into the night alone, are you, good sir?'

With his free hand Temper drew his gauche and thrust at her. She snatched his wrist and twisted. He howled, struggled, fought, but the hand numbed and the blade dropped from his grip.

He fell, tried to roll, but she remained on top of him, wrapped as tightly as a winding sheet. Glancing down, Temper saw, horrified, that it was no longer two legs that squeezed the breath from him, but rather a single snake-like limb that encircled his chest down to his knees. Already his ribs felt crushed from the pressure. Moonlight shone from glistening scales. He would've shrieked had he breath for it. Holding her

121

head away from his neck, his arm and hand burned as if aflame. Fraction by fraction the face inched inward, lips pulled back from tiny serrated fangs, her eyes mocking all his strength.

Gasping, panting, he spared one short breath to shout, '*Help me!*'

She let out a girlish giggle. 'None will help you this night. Tonight belongs to the hunters of Shadow. Can't you hear them call their hunger?' Forcing herself close, she cupped one hand behind his neck. 'Now, let me show you my hunger. You will enjoy it much more than theirs. I promise you.'

Temper poured every ounce of strength into his arm but now her greasy hair brushed at his face. His own blood dripped from her mouth onto his cheek and burned there as if turned to acid. A hiss gurgled from the creature's throat. Temper wrenched his face away as far as humanly possible.

The thing snarled and whipped over him suddenly. Its hair was yanked from his face. Temper glanced back: a fist had gathered up a handhold of the creature's hair and was pulling back its head. The thing hissed, writhed and spat wordlessly. Its neck was bent backwards to an impossible angle. Its eyes glared blackest fury. A long blade came down in front of the neck, rusted, its edges uneven, more like an ancient iron bar than a sword. It sawed into the pale flesh inches from Temper's face. The neck parted with a wet, ragged scission like a rotten fruit split from its stem, and hot fetid blood gushed out onto Temper. The thing spasmed, pulled away, its arms beating at him, its snake limb lashing the stones.

Temper threw himself aside, slapped at his cheeks and eyes where the corrupt blood stung as if poison. 'Gods! Aw, gods!' On his knees he vomited, groaned, wiped his mouth and lay dragging in great lungfuls of welcome air.

Whoever had rescued him stood over the butchered corpse. Headless, the body still twitched. Like a leech, Temper

122

thought, and almost heaved again. Slowly he got to his feet and spat to clear his mouth. 'My thanks, stranger.'

The man said nothing. In the shifting moonlight Temper now saw that perhaps things had got worse. Who or whatever his saviour was, it wasn't alive. It was a walking cadaver, desiccated, wearing shredded armour, its dried flesh curled back from yellowed teeth, its eye sockets empty and dark. In one hand it held the head, blood dripping, black hair matted.

'Disgusting parasites,' the thing said in a voice as dry as sifting sand. It tossed the head aside where it rolled under an empty vendor's cart.

Temper pulled his gaze from where the head had vanished. 'Yeah. Damned disgusting all right.'

'Please do not think they belong to Shadow. They are trespassers. Like you.'

'Like me?' Temper eyed the thing. It resembled an Imass warrior, though taller and slimmer. He wondered why it had stepped in. 'Who do I thank for my life?'

The being inclined its head a fraction. Temper heard dry flesh creaking like leather. 'Edgewalker.'

'Temper. So, what now?'

Edgewalker gestured a skeletal hand to the shops and houses lining the way. 'You'd best remain inside. The dwellings will be respected, mostly.'

'Sorry, but I can't do that.'

Edgewalker shrugged ever so slightly. 'Then I wish you better luck.'

'Many thanks.' Temper backed away. The being, who or whatever it was, remained where it stood. At the end of the street Temper paused to peer back but he, or it, was gone. He gave his own shrug and started on, heading for a public well he knew to be nearby. He had to wash this filth from himself.

*

At the broken fountain dedicated to Poliel, Temper rinsed bucketful after bucketful of freezing cold water over his head. He then jogged onto Toc Way, but before long he slowed and looked about. Shouldn't Stone Lane be right ahead? He squinted into denser patches of night. The rows of houses and shop fronts did not look familiar. Something tonight seemed to be tricking his sense of direction, causing him to even doubt where he'd just been.

He drew off his helmet again, pushed back his wet hair, and wiped the remaining cold water from his face. Had he some-how turned around? But where? The way twisted between the uninterrupted rear walls of shops and houses. A shockingly brisk breeze gusted at him and he heard the rasp and creak of numerous branches lashing in the wind. Yet the island was practically deforested. The surge of the surf . . . where had it disappeared? These last months he had worked, eaten, and slept to its reassuring beat. Was the heavy mist obscuring it? Yet the winds were fierce tonight; contrary.

He started up a cobbled rise. No matter the twists and turn-ings, *up* led to Mock's Hold, and that had to be the mercenaries' target. There couldn't be anything else to interest them on the island.

After a number of turns the ground levelled and Temper lost his way in a maze of narrow lanes he'd never before come across. Scarf-thin wisps of cloud scudded overhead and the full moon, a pool of suspended mercury, dazzled his vision. Only Mock's Hold squatting high upon its cliff, silver and black in the monochrome glare, reassured him that he was indeed still on Malaz. Otherwise he would have sworn he'd wandered into another town, another country.

Dry hot air tickled the nape of his neck and he rubbed at it; his hand came away gritty with sand. Sand? Where in the world had that come from? He stood still, rubbing the grains between thumb and forefinger as he looked about. Hadn't the moon just been to the left of the cliffs a moment earlier?

A deep bull-like snort reverberated up the narrow lane behind him – the distant cough of an animal scenting spoor. Then came a grinding of claws over stone. Temper swallowed, backed against a wall. Automatically his hands moved to check his weapons. A door stood to his right and he hammered at it. No answer. He pounded the sturdy planks again. A voice spoke, but in no language Temper had ever heard before.

'Open up,' he growled.

The voice croaked again and this time Temper recognized a word: hrin. *Hrin?* Hadn't someone once told him that was an ancient word for revenant?

His mouth dried from a new sort of fear – the dread of one's senses corroding. This was his worst fear of the Warrens: the way they could twist the mind. A physical enemy he could face, but insanity? How do you fight that? Old Rengel's warning echoed: *'The bloodshed summoned it. Fiends and worse rule this night!'*

He turned and ran. Flint cobbles jarred under his feet. Boarded shop fronts passed, blind and forbidding. From far away a bell rang mutely, as if from a ship at sea. He stopped, listening. The third bell of evening. To the left a lane curved steeply downwards, the roofs of warehouses just visible beyond – the waterfront, Temper realized, but shrouded in fog. While he watched, the dense bank rose like an unnatural tide, clearing the warehouses and crawling up the lane.

He backed away, turned, and sprinted uphill. Up, just keep going up. That's where he'll find them. But then what? What could he—

An explosion of sound, a blood-freezing howl that made him stumble and clasp his hands to his ears. The agonizing call rose and fell like the inconsolable keening of the dead. Temper pulled his weapons though he could see nothing of the beast – nor hope to accomplish anything against such a monster.

Togg protect him. Had it scented him? Did it smell at all? Perhaps it followed some other kind of less mundane spoor. He saw the fog still rising and ran on.

The rutted lane he followed crossed a narrow stairway. He started up then stopped. Noise carried from below: something shuffling through the mist obscuring the lane. His first urge was to make a stand at the crossing; put an end to this un-manning fear and anticipation, one way or another. Yet his experience, the accumulated wisdom of decades amidst the smoky tumult of battle, warned against it. What reason had he to believe that whatever was down there knew of him, or even sought him? Why force a confrontation by blocking this narrow passage? Snarling under his breath, he backed up the stairs, weapons held ready.

The worn steps ended at a shoulder-width cleft between buildings facing Jakani Square. Temper felt his way along the walls and out onto the square. It was a shifting sea of mist, the cobbles treacherous beneath his feet. Echoes of his steps returned distorted and hollow. A gust cooled his face and through the mist he glimpsed house fronts looming dark, shadows flitting past so fast he couldn't follow them.

From the gloom came a mewling. He adjusted his grips and tried to steady his breath. A scrape and scuffle there, from the alley, a hunched shape advancing with agonizing slowness.

He readied himself, one blade held high, the other low. Yet he hesitated to attack; something wasn't right. The figure came forward unsteadily, weaved side to side, shuffling. Temper had heard enough of the animal sounds of injured men to know it well. The man – for it was a man – hugged himself as he limped. His arms were crossed tight around his stomach as if he carried a precious gift. Temper lowered his weapons. What was this? Some sort of damn fool trick?

Closer now, the man kept coming and Temper gave ground to him, shouting, 'Stay!'

The man halted. The head tilted to one side. His mouth worked, a soundless black void in the night. One arm rose, stretched out to him. Temper heard the viscous suck of half-dried blood tearing, and then a braided mass slopped from the man's stomach to the pavement – the coils and glistening viscera of his entrails. The man collapsed.

Temper tried to moisten his mouth but couldn't untrap his tongue. He advanced, prodded the corpse with the point of his weapon. Dead. Long dead, or so it seemed to him.

'*Listen to me,*' the corpse whispered.

Temper snapped his swords to guard.

One hand, slick with gore, urged him closer.

'The hound,' it moaned. Temper leaned forward. He detected no air escaping the mouth. 'It killed me. Killed us all.' This man, he realized, was one of the gang of mercenaries that had captured him. 'And it . . . it . . .' The hand urged Temper even closer. He lowered his head and the hand snatched at his sleeve. He tried to brush it off but the fingers clung like hooks.

The dead face leered a carious grin. 'And . . . it's following me.'

'*What?*'

'Now . . . you're dead, too.'

Temper looked up to where a wet red trail of blood led away from the corpse. A track that wove and pooled back to the stairs he'd just climbed. 'Bastard!'

The corpse gave a mocking laugh.

Temper tried to rise but the hand still gripped him. 'Scum.' Temper hacked the hand from its limb. It spun away, poised for a moment mid-air, then slapped down onto the stones.

Low panting tolled up the narrow stairway. Temper backed away, scanned what he could of the square. It boasted some seven main lanes radiating out. Before even thinking he was sprinting for the nearest exit.

Up constricted lane after lane he fled in panic. His lungs

flared and his throat was rasped raw. Slowing, gasping for air, he admitted his mistake. Fool! You can't evade the damned thing. Stand and fight. He turned and pressed his back to a wall of chiselled stone boulders. It chilled the steel lobster-tail guard at the nape of his neck. Gulping down great mouthfuls of air, he tried to calm himself. Don't wind yourself before a fight; conserve energy. Ha! Too late for that. He was acting like a pimply conscript facing his first engagement.

Beams of moonlight now split in half shuttered buildings across the way. From a nearby house an old woman wailed prayers to Burn the Preserver. A distant scream sounded and was cut off. Temper wiped at his face and pushed himself from the wall. Not the best spot for what he had in mind; he needed more room to manoeuvre.

Two turnings brought him to a wide length of esplanade that served as a morning market. Temper now knew where he'd ended up: close to the concourse that led to Reacher's Way. Rats scampered from him as he chose a spot close to the middle gutter and kicked the rotten litter from underfoot. Crouched low, he swung his arms and rolled his shoulders.

He could hear it out there past the gusting wind, chuffing and snorting. Gods! It sounded as big as a horse! An urge was on him to kick down a door and get behind solid walls. Yet what could he do in one of these tiny shops? Hide under a table? The beast would trap him like a cornered rat.

A brassy call rolled in with the wind, rising and falling like a wolf's plaintive cry. Temper tilted his head and listened. Had it run off? No, from up the lane he'd taken came the grating of claws over stone. Hood's teeth! More than one of the beasts!

He watched as the shadows swirled beneath the driving cloud cover and prayed that iron could harm the demons. Often it could when backed by enough strength. Like the time Urko, a commander famed for his brawn, dismembered an enk'aral during the campaigns in north Falar. But he was no Urko. He could only hope for one good shot. A shame, really. He'd always thought to fall fighting, but he would have wished for a more even match.

Now all was silent. He'd lost track of the thing in the shadows – assuming the noise he'd heard had been the beast. He listened, arms tensed, waiting for it.

Claws scoured stone, rear and left. Temper risked a glance but saw nothing.

Then he caught the sharp snick of talons and hurled himself to the side, swinging his blade only to dash sparks from the cobbles. As he fell he saw a hound bigger than a Fenn mountain lion snapping shut jaws where he'd stood but a moment before. The brute loped on, its nails furrowing stones. Temper caught one glimpse of a shaggy brown pelt and a scarred rear limb before it leapt again, dissolving into shadow.

Crawling to his feet, he gazed into the patch of darkness where the hound had disappeared. Not fair. *Not bloody fair, my friend.* He swore then to hurt the thing before it tore him limb from limb, never mind the hopelessness of ever achieving that.

From all around now came the sound of bestial claws. A cold wind brushed the square of clinging mist, but he still couldn't spy it. Then, across the way, he caught a deeper shadow in the gloom. Eyes the colour of heated amber flashed open, and a growl that the shook windows in their frames rolled over him. It raised the hairs on his neck, but now at least he knew: the full frontal assault.

It surged towards him, astounding speed in the stretch of its stride. It was on him before he could decide whether it was real or an illusion.

He managed to ram his hand and weapon, hilt-first, into the beast's maw but its onrush snatched him from his feet and dragged him clattering and bouncing beneath its massive chest. The iron scales of his armour gouged through his shoulder. The monster's fangs closed on his forearm, grating against the bones. Temper roared at the searing pain.

The beast hauled him to a wall and shook him as a terrier might a rat. It would rip his arm off in a moment. Channelling all his pain into one ferocious effort, he swung his free hand up and smashed the iron pommel of his weapon down on the fiend's skull. It rang like a bell, and the beast jerked and snorted as if it would release its grip. But then it merely coughed, sending a blast of hot fetid air into Temper's face. It heaved forward, dragging him over the cobbles, smashing him into walls and battering his body against timbers as it loped through the labyrinth of alleys. Stone steps gouged his back and cracked against his knees. He threw up a gout of froth and blood. Screams followed him and as his mouth filled with his own bloodied vomit, Temper knew the cries weren't just his.

Eventually the beast wearied of the game and let him roll away. Crippled, his arm broken and mangled, he was past pain and long past fear. He was in a place he hadn't known since his last battle nearly a year ago, and it was like a strange reunion. He was floating, euphoric. It was the place he retreated to during the worst of his engagements. Where all his strength and resilience flowed unbound. Where his body moved like some remote automaton of flesh and bone; where no injury could reach. Lying broken and dirt-smeared, he bared his teeth at the hound.

It towered over him, heaving great bellows of hot air, its coat a mangy reddish brown, grown tangled over the scars of countless battles, its eyes blazing.

With his good hand, Temper edged a dirk from its sheath at his hip. End it! he urged the lantern eyes. *Do it now!*

The head lunged toward his chest. Temper thrust the dirk up point-first into the open maw. The beast recoiled, hacking and snarling. It shook its muzzle; sprayed blood and saliva.

Temper tried to laugh but could only gag. He held the blade up. *Got you!* Hurt you, you Hood-spawned bastard!

Pawing at its mouth and chuffing, it ran in circles, shook its enormous skull, then smashed into a wall of whitewashed plaster that crumpled. The beast turned back to glare at him. A mere wasp's sting, Temper admitted sadly. His arm fell and the weapon clattered to the stones. Dizziness and a black onrushing wind smothered his senses. From a vast distance, he watched as the beast coiled for another spring.

He must have lost consciousness, as the visage he avoided through every battle and duel now gazed down at him. The Hooded One himself, come at last to collect his spirit. Temper wished he had the strength to spit at him. A cowl of darkness descended over him, and he felt himself falling, on and on until he was smothered in night and knew nothing more.

You can't find me. You won't find me. You'll never find me. Arms wrapped tightly about her knees, Kiska rocked herself back and forth, back and forth. *Never find me, never find me.* She sat in a tiny hut while a silent rain drifted down around her. She rubbed her chin over her hurt knee.

Who can't find you? she asked herself.

No one. Not one person ever. None of the kids she played hide and seek with. None of the local thieves she competed against. Not even Auntie when she tried her magic. But she could find anyone. She always did. Auntie said she had a talent for it.

And what else can't find you?

Kiska rocked for a time. She hummed to herself. *No one. No one.* A whimper sounded from her side and she glanced down. A dog lay curled against her haunch. A large dog. It peered up at her with sad eyes full of fear.

Kiska sighed, freed one arm from its grip of her knees and

stroked the dog. It whimpered again and huddled closer. She nodded in agreement.

I think *they* could find you, girl, she told herself. If they wanted to.

She sighed again and massaged her knee where her black pants were torn and blood had dried in a rough crust. She flexed the leg and winced at the pain. The dog whined its alarm.

Can't stay here forever.

She rubbed her eyes. Stay here.

On this island? *Forever?*

'A living death,' Kiska whispered into the dark.

The dog cocked one ear. She peered down at it. Sorry, boy. I just can't hide any longer.

She pushed herself to her feet. She had staggered into an out-house, a boarded shack hardly larger than an upright coffin. She looked out over the half-door. Boards covered the rear windows of a house belonging to a young family Kiska knew. They exported dried fish and were quite well-to-do. They even had an outhouse in their vegetable garden.

So here she was. The biggest night of her life and she was hiding in a shitter. Everything she wished for all her life had materialized and what has she done? Run away!

The dog rested its head on one of her muddied slippers and peered up at her. Kiska searched her pockets and sheaths. A length of cord and a scarf, needles, cloths soaked in unguents given to her by Agayla. This was all she had left. She unfolded one cloth and pressed it to her knee. She hissed at the pain. Yet who could've guessed at the vast difference between hoping for action, and the sight of a man's head bursting like a melon in the maw of some monster from another realm? No wonder she'd found herself throwing up in a back alley.

That man from the Imperial cutter . . . he hadn't been afraid to walk the streets. He'd faced down an entire nest of cultists.

132

And he must've known what he was walking into. She was certain of that. Yet he had come. Oleg said his message had to get to him, a message he believed vitally important. But he was mad. Agayla, though . . . she'd also sent Kiska after him.

Her hand found the flattened scroll at her chest. This was for him. Had he reached the Hold yet? He must have – but who could be sure on a night like this? And the gatekeeper – Lubben – he would let her know if he had. He might even let her in. If she played it right.

Kiska opened the door. The dog whimpered afresh. Looking back, she saw it still curled on the privy floor, unwilling to even push its nose past the threshold. She bid goodbye and headed for a shortcut she knew to Rampart Way.

The night had turned unearthly still. Even her slippers and the whisper of her breath sounded deafening. Then suddenly, randomly, a hound's baying shattered the calm, causing her to shrink. But other than these terrifying moments – each of which she was certain would be her last – it was as if the night stood frozen. Only the moon appeared to move, watching her with its silver eye as she made for the waterfront where the shore lapped the cliffs and the oldest wharves ceased at a thatch of rotten piers.

She climbed the slick stones jumbled at the cliff's base. Salt spray beaded on her shirt and the waves beneath her murmured, unnaturally subdued. Her cord-soled slippers gripped the broken rock, but her hands slid, cut open on its knife-like edges.

Soon she reached the barest lip in the uneven stones – an animal path dating back generations to when wild goats still clambered over the island. The track was long forgotten and invisible to those beneath and above. She fancied it was the mystery behind the phantom departures and arrivals of the island's pirates.

She carefully edged her way up the slick rock ledges, most no wider than her foot. Thorned brush choked the route, forcing her to ascend behind or over. But she knew the way blindfolded, as she'd often climbed it at night. It led to her favourite spot on the island – after Agayla's rooms, that is.

The mist closed in like a shroud. The bay, some hundred yards down, lay smothered in low-lying fog. In the southern sky, lights flickered green and pink, reminding Kiska of the legends of the Riders who rose in winter to tow sailors to their doom. She also remembered the tales of ghosts and revenants said to haunt the Hold above. Even these cliffs boasted an entire host of spirits – drowned sailors deceived into drawing too close to the shoals, tricked by her ancestors, wreckers and pirates all. It was said you could still hear their moaning at night, seeking vengeance on their murderers. She'd grown up on such yarns and believed not a one. Including those of a certain demon-haunted Shadow Moon . . .

When her outthrust hand told Kiska she'd reached a depression in the veined granite, she threw herself into the opening she knew awaited ahead. She gasped for air, and not just from the strain of the climb. Her clothes clung to her, heavy and damp. The air retained the rich fetor of rotting humus and bird droppings. Kiska leant against one inward-canted wall to steady her breath. The crevice she stood in couldn't really be called a cavern: it was more like a ragged cleft in the living rock of the island, a jagged fissure that shot straight into the cliff. Her heel dislodged chips of stone that shifted and crunched. She'd found places within where there was no floor to speak of at all, just a thinning skim of darkness descending straight down to a finger's breadth.

She had played here as a child. It was her secret hideaway, though she had the feeling Agayla was aware of its existence. She'd explored every inch of the radiating cracks and the galleries of narrow, vertical faults. And though island legends

134

told of secret caves and hidden troves of gems and gold, she'd found no trace of them. Broken decayed slats and bits of salt-dissolved iron scattered here and there were all she'd kicked up as reward for her efforts.

Overhead passed a portion of Rampart Way; it would be a difficult final climb. She rubbed warmth back into her hands and felt the burn of cuts as circulation flowed into salt-encrusted wounds. Perhaps she should wrap them in lengths of cloth. But what if it should slip or come loose?

Noise clattered from without. Kiska pressed herself against the cliff wall and listened: fabric brushing over stone, falling pebbles. Someone climbing outside. She edged farther into the cavern. As she did so, a shape from within loomed in the narrow stone confines like one of the revenants she'd heard tell of.

An instant of soul-clutching dread slowed her enough for the figure – a flesh and blood man – to grasp her hand. She almost smiled at such a mistaken move and used his resistance to snap a kick to the opposite side of his head.

The man grunted but held on. Kiska lost her grin.

A foot lashed out and cracked against her wounded knee. She bit down a shriek of stabbing pain as the leg gave way. He released her hand as she fell.

'Don't struggle,' he told her.

She stared up at him; here in the dark he was mostly shadow, but there was something familiar about him.

He shook out a slim length of cord and stepped over her. Her every instinct wailed against being bound again, and she lashed out with her good leg, catching him high in the inner thigh.

A loud hiss escaped his lips, yet he bent over her again.

Kiska covered her face, cried, 'No, please!' She slipped the knife from the back of her collar. Before she could use it his booted foot came down on her wrist and something hard like a knout of iron smashed against her temple. The cavern's

135

darkness exploded into a dazzle of red and yellow pinpoints that shimmered and faded slowly.

'You've a few moves,' he allowed, grudging, 'but you're out of your depth here, child. Don't make me kill you.'

Kiska blinked against the lights befuddling her vision. 'Who in the Lady's Pull are you?'

The man ignored her. 'Turn your back,' he told her.

She obeyed and he tied her wrists together. Another figure climbed up into the opening and the man moved to his side. They spoke and against the light of the moon Kiska recognized him. The flat, scarred face, cat's whiskers moustache: the body-guard of the very man she sought.

She laughed. The men ignored her, continued speaking in low tones she couldn't catch. The newcomer was sent out again. The Seti tribesman returned to her. He pulled a black cloth from within his cloak. Kiska recognized the cloth and where it would be thrown.

'I have a message for your master,' she said as he readied the cloth for her head. The hands hesitated a fraction of a heart beat, continued down.

Darkness enveloped Kiska. 'The man he met in the garden is dead,' she said, too quickly and loud for her liking. Her heart hammered.

Silence. The sullen lurch and suck of the surf beneath. Kiska listened: not even the clatter or shift of stone chips underfoot. Nothing. Was he still there? Was anyone? Would they leave her here? Perhaps it was a sort of twisted kindness. After all, she'd be safer tied up here than roaming the streets tonight.

A hand took hold of the hood at its uppermost fold. It gently lifted up and away from her head. Her hair caught at its coarse weave.

A man crouched before her: a long, narrow mahogany-tanned face that appeared oddly seamless, bland even. Sunken, dark, black-ringed eyes. Brown pate shaven but for a long braided queue at his shoulder. A straight slash of mouth. Lips Kiska imagined shattering should they be forced to smile. Her quarry.

'I'm told you have a message for me.'

He spoke aristocratic Talian with a hint of an accent she couldn't place. As out of place on this island as gold in a fish's mouth.

He waited, expressionless. Kiska found her voice. 'In my shirt.' She tried to raise her arm but only wrenched her wrist.

He raised one hand. 'May I?'

'Yeah – yes.'

He wore black leather gloves, his fingers long and thin.

'No!' barked the bodyguard. He yanked her away by the back of her collar then rummaged at her shirt. His hand brushed her small breast. She smiled to unnerve him but his eyes remained empty of emotion.

'Hattar . . .' her target murmured reprovingly.

She peered up at him. 'Yes. *Hattar.*'

He found the scroll then shoved her over and pressed one knee down on her shoulder. His weight drove all breath from her. The scroll crackled as he tore at it.

'Hattar,' the man sighed, 'you cannot read.'

Hattar grunted something.

'Let her up.'

Unwillingly, he eased his weight. She gasped a deep breath, choked on dust and dirt she sucked in. Her side ached, pressed firmly into the uneven stones.

'I will speak with her.'

'Hunh?'

'Raise her up.'

'My Lord . . .'

Silence. Kiska waited. A look from *the Lord* perhaps? A gesture? Hattar knelt within her sight. He held a wicked curved blade to her face. His other hand twisted a grip in her hair. He brought his scarred nut-brown face close to hers.

'You and my master will speak,' he whispered. 'But this dagger,' and he wagged it before her eyes, 'if you twitch, it will reach your heart through your back before you are even aware of it tickling your pretty soft skin. Do you understand me?'

She nodded, wide-eyed.

Hattar returned her nod. He raised her up and shifted her round. His master held the scroll in one hand and was tapping it against the other. The lips were curved downward ever so slightly. 'My apologies for Hattar. He takes his duties very seriously.'

Kiska almost nodded, stopped herself. 'Yes. He does.'

The man sighed, rubbed his fingers over his eyes. 'What is your aunt's name?' he asked suddenly.

'Agayla.'

'What does she do at Winter's Turn – Rider's Retreat, I understand you sometimes call it here.'

Kiska stared. Had she heard that right? Winter's Turn? She almost shrugged but felt a prick to one side of her spine and held herself rigid. 'Ah, she . . . she consults the Dragons deck for the coming year.'

'Yes. Many do. And?'

A test. He was challenging her obviously. Why Winter's Turn? What was so . . . she remembered then. One eve sneaking down the stairs and watching from the cover of the landing while Agayla sat up all night, from midnight's bell till dawn's light. The side to side woosh of the shuttle. The click and rattle of the loom. Weaving. All night. Kiska licked her dry lips. 'She weaves.'

Her target nodded. 'And what is your name?'

'Kiska.'

The brow arched. 'Your real name?'

'What? Is it in there?'

He just waited, patient. Kiska could sense Hattar at her back eagerly tensed for the killing blow. 'Kiskatia Silamon Tenesh.'

He nodded again. 'Very well, Kiska. You may call me . . .
Artan.'

'Artan? That's not your real name.'

'No. It isn't.'

'Ah. I see.' Kiska stopped herself from asking his real name;
he wouldn't tell her anyway.

Artan opened the scroll. He started ever so slightly, surprised, and Kiska decided that whatever was written there
must be startling indeed to have broken through his iron
control. He let out a breath in a long hiss while tapping the
scroll against his fingertips.

'Does she say how I saw your meeting?' she asked.

Artan did not answer. It seemed to Kiska that his gaze stared
into the distance while at the same time was turned inward in
meditation.

'Artan?'

He blinked, rubbed again at his ancient, tired-looking eyes.
As if struck by a new thought, he studied her. 'No. That is not
its message.'

'Then what does it say?'

He held it out to her, open. 'Does this mean anything to
you?'

There was no writing on the scroll. Instead, a hasty rectangle
was sketched on the parchment. Within the rectangle was
drawn a spare stylised figure. Kiska couldn't quite make it out.
A mounted warrior? A swimming man?

Curious, she looked closer: blue, she saw. Gleaming
opalescent colours. Plates of armour shining smooth like the
insides of shells. And ice, the growing skein of freezing scales.
'I see ice,' she breathed, awed.

'Truly?' Artan plucked it back. It withered into ash in his
gloved hands. He brushed them together. The gesture troubled
Kiska; she'd seen poor street conjurers use the same trick.

'So. Your message?' he asked.

Kiska stared. 'Wasn't that . . .'

Artan cocked a brow and Kiska saw that she was right: his mouth did little more than remain a straight slash. 'No. That was her message. Not yours.'

'You know her?'

'We've met. A few times . . . long ago.'

'Really? Well, my message is about Oleg.'

Both thin brows rose. 'You know his name?'

'He told me.'

'I see. Go on.'

'I, ah, I followed you to your meeting with him.'

Artan sent a look over her shoulder to Hattar. Rueful? Accusatory? A growl sounded behind her.

She hurried on. 'After you left he was killed by a man in grey robes.'

Artan's lips almost pursed, the dark eyes narrowed. 'Then pray, how did he tell you his name?'

'Ah. Well. You see, I waited, then went into the garden and looked at him.'

'And he spoke to you?'

'Yes.'

Artan sighed. 'The Shadow Moon. Of course. What did he say?'

Kiska frowned. 'Well, it was strange and rambling. And the words – I don't know what they mean. Anyway, Oleg said the message was for you.'

Artan jerked, surprised. 'He named me?'

'No. He said it was for the man who was just with him. And he – well, he did call you an irresponsible idiot.'

Artan allowed his lips the slimmest cold upturning that could generously be called a smile. He touched his gloved fingers to his lips. 'Go on.'

'He said that, ah, that now he was dead he could see that he'd been right all along.'

140

'A rather unassailable position,' Artan observed dryly.

Kiska continued: 'He said that Kellan—'

Something cracked off her skull from behind.

'Hattar!'

Kiska blinked tears from her eyes.

'My apologies,' Artan said, 'I should have told you. We do not say that name.'

'Obviously. Well, what I was trying to tell you was that he – that is, Oleg – said only fools think *he* is returning for the Imperial throne.'

Artan's gaze rose past her shoulder to Hattar. 'Then, pray, what is he returning for?'

'For a different throne. For the throne of Shadow.'

Artan's jaws tightened – the masked expressions of a lifetime of guarding one's thoughts. 'I'm sorry. But this is nothing I haven't heard from Oleg before.' He stood, brushed at his pants.

'It's true!'

'I'm sorry, Kiska. But how do you know?'

'Because someone else confirmed it.'

Artan paused. His face did not change, but Kiska could tell she had caught his interest. 'Who confirmed it?'

'While I was in town I was swept up in something – a Changing – and I was in Shadow. I met someone there. An old creature like a walking corpse, or like an Imass, named Edgewalker. He said many people have tried for the Shadow throne.' She waited expectantly, but the information seemed to signify nothing to Artan.

'And did he say . . . the emperor . . . would?'

'Well, no. He just wasn't surprised. He—' Kiska's shoulder's slumped. Damn! *She* had told *him*!

'I'm sorry. I need more evidence than this.'

Artan was right, of course. It was all just the babbling of a man who'd admitted hating Kellanved. She was a fool to have believed him.

'We must be going.'

'Wait! He said that during this *conjunction* the paths between realms are accessible.'

Artan nodded. 'Yes. But that was not our dispute. I acknowledge it, in theory.'

'Ah, yes. Well, Oleg said that during *transubstantiation* existed the greatest possibility for . . . ah . . . for entombment. That then lay the greatest opportunity to entrap him. That you should act then.' Kiska frowned. 'Do you know what that means?'

Artan sighed. 'It's all thaumaturgic theory. His own research. I'm not so sure of it myself. Was that all?'

'No. One other thing.'

'Yes?'

'Well, this last bit sounds kind of silly to me.'

'Just this last part?'

Kiska laughed nervously. 'Yeah, well. He said don't be fooled by appearances. That he plans on *losing all* to gain everything. That defeat would seal his victory.'

Artan rubbed at his sunken eyes with thumb and forefinger. Kiska wondered if the gesture was a habit of which the man was not even aware.

'Poor old Oleg,' Artan sighed, 'Hedging and oracular to the end. Thank you, Kiska. I'll keep these speculations in mind.'

'But I'm coming with you, aren't I?'

'Great One below, no.'

'*What?*'

'Hattar, tie her up more securely.'

'At once.'

'Wait—'

A gag whipped across her mouth and yanked tight. The plainsman tied her elbows to her sides, pushed her down and bound her legs.

From the cavern opening Artan said, 'Goodbye. Give my regards to your Aunt.'

Kiska cursed him through the gag. Hattar stood over her. He studied his handiwork. They were alone in the cave.

He knelt beside her, took out his fur hat and pulled it down over his long oiled hair. 'If you are any good, you'll work your way out of these bindings. If you do, don't follow us. If I find you pursuing us again, I'll clip your feathers, little bird. You understand?'

She cursed him to the most distant of Hood's Paths. He chuckled – at her predicament she supposed – and left. She was alone.

For a few moments she lay still, listening to be sure she was indeed on her own and that he wasn't watching from the opening. Then she concluded this was foolish, that he wouldn't hang around here with his master gone, and began wriggling. She twisted and waggled her hands to wedge a thumb at just the right angle against a rock, then pressed. It dislocated with a crack and a familiar jab of pain. Then, using the edges of stones – even the walls themselves – she teased and plucked and coerced the rope coils at her wrist down toward her fingers. After that it was easy to accomplish the rest.

Throwing off the rope at her legs, she was free. And in much less time than that bastard Hattar planned on, she was sure. Not pursue them! She'd follow all right. She'd get ahead of them! She'd show what she could accomplish. No one left her trussed up like a prize pig at a banquet.

She'd climb up to Rampart Way, then sneak into the Hold. Climb the wall itself if she had to. Just as she did years ago to see if she could. Aunt Agayla's warning then flashed into her thoughts: *do not enter the Hold!* But Artan would be there. And besides, if there were great things happening, and even greater powers contending, no one would pay her a mind.

CHAPTER FIVE

OLD ENEMIES, OLD FRIENDS

A LONE ORANGE EMBER FLICKERED DULLY WITHIN A maelstrom at the heart of an icy ocean. It bobbed and surged with each heave of the fisherman's oars that cracked and clattered off chunks of ice. Circling at a distance, Riders plunged and reared, darting in close then submerging. Javelins of ice hurled at the skiff burst into clouds of mist. The fisherman forced his chant through lips frozen to his teeth.

One Rider dared to lunge within the circle of calm surrounding the fisherman. Wave-borne, it reared close only to howl and beat at its arms as its glittering pearl armour melted, then it plunged beneath the boiling surface. Far off, amid the whitecaps and rafts of ice, five indigo-robed Riders watched, conferring. They cradled amethyst wands at their chests. Cold pulsed from them as an expanding sphere. Kneeing their churning wave-mounts, they dispersed. One raised its wand to the south.

Out of the heaving waters from far under the clouds came yet another crag of ice, this one the smallest of the flotilla. Riders at all sides shepherded its progress. The fisherman rowed on oblivious, back hunched, his whole being focused on the effort of rowing and his song. The berg loomed closer, a dark shape frozen at its heart.

The instant vapour burst from the iceberg's leading spur the Riders plunged beneath the ice-mulched surface. Water poured in torrents down the crag's shoulders while the gale tore streamers of frost smoke from its peak. When a shard of glacial emerald calved from its front, it raised a fountain of spray that rolled north to the skiff and disappeared under its bow. Now from the heart of the berg jutted a prow of wood. Water streamed from it, driving wisps of cloud into the wind. Caught in a mountain of ice, it bore down on the tiny skiff.

The fisherman, his back against the thrashing wind, continued rowing as the berg entombing *Rheni's Dream* shattered and slid into the waves. He chanted on even as the prow of *Rheni's Dream* loomed over him. He was pulling on the oars as the skiff was smashed to shards and the glowing brazier extinguished in an explosion of steam as it was driven beneath the waves. *Rheni's Dream* bore on, listing, its planks heaved and warped. Caught broadside by a massive wave, it rolled further, seemed to hesitate, then ploughed into the sea. Amid the wreckage left behind one oar floated. A sheath of ice gleamed over it already. Stormriders surged past the wreck. Some raised their ice-lances high overhead and brought them down, pointing north. At the horizon of cloud and storm-tossed sea, lightning revealed a dark smudge of land.

High combers flung themselves against the south shore, driven by a freezing wind. A woman, her long black hair and layered skirts snapping, picked her way down the rock-strewn shore. She held a woven shawl close at her shoulders as she took a footpath down to a driftwood and sod hut just above the strand. Pushing open the wooden door, she peered into the dim interior. Within sat a woman, motionless, facing the door, knitting forgotten in her lap. Her bright white eyes glowed in the darkness.

The woman at the door shivered. 'It's me, Agayla.' Her breath hung in the cottage's frigid air. She stepped closer; hoar-frost crackled beneath her shoes. Ice crystals glittered on the blackened logs in the fireplace. Frost layered the sitting woman's lips and eyes.

Agayla reached out to gather up the knitting but the wool shattered into fragments.

In what little moonlight penetrated the churning clouds, Agayla walked the edge of the strand where driftwood and old planking lay beached by the high waves. Steam rose from the freshest seawrack of dead fish and seaweed. She gazed steadily to the south, to the horizon of sea and cloud where past the foam of whitecaps flashed a bright glimmer of emerald and azure. Her route took her to a point of tall rock overlooking the shore. Another figure stood there already, an old man in shapeless brown robes, bald but for a fringe of long white hair that whipped in the wind. Arms crossed, he scowled southward.

'Have you ever seen anything like it, Agayla?' he said without turning as she drew near. His words reached her easily despite the roaring wind.

Skirts raised in one hand, Agayla picked her path carefully over the rocks. 'There has never been the like since the earliest assaults, Obo.' She stopped beside him, pulled her shawl tighter.

He grunted, glowered even more deeply. 'And the fisherman?' Obo asked, cocking a brow at her.

'Overcome. He was out there all alone. They knew how naked we are. They could sense it.'

'That fool, Surly, trying to outlaw magery on the island. Why didn't she stop to consider why this island should be such a hotbed of talent? Wind-whistlers, sea-soothers, wax-witches, warlocks, Dragons deck readers. You name it. The Riders dared not come within hundreds of leagues.'

'She didn't know because no one knew, Obo,' Agayla observed.

He spat to one side. 'I'm leaving. We can't stop this.'

She lanced him a glare. 'Certainly. Run back to your tower. We both know you could keep it secure. But what of the island? How would you like living on a lifeless rock continually besieged by the Riders?'

He sniffed. 'Might have its advantages.'

Scornful, she shook her head. 'Don't try *that*. You've anchored yourself here in your tower and it sits on this island. You have to commit yourself. You've no choice.'

Obo's mouth puckered as if tasting something repugnant. He raised his chin to the south. 'We can't win anyway. The two of us aren't enough.'

'I know. That's why I asked someone else.'

'*What?*' Obo spun to her. 'How dare you! Who? Who is it? Who's coming? It's not that raving lunatic is it?'

'By the Powers, no. Not *him*. He's chosen another path in any case. No, it's someone else.'

'I don't like it.'

'I knew you wouldn't,' Agayla sighed. 'In the meantime we must still resist.'

'If I don't like who you've asked, I'll leave. I swear.'

'Yes, Obo.'

As if caught in a sudden gust, Agayla wavered, took a step back to steady herself against an invisible pressure. She reached behind to a waist-high rock to brace herself and leaned against it, massaging her brow. 'Gods above. I've never felt anything so strong.'

Nodding, Obo crossed his arms again. 'Single-minded bastards, ain't they?'

*

Temper opened his eyes to find himself once again at the siege of Y'Ghatan. It was his old nightmare. The one that he relived over and over, dreaming and awake. Yet it had been a long time since it had returned, and it troubled him that he should find himself here now once more.

He heard cloth lashing and snapping in the unrelenting wind, orders barked from somewhere nearby. The air stank of burnt leather and rotting flesh. His doubts and lingering sense of unease dispersed like a pan of water left out under the burning Seven Cities sun. Serried ranks of Malazan regulars stood, backs to him, before a flat field scoured by blowing sand. Bodies dotted the plain and a forest of spears and javelins jutted from the ground at sickening angles. Through the dust rose the dun walls of the first escarpment to the four levels of the ancient ruins. The fortifications looked to Temper like nothing more solid than simple rammed earth. Beyond, the jagged incisor-like ridges of the Thalas Mountains darkened the northern horizon.

Flags snapped in the strong wind. Orders carried, distorted by the wind's own voice. Soldiers marched. Temper squinted into the dust, pushed back his helmet and hawked up grit. A canteen thumped against the chest of his scaled hauberk. He took it with a nod to the bearded and armoured man at his side. 'Thanks, Point.'

'What in Burn's Wisdom are we doing in this god-forsaken waste?' Point grumbled as he drew on his own helmet, an iron pot bearing cheek guards embossed to resemble the jaws of a roaring lion.

Temper said nothing. There was little to say. Point grumbled about everything; it was his way. Across the lines mixed Gral, Debrahl and Tregyn of the Y'Ghatan guard rode back and forth, shouting insults hoarse and unintelligible from this distance, clashing their swords against round bronze-faced

149

shields. Temper turned to examine the rippling white walls of the command tent. 'The last one, he says.'

Point snorted. 'Not in this rat's nest of a land. There'll always be another, and another. These people will never face the truth.'

Temper watched the snapping cloth, the marines standing guard at the entrance, and his four brother bodyguards waiting next to them. 'Maybe so. But he says it's *his* last.'

Point glanced at him, his eyes narrow within the shade of his helm. 'You don't *really* believe that. He's always sayin' that.'

'I don't know. That Bloorgian priest, Lanesh – you've heard the things he's been ranting.'

Point slapped the sword sheathed at his side. 'That pig. He's just eaten up that Dassem's closer to Hood than he'll ever be. Ferrule says we ought to gut him, and for once I agree with that murdering brute.'

Temper straightened as the tent flap was thrown back and officers filed out. 'Here they come.'

Dassem stepped out, his horsehair-plumed helm under one arm. The four others of his 'sword' bodyguard met him there. Soldiers nearby in the ranks shouted, 'Hail the Sword!' Dassem raised a gauntleted hand in answer. A few of the mage cadre emerged: old man A'Karonys with a staff taller than he was; the giant Bedurian; the woman Nightchill; and the short bald walking stump of a man, Hairlock.

Point murmured, 'I wish the old ogre was still around. He always kept that bitch in check.'

Temper grunted agreement. The *bitch*, Surly, remained hidden within the tent. Talian and Falaran Sub-Fists and commanders came out and headed to their posts. In their wake they left messengers running with last minute orders. From behind the city walls horns sounded distant alarm. After a last dust-ridden pass and javelin toss, the harrying Y'Ghatan cavalry withdrew.

The assault lasted through the entire day. The thunder and roar of battle rose and fell as flank commanders probed the defences, searching for a weakness. Smoke and the stench of burnt flesh washed over Temper as A'Karonys lashed the walls with flames, only to be pushed back by what remained of the Holy Falah'd. Ranged around Dassem, Sword of the Empire and commander of the Imperial forces, Temper and his brethren watched and waited through the day's punishing heat for the time when the Sword would commit itself to the field. Runners came and went, conveying intelligence to Dassem, relaying his orders. A company of saboteurs emerged from the churning winds. Caked in dust but grinning, they saluted Dassem. Somewhere, the defences had been breached.

Slowly, step by step, the regular infantry advanced. They scrambled up the first incline of the lowest terrace to the broached first ring of walls. Here the Imperial sappers had done their work, undermining and blasting entire sections. So far, the defenders held a death-grip on these breaches. Piled cask and timber barriers went up at night, while each day the Malazans tore them down. Scaling a siege ramp, Temper calculated that every footstep taken up the dusty rotten slope cost a thousand men. An impenetrable cloud of reddish dust obscured everything. Ahead, muted screams and the thundering clash of arms reached him through the gusting wind.

Temper scanned the next walls – no more than heaped sun-baked mud bricks. Why here at this pathetic backwater? Why had the surviving rag-ends of insurrectionist armies and a last few newly anointed Falah'd converged here? Prisoners boasted of its extraordinary antiquity and named it the hidden progenitor of all the Holy Cities themselves. A convenient claim now that all the rest had fallen, and a sad one too. It spoke of just how far a proud civilization had been reduced. The last undignified scrambling of a defeated people.

Dassem gestured to his signal corps and the messengers

stopped coming; he had turned over the battle to the sub-commanders of the Third Army: Amaron, Choss, and Whiskeyjack.

Temper approached. 'The last one then?'

Dassem glanced over, his dark eyes softening. 'Aye. The last.'

Temper thought of all he had heard whispered from so many sources – of Pacts and Vows sworn to the Hooded One himself. Steeling himself, he ventured, 'You can't just walk away.'

Dassem slapped at the dust coating his long surcoat of burgundy and grey, the Imperial sceptre at its chest. 'That's the last of my worries, Temper. There are plenty of others all too eager to do his work. Lady knows, they're practically lined up.'

'It can't be that easy.'

'*Easy!*' The First Sword's black eyes blazed and Temper jerked back a step. Dassem passed one gauntleted hand across his eyes as if wiping away a vision of horror. His long black hair, plaited back and tied at his neck, lashed in the wind like the horsetail plume at the helmet under his arm. He shaded his gaze to scan the battle. 'He made a mistake,' he whispered aloud.

Temper wondered: was this *meant* to be overheard?

'All that has ever mattered to me has been taken. I have nothing left to lose . . .'

Though he ached to take his commander's shoulders and shout – *But what of your own soul, Dassem?* – Temper held his tongue.

He sensed he had pushed as far as he dared, had been given all that this man was prepared to give. Besides, what did he know of pacts made in his grandfather's time? Or of Hood's murky intentions, for that matter?

A roar went up from thousands of throats as the Malazan regulars of the Third Army pushed on through the next level of the layered defences.

'Soon, now. We'll see Surgen soon,' Dassem said under his breath. His lips drew back from his teeth, his features tensed, eager. Although they were the enemy, Temper found himself pitying the soldiers ranged against them. Dassem drew on his helm and started forward. Temper and the rest of the Sword – Point, Ferrule, Quillion, Hilt and Edge – fell in around him.

As they advanced, Temper kept a look ahead for Surgen – Surgen Ress, the man who claimed to be the last of the Holy City's patroned and anointed champions. Never mind there were only seven Holy Cities and that all seven champions had fallen to Dassem's sword. He gave life to Y'Ghatan's claim to be the eighth Holy City, hidden, but the eldest. Temper wondered just how long such a pretence could last.

Wounded soldiers, some carried, others staggering, appeared out of the wind-lashed dust like summoned spirits. All paused at the sight of Dassem's black horsehair plume. Those that could, saluted; most simply watched them pass with battle-dulled eyes.

They reached a second tall earthen embrasure and its ramp. Corpses lay thick upon it: Malazan infantry in scaled armour under grey surcoats; Seven City defenders lying in droves, robes and headscarves tossing in the wind, brown limbs askew. Crossing the second wall defences, Temper and his brothers tightened their protective ring.

Sweat soaked the padding under Temper's armour and dripped from his brows. Grit scoured his mouth as dry as baked stone. He blinked, his eyes burning and watering in the dust. The screams and clash of arms deafened him as always, but he stood more relaxed than at former engagements. He knew that the surviving Seven City priest-mages, the Falah'd, could not strike so long as they were held in check by the Malazan cadre mages.

A runner reached them, saluted. 'Surgen has taken the field. Right flank.'

Dassem dismissed him, eyed his bodyguard. 'I'll try not to let him slip away this time.' Temper and his brothers smiled as Dassem drew his sword. They advanced to the right.

The regulars parted to allow them passage. Dassem stepped to the front while Point and Edge took his flanks. Temper, Hilt, Ferrule and Quillion fell in to guard his back.

They reached the front lines. Sergeants directed Dassem through the swirling maelstrom of dust and struggling bodies to Surgen's position in the lines. Spying Dassem's plume the Y'Ghatan soldiers howled, suddenly berserk with fury. They launched themselves forward in a frenzy, as if meaning to bury the ranked soldiers. Temper knew that those who engaged Dassem and fell had been promised a blessed martyrdom. Then, from the screen of blowing dust, appeared Surgen's escort of twenty hand-picked bodyguards, in red headscarves and bearing facial hatch-lines. Dassem committed himself to the front. The Y'Ghatan infantry pushed in like a crushing wall. Soon, in the sweep and shift of battle, Temper found their position enisled by Seven City defenders.

At first he was not worried. It had happened before, and would no doubt happen again. He was certain even now Malazan regulars were counter-attacking to reach them. Surgen appeared, clashed briefly with Edge, but it was clear that Edge was not the man Surgen wanted, and so he pulled back to move on to Dassem, who stood alone, none daring to engage him, or those who did lasting no longer than a single exchange.

The blades met, ringing continuously. Surgen's escort pressed around Temper, eager to hack down him and his brothers to encircle Dassem. But such tactics had often been attempted. Temper fought a careful, defensive duel with sword and shield. Heavily armoured, he did not exert himself but rather delayed and deferred, waiting for an opening to fell his opponent. And ultimately, secretly, his advantage was that he knew: he had only to last long enough for Dassem to finish his man.

At first it went poorly for the defenders. Dassem bore Surgen back and the Sword advanced with Dassem, covering him against all comers. Seemingly overborne, the last of the Seven City champions continued to retreat, step after step. Still Temper waited for the Malazan regulars to reach them. Yet this day the Y'Ghatan defenders, citizen-soldiers bolstered by veterans of all the other smashed native armies, held where before they had broken.

Dassem advanced and Temper finished off the last of the escort guards opposing him, then edged sideways to close the gap.

Surgen attacked with both swords and Dassem countered, his blade a blur. Then a flash across Temper's vision and Dassem gasped, bowed forward as if cradling a wound. Another attack? An arrow or bolt? Temper couldn't be sure what he saw. Surgen was also startled, but instantly pressed his advantage. One-handed, Dassem fended off the blows while grasping at his chest. Quillion and Edge broke formation to interpose themselves.

Then Hood's Own Paths cracked open upon them.

Smelling the blood of a champion who'd stood for as long as any could remember, Surgen, his remaining escort, and the regulars lunged in upon them. Quillion and Hilt fought fanatically as the Sword attempted to retreat as a unit. But only Dassem could match Surgen, and so Quillion fell to the twin swords of the anointed and Holy-patroned champion.

Temper bellowed for relief but his voice was lost in the defenders' frenzied shouts. Dassem struggled, head hanging, staggering. Neither Temper nor any of his remaining brothers could spare an instant's concentration to help steady him. It tortured Temper to feel the man stumble against his back as they withdrew, pace by pace, over the uneven ground.

What had struck him? Temper wondered, blazing with fury.

Who could have reached him? How could it be that on this day, at this hour, the Y'Ghatan soldier-citizenry defeated Malazan professionals? What gave them the backbone?

Surrounded, they struggled to retreat. Temper could only shield-bash continuously, slashing any hands that grabbed at the sharpened iron edges of his shield. For a moment, the five of them surfaced intact like a wave-tossed piece of wreckage. Then they were four: he, Dassem, Point and Ferrule. They held for heartbeats longer until Surgen broached the crowd like a bear scattering a pack of dogs. Though apparently injured near to death, Dassem still easily parried and dropped the regulars. Point moved to intercept Surgen while Temper and Ferrule fended off the encircling mob.

And still the Malazan regulars had yet to push through. Point faced Surgen. Temper saw little of the duel – he was too busy staving off Seven City infantry throwing themselves against him in a desperate bid to bear him down. Glimpses convinced him of Point's brilliance: the man outdid himself, lasting more exchanges than Temper believed possible against a patroned champion. Temper bellowed again for the Malazan regulars; short of friendly forces sweeping over and rescuing them, he knew each would die in turn under Surgen's blades.

Point fell. Temper roared in rage as Point had fought beautifully; there was no justice in his defeat. He used that searing fury to break into the gap. Of the duel that followed, he never forgot Surgen's hot eyes fixed at a point past his shoulder . . . on a crippled Dassem just beyond reach.

Sensing the end was near, the Seven City regulars drew back to give Surgen room. He pressed forward confidently, contemptuously even, and that made Temper all the more stubborn. The blows rained down. He simply hunched low like a shack in an avalanche, determined to remain, no matter what was thrown at him.

Surgen punished him for his temerity. Yet, Temper hung on.

Surgen was incredibly skilled, almost as strong as Temper, and far quicker. Facing the champion's ferocious eyes, his mouth open as if already tasting Dassem's blood, Temper abandoned any hope of surviving. He gave himself up as dead already and determined to remain standing merely long enough to deny Surgen the satisfaction of victory. He parried the man, using his bull strength to bear Surgen back whenever possible. Thrust through the stomach, Temper merely grunted and swung for Surgen's head. But such was warrior's speed that Surgen simply snapped back his head, taking only a cut across the bridge of his nose. Surgen pulled away then for an instant, stunned Temper hoped, for he could no longer see clearly through the pink mist of sweat and blood fogging his eyes.

He waited, gasping in air, still giving ground while Ferrule, bellowing, thrust everywhere, surrendering to blind battle lust. Dassem staggered, parrying like a drunk, yet still able to defend himself against the common soldiery.

Surgen howled holy outrage and lunged at Temper again. The attacking blade was a blur. Temper could only wait to see what the man intended for the damage was done: he could feel his life leaking down his legs in a warm wet tide. His shield shattered under Surgen's punishment and Temper released his sword, grappling the man's wrist. The champion spat into his face, 'Die! Die!'

Temper smiled blearily at him. 'Fast as I'm able, friend.'

Enraged, Surgen swung at him again, fought to tear loose his arm, but no one, not even Dassem himself, could break Temper's iron grip.

Surgen glared past him: his eyes widened; he yelled incoherently. Temper, his vision blackening, felt his grip weaken. Surgen wrenched free, backed away. A tide of Malazan regulars swept over them. Arms took Temper and lifted him from the field. He let himself go then into that darkness, knowing he'd won his last battle – that once again he'd stood long enough . . .

Temper waited for the old nightmare to end. He always woke after that moment, his heart hammering, short of breath. But this time the darkness didn't come. Surgen still tore at him, workmanlike, as if butchering a slab of meat. And now, instead of a gilded bronze helm, he wore a grey hood. The certainty of death clutched Temper's throat. The hooded form leaned over him, smothered him in a different sort of darkness. Temper couldn't breathe. Death pressed down upon him like a vast weight, crushing his ribs, heavier, till he felt nothing of himself was left. Still he struggled to fight. If only to twitch a finger, to spit into the face inside that hood.

Temper inhaled. Cold air jarred his teeth. His chest expanded, fell, rose again. Light returned to his vision, blurred at first then clearing: once more he watched clouds massed before the frigid stars of a night sky.

Someone spoke from beyond his vision, saying dryly: 'You're a very stubborn man.'

Groaning, he turned his head. A man hooded in ash-pale robes sat above him on a stone block. Temper wet his lips, croaked, 'Who in Fener's own shit are you?'

'I would ask you the same question but believe I have my answer.' The man hefted an object: Temper's helmet. He turned it in his gloved hands as if critiquing the workmanship.

Temper moaned, let his head fall back.

'My people saw your duel with Rood. They were impressed. They, ah, intervened and fetched you here.'

Temper experimentally raised his right arm. He studied the hand, rubbed his eyes. 'Rood?'

'The Hound of Shadow. You surprised him. Too much easy prey recently, I should think.'

Temper attempted to sit up, groaned again. He wondered: how does one intervene against a demon like that?

'I had them heal you – after I saw this.' He tapped the helmet. 'A very unusual design.'

The helmet thumped onto his stomach. With a gasp, Temper sat up.

The man stood. 'You should get rid of it. Too distinctive.'

Temper grimaced. 'It's the only damned one I've got. And the question still stands: who are you?'

The man ignored him. He studied something in the distance then waved him up. 'Time is short. Suffice it to say that we have a common enemy in the Claws.'

Temper grunted at that. He carefully pushed himself upright. He examined his arms and wondered at the flesh made whole beneath the broken iron links and shredded leather under-padding. Forced healing of this magnitude stunned him. It was unheard of. He should be prostrate in shock, his body convinced he was crippled, if not dead. What had they done to him? At his side lay all his weapons and both gauntlets, one mangled and in tatters. He re-girt himself, hissing and wincing at limbs stiff and numb, shocking jolts of pain from every joint. The man merely watched, his face disguised in darkness.

They stood in Mossy Tors, a glade the town had encroached on as it grew inland. Temper spotted others, male or female, clothed in the same shapeless robes standing guard among the birch copses and jumbled stones. 'Well, whoever you are,' he grudgingly admitted, 'you're out in force.'

'Yes. This night is ours. We control the island two or three nights every century.'

Temper tried to get a glimpse into the shadows within the man's hood. There was something very odd about his accent. But it was as if the cowl was empty. That shook him: too reminiscent of the Claws . . . and his dream.

Another figure approached, almost identical to the first, and the two spoke. Their hoods nearly touched as they bent together. Both stood unnaturally tall and slim within their robes, and they conversed in a foreign lilting language that made Temper uneasy. He'd encountered a lot of languages in his travels, but this was not like any of them. That, the healing, the undeniable fact that they must've done something to yank him free of the hound, and the man's claim that they ruled this night, put Temper in mind of what he'd heard of the cult that worshipped Shadow. A sect steeped in sorcery and patron to assassins. And evidently, an organization hunted by the Claws. That made sense. Professional rivalry, he supposed. He recalled another organization of assassins, started up by Dancer at the inception of the Empire: the Talons. Surly's Claws, so it was said, began later as a pale imitation of that secret society. He'd also heard murmurs that since Kellanved and Dancer's absence, Surly's organization had moved to fill the void. That people loyal to the old guard had been disappearing. He'd never considered himself particularly loyal to Kellanved or Dancer; it was Dassem he'd refused to betray that day at Y'Ghatan. He'd survived, gone underground. Watching these two, he wondered if they too had served, though sure as Hood he'd never ask. He cleared his throat. The one who'd addressed him earlier turned to examine him. 'Come.' He waved for Temper to follow and abruptly started across the stone-littered meadow.

Surprised, Temper stood frozen until two others in the same shapeless garb approached from either side. The slimmer of the pair walked with an arrogant, cocky swagger that made Temper want to slap him. Scorch marks marred his robes at the front of and along the edge of his hood as if the fabric had been dropped in a fire. The stockier one motioned him to move on ahead with a hand that was hairy and wide-knuckled like a blacksmith's or a strangler's.

He was led to a rise overlooking the east quarter of the old town. 'What do you see?' the one who'd woken him asked.

Temper hesitated. What did the man want from him? Then, reluctantly, he scanned the quarter. Fog, thick as low clouds, clung to roofs and snaked through the streets. It seemed to converge around the general block of the Hanged Man Inn – and the neighbouring Deadhouse as well.

Staring now, he could just make out lights, an eerie blue-green nimbus that sometimes accompanied manipulation of the Warrens. How many times had he witnessed that same glow burst, spirit-like, over battles? And how many times had he ducked, experiencing the same cold knot in his stomach, because here was something all his skill could not combat? Rolling up from that same quarter, like a distant blast of alchemical munitions, came a hound's deep-chested call.

'What is it?' Temper asked.

'Some say a door,' the man told him, his tone thoughtful. 'An entrance to the realm of Shadow. And he who passes through, commands that Warren as a King. A stunning possibility, yes?'

Temper gave a knowing nod. 'So that's what all this is about. You're going for it.'

A silken laugh whispered from within the hood. 'No, not I . . . I haven't near the power. And it is too well defended. The hounds are only the first of its guardians. But another might try before dawn, and for that we are readying.'

'And what's that to me?'

'You could help.'

He nodded again, this time with scorn. 'And if I refuse?'

The hood regarded him and he stared back, trying to find the man's eyes in the darkness. The silence grew in length and discomfort. Temper rubbed the scar crossing his chin.

'Then you may go,' the man said.

Temper scoffed. 'What? Just like that?'

'Yes, just like that. Two of my people will escort you to wherever you wish.' He pointed past Temper.

Glancing to one side, Temper saw his earlier guards waiting nearby, at a length of mossy wall. 'Anywhere?'

'Yes.'

'Then I'm going to take you up on that.'

'Fare you well, soldier,' and the man gave a salute at his chest, the old sign of the Imperial Sceptre.

Temper dropped his hand from the scar that slashed down his cheek to his chin. 'I don't suppose you want to know what I think about your chances.'

The hood cocked to one side. 'Don't be foolish, Temper.'

'Yeah. I suppose so. My thanks for the healing.'

The hood inclined a goodbye. Temper backed off a few steps, as if worried that at the last moment they might change their minds, then started for Riverwalk. His two escorts fell into step behind him.

All the way up Riverwalk, Temper's back itched as if he were under the Twin's regard. He couldn't shake the suspicion that these two had been sent along to leave him dead in a ditch. Stupid of course: they could have simply left him for the hound. But the old habit of a healthy paranoia wouldn't leave him alone.

Finally, it became too much and he abruptly stopped and turned. Back about ten paces, the pair stopped as well. The slim one struck a pose, crossing his arms as if bored by the whole thing. The stocky one waved him on.

'Nothing to say for yourselves, eh?' Temper taunted, but then resumed his walk. The damned prophecy of the Return, he told himself, that was what all this was really about. Not this Shadow gateway bullshit. They'd gathered for *him* tonight. For Kellanved to return and claim the throne of Empire. It was still his after all. And Temper had to admit it was hard to swallow that he'd just disappear to let Surly – or anyone – usurp it. If he was yet alive, that is.

Pure blind bullshit. Or in this case, hound shit. Come dawn, their predicted millennium would fail to appear and they'd fade away, like so many cults before them. Temper had never been a religious man himself. The old standby patron gods of soldiers, Togg and Fener, had always been more than enough for him. The rest of that dusty theology just made his head numb: Old versus New; the rise and fall of Houses of influence; the eternal hunt for Ascension. Still, it was troublesome to see someone as clearly sharp and organized as that robed fellow swallowing it all.

He turned north onto Grinner's March. Rampart Way rose into view through the mist, making Temper smile. That, and the thought that he now had a ship-load of questions for Corinn when he found her. He counted on getting answers from her. Hood's bones, she owed him an explanation. *I saw*, she'd told him; seen the breaking of the Sword. Why? To shock him into cooperating? He sent a short prayer to Togg that somehow she'd managed to escape all this.

As he laid a hand on the cold granite wall of Rampart Way, he turned to his two escorts. They'd stopped a few paces back, side by side.

'What? Not coming?'

The slim one's hood rose as he peered up at the Hold. 'You'll find only death there tonight.'

Temper wanted to laugh that off, but the man's words sent a chill up his spine. He waved them away. 'Maybe. Run back to your master and let him know where I went.'

'He knows.'

Temper watched them. They remained motionless. He stared back for a time longer, then, snorting his impatience, started up the steps.

Grumbling, Temper strode up the wet stones. What a pack of moonstruck fools! As if there was anything to all that charlatan cant about a *Return*. It was damned embarrassing, that was what it was. A bunch of spoiled aristos probably. None of whom had ever shed a drop of blood in the fields. Never saw Kellanved murder thousands when he brought down a city wall, or his pet T'lan Imass warriors slaughtering entire towns. Good riddance to that wither-legged Dal Honese elder and spook of a partner, Dancer! In his career Temper had met and fought a lot of men and could honestly say: none scared him as much as those two did.

Dassem spoke of the Emperor rarely, but when he had, it was always with the greatest care and wariness. He had told one story of entering a dark command tent during the Delanss pacifications to inform Kellanved of the dispersal of the troops. While the two spoke an aid brought a lit lantern into the shadowed tent and Dassem discovered himself alone. Later, he learned from Admiral Nok that on that day the Emperor had been at sea, on board the *Twisted*. Dassem said this was characteristic of the old man: no one should ever be certain where Kellanved stood – in anything . . . or on anything.

Temper had seen him now and then, distantly, during marshalling of the troops: a small black man with gnarled limbs and short grey hair. Or so the pretence. At first glance he looked like nothing more than a withered-up old gnome. Yet one look from him could be enough to drive anyone away as if struck, or if wished, crush them to their knees. Temper had to give him that much.

But Dassem, Sword of the Empire, *he* had looked out for the men. By the Queen, the army literally worshipped him! All those others – Surly and the rest – knew it too, even then. He'd seen it in their eyes the times he'd accompanied Dassem to briefings. Surly and the other lackeys knew only the rule of fear. But Dassem, with praise here, or a chiding word there, could capture a man's heart. And he led from the front; in every battle. Soldiers shoved each other aside just for the chance to fight near him.

At a switchback Temper paused. The night closed in on him, black, hollow, and surprisingly cold – a chill that seemed to broach his soul. Downhill, the fog obscured the slopes and hung over the town. Icy rain brushed him and he wiped at his face. Damn, it was raw! His bones ached. What time was it now? Four bells or five? He couldn't remember hearing the mole lighthouse for some time now. Gods, he was weary. Leaning against the wall, he wondered just what it was he hoped to accomplish. He stared out into the lazy wisps of mist and the strangely dull stars, and he remembered that other night. The night close to a year ago when he and Dassem died.

He'd awakened in an infirmary field tent. An officer's facility, small and empty, unlike the ones they stuffed with regulars while the overflow simply stacked up outside. Ferrule sat beside him on a travel chest, as short and hairy and vicious-looking as ever. He wore a thick leather vest over a cloth jerkin. Two dark shapes stood at the closed flaps: Claws.

'Back with us, hey?' Ferrule grinned, slapping his leg. With his left hand, hidden by his body, he signed: *they've made their move.*

Temper answered with a faint nod, smiled. 'Yeah, whole again.' *Their move.* The six of them had always known it would come. They had spoken of it, planned for it, dreaded it. But now they were only two. Two against all Surly's Claws.

'Where is he?'

Ferrule jerked his head to the flaps. 'Taken for special treatment. Tried to stop them, but . . .' He shrugged.

'The wound?'

'Damned bad. Worst yet.' Ferrule opened his vest a fraction revealing the hilts of two knives. *We have to get to him.* 'How do you feel? I made them heal you up. Raised Togg's own stink about it,' he laughed. *Can you make it?*

Temper signed to Ferrule: *I'm with you.* 'Feel like a

new-born kitten. Help me up. We have to check on him.' He'd exaggerated only a bit. Surgen had pretty much cut him up into a walking corpse. Forced healing and bone knitting was wondrous, but it was just as traumatic as the wounds themselves: he felt as if he'd been tortured for weeks. He bit back sour vomit. Sweat beaded all over his body, trickled down his face. Yet he was alive, and he had sworn his life to Dassem. If the Claws were behind this attack, then as far as he was concerned they had made a huge error in not killing them all immediately. Surly's hands were probably tied – too many must have witnessed their survival.

Ferrule grunted, 'Don't faint on me,' and passed a knife while helping him off the cot. Temper leaned on Ferrule's shoulder, both for effect and because his knees shook, barely able to support him.

Flanking the entrance, the Claws exchanged glances. Both were male and dressed for combat rather than in the loose black cloaks they always wrapped themselves in when allowing themselves to be seen. Their unofficial uniform consisted of dark dyed cloth, tall leather boots, trousers, loose jerkins, vests and gloves. Their long hair hung gathered down their backs. Each carried an arsenal, but concealed in pockets and folds. The tiny, understated silver Claw sigils glittered at their left breasts.

Temper shuffled across the tent on Ferrule's arm, exaggerating his weakness, though probably fooling no one. Ferrule's rock-like solidity reassured him. It would be good to have him at his side for what was to come. They'd given the hairy, muscular Seti plainsman the name Ferrule because he preferred to fight in close. After any battle the blood literally ran from him.

The Claws shifted to stand side by side. 'You're to remain. Recuperate. The Regent's orders.'

Ferrule slowed. 'We're leaving, lads. Stand aside.'

'Orders, soldier. Don't challenge her authority.'

Under his arm, Temper felt Ferrule flex, readying for action. 'Stand aside,' he warned, his voice level, 'or we'll carve through you like we did the Holy Guard.'

The Claws exchanged one quick glance. The one who'd spoken flicked his hand.

'Spell,' Ferrule snarled. He snapped out the hand he'd held behind Temper's back and a knife flew. Temper flung himself ahead and to one side. Something clipped his arm, the dressing ripped. He rolled, came up where the Claws had stood and though dizzy, snatched out in time to grab an ankle of one as he tried to call up his Warren. Losing his balance, the man fell and lost control of the forces he'd tried to summon. Wracked by lancing pain, his vision darkening to a tunnel, and just plain furious, Temper stabbed the man in the groin then lunged for a lethal throat jab. But the Claw wriggled aside and Temper's blade merely nicked the man's chin.

Amazingly, the Claw stood. Temper was slowed because he'd discovered his right side was smeared in fresh blood, and something long and sharp stuck entirely through his upper arm. How in Hood's name had that got there?

A knife appeared in the Claw's gloved hand. Temper lashed out for his legs, but it was a feeble effort. As the Claw bent his wrist back for a quick snap-throw, Ferrule slammed into him. They went down together in a flurry of limbs, swinging, racking, grappling. And though more blows were exchanged than Temper could keep track of, it was over in a few seconds.

Ferrule rose, grinning. One ear hung loose, nearly torn off. His shirt was flayed and his chest dressings hung in tatters.

'Wind's Blessing!' he sighed, as if he'd just drained a mug of beer, 'I've been aching to do that for years.'

Temper groaned, stood. He poked at his arm. 'Am I everyone's target today, or what?'

Ferrule examined the wound then eased the blade free.

Temper muffled a shout of pain, hung onto the man's shoulder to keep from falling. Ferrule, admiring the long lethal stiletto, whistled. 'Might've got you in the heart.'

'Thanks a lot.'

Ferrule sat him down and began redressing his arm. Temper watched the big man work, all the while feeling embarrassed by his performance in that quick and dirty fray. He didn't think he'd be much use in what was to come.

Ferrule checked the entrance, reported that it looked like they were under unofficial quarantine for the night. He said he saw where they'd taken Dassem, then set to cleaning himself up and collecting useful weapons from the Claws. Temper sat and shook his head. Clearing his throat, he said, 'Look, Ferrule. Seems like I'm not going to be too useful. Maybe you should go it alone.'

Ferrule looked up from one Claw corpse. There was something in his eyes: wonder? Disbelief? He came to Temper's side. 'Not much use! That you're alive is a miracle. Do you know what you did?'

Temper shook his head, uncertain.

'You stood against Surgen! It was amazing! I didn't see the half of it, but everyone's talking. I heard them through the tent. He was a Holy City patroned champion! Mage-abetted. Temple anointed. And you stonewalled him! I thought we'd had it, but you saved our hides. I even heard talk that maybe you had a patron up your sleeve—'

Temper laughed that off.

'No. I mean it. You come out of this tent looking like the ugly block of granite you usually do and everyone'll back off. I mean it.' Ferrule waved to the corpses. 'Don't you think it was strange the way those two panicked? You, us, we impressed the shit out of some people today. People who thought we were sure to be dead.'

That had troubled him as well. It had been too easy. The

Claws had acted as though they were facing opponents of unknown potential. They'd tried too hard to keep their distance. He nodded, squeezed Ferrule's arm. 'Very well. Hail the Sword.'

Ferrule gave a grin of savage glee. 'Just the three of us now – but three times enough, I say.'

Outfitted and cleaned up, they pushed aside the tent flap and boldly set out across the infirmary quarters of the encampment. The night was warm and dry. The branches of a nearby olive orchard rustled in a weak wind and a sliver of moon shone down like a yellow scimitar blade. Torches burned at every major intersection of the tent city, but few soldiers moved about. They greeted each sentry and some, recognizing them, called out, 'Hail the Sword!' Ferrule raised a fist in answer.

'They'll know we're coming,' Temper complained.

'The more witnesses the better.'

Temper grunted at the wisdom of that. Ferrule guided them to a private tent near the edge of the infirmary quarters. Lamps glowed within and two Claws stood at its closed flap. As they approached, the sight of open surprise and confusion cracking through the assassins' legendary control warmed Temper's heart.

Side by side, they walked right up to the Claws guarding the entrance. 'We've come to see Dassem,' announced Ferrule without slowing, and he waved to soldiers watching from nearby tents.

After the briefest hesitation, one Claw inclined his head and stood aside, opening the flap. Ferrule eyed the dark opening, perhaps not liking their cooperation. Temper felt a twinge of doubt; what if they'd simply moved Dassem again?

Inside, clay lamps gave a low, guttering light. Dassem lay on a cot as if dead, his torso wrapped in dressings. The amber light gave his dark skin a rich lustre, as if he were a statue of bronze. Temper paused, sensing someone else in the darkened recesses of the tent.

Fabric whispered in the dark.

'Hail the Sword,' said a woman's voice.

Surly stepped from the shadows, three Claws just behind her. Temper had rarely faced her this close. She wore her typical shirt, sash, pants, and her feet were bare. The woman's plain face was flat and narrow, tight with concentration. Her hair was cropped short in the fashion common to the many women who served in the Malazan military, and her hands bore dark calluses. She struck Temper as all hard edges. As the third most powerful individual in the Empire, Temper supposed she had to be.

The three Claws with her Temper knew by name and reputation: second-in-command Topper in his signature green silks; Possum, as beady-eyed and narrow-faced as his namesake; and Jade, a dark-hued Dal Honese female, and one of the most vicious of the crew.

Ferrule and Temper ignored Surly and her aides, crossing to Dassem's cot. Temper felt for a pulse, sensed nothing. 'Is he alive?'

'For the moment,' Surly responded. 'He flutters on the edge of his patron's realm. One would think Hood should be eager to embrace him.'

Ferrule and he exchanged glances, turned on Surly. Temper saw Ferrule sizing up Possum. Balanced forward on the balls of her feet, Jade seemed ready to throw herself at Temper.

Surly raised a placating hand. 'A change has been decided upon. Choss has been field promoted to High Fist and interim Commander of the Third.'

Ferrule scoffed but Temper let out a long thoughtful breath. Choss was a name that just might please the majority. The officer cadres respected him, and he was a skilled strategist. He was also unpatroned. Just a regular soldier – no threat to Surly.

Temper licked his lips. 'But you still need Dassem. Choss is no champion.'

Surly frowned a negative, shook her head. 'No, Temper, you still don't understand. Things are different now. Even as we speak, Surgen succumbs to his wounds. It isn't the most decisive victory, but it will be a victory. And disheartened, without time for a new ritual of Anointing, Y'Ghatan will fall. No more champions. They're too expensive. Too . . . vulnerable.'

Snarling, Ferrule would have launched himself, but Temper gripped his shoulder. 'And what of us?'

Surly raised her brows, surprised and impressed by Temper's pragmatism. 'What is it you wish? Rank? Titles? A regional governorship?'

Ferrule squeezed Temper's wounded arm in a ferocious grip. Temper bit his lips to keep from shouting. Pressing his hand into Ferrule's back, he arranged his fingers in a sign: *wait*.

Temper managed in a controlled voice, 'Dassem's life, for one thing.'

Surly nodded. 'That *might* be arranged.'

Her response decided the night for Temper. It seemed neither of them had any intention of keeping their word. 'No witnesses' was almost Surly's credo. The Claws never left anyone alive. It was part of their terror tactics. He also believed that she knew he wouldn't sell out, or frankly didn't care either way. Yet they had their roles to play, a charade to complete.

'Okay,' he breathed out long and slow. 'We'll stay with him. For the meantime.'

Surly pursed her lips. Temper could almost see the plans and various options spinning through her thoughts as she eyed him and Ferrule. Her gaze lingered at his wounded arm and something changed in the set of her shoulders; she inclined her head a fraction. 'Very well. You may discuss the particulars with

171

these two representatives. Possum. Jade. Take care of these gentlemen. Topper, accompany me.'

The two Claws edged forward a half-step. Surly crossed to the entrance, the cloth of her pants brushing soundlessly. As she turned away, Temper glanced to his own arm: fresh blood soaked the new dressings. So. She figured her best should be enough to finish the job.

Topper held open the tent flap, with a half-bow of farewell Surly exited. Ferrule and he caught each other's eyes. Ferrule, legs flexed, arms crooked, looked like a bear ready to pounce, and he winked, the same old supremely confident brawler. Temper couldn't muster the same relish for this fray. His fears were confirmed when the two Claws guarding the opening stepped in as their commander left. Possum waved as if tossing something down and suddenly the camp sounds from beyond the tent walls ceased as if snatched away.

Shit, Temper fumed, *that guaranteed privacy*. He decided to pursue the one mad chance he'd thought of while Surly made her own evaluation of the situation.

'Guard me,' he snapped to Ferrule. In one motion he stepped, knelt, and raised his knife in both hands over Dassem's chest. *Fluttering at death's door*, Surly had said. He prayed that was an inadvertent truth, for Hood was the patron god Dassem has sworn his soul to – *sworn then rejected*.

He heard Ferrule parry the first attacks behind him as, in that same motion, he plunged the knife down with all his strength.

'Stop him!' Possum snarled.

Something smacked off Temper's skull.

Dassem's hand snapped up, grabbed Temper's arm, and tossed him aside. Dassem sat up. Temper crashed through a cot and thumped to the beaten earth. Blood blinded one eye and warmed his face. He watched the rest of the melee on his side, stunned, fighting unconsciousness.

Foolishly, perhaps misled by their numerical advantage and Dassem's weakened condition, the Claws chose to finish things here. Not that Temper could blame them. After all, they hadn't fought side by side with Dassem as he and Ferrule had. They had never seen up close just what the First Sword was capable of. That, and Claws tended to overconfidence.

It all registered like slow deliberate dance steps to Temper's fading vision. Ferrule spun aside, spurned by Possum. Blood arched from his wounds as he fell. The other three closed on Dassem who lunged at the nearest. In one motion he simply reached out and crushed the man's throat then turned, holding the corpse before him.

Regardless, Jade and the other closed. Possum – wisely, if belatedly – backed off. Rather than use the body as a shield Dassem threw it as easily as a horseshoe at both lunging Claws. They fell in a heap. Temper could tell how angry Dassem was by the extravagance of that gesture and the way he scowled his disgust.

He kicked Jade across her head, tore a weapon from her hand and pulled it across her throat. The other Claw guard lay where he'd fallen, stunned.

Possum tried to access his Warren, but broke off to dodge the knife Dassem threw. The two closed and Possum met Dassem with daggers in either hand. They circled, Possum feinting, Dassem weaving, dodging. Temper had to admire Possum's form; it was the best he'd seen, but the man had made a fatal mistake in not breaking off the instant Dassem revived. Arrogance, perhaps.

Dassem closed, yielding a cut across his side to grab one hand. They spun, pivoting on that fulcrum and again Temper was amazed by Possum's moves. But Dassem's skill, strength, and speed, though all sapped, still proved too great for Possum's will and razor-honed training. Dassem broke the wrist, twisted the arm around, and jammed Possum's own blade onto his chest. He collapsed, and camp sounds returned to the tent.

Temper smiled at their victory and gave in to the cold hard darkness that pulled at him like the embrace of deep water.

As the night progressed he fluttered into consciousness now and then. Pain in his stomach jabbed him awake once and Ferrule, his face close, strained and pale, motioned for silence. He saw tents and wagons once, dark, unmanned. Later, a field of tall grass whispered and hissed as pain shocked him awake again and Dassem, wearing a broad cloak, examined him, smiling his encouragement.

Travelling only a few leagues each night, they escaped. They walked north through passes of the Thalas Range to the coast and stole a small fishing launch. This they sailed by turns night and day, north-east out to the Sea of Dryjina, then south. A month later they landed, thin, sunburnt, bearded, on the Seven City coast south of Aren. Here they parted ways. Temper and Ferrule planned to take the boat south to Falar. Dassem did not intend to go with them.

They had stood together on the rocky shore, none wishing to speak. They wore loose robes now over trousers and tunics. White home-spun cloth scarves wrapped their heads and masked their faces. Of his former life, Temper carried only his helmet wrapped in his blanket bedding. Dassem had presented it to him when he awoke.

Temper stood with arms crossed, fixed his sight on a distant mountain range. 'So,' he said to Dassem, 'it has to be alone, does it?'

Dassem gave a tired nod. It was an old argument.

'What will you do?'

'Travel. Head west.'

'What in Togg's name could possibly be out there?' Ferrule snapped, furious as usual when thwarted in anything.

Dassem's smile cut at Temper's soul, so wintry was it. 'Something. Something's out there. Maybe what I'm looking for.'

Temper cleared his throat. He thought of Dassem's own whispered words and the rumours he, Point, and Edge kept track of, regarding a purge among the highest levels of the cult of Hood. 'I'd wish you luck, but I'm not sure you should find what you're looking for.'

That got a sharp look, but Dassem relented with a pained expression that seemed half-agreement. 'I suppose we'll see.'

'A pox on all of it!' Ferrule snarled, and threw himself into the surf. He lurched out to the anchored boat. Grasping the side, he shouted back, 'If you must travel half of creation, look me up on the Seti plains.'

Dassem waved farewell.

Temper stepped up and they embraced. At the shore he tried one last appeal, though he knew it was useless. 'Retire with us. Set your feet up.'

'There are things I must do.'

'Yeah, well. Be damned careful.'

Dassem laughed. 'I will.'

'You ain't got us to watch your back no more.'

'I know.'

Still Temper could not bring himself to part from the side of the man he had sworn to give his life for. 'I could refuse, you know. Follow along.'

Again the sad smile. 'I know.' He squeezed Temper's shoulder. 'But you will die if you remain with me. This I know. Stay with the fight, Temp. There is a good chance you will live a very long while yet.'

Temper's breath caught. 'You have seen this?'

Dassem released his shoulder, motioned him on. 'Go. That's an order.'

Temper pushed his way out through the surf. Ferrule and he

set the sail. As the dusk gathered between the boat and the rocky shore, they waved farewell. Dassem raised an arm in one long continuous salute. Finally, the dim figure turned away from the shore and disappeared among the trees.

After a time, while they sailed along the coastline, Ferrule asked, 'What in Fener's tusks is so damned important? Why can't we go with him?'

'I think he's going where we can't follow.'

Ferrule peered back over his shoulder at Temper as if wondering just how serious he was. Temper wasn't sure himself.

It wasn't until weeks later on the island of Strike that they heard the official version of that final day at Y'Ghatan. It seemed that the three surviving members of the Sword, weakened by their wounds, died in a night raid by fanatical Holy City Falah'd, who after withdrew to the city, taking Dassem's body with them.

That same night Surgen died in a manner never fully explained. Three days later the city fell. By all accounts High Fist Choss acquitted himself well. Dassem's body was never conclusively identified and the Empire never did get around to appointing a new First Sword.

At the top of Rampart Way Kiska found the Hold's towering iron-studded gates closed. No lantern or torchlight shone from the slits of the machicolations to either side. Normally, the glinting barbed tips of crossbow quarrels would have tracked her movements and the watch captain would have hailed her long ago.

Cut into the timbers of the left-hand gate, the tiny thieves' door stood ajar. Something lay jammed at its bottom. Kiska slid along the timbers until level with the opening. A forearm, bloodied palm up, stuck out as if offering a macabre greeting. She peered through the gap. It belonged to one of the mercenaries who had kidnapped her. He was dead, the leather armour at his back stitched by cuts. From the way he lay he must have been trying to escape. Darkness obscured the entrance tunnel and she knew she was now outlined by the moonlight glowing behind her. Slipping in, she stepped to one side and stopped dead, listening.

Nothing but the faint and distant surf. The stink of blood and voided bowels filled the enclosure. As her eyes adjusted to the dark, the twisted shapes of two other mercenaries distinguished themselves from the cobbled lane. Perhaps they'd been left behind to guard the gate and since then, someone had come and made quick work of them. She knelt: a dark trail of blood, still sticky to the touch, traced where one of the men had dragged himself just short of a small side-door in the tunnel; the entrance to gatekeeper Lubben's quarters. She followed, stood over the body, and listened at the door. After a few heartbeats she was about to step away when the scuff of a shifting foot reached her. Someone was within, perhaps listening just as she was. Did she want to know if it was the hunchback or his murderer? No, she'd leave that alone. Somewhere ahead Artan must be . . .

The door whipped open. A thick arm and a hand the size of a small shield grabbed the front of her shirt and yanked her in. A hatchet blade shoved under her chin jammed her against the wall. Close hot breath reeking of wine assaulted her.

'Oh, it's you, lass,' Lubben growled. He squinted through his good eye then released her and pushed himself away. 'Sorry.'

Kiska caught her breath, straightened her shirt and vest. The room was no more than a nook. A hole overlooked during the fortress's construction – too short for her to straighten, though tall enough for the hunchback gatekeeper.

'By the Elders, child. I thought you'd better sense than to come here tonight.' He shoved her aside, closed the door, slammed the bolt.

'What's happening upstairs?'

Lubben thumped down into a chair beside a brazier of glowing coals. He took a pull from a skin, wiped his mouth on the sleeve of his stained leather jerkin.

'Don't know and don't care.'

Kiska stood near the door, shivered in the damp air. 'But you must have some idea.'

Lubben laughed, coughed hoarsely. 'Lass, I've ideas all right. Plenty. But here they stay.' He tapped one blunt finger to his temple.

'Well, I'm going to find out.'

Head tilted to one side, he eyed her as if estimating the degree of her insanity. He pointed to the door. 'Be my guest.'

Kiska hesitated. 'You mean you're just going to sit here?'

'Indeed I am.' Grinning, he took another pull from the skin. 'Listen. It's a war up there – no prisoners. You understand? This ain't your regular social affair.'

'Fine. I'll go alone.'

Lubben frowned, shoved a wood stopper into the skin and set it down on the floor. He cleared his throat, spat into a corner. 'You could stay here for the night, y'know. Been safe enough so far.'

Shifting to warm her hands over the brazier, Kiska shook her head. 'No. Thanks. I've got to look into this. There's . . .' She stopped herself, decided against revealing names or just what might be at stake. 'This is important. I've got to know what's going on.'

A deep-throated chuckle shook Lubben. 'I'm thinking that's what everyone would like to know.'

Kiska got the feeling that Lubben knew more than he was revealing. He'd been the Hold's gatekeeper for as long as she could remember. As a child she and her friends had often gathered at the open gate, daring each other to tease the 'hunch' with his crablike walk and the great ring of keys rattling at his side. Remembering that, Kiska felt her face burn with sudden embarrassment. To think she'd almost called him a coward for hiding in his cell. Who was she to judge?

She sighed. 'All right. I'll be going then.' Lubben nodded, stared at the sullen coals as if reviewing his own painful memories. Struck by a thought, she turned from the door. 'Can you lend me a weapon?'

He grunted, pulled a dagger from the wide belt at his waist and handed it over. She took it: one of the meanest-looking blades she'd ever seen on a knife – curved like a hand-scythe.

'Thanks.'

He grunted again, his gaze averted. She unbolted the door.

'Lass . . .'

She turned. 'Yes?'

'You keep your back to the walls, you hear?'

'Yes. I will.' Slipping through the door, she pulled it shut behind her.

The bailey stood empty, unguarded. Just inside the fortified door to the main keep she found four more dead mercenaries. Among them was one of the scarred commander's picked veterans. No visible wounds – it was as if they'd simply dropped dead. Her back prickled at the possibility of a Warren-laid trap such as a ward. If so, she prayed it was now spent. She wasn't sure how many men had escaped the hound's attack: maybe fifteen or twenty. By her rough reckoning that left ten men, including their commander and the woman she believed to be a cadre mage.

In the reception hall the light was low. The candles had burnt out, leaving only oil-lamps guttering here and there along the walls. Deep shadows swallowed most of the chamber, gaps so dark someone could stand within and she'd never know it. A circular stone stairway hugging the wall started on her right. The high official and her Claws had taken over the top floors of the keep.

With Lubben's warning in mind, she eased herself along one wall. In the darkness her foot pushed up against something at the base of the stairs. She crouched down. One of Artan's two remaining guards, dead, a throwing spike jammed into his throat. Hood's breath! At this rate no one would be left alive. And who was doing all the killing? So far, the murders stank of the Claws.

At the second-floor landing a single oil lamp cast a weak glow upon a scene beyond her worst nightmares. The dead lay in heaps, most of them from the mercenary band. Smouldering tapestries and scorched furniture sent wisps of smoke into the air. She gagged at the sweet odour of burnt flesh. Eviscerated and blackened, the head and upper torso of a Claw hung through the smashed planking of a door. Another Claw lay sprawled amidst the thickest pile of dead, virtually hacked to pieces. It looked as though another one of those alchemical bombs – Moranth munitions – had been touched off in the enclosed quarters.

Holding a portion of her cloak over her nose and mouth to keep out the worst of the stench, Kiska stepped over the bodies to cross the landing. A hall led to a second flight of stairs. Another veteran lay on the floor in a pool of blood, throat slit. From the number of corpses, it looked like the commander couldn't be left with more than a few survivors at most. The woman didn't appear to be among the bodies, nor Artan or Hattar.

Blood dripped down the worn stairs, sticking to her slippers as she followed the curve of the inner wall. She halted just short of the top behind the body of a man who'd dragged himself up from the carnage below. She recognized the lozenged armour: it was the sergeant who'd captured her at Mossy Tors.

She stepped over him and crouched, head level with the

landing above. She paused to listen. Silence. Profound and utter quiet. It made her back itch. Was everyone dead?

A sough and a slip of cloth sounded beneath her. She looked down, the hair at the nape of her neck rising. The mercenary was not dead. While she watched, a hand rose then snapped at her ankle. She nearly shrieked aloud. It yanked and she fell back onto him, her head cracking on the stairs. Stars and tearing pain half-blinded her. The mercenary's arm rose and she blocked his feeble blow, though the effort sent her sliding backwards down the stairs.

The grip on her ankle weakened and she jerked her leg free. The mercenary lay slumped on his back. Half the flesh of his face had been burned away. He glared at her. 'You again,' he chuckled. Oddly, he merely sounded tired.

Kiska snapped, 'What in K'rul's pits are you trying to do?'

That roused him. He grimaced, foam on his torn lips. 'What're we trying to do? Bring back the old glory! Return Malaz to its true path! You know nothing of how it was. *He* came to us. *He* promised us!'

The man coughed up blood, his eye lost focus, then found her again. Kiska did not need to ask who *He* was. 'And what happened?' she whispered.

'A damned free for all, s'what. Claws comin' out of the woodwork like roaches. Don't know how many left. Too many is my wager. She came ready for anything.'

'She? Who is she? Tell me.'

Kiska shook him, but his eye closed and his head eased back to the stairs. His last breath hissed: '*Surly.*'

So. There it was. Yet he could be wrong. He might be mistaken. It was possible confirmation of what she'd suspected but dared not believe. And now that she knew, or suspected that she knew, fear replaced curiosity. Agayla, Artan, even Lubben, they were right: she had no business here. This was between what everyone in Imperial service called the *Old*

Guard. She – and anyone else – would be killed as unwanted witnesses to old grudges.

Kiska shrank back down the stairs. At the bottom she leapt back into shadow, spotting someone coming up the hall. Smoke still hung thick in the air, and the lamps cast poor light, but even at noon on a clear day the figure would have sent shivers of dread up her spine. It looked like a hoary shape out of the legendary past, ripped from its grave by the Shadow Moon.

Two curving longswords out, crouched, the apparition strode heavily through the wreckage. In archaic armour that might've been worn decades ago by the Iron Guard or the Heng Lion Legion, a battered, lobster-tailed and visored helmet covered its head. And Kiska was thankful for that, for no one could have survived the ferocious wounds the mangled armour betrayed. Steel scales swung loose from the torn leather and padding. Iron rings clattered to the stone floor as it lumbered forward. Surely this was one of the horrors hinted at in the legends of the Shadow Moon. A demon, or an inhuman Jaghut tyrant clawed from its rest, lusting to settle ancient wrongs.

Kiska couldn't move: there was no way past it, and she couldn't go up. While she watched its implacable advance, a shadow flickered at the edge of her vision. Something thudded from the figure's layered armour. It grunted, turning awkwardly sideways in the hall like a battered siege tower, one weapon ahead, the other to the rear.

Two shapes emerged from the shadows before and behind the figure.

Claws. Needle-thin blades gleamed in their hands. The figure glanced behind, then returned its attention to the front.

Kiska watched appalled while whatever the thing was shifted to forge ahead. Its body language shouted *lunge* in footing and balance, and the forward Claw yielded a half-step. Incredibly, at that instant, the armoured giant spun then sped behind as swiftly as a naked runner. The rear Claw parried a blur of blows. The figure pressed on, head-butting the Claw with his steel helm. Stunned, the Claw reeled back, then, as he fell, the figure slashed, ripping open his gut.

A thrown blade slammed into the armoured back and jammed. Snarling, the warrior whirled around. It and the Claw stood facing each other, poised. Like a boar readying for a charge, the warrior rolled its shoulders. It pointed a mangled gauntleted hand at the Claw. 'I'll have your head this time, Possum.'

Kiska felt a chill from her scalp to her toes. Clearly, this Shadow-summoned fiend could not be stopped. No normal soldier went around dispatching Claws or vowing their destruction. Perhaps it was a warrior from the Emperor's terrifying T'lan Imass legions. They were said to wear tatters of their ancient armour and to be as irresistible as a typhoon.

The Claw laughed. 'Then come. I'll await you above.' He stepped back into darkness and disappeared.

Alone, the figure snorted its disgust. It rubbed its back against a wall like a bhederin scratching itself. The knife clattered to the stones. After that the warrior rolled its shoulders once more and clashed its swords together as if gathering itself to slaughter anyone it found.

Kiska dashed up the stairs past the dead mercenary.

At the top stretched another hall like the one below. This one however displayed no trace of conflict. She knew it held the rooms of senior officers, the military tribunal presided over by Sub-Fist Pell, and a private dining room. The appointments were stark, befitting a military garrison: clay wall lamps, a few hanging banners and moth-eaten standards. Narrow hall tables bore funerary vessels, spent candles, and miniature stone statues of soldiers, the sight of which reminded Kiska of the demonic warrior behind her. The furthest door stood ajar. She pushed it open and slipped into the darkness.

Though she'd never visited, Kiska knew this for the private dining room where Sub-Fist Pell entertained visiting ship captains and other officers, and where long ago pirate admirals once drank with important hostages dragged out of the dungeons below.

She backed slowly into the room. Vague outlines of tall-backed chairs swam into view along the walls. Trying to slow her pounding heart, Kiska took deep breaths. This was obviously the largest room on this floor, but she felt crowded, as if she weren't alone. She stopped moving, poised to turn on the balls of her feet. Sensing something behind her she spun to stare up at Hattar's flat, anger-twisted face. As a warning he raised a finger for silence, then waved her to the rear of the room. Backing away, she bumped up against someone who steadied her. It was Artan.

She turned to him, started to speak, but he pressed a gloved finger to her lips. She clamped her mouth shut, nodded.

He leaned his mouth close to her ear, whispered, 'You shouldn't have come.'

'Something's coming. An armoured demon like a T'lan Imass. Unstoppable. It defeated two Claws.' Her eyes had adjusted to the gloom, and she saw his brows rise in disbelief, or surprise. She also caught hand signals flying between Artan and Hattar. That startled her; earlier, Hattar's night vision had struck her as poor. It must since have been augmented. By Warren perhaps. Two long knives at hand, the plainsman took a position just behind the door. Artan drew her farther back into the long room, to a corner where, through the open door, they could see a section of the lamp-lit hall and the base of the steps to the top-most floor, occupied by the High Official – Surly.

They heard the armoured fiend long before seeing it: slow, heavy tread, torn scales and strapping rattling the walls.

As it loomed into view in the doorway, Artan's breath caught. Kiska wondered if it was in recognition, fear, or both.

'You were right,' Artan murmured, his voice a bare whisper, 'a ghost out of the past indeed . . .'

Filling the hall like an animated statue, the shape turned to the stairs. It rolled its head in the large helmet, slashed one blade through the air at the base of the narrow curving stairs. Then, swords clashing up into guard, it flinched away.

Someone stepped down from the stairs and into view. A slim figure in an iron-grey cloak. A cultist! Kiska shot Artan a questioning look, but his eyes were wide with amazement. She turned back to the doorway.

The two appeared to be negotiating. Clearly, they knew each other and no love was lost between them. The cultist's voice was a soft murmur, the warrior's a hoarse rumble, both echoing in the stillness of the hallway until, eventually, they seemed to come to some sort of an agreement. The cultist lazily waved one hand and a third shape appeared, prone on the hall's floor. The armoured being, not lowering its attention from the cultist, nudged the figure with its foot. The new arrival responded groggily. It was the dark woman, the mercenary mage, in her black silk shirt and brocaded vest. After a few more exchanges, the armoured figure sheathed its weapons and lifted the woman to its shoulder. It retreated back down the hall, out of sight.

Why take the woman? Kiska wondered. Some kind of sacrifice? She released her breath. It was over. The ancient revenant was gone. Artan, though, gave her arm a painful squeeze. She peered up.

Gaze nailed to the doorway, he mouthed, *Be still*.

She looked. Whoever the cultist was, he'd turned and now stared straight at them through the door's narrow yawn. Yet standing in the lamplight it should have been impossible for him to see them hidden in the dark. At her side, Artan stood as tense as a drawn bow. He swallowed, breathed aloud in wonder, 'By the Autumn Worm. It is *he*.'

185

When he'd entered the Hold's main gate Temper had drawn his twin curved longswords at the sight of the four corpses. He recognized them as members of Ash's rag-tag platoon and noted there were no ex-Bridgeburners among them. Ash was obviously holding his best close to hand. He hoped fervently that Corinn counted among those.

He paused at the door to Lubben's quarters, wanting to see if the hunchback still lived, but reconsidered. If alive, there was a chance Lubben might recognize his helmet. There was no telling – the old souse was pretty damned canny in his own way. So Temper passed by the door, stepped out into the empty bailey. He thought of checking the barracks, but dread of what he might discover urged him away. The Claws had perpetrated worse atrocities in their history than the slaughter of one small garrison. After jogging across the bailey, he pushed open the keep's door with the tip of one sword. More dead chaff here. The Claws, and perhaps even Ash, were thinning their ranks of expendables. He could just imagine Ash figuring that, Twin's chance, the boys might actually get lucky and kill a Claw or two. Pausing, he tightened his helmet strap, adjusted the frayed rag-ends of gauntlets and shook his shoulders. This was it. Upstairs was the 'High Official', her Claw bodyguard, possibly a friend, and perhaps two spectres from his past who had yet to answer for a betrayal they did nothing to prevent. He concentrated, emptied his mind of everything but the objective at the top of the tower.

Ten heart beats later his old fighting calm slipped over him like a familiar protective cloak. He felt good. Damn sore, but strong. He started down the entrance hall, knees bent, weapons ready. He didn't have far to go. At the main reception chamber he felt a prickling of warning and threw himself against the wall. Something disturbed the air only to disappear, swallowed by the shadows. He began sliding along the wall for a corridor that led to the stairs.

A shape rippled into view at the centre of the chamber. A Claw – female – her chest slashed by savage wounds, blood soaking her pants. She stood before him empty-handed, staring glassy-eyed.

Through the forward sweep of his cheek-guards, Temper frowned. As he edged along the wall he wondered if she even saw him. When only a few paces separated them, the Claw began weaving her hands in front of her. The distant lamp flames guttered and a cold wind brushed Temper's face while a pool of impenetrable night grew before the woman. Horrified, he recognized a summoning of the Imperial Warren. At any moment anything could emerge: Claws, an army, or a demon. Temper launched himself forward to the floor and slashed the Claw's feet out from under her. She collapsed and the portal snapped shut. Rolling, he straightened and thrust down. Both blades tore their way into the Claw's bloodied chest. Still silent, she pawed futilely at Temper's blades, weaker and weaker, until she sighed and her arms fell.

His heart racing, Temper pushed himself to his feet. Gods! Though half dead that Claw had almost finished him. He swivelled to cover the chamber. Why not a more active use of the Warrens? It occurred to him that perhaps this night, during the Shadow Moon, drawing upon them might be the greatest risk of all. Sensing himself alone, he wiped his blades across the body and continued on.

Carried by pale smoke a familiar stench drifted down the stairs. It transported Temper back to the countless battlefields he'd strode. No matter where the war, in forest or desert, the smell of death was always the same. As he stepped up onto the landing he felt he'd arrived home. As if the brotherhood hadn't been shattered. As if he still campaigned with the

Sword. He almost sensed their presence at his back like a firm hand urging him on.

Two more dead Claws lay among what looked to be the majority of Ash's remaining company. It must have been an ugly knife-fight that ended when one of the Bridgeburner veterans touched off an alchemical anti-personnel Sharper or explosive concussive right in everyone's faces. Those boys always did play rough. He didn't see Corinn or Ash among the bodies.

Up the hall past the wreckage Temper thought he saw movement on the stairs ahead, but it might've been the oil lamp's flickering flame. He paused, flexed for action: the Claws had disputed this stretch of hall before so perhaps they'd—

A thrown weapon hit and deflected from his back. He struck a sideways guard position: one sword high to the front, the other low to the rear. How many of the damned murderers could be left? A normal Claw cell numbered five. Leaving two. But if that was a Fist upstairs, or someone of even higher rank, she wouldn't have travelled with less than two cells in attendance.

A Claw appeared before him and he knew instinctively that another had come out behind. But he looked back anyway, confirming it, because he didn't want them to suspect his knowledge of their tactics.

The front one closed a few paces, two parrying gauches out. There was something eerily familiar in his walk and carriage, but Temper ignored that for the moment, thinking through his options. Having passed the aftermath of an old-style drag-out brawl, he felt inspired. These two probably expected a dumb-grunt lunge up the middle, so he'd be accommodating. He gave them that, then reversed, charging flat-out. The rear Claw hesitated, thrown for an instant. Temper overtook him, head-butted, sliced him across the middle and began to turn back in the same motion but wasn't quite quick enough. A thrown dagger slammed low into his side.

The wound staggered him, but he gave a show of shrugging it off. He must be facing a Claw commander – damned few people could throw a weapon through a thumb's breadth of bone stripping and boiled leather.

A commander, and familiar! He'd heard that beady-eyed bastard still lived. Temper rolled his shoulders, partly to try to dislodge the knife, partly to think of his next move. He needed time, so Twin's luck, he might as well try it. He pointed to the Claw.

'I'll have your head this time, Possum.'

The Claw laughed, acknowledging their mutual recognition. 'Then come. I'll await you above.'

Well, gods below. He'd guessed right.

Possum took one step to the rear, as if putting his back to a wall, then slipped into the gloom and disappeared.

Temper held himself utterly still. Had that been a mere distraction? Would he come for him through another shadow, like that blasted hound? He let a breath hiss through his teeth. No sense worrying. What would come, would come. He limped to a wall to try to pry out the damned knife. Luckily, the armour had absorbed most of its thrust. At a joint of the wall's stones he felt the hilt catch. He slid sideways and bit back a shout as it pulled free.

Damn that hurt!

He thought he heard steps on the stairs and wondered if that disappearing act had been for show, and only now did Possum run up the steps. That would be funny: Possum scurrying off like a rat. Temper chuckled, sucking in air, sweat dripping from the tip of his nose. He clashed his swords together to hurry the bastard on.

Gathering his breath he straightened, crossing the hall and climbing the stairs, all the while testing every space before him with a blade. He hesitated at the landing. So far he'd hoped to avoid going all the way up. He thought he'd have come across

189

Corinn by now, dead or alive. Had Ash and his company made it all the way to the upper floors? He had to admit that he thought it unlikely. Were they hiding in a side room? Probably not. Ash had struck him as a fanatic, not the least troubled by the odds he faced.

Unhappy about it, Temper decided to push on. Wary of Warren-anchored traps, he slashed the air at the next stair-way. Shadows over the steps rippled like heat waves. Temper backed off, swords raised. He prayed to Fener it wasn't another hound.

A shape took form, that of a slim figure, male or female, in a hooded robe like the Shadow cultists in town, only of finer material that seemed to shimmer. It stepped lazily down the stairs and in those few movements Temper recognized whom he faced. Rarely had they met, but Temper knew him beyond a doubt from the tired, almost bored stance – the carriage of absolute arrogance. It was Dancer, Kellanved's co-conspirator, bodyguard, and the top assassin of the Empire.

This could be it for him. No one could match Dancer. The man was an artist at murder. In fact, so subtle was he that many had forgotten that Kellanved had a partner. The worst kind of killer: the kind no one notices. And the slippery bastard was supposed to be dead, too.

Temper decided to break the stand-off. 'Are we going to go a round?'

Dancer gave a nonchalant wave that utterly dismissed Temper as if he weren't worth the trouble, and reminded him that he had much more important matters to deal with.

'You wouldn't agree, Temper,' he said in that soft patroniz-ing voice, 'but we're on the same side.'

Temper decided against scoffing. He'd play this close to the chest. Dancer was like a viper that could squeeze through the smallest opening. He said nothing, waited, watched.

'A lot of care and energy have gone into arranging tonight's drama. It's invitation only and I'm the gatekeeper.'

Temper wet his lips, thought of Corinn. 'A woman came up before me, ex-mage cadre. Where is she?'

'I have her.'

'You?'

'Yes. Her and Ash. *They* remained loyal and came to serve.'

'Give her to me and I'll go.'

Dancer's laugh whispered like falling sand. 'Why should I? You'll go anyway, Temper. You've no choice.'

Temper hunched, took a fresh grip of his weapons. 'Give her up, Dancer.'

'Don't be a fool.'

Damn the man for stacking the deck! He decided to try negotiation. 'I'm not the one acting the fool here, Dancer. You're leaving me no choice and that's not smart. Everyone has their pride. I can't just turn around now.'

'But you see,' Dancer whispered, 'there is a choice.'

Inwardly, Temper groaned. Dancer had simply been demonstrating the strength of his position. Corinn was nothing to him; he wanted something in return. Through clenched teeth Temper ground out, 'And that is?'

'One last fight, Temper. One last service from the last shard of the shattered Sword.'

The last? Something stabbed at Temper's chest. Truly the last? He seemed unable to breathe. Then Ferrule – even Dassem – dead?

'What is it?' he murmured, vaguely aware that he'd lowered his weapons.

'I relinquish the woman. You return to Pralt who commands my servants in town. I understand the two of you have met already; that should make things easier. There, you do as he says. Understood?'

Temper nodded. Perhaps Dancer lied, but why should he bother? Maybe for all he knew Temper was the last. 'And do *what*?' Temper asked sharply, suddenly remembering where he was and with whom he negotiated.

'Nothing distasteful. A battle, Temper. What you're best at.'

He grunted. 'Very well. Where is she?'

Dancer waved to the floor. 'Right here.'

Corinn appeared from the shadows at his feet as if a blanket of night had been pulled from her. Temper extended an armoured foot, nudged her. All the while he kept an eye on Dancer. Corinn moaned, stirred groggily.

Grumbling irritation at himself and his position, Temper slammed home his weapons and lifted Corinn over one shoulder. He faced Dancer.

'You two mean to retake the throne?'

The hooded head tilted to one side. Temper imagined a teasing smile. 'We're not here for a lark; you know that. But even from the beginning we didn't want such an unwieldy entity. A kingdom, an Empire. These are just symbols. Kellanved and I see much further. We've always been after greater things.' Dancer waved him away. 'Go. There's a nasty little battle brewing in town. I think you'll find it amusing.'

Temper edged away; he wanted to ask about that battle but decided he was afraid of the answers. Backing up the stairs, Dancer dissolved into shreds of shadow and was gone.

Corinn's flesh was cold to the touch. He adjusted her on one shoulder and started down the hall. What Dancer had said more or less agreed with own conclusions about the Emperor and his cohort. To his mind most people, like Surly, viewed control – political or personal – as the highest ambition. But men like Kellanved and Dancer were after Power, the ineffable quality itself. Heading a kingdom or an Empire was just one expression of it. They'd done that and now wanted more. What had that cultist, Pralt, said? That the control of a Warren was in the offing? Now there was a prize!

*

Temper paused as he stepped out into the moonlit bailey. He touched one hand to Corinn's cheek. The flesh felt like damp clay. What time was it now? He scanned the sky: the moon would soon sink below the walls. That is, if the laws of celestial movements still held. Could it be near the sixth bell? Of course, there was no question of not following through with his word. If the island belonged to the cultists for the night, and they belonged to Dancer, then nowhere would be safe for him. And he had to admit he was curious. Too bad he couldn't just go as a spectator. He adjusted Corinn over his shoulder. He had to get her somewhere quickly that was safe, and the nearest place was one he'd prefer not to visit. But it seemed he had no other choice.

Temper stopped at the main gate's tunnel and gave Lubben's door a kick. 'Open up!'

A voice snapped, equally impatient, 'Go away!'

'Open up, Lubben, you pox-blinded lecher!'

'Hey? What's that?' Uneven steps clumped up to the door. 'I know that voice. Who's that to speak of lechery when he's too old to remember it?'

'Old!' Temper ducked his head, peered about the tunnel, then leaned to the door. 'Open up you hunchbacked freak of nature. This is no time to be ashamed.'

'Ashamed!' The door whipped open. Lubben glared out, bleary-eyed, a wineskin in one hand. He blinked, stared at Temper's helmet, then blinked again at his burden and backed away from the threshold. Temper pushed in, hunched under the low roof, and dumped Corinn on the straw mattress. Wine fumes swirled in the closed room as potently as in the Hanged Man on a busy night.

Weaving unsteadily, Lubben scratched his stubbled chin. 'Who's this then?'

'She's a vet, ex-mage cadre.' Temper pulled off his helmet, squeezed Lubben's shoulder. 'So keep your hands to yourself.'

Lubben snorted, thumped down onto his chair. He eyed Temper suspiciously. 'What're you mixing yourself up in now?'

'Nothing.'

'Don't give me that nothing crap.' He crooked a finger at the helmet under Temper's arm. 'You've had your head down for a long time friend. Raise it now and you'll get it chopped off.'

Temper replied with a fatalistic shrug, then said, 'You're the second one to tell me that tonight.'

Lubben shook his head sadly. He waved the skin; wine sloshed within. 'Well, be gone with you then. You sorry-assed fool. Listen,' and he looked up, his eye bloodshot, screwed nearly shut. 'I thought we had an understanding. You and I. We were gonna hang around long enough to piss on all their graves.' He waved the skin up to the ceiling.

Temper laughed. 'And I still mean to.'

Lubben snorted his scorn, shook his head. 'You're being used again.' He pointed the skin at Temper. 'Used like before. They don't care if you live or die, so why should you give a damn for them?' He drained the skin and threw it, limp, into a corner.

Temper had nothing to say to that. He knew it. He pulled a dirty wool blanket over Corinn. 'Keep her here, Lubben. Till dawn.'

Lubben nodded tartly.

Temper turned to the door. 'See you later.'

'You say she's mage cadre?' Temper turned back. Lubben sat scratching his chin, eyeing Corinn.

'Aye.'

'What outfit?'

'Bridgeburners.'

Lubben arched the grizzled brow over his one good eye. 'Well I'll be damned.'

Temper hesitated, wondering what the battered old hunch-

194

back was getting at, then shrugged it off. 'Right. So watch yourself.'

Sitting back in the creaking chair, Lubben answered with a crooked smile. 'Oh, yes. I mean to.'

Temper pointed one last warning at Lubben, then ducked out of the low doorway.

CHAPTER FIVE

FEINTS AND FATES

FROM KISKA'S SIDE ARTAN SIGNALLED THROUGH THE darkness to Hattar, who obviously couldn't believe what he was being told. Artan signed again, insistent. Furious, Hattar slammed his weapons into their sheaths and stepped away from the door.

A soft laugh echoed all around the room; it whispered from every shadow. Kiska felt a familiar prickling at her neck and recognized the feeling for what it must be: the accessing of a Warren. She'd felt it a number of times with Agayla, when her Aunt sat with her legs curled under her as she dealt the Dragons deck. This time, however, the sensation was much more intense: dislocating and eerily sentient.

Beside her, Artan breathed deeply and shifted his stance, obviously readying for a confrontation he hadn't expected or wanted.

'A wise decision, Tay,' murmured a voice like fine cloth brushing across itself.

Kiska bit back a yelp as the voice seemed to whisper from every shadow – even from over her shoulder, though her back touched the cold stone wall.

Standing in the open hall, the cultist pushed back his hood. The face and head were unremarkable: bristly short black hair, narrow fine features. No scars. The eyes, though, shone like jewels of jet. He stepped into the room, glanced at Hattar and smiled. The expression, dismissive, set Kiska's teeth on edge.

Artan's – *Tay's?* – hands clenched into fists at his sides. 'Evening, Tay.'

'Evening.'

Kiska shot Artan a quick glance. Tay? Surely not Tay, as in Tayschrenn? Imperial High Mage, greatest of all talents aligned with the Empire!

The robed man chuckled lightly. His one-sided smile deepened. He seemed barely able to contain himself, as if at any moment he'd break out laughing at a joke known only to himself. 'And what brings you here this night?'

'As always,' Artan replied, 'concern for the Empire.'

The man cocked a brow. 'So you still cling to that worn conceit of neutrality. Always the dutiful one.'

'I serve the long term, as always.'

'The long term? You serve yourself, Tay.' The eyes flicked to Kiska. 'And who is this?'

The dark pits of his eyes fascinated Kiska; she wanted to answer. Suddenly she wished to tell this man everything about her. Artan's hand snatched painfully at her forearm. She winced, kept quiet.

'She's with me.'

The smile broadened. 'Always an eye for talent, hmm, Tay?'

Artan remained silent, clenching his jaw as if hardening himself to the baiting. At that, the man's smile dulled to a bored expression, the edges set into disappointment. He sighed. 'Stay here if you mean to stand aside, Tay. Don't move until it's over. Anyone upstairs is a participant ... understood?' Artan nodded. The man inclined his head. 'Till morning, then.'

'Perhaps.'

The secret smile reappeared. 'Yes. Of course. Perhaps.' He turned and walked away, through the door and around the corner, as if to ascend the stairs.

Kiska stared at where he'd disappeared. She yearned to check if he'd really gone. 'Was that really *him*?' she whispered to Artan.

Signing to Hattar, Artan pulled out a chair and sat wearily at the long dining table. Hattar closed the door.

'We should be safe here,' he said while massaging his brow. The confrontation seemed to have left him exhausted, which surprised Kiska, as earlier she'd witnessed mere irritation and contempt when faced with over fifty cultists.

He gestured for Kiska to sit. 'Really him?' he repeated. 'Not in the flesh, if that's what you mean. That was a sending . . . an image. He's obviously stretched very thin tonight. Understandably so.'

'He called you Tay.'

'He did.'

Kiska licked her lips. 'As in *Tayschrenn*?'

'No,' growled Hattar.

Artan – Tay – waved a tired hand at Hattar. 'Yes.'

By the gods! Here she was, sitting next to one of the greatest sorcerers of the age. Greater, many said, than the Emperor himself. There was so much she wanted to ask, yet how could she, a nobody from nowhere, dare to address such a personage? Kiska reflected with growing horror on her behaviour towards him. How had he put up with her? She watched him side-long: suddenly he'd become something alien, utterly separate from her own life.

A candle flamed to life at the door. Hattar touched it to a candelabra at the dining table and warm candlelight brought the room's centre to life. Wide tapestries – war booty probably – insulated the walls, interspersed with shields, banners, and a multitude of pre-Imperium ships' flags in a riot of colours and

199

designs. Tayschrenn sat at the end of the table furthest from the door, in a high-backed, dark wood chair. Kiska took a chair along the side, situated between the table and the wall. Hattar returned to watching the door.

Kiska cleared her throat, whispered, 'So what now?'

'Now?' Tayschrenn sat back, let out a long slow exhalation. His eyes appeared bruised and sunken. 'Now we wait.'

Kiska nodded, glanced to the ceiling. 'It's quiet.'

Tayschrenn's shoulders tightened at that. 'The Malazan way,' he breathed. 'The murderer's touch. A brush of cloth. A sip of wine. The gleam of a blade as fine as a snake's tooth. Your name whispered just as you fall into sleep.' He shook his head as if sad or regretful. The candlelight reflected gold from his eyes. He asked abruptly, 'What of you, then?'

Kiska started. 'What? Me?'

'Yes. Tell me about yourself.'

Kiska's cheeks burned in embarrassment. She lowered her head. How could he be so relaxed when, just overhead, the Abyss itself seemed ready to open up? 'Me? Nothing. There's nothing to tell. I was born here. My father died at sea when I was young. I hardly knew him. He was a sailor. My mother is a seamstress.' Kiska glanced up. Tayschrenn was watching her over steepled fingers. The sight dried her throat.

'And your mentoring?' he asked. 'How did that start?'

She swallowed, blushing again, but couldn't help smiling. 'By accident, you might say. I broke into Agayla's shop and she caught me.'

Tayschrenn leaned back and laughed. His shoulders lowered as tension drained from them. He grinned and Kiska suddenly couldn't be sure of his age. His guarded features bespoke a lifetime of watchfulness and calculation. The laugh and smile melted decades from the man.

'I was very young,' Kiska added, piqued.

'You must have been, to try to steal from her.'

'You said you'd met. You know her?' The idea fascinated Kiska. Agayla, familiar with such heady circles of power – like a secret other life.

Tayschrenn shook his head. 'Really only by reputation. You could say we're colleagues.'

Kiska sat back. Well, colleagues; that was something! Amazing that she knew someone Tayschrenn considered a colleague. What would Agayla think of being called an associate? Actually, knowing her, she might not be pleased. She rarely spoke of politics, but whenever the subject came up the heat of her scorn could curl the dried roots hanging from the rafters.

Out of the corner of her eyes Kiska watched this man as he sat separated by mere breadths of dressed stone from the encounter that might well decide his fate. He seemed unnaturally calm, even contemplative: one long index finger stroked the bridge of his hatchet-sharp nose. His gaze appeared directed inward. Perhaps he pondered the outcome and his own personal fortunes. But then, perhaps not – he'd named himself neutral in the matter. Agayla sometimes called the Imperial mage cadre – which Tayschrenn veritably ran – the Empire's glorified clerks. As such, he should be indifferent to whoever actually occupied the Throne. That is, short of his own personal ambitions.

Despite the tension, Kiska felt herself becoming restless. She fought an urge to fidget and looked at Hattar. Even he, the savage, flat-featured son of the steppes, had succumbed to the charged atmosphere. Kiska watched his gaze rise to the square-cut stones above them. His eyes glistened as he examined the cracks for some hint of what was happening above.

Kiska licked her dry lips, cleared her throat. 'What,' she whispered to the High Mage, 'what are you thinking?'

Tayschrenn's eyes, gold in the candlelight, shifted to her.

From deep within them awareness swam to the surface. 'I am wondering,' he began, his voice low, puzzled, 'just who is trapping whom. Surly has set a trap above for Kellanved. But he picked the time and place long ago – who knows how long – and has been preparing all the while. So perhaps this trap is for her. One she likely recognizes, but one she cannot avoid. She *had* to come. They *both* had to come.' Then he frowned. The lines bracketing his mouth deepened into furrows. 'And what could he and Dancer hope to gain? Their followers have been killed or scattered. No organized support remains but for Dancer's Shadow cult, and they gone to ground and so few. Their authority would not be accepted by the Claws – or the governing Fists – should they return.'

'And Oleg. What of his message?'

The magus actually grimaced, touched one temple as if to still a throbbing vein. 'Yes. Oleg. Our hermit mystic. A self-mortifier and flagellant. Driven insane, perhaps, by his own blunted ambition? Or a prophet foolishly ignored?' He sighed. 'If I follow the lines of his reasoning accurately, they lead to suicide for Kellanved and Dancer. That I simply cannot accept. I know those two and neither would allow that.'

Suicide? No, she couldn't imagine that either. Not those two. Kellanved had clawed his way to power over too many obstacles. He would destroy anyone or anything in his path. It was his signature.

Tayschrenn stirred, his head rising like a hound at a scent. 'Listen,' he whispered, glancing up.

Kiska bit her lip, scanned the ceiling. The waiting, the dread and uncertainty, had stiffened her shoulders and neck. Immobile for so long, her bad leg felt as if it had fused at the knee. Shifting, she flexed it and eased the tension from her back. What was happening now? Peripherally, she noticed Hattar gliding cat-like and protective ever closer to them, his weapons bared.

'How will we—'

Tayschrenn raised a finger to his lips. '*Listen.*'

Kiska strained to penetrate the quiet. The subtle throb of the surf shuddered through the rock. Dust falling and the stones losing heat to the night brought ticks and trickled motes from the walls.

Then she heard it. A distinct tap and faint shush – tap-shush, tap-shush – crossing the ceiling, side to side.

Kellanved.

She'd never seen him of course, but had heard many descriptions – some contrary, most vague. Many mentioned his walking stick and his slow gait, but all told of his extreme age and the black skin and curled silver hair of a Dal Honese elder from the savannah of south-western Quon Tali. And, of course, there was his taste for grey and black clothing.

As if to confirm Kiska's suspicions, Tayschrenn and Hattar caught each other's gaze.

An overpowering sensation of pressure bore down upon her like an invisible hand. She sensed something enormous nearby, silent in the dark, like a Talian man-of-war passing within arm's reach. A gravid deadly presence too huge to grant her notice. She glanced to Tayschrenn and saw him grimace, fingertips pressed against his temples. A droplet of blood fell from his nose.

It's *him*, she thought, amazed. *Even I can feel it.*

The pacing – for that is what it seemed to Kiska – abruptly stopped. A long silence followed. She imagined conversation and wondered how desperately Tayschrenn might wish to know its content. Then again, a man like him might be bored by what could be little more than an exchange of warnings and mutual threats.

The limestone blocks of the ceiling jerked then, like child's toys, and dust showered down. The soundless impact drove Kiska down into her chair and popped her eardrums. The candles snuffed out. Metal rang from the stones above. Weapons, Kiska imagined. A thumping and clatter as of bodies falling. A shout – a wordless roar of rage – that faded into silence. In the charged calm that followed, she barely breathed.

Light flared up. Hattar, calm and phlegmatic, relit the candles. Kiska could not believe the man's aplomb.

Then a woman's shrill scream tore through the solid stone, and Kiska leapt from her chair. She glanced to Tayschrenn but his clenched features revealed nothing. Was that the end of Surly? Had Kellanved and Dancer won? Yet the scream held no note of despair or death. Instead it spit frustration and venom.

Tayschrenn cleared his throat. He dabbed a cloth to his nose and pushed back from the table. He stood, adjusted his cloak at his shoulders and signed something to Hattar. The Seti plainsman glanced at her. The narrow slash of mouth under his flattened nose twisted into a sneer. Tayschrenn, crossing to the door, failed to notice his guard's reaction.

Hattar stepped up to block the doorway and Tayschrenn stopped short, surprised. He signed again. At the table Kiska wondered what was going on; whether it could mean any threat to her. She suddenly felt keenly aware of the weight of Lubben's curved knife at her side. But these two intended no harm to her, surely?

Hattar, hands clamped at the grips of his sheathed knives, glared at Kiska, spat, 'No.'

Kiska stood, moving to centre the table between them and her. She massaged her hip where she'd struck her side. What was this – housecleaning? Was she to be silenced? But why should Hattar refuse that? She imagined he'd relish the chance. Yet why wait till now?

Tayschrenn signed furiously. Hattar just smiled, showing sallow teeth. He shook his head. Tayschrenn half-turned to her. He appeared bemused and annoyed.

'Well,' he observed, eyeing her. 'Something of a quandary. I must go upstairs. Hattar refuses to stay here to guard you and I think it still too dangerous to leave you alone.' He coughed into one fist, cocked a thin brow. It was as if he were guessing her thoughts. 'How would you suggest we resolve this?'

Kiska wet her lips. 'Take me with you.'

Tayschrenn turned to Hattar as if that settled the matter. Hattar scowled ferociously. He snapped a sign: negative, Kiska assumed. Tayschrenn answered with a shrug that said it was indeed settled. He waved Kiska to him.

'You will stay with me. Stand to one side and back two paces. Say nothing and take your cue from Hattar or myself in all things. Do you concur?' Hardly able to breathe, Kiska nodded. 'Good.' He looked to Hattar. Grudgingly, the plainsman edged aside from the door. Tayschrenn passed through. Kiska approached. The Seti warrior said nothing, though his hot gaze bore into her skull.

Side by side, she and Hattar climbed the stairs behind Tayschrenn. She felt as though she'd been inducted into the magus's bodyguard. And come what may, she suddenly realized, she'd do her best to honour that trust. She prayed there'd be no need.

Hattar watched her sidelong. His lip curled away from his sharp teeth in a sneer of contempt. She glared back. Looking away, he snorted a laugh that said, *just you wait*.

Light flickered up ahead. These halls were warmer, cosy, and inhabited. They stepped up into a richly appointed hall faced at intervals by doors of polished wood. Sub-Fist Pell and his inner circle had occupied these rooms for the last seven years, but not on this night. She wondered idly just where he was, then dismissed the thought. He'd probably locked himself downstairs in the wine cellar or was passed out in his bunk.

Tayschrenn walked steadily, unhurried, down the hall. They passed silver mirrors and portraits of men and women she didn't recognize, mounted boar heads, trophy swords and captured heraldry the likes of which Kiska had never seen before, except for the black vertical bar and pale blue wave of Korelri far to the south. Warm firelight spilled from an open door at the hall's far end, sending shadows rippling and dancing madly. A draft of cool air brushed Kiska's cheeks and she heard, distantly, the surf murmuring far below.

At the entrance Tayschrenn paused, blocking Kiska's view. The draft, stronger here, billowed his cloak. He waved a sign to Hattar then entered. Hattar grunted, plucked at Kiska's sleeve and motioned for her to stay close to him. Kiska swallowed and steadied her breathing. Hattar's lip curled again as if he expected her to faint on the spot.

Heat struck her at the doorway like the blast from a stoked stove. That, and the stink of smoke mixed with the sour iron tang of spilled blood. Hattar moved to one side of the doorway. Kiska stepped to the other and pressed her back against the warm stones.

It was a long rectangular room. She wondered if perhaps it was some kind of a reception chamber. Now it was devoid of furniture and ornament. A roaring fire filled the huge hearth towards the left inner wall. Over the floor, here and there, corpses lay like discarded clothes. By a broken set of doors leading to a balcony they were gathered more thickly. Claws, all of them. Kiska counted twelve.

At the centre of the room a woman sat in the chamber's only furnishing: a plain wood chair. The woman's brown hair was cut short, military-style. The bluish tinge of her skin marked her as Napan. She wore a green silk shirt, torn and blood-spattered, a wide sash of emerald green, and loose pantaloons gathered snug at the ankles. Her feet were dark and calloused as if always bare. A Claw, kneeling at her side, was wrapping her hand in dressings. Kiska recognized him as the one from the duel with the armoured colossus: Possum.

Surly. Kiska was struck by how small she was, and how calm and self-possessed. One could hardly guess she'd just faced down the two most dreaded figures of recent Quon Talian history. But then, she was third on that list.

Tayschrenn crossed the long room towards her. An ironic smile tilted one edge of her mouth as she watched. Halfway, the magus stilled, peered down at the bare stone floor. Kiska looked also but saw nothing, just a fine swirl of spilled red powder. From Kiska's side, a hiss escaped Hattar. The plainsman's jaws worked and his hands were white fists gripping the bone handles of his long-knives. Slowly, carefully, Tayschrenn gathered up his cloak and shook the dust from its edges. He continued on, stepping over the corpses as if they were no more than puddles in a muddy street. Just short of Surly, he bent to the corpse nearest the chair and lifted its head. Kiska recognized the body.

'Ash,' said Surly. 'Ex-Lieutenant of the Bridgeburners. And one very determined man.' She raised her bandaged hand. 'Acid.'

Tayschrenn straightened from the body and turned to the smashed balcony doors. Reaching them, he glanced out. 'Gone, then?'

Surly nodded, but sharply, as if things hadn't gone exactly as she wished. On the floor, just before the balcony, lay a stick amid the spattered blood. A walking stick of dark wood, ebony perhaps, with a silver handle. Kiska stared. Gods! Was that it then? Was he dead?

A second surviving Claw stepped out from the shadowed balcony. Unusually tall, he favoured one leg and cradled his right arm at his breast, wet with dripping blood. His hood was down, revealing long startling white hair, a dark face, hooked nose with a goatee and black glittering eyes. Kiska had never seen him before.

'Organize a search for the corpses,' Surly told Possum. He

bowed and backed away to the door. Kiska watched him side-long as he passed and saw that he now bore a slash across his shirt-front, and that blood smeared his cloak. But his hood-shadowed face did not turn to regard her. It was as if the man had his mission and all else was mere dross.

Tayschrenn stepped out onto the balcony. The railing of low stone arch-work had been broken or blasted away, leaving a large gap into open air. He peered out and down, a gloved hand at the shattered edge. In the wind his cloak billowed and fluttered, and from below came the muted beat of the surf.

He returned to Surly, his boots scraping over the littered floor. 'You can't be sure—'

'Certain enough,' she snapped. 'Absolutely. It is over and done. Finished. I'm surprised you bothered to come.'

Glancing back at the balcony, Tayschrenn murmured, 'I was truthfully drawn here for another reason – if you must know.'

Rage flared like dark fires in Surly's eyes and her good hand shot out to the High Mage as if she would crush him in her fist. Kiska almost shouted a warning, but as quickly as the fires rose so were they banked. She gave a small, low laugh. 'Play the pompous lord to your underlings, Tay, not me. That you are here belies your words.'

The magus turned to her. Kiska watched him blinking, as if he were utterly unaware of the woman's reaction. Yet how could that be? The two of them had worked, fought, and schemed together for generations. They must know to a hair's breadth how far they could goad each other. Clearly, Tayschrenn wanted to remind Surly of something.

His shoulders rose and fell in a slow, indifferent shrug. 'If you insist. Still, it would seem—'

'I don't care how it seems to you.' She studied her bandaged hand. 'It is over. I am Imperial Regent no longer. I will take the Throne, and my new name to rule it by. What say you to that?'

He said nothing. Kiska imagined he had already carefully thought through all possible outcomes.

'Hail the Empress,' prompted the Claw from the balcony, stroking his neck with a hand in a green leather glove. Tayschrenn eyed the man, who offered a predatory smile in return. There was open dislike here between Tayschrenn and these pet servants of the throne. Kiska wondered how such a meeting would have developed years ago, with Kellanved and Dancer also present. Likely a nest of vipers.

Tayschrenn gave a short bow. Kiska couldn't tell if it was genuine or mocking. 'Indeed. Hail,' he echoed.

Surly answered with a curt nod, all business. 'Good. Now, we have much to discuss...' She inclined her head towards Hattar and Kiska, whose heart lurched at the attention.

Tayschrenn waved to the Claw. 'And what of him?'

A thin smile tightened Surly's lips. 'The Claw is now part of the command structure, Tay. Each one speaks with a measure of my personal authority; each will be, in a measure, my representative. Topper will stay.'

Tayschrenn bowed as briefly as before and backed away. To Hattar he said, 'Your task is done for the night. Take her and return to the dining hall. Get some sleep. I'll join you later.'

Hattar's jaw tightened in distaste, but he nodded. Waving a brusque farewell to Kiska, Tayschrenn turned away. Hattar motioned to the hall, pushed her ahead of him. Startled by the abruptness of it, she peered back over her shoulder. Was that it? Not even a goodbye? Hattar urged her on with a jab at her back.

In the hall, Kiska glared and hissed, 'Couldn't I get a word in?'

The plainsman's face remained set. 'Not now. Tomorrow.'

Kiska relaxed, ceased resisting. 'Okay.' She walked on. 'I just don't want to be shaken off, you know. I went to a lot of trouble to talk to him.' She laughed at the thought of that.

'Hood's own trouble.' But Hattar had set his face ahead, ignoring her. Kiska shut up. Here she was complaining to the one fellow who couldn't possibly give a damn.

In the dining hall, Kiska watched while Hattar blocked the door with a chair, lit the candles, and sat. He thumped both booted feet onto the table, then untied his belt and lay it before him so that the sheathed knives rested within reach.

Kiska eased herself down into a chair across the table. 'What was that about the red dust upstairs? What was it? Poison?'

Hattar's gaze had been directed up at the ceiling. Now it swung down to her. The eyes were slitted, unreadable. 'You ever heard of Otataral ore?'

'Something about magic?'

'Magic deadening.' His gaze returned to the ceiling. 'Upstairs, in that room, he's helpless.'

She blurted, 'Then Surly must have seeded the room, or thrown it, and Kellanved—'

Hattar's nod was savage. 'A great leveller that. Just knives and sheer numbers after.'

Kiska was silent, trying to imagine what it must have been like: the crippled Kellanved a useless burden in any mundane battle. Dancer struggling to both fight and protect him. The two retreating to the balcony, desperate to escape. How many dead had she seen? Twelve? She shook her head, awed. 'Now what?'

'Now nothing. We wait.'

Biting her lip she watched Hattar as he stared off into the darkness. After a moment, she asked, 'You've disliked me from the start. What have you got against me?'

A slight clenching of his mouth seemed to betray that he was debating whether to reply. Then he growled, 'I lost three good friends tonight. You've too high an opinion of yourself if you think you've got anything to do with my mood, lass.'

210

She looked down, her cheeks flushing. Who did he think he was – but then, who did *she* think *she* was? From his view she was just a meddlesome civilian – and a girl at that – nothing more than a security risk, and an impediment to his sworn task.

She clasped her hands together, studied the dusty tabletop. 'I'm sorry. You're doing your duty. I see that. But I'm not going to disappear just for your convenience. Dammit, I've gone through a lot tonight. As much as you, maybe. It has to be for something!' Looking up, she wiped at her eyes, damned the tears of frustration. She glared at Hattar, daring him to dismiss her, then gaped in utter disbelief: the plainsman's head hung back, mouth open, and his chest rose and fell steadily. Asleep! Well, damn him to the Abyss! How could he?

Watching him doze, she felt her own eyes droop. Her knee and shoulder and side all ached fiendishly, calling for rest. Sighing, she pushed back from the table and set to building a small fire in the hearth from kindling and split logs piled to one side. Soon it caught and she gathered her cloak about her and sat with her back to wall. Uncertainty for her safety still nagged at her, but her exhaustion swept over worry, and her chin sank eventually to her chest.

At the bottom of Rampart Way the two cultists who had escorted Temper to the stairs stepped out from the darkness to meet him. He ignored them. The slim one let fall the slightest of chuckles as Temper passed, as if he'd personally had a hand in the slaughter above and knew all the secrets those lips were sealed to protect. The conceit enraged Temper. He pulled short and turned on them; neither had earned the right.

They stopped, but much closer than before – arm's reach in fact. The slim one jerked his hooded head back up to the Hold. 'A waste of time, yes? As I said, now you serve my master.'

'You should learn a little respect.'

211

The man glanced to his companion, laughed outright. 'You've been sent by our master to run an errand, soldier. Do it and shut up.'

'If Dancer's your master, then yes, I made a deal. But it doesn't include putting up with mouthy pups like you.'

Temper's fist lashed out and caught the cultist on the side of his head.

The scorchmarked hood flew back, revealing a young man with cropped blond hair and beard. He stared, amazed past words, blood welling from the torn flesh of his cheek. He drew a knife from within his robes. Without comment, his stocky partner stepped aside. The youth wove the weapon before him in a backhanded grip. 'Pralt warned us you're a dangerous man, soldier. I say you're just a tired old relic. I'm going to send you to my master.'

'You talk to much to worry me, boy.'

Snarling, the cultist lunged. Temper was almost caught off guard. He hadn't believed he'd actually attack. The blade caught the edge of a cracked iron scale, nearly reaching the gap in the hauberk's underarm. Temper clamped one gauntleted hand at the fellow's neck and squeezed. The knife racked his side. He grabbed the hand and twisted the blade free, then pushed it into the youth's stomach. The knife slid in just below the ribs. The cultist shuddered, gagged a half-throttled scream.

Temper shook him by his neck, then let him drop in a heap. The youth lay curled around the knife like an impaled insect. He moaned. Temper faced the other. 'Let's go,' and he started down toward Cutter's Strait. After a few moments footfalls announced the stocky one following.

Long before Temper reached the houses of the old quarter surrounding the Deadhouse and the Hanged Man Inn, he saw signs of the battle ahead. The frigid night fog had thickened – unnaturally so – but through it bursts of phosphorescence

212

flickered. Hidden beyond, the hounds howled, a number of them, drowning out the brittle crackle of raw energy and small eruptions.

It reminded Temper of the worst kind of engagement he'd known: mage duels where more died from the side-blasts of unleashed Warrens than from sharp iron. Ahead, a cultist emerged from the fog and stood motionless, apparently waiting for him. The figure motioned him forward into the churning wall. Clenching his jaw, Temper continued on and the cultist fell into step at his side. His old escort stopped outside the barrier, implying a hierarchy within the organization. Perhaps those inside were initiated into higher secrets. Or, Temper reflected, maybe they were those the cult wouldn't mind losing if this gambit went to the Abyss.

The opaque fog obscured everything. Buildings vanished, then the cultist at his side. He wondered if perhaps he'd just been escorted into a portion of the Warren itself. Musing on that, he was unprepared when something like a bat launched itself out of the mist. He yelped, ducking, and the ghostly shape of his escort appeared at his side, gesturing. The thing folded up upon itself and flapped off. Temper was shaken: it appeared to be nothing more than a patch of fluttering shadow. He leaned close to the cultist who smiled back from within his hood. 'Where are we?' he growled.

His escort shrugged. 'Nowhere, strictly speaking.' He waved Temper on: 'Come, we haven't much time.'

As they walked on Temper was startled to find himself climbing the slow rise of a cobbled road. Here the fog was thinner, and after a few more paces he and his escort emerged from the worst of it. Ahead, at the top of the shallow grade, sat the Deadhouse and the crumbling wall surrounding it. All around waited cultists. As for the rest of the town, it was nowhere in sight, erased by the haze. It was as if he, the assassins, and the House had been transported to another isle.

High clouds masked the sky, making the light eerie and diffuse like early dawn, spilling from no discernible direction. At the front gate a knot of cultists had gathered and his escort led him to them.

Temper eyed the Deadhouse. The dark shuttered windows betrayed no hint of what might be going on within. Instead it was the grounds that captured his attention: the dead black branches of the trees twitched like jerking fingers, and the bare earth bulged and heaved as if something stirred beneath. Temper smelled a dustiness in the air, as of a long-sealed crypt, and over it the ozone stink of power like the constant low discharge of a channelled Warren.

A cultist in pale robes broke away from the group and met Temper. He waved off the escort.

'Pralt?' Temper asked.

He nodded, inviting Temper to accompany him to the wall of heaped stones.

'So this is it then? Shadow?'

'No, not properly. More of a bridge. A midway stage created by tonight's special conditions.'

'The hounds?'

'We've left them behind. No need to worry about them. We've other things to occupy us.'

Temper detected the irony of a massive understatement. He stopped short, rested his fists on his weapons. 'Okay. I've played along so far. But now that I'm here, what's the arrangement?'

Pralt faced the grounds, then turned to Temper. Even standing this close, Temper saw only darkness filling his hood and that aggravated him. The assassin folded his arms, slipping his gloved hands into the robe's wide sleeves as if he were some kind of priest. 'An assault on the House. Simple as that.'

Temper scowled. 'Defences?'

'Ah, yes. You've hit upon the main worry. No one knows

just what the House is. Some claim it's simply a gateway. Others say it's an entity itself, one that straddles the realms. Whichever the case, we are by no means the first to try to master it. Through the ages countless have attempted and all have failed. And all who failed are now enslaved by the House to its defence.' Pralt was silent for a time, letting that fact sink in. 'Ingenious, yes? As time passes its defences actually gain strength. Impressive.'

Temper stared, speechless, then laughed his utter disbelief. 'You can forget it, Pralt. There's no way this shabby outfit can win this one. You're in over your heads.'

The hood nodded as if the man agreed. 'Oh, yes. We haven't the firepower to defeat the House. But that has never been our goal.'

Now Temper frowned. He hadn't liked the way this was headed before; now he was sure he would hate it. 'I ain't no one's stalking horse.'

The hood faced him directly. After a moment Pralt said gently, 'That's all you've ever been, Temper. Even the Sword was nothing more: a banner to draw the notice of the strongest enemy. Bait to tempt them out.'

Temper's fists clenched reflexively, but he took a deep breath, allowing the comment to pass. Dassem used to speak of that. Called himself the army's lightning rod. And they'd all known it too: he, Ferrule, Point, and the rest. But they hadn't minded at the time because they were young and believed Dassem couldn't be beaten by anyone. So what did it matter? Let all comers try; the Sword would always prevail. Little thought or care did they give to those profiting from their blood and lives.

'Strong words,' Temper finally growled, staring off at the House, 'from someone who expects my cooperation.'

'Nothing we say now can change the past. And you gave your word.'

Temper snorted, pulled off a gauntlet frayed by hound's

teeth. He rubbed his index finger over the puckered scar at his chin, nodded. 'Yeah. I suppose I did at that. All right. Let's go.'

Pralt invited him to walk to the gate. Temper slapped the gauntlet to his thigh, thinking: *so, a diversionary sortie*. A quick in and out. That meant the real assault would come from another direction, and run a much lower profile. He figured he knew who that would be.

Before the gate they joined the other cultists. Temper studied them. This was it? Just the six of them? Pralt and his companion spoke once more, hooded heads nearly touching. Temper, uneasy, rested his hands on the iron pommels of his swords. Was he just an extra hand or was something else in the offing? He didn't have such an inflated opinion of himself to believe that they needed his participation. Or that they'd even planned for it. No, this had the feeling of something thrown together. A last-minute change. Now he was certain he hated it. But he'd given his word; he at least had his honour. He'd step in, but would back out once it got too hot for his liking. And he had the feeling it wouldn't take long to attract that kind of heat.

Pralt and his friends broke off their talk. Hand signals flew between them. Temper couldn't interpret the sign language – it was not Malazan standard. He didn't like that at all. It made the back of his neck itch.

Pralt turned to him. 'Get ready. You'll take centre point between Jasmine and me.'

Temper nodded to Jasmine who answered with the slightest inclination of – her? – hood. He drew his longswords, eased his shoulders to loosen them. Pralt approached the plain wrought-iron gate.

A shout from behind made Temper start. '*Do not enter those grounds!*'

He turned. There stood Faro Balkat and Trenech. They

looked the same as they had ever looked: Faro frail, rheumy-eyed, and Trenech dull and bhederin-like. Only now Trenech carried a wicked pike-axe, its butt jammed into the ground, and Faro had clearly shaken off his drugged stupor. A number of cultists came running up, surrounded the two. Faro ignored them as he had the soldiers earlier at the Hanged Man.

Pralt faced them, gave a stiff bow. 'Our mission does not cross yours,' he called. 'Why are you here?'

Faro's mouth drew down in disgust. Temper had never seen the man looking so lively. 'Do not play games with me, shadow-slave. By crossing the barriers you weaken them, and that is not to our liking.'

Pralt shrugged. ''Tis regretful, but I know the confines of your roles, and you cannot stop anyone from entering the grounds.'

Faro's gnarled hands clenched at his sides. 'That much is true.' He stepped closer. 'I ask you not to do this. You play with forces of which you have no conception.'

Shaking his hooded head, Pralt turned away. Temper stared at the man hard. What did this promise for him?

'They are waiting,' Jasmine whispered, urgent. 'We must act now.'

Pralt faced the gate.

'Soldier!' Faro called. Temper turned. 'Do not enter. You'll not return.'

Temper raised a sword in a farewell salute. 'Sorry, Faro. Gave my word.' He spoke with as much bravura as he could muster, though his stomach was clenched in the certainty that he was already more committed than he wished.

The gate rasped under Pralt's hand, rusted with disuse. Faro fell silent. Trenech hefted his long pike-axe.

A path of slate flags led to the front steps past bare mounds that reminded Temper of hastily dug battle graves. It was quiet so far, the House dark and lifeless. Pralt and Jasmine advanced to either side and Temper followed. They appeared unnaturally relaxed, without any weapons in evidence. About halfway up the walk they stopped. Pralt turned to him.

Temper stared back, uncertain, licked his dry lips.

'This is as far as we go,' Pralt said. He sounded strangely solemn. 'This isn't what I had in mind, and I'm sorry. Dancer's orders. Goodbye, soldier.'

Pralt and Jasmine disappeared. Temper spun: the three others were also gone. It was as if he'd walked in alone. The ground to either side of the walk heaved. The moist bare earth crumbled and steamed while above the tree branches flailed, creaking. Blue-green flames like mast-fire danced over them and along the low stone walls. Trenech now blocked the gate, pike-axe lowered. Faro stood behind. Beyond, gathered together once more, stood the cultists – Pralt and Jasmine included – watching, arms folded.

Temper pointed a sword at them to shout that he'd have their hearts out, when a loud grinding rumbled from the House. He turned, flexing, weapons ready. The door scraped open, dust falling from its jambs. Darkness yawned within only to be filled by the advance of a giant figure.

Betrayed. The last assault on Y'Ghatan all over again. *He hadn't learned a damned thing.* Temper threw back his head and howled an incandescent rage so consuming that every fibre of his body seemed to take flame.

Agayla and Obo occupied a point of rock suspended within a channel of raw streaming power. The surf had risen over the strand, punishing the rocks above. The wind lashed sleet at them, yet it parted before their small circle of calm like dust brushed aside. Overhead, a roof of clouds skimmed the hill-tops, eclipsing the sky, and extended inland to enshroud the island. To the distant south thunderheads towered ever higher, roiling and billowing, lancing the seas in a constant discharge of lightning that lit the lunging dance of the distant Riders.

A sense of presence behind him brought Obo's head around. He fixed his gaze on the bare hillside where two figures descended. One motioned for the other to remain among the rocks and continued down alone, his dark robes flapping in the wind. The second moved to shelter in the lee of a tall plinth of rock and squatted, elbows at his knees, his shirt shining wetly. 'Someone's comin'.' Agayla did not respond. Obo turned to her: she sat hunched forward, hands clutched at her head as if to hold it from bursting. 'Your boy, Agayla. Looks like I lose my bet.'

She looked up but with eyes empty of understanding. Slowly, awareness awoke within. She blinked, squared her shoulders and pushed herself upright. 'Good. Very good.'

As the figure drew near, his bald scalp gleaming, Obo mouthed a curse. 'So. It's him. I don't trust this one. The stink of the Worm clings to him.'

'He is free from all bindings, Obo. I wouldn't have approached him otherwise.' She bowed to the newcomer. 'Greetings, Tayschrenn.'

Tayschrenn answered the courtesy. 'Obo,' he offered. Obo turned his back. Tayschrenn gestured to the south. 'This is incalculably worse than I imagined.'

Agayla nodded. 'We *are* masking most from the island. Appalling, isn't it?'

'Reminds me of the Emperor at his most brutal.'

Obo barked, 'He was a fool with a sharp stick compared to this!' He glared at the two of them. When Tayschrenn returned his look, he jerked away to stare south once again. What he saw there made him flinch.

Tayschrenn took in Agayla's exhaustion and Obo's rigid stance; he invited her to sit. 'You're losing.'

Agayla merely gave a tired nod, too worn even to pretend.

219

'Yes. Before the dawn we shall fail. That is . . . unless you commit yourself.'

'Yet some force was forestalling this. Where are they?'

'He has been overcome.'

'*He?*' One against all this? There is no one. Osserc, perhaps—'

Obo snorted again.

Agayla merely massaged her fingers across her brow. 'Really, Tay. You, above all, should know there are ancient powers, those that see past your and Kellanved's empire-building as just another pass of season. The paths to Ascendancy are far more varied than you imagine.' Sighing, Agayla straightened. 'But now is not the time for that. Surly's campaign against magery had left him sorely diminished. A fraction of talent remained to draw upon and so he was overwhelmed.'

'She had no way of foreseeing the deeper consequences of her actions.'

'You did.'

Obo spun around. '*Is that so?*'

His face a mask, Tayschrenn clasped his hands at his knees. 'I did have some presentiment of it, yes. Unease at the alteration of such an age-old balance of power.' He met Obo's glare. 'But I swear upon the Nameless Ones I had no suspicion of anything this profound . . . this . . . perilous.'

Looking at Agayla, Obo spat. 'And this is the one you would approach.'

The strength of the anger that clutched Tayschrenn's chest in response to Obo's scorn surprised him; no one treated him in this manner. He had tolerated Kellanved's mockery and now ignored Surly's mistaken rivalry, but no one ever spurned him with contempt. From a pocket in the lining of his cloak he drew out a pair of wet kidskin gloves and struggled to slip them over his hands. Clenching and unclenching his fingers, he reflected that Obo was, after all,

Obo. The man would slam a door in the face of Hood himself.

Agayla merely watched, her gaze weighing. Tayschrenn shook the uncomfortable sensation of being judged – and found wanting.

'Yet you allowed it,' Agayla observed, speculatively.

Tayschrenn accepted the opening to explain. 'To have opposed Surly's orders would have aroused unnecessary suspicion.'

'Suspicion of . . . ?'

'Collusion, communication, sympathizing with *him*.'

'Ah. I see.' She pushed the strands of wet hair from her face, wiped a hand over her brow. Tayschrenn would have offered a cloth had he anything not already sodden. She sighed, peered up at him. 'Poor Tayschrenn. One day you will wake up and abandon this petty politicking and manoeuvring. It will burn you so many times, and you will scald so many others before you discover wisdom.' The woman's dark eyes probed his awareness. She whispered, 'You have not yet even journeyed far enough to wonder on the cost, have you?'

Tayshcrenn stared – never, not since his training in the temple, had anyone brushed aside his defences with such ease. He shook himself. 'Do you wish my aid or not?'

'That is just it, you see. We may not want *your* aid.'

Staggered, Tayschrenn wiped a hand across his mouth. Here stood two powers – yes, he could admit to that, *powers* – facing annihilation under the heels of an enemy of incalculable might, and *they would reject his aid*?

'But, the island . . . thousands of souls.'

'Oh, come. More died at the fall of Unta alone. Do not pretend their fate concerns you. No, if we fall then you will *have* to commit yourself, won't you?'

'Would I? You say I care nothing for these lives, yet I would commit myself to their defence? I am sorry to disappoint you Agayla. I would stand aside.'

Obo, silent for so long, snorted his derision at that.

'Oh?' Agayla breathed, turning her face to the south. '*Would* you?'

Her gaze drew Tayschrenn's own. What he saw drove all conscious thought from his mind, as if a veil had been ripped aside, and now he saw for the first time the appalling truth of what, to normal senses, resembled a storm-front of unprecedented scale. The weather was the mere side effect of a much more profound battle between contending Realms. Summoning his Thyr Warren, he probed the work of the Stormriders' mysterious sorcerers, the Wandwielders. It appeared like a curtain of energy, a replica of the shimmering light that sometimes played above the northern night sky. Streaming down from the heights of the atmosphere, it cut a dividing line that, unlike most human theurgical manipulations, did not end at the water but plunged downward through it. With his inner-eye, Tayschrenn followed its dizzying descent and was horrified to see it continue unbroken, down through the depths of the cut into unplumbed crevasses, where he glimpsed a glowing heart of otherworldly ice. A heart that, as he watched, throbbed and swelled. He broke away, dazed by a vertiginous sense of power such as he had known only once before – as a supplicant before his old master, D'rek, the Worm of Autumn that gnaws at the World.

'You may choose to stand aside, Tayschrenn,' Agayla observed. 'Malaz would fall, no longer a barrier forestalling the Riders' expanse. That *is* the ancient worry, is it not? That free of the confines of the strait, they would dominate the seas? A menace to all?'

Tayschrenn nodded warily, uncertain of her point. 'Yes. Of course.'

Shuddering, she crossed her arms then met Tayschrenn's gaze squarely. 'But what if it was not the island itself they sought? Think on it. What sits in Malaz, within a stone's throw of the shore? What if this was not some mindless storm seeking escape, but a calculated reach for power, for influence?' She swept an arm out to the horizon-spanning cataclysm of sky and sea. 'Tell me, Tayschrenn – could the House withstand all *this*?'

He stared, stunned. The *House*? What could it be to these alien beings? Yet . . . what were they to anyone? An enigma. A focal point of power and potentialities. That much was certain: *it was possible.* Perhaps the island was not simply *in their way.* Perhaps they wanted it; wanted the prize it held. Tayschrenn damned the sorceress – she and all others aligned with the Enchantress – their eyes saw everywhere. Yet he had to help. He could not risk the alternative she had set before him as, he was certain, she'd known all along.

'Very well, Agayla.' He bowed his head. 'You win. You shall have all my strength. Every ounce I possess. The Riders must be contained.'

'Don't expect me to get all slobbery,' Obo muttered.

At first Kiska thought it a dream. A tingling prickled her skin. She felt as if someone were watching her. Slowly, awareness of just where she slept trickled into her thoughts and she snapped awake.

A dark woman bent over her, hands out as if grasping for her. Kiska jumped to her feet and the woman flinched away, startled. Kiska's hands flew reflexively to her waist, sleeves, and collar but came away empty. She snarled, arms raised.

The woman straightened, held out open hands. 'Hold on, child. You gave me quite a start there.'

Kiska glanced around. Hattar was gone, as was his weapon belt. Embers glowed in the hearth and the candles had burned low. Her own blade lay sheathed on the table. Someone stood in the doorway: it was the hunchback, the very man who had lent her the weapon.

223

'*I* startled *you*?' Kiska laughed. She straightened, wincing at the pain that lanced her side and knee.

The woman was the Napan mercenary mage. She nodded. 'Yes. You were under a light ward – a healing slumber. I was only testing its strength but you awoke and broke it easily. Your resistance is unusually strong.'

Kiska snorted, dismissing the woman's words. What was she really up to? Where was Hattar? Or Tayschrenn, for that matter? 'Where is everyone? What time is it?'

The woman knelt to warm her hands at the hearth and, Kiska supposed, to reassure her. 'We were hoping you could tell us. No one's here. The hold is empty. And the time?' She shrugged. 'After the tenth bell of the night, I believe.'

Kiska picked up the weapon and tucked it at her side. 'If you want answers just go upstairs. I'm sure the Claws would be happy to help you.'

The jangle of steel announced the hunchback's shambling advance. In the hearth's faint glow Kiska saw that he wore a rusted and battered steel pot helmet. Armour hung from his bent frame in layers of mail folds with steel scales at the shoulders, chest, stomach and arms. He also carried a long-hafted throwing-axe. Kiska stared, appalled, certain that any normal man would've collapsed under that load.

'She means you no harm, lass,' he growled. 'Everyone's gone. What do you know of it?'

She looked from one to the other. 'What does it matter? It's finished. Surly won.'

The woman flinched. 'You were there? You saw it?'

Then Kiska remembered with whom she spoke and her breath caught. 'Oh, and Ash. I saw him. He's dead. I'm sorry.'

The woman brushed back her long hair, sighed. 'I'm not. The man's better off dead. He should have died a long time ago. These times were not to his liking. Still, I owed him a great debt.'

Kiska looked away. 'Well, I'm glad you're okay.'

'So you saw *him* as well?'

Kiska rubbed her arms to warm them against the unusual cold. She felt chilled and hungry but refreshed, as if she'd slept a full night. Even her knee felt strong, throbbing and stiff, but firm. 'No. I didn't see that. But I was there just afterwards. Surly said Kell— that they fell from the balcony, down the cliff. No one could survive that. It's a hundred fathoms.'

Lubben and the woman eyed each other, clearly sceptical.

Stung, Kiska stepped away. 'It was good enough for Surly. She said it was finished. Even—' she stopped herself, swallowed. 'Well, everyone agreed.' But as she said it, she wondered. Where were Hattar and Tayschrenn? Or Surly? Had Tayschrenn laid that spell upon her – if a spell it had been, as the woman claimed? Had they lied about the end of things? If so, it couldn't have been because of her presence. No, they must have had other reasons, and no doubt different reasons at that. They may have lied to each other out of habit. *The Malazan way*, she remembered Tayschrenn whispering with biting irony. And now in the High Mage's words Kiska heard a measure of self-disgust as well. Rubbing her hands at her sides, she looked away. 'I guess I don't know. I *thought* everything was over.'

'Well it isn't,' said the woman, sounding oddly angered. 'That's for sure.' Kiska looked at her, puzzled. 'There's an immense disturbance among the Warrens here,' the woman explained. 'I can feel it as strongly as the storm breaking over the island. That's probably where everyone's gone.'

'The Deadhouse,' Kiska breathed, remembering Oleg's words.

The woman eyed her sharply, taking her measure a second time. 'Yes. The Deadhouse. All this,' and she pointed upstairs, 'was probably nothing more than a diversion. A side show.'

'But all the dead. And Ash, too.'

The woman turned to the embers. 'Nothing like a massacre to confirm appearances.' She took a poker from a stand beside the hearth and raked the remaining coals, spreading them among the ashes. 'There's nothing more to learn here, Lubben.' She spoke with a strength of command that surprised Kiska. 'We'll go to the House.'

Lubben grunted his assent, cradled the axe to his chest. That the independent, cynical hunchback should submit so easily to orders from the woman struck Kiska as very telling. Back at the Inn, she'd acted as if second in command to Ash, who, if Surly was to be believed, had been an officer of the Bridge-burners. She might be of rank equivalent to a company commander herself.

'Take me with you,' Kiska blurted.

The woman smiled at Kiska's eagerness but shook her head. 'No. It's too dangerous.'

'I can be of use. I know things.'

The woman eyed her, tilted her head to one side. 'Such as?'

Kiska wet her lips, tried to recall everything important Oleg had said, together with all she suspected herself. 'I know that we'd have to get there before dawn, but that use of a Warren would be dangerous because the hounds are sensitive to them and might even travel them at will. I know that there's an event occurring focused on the House. And that,' she paused, trying to remember the word Oleg had used, 'that it might be a portal to Shadow—'

'*Enough!*'

Kiska stopped short, surprised. The woman raised a hand apologetically. 'Sorry. But some knowledge is best not hinted at anywhere at any time.' She turned away, began pacing. Kiska watched, tense, desperate to press her case, but afraid she might just annoy her.

'I'll keep an eye on her,' Lubben offered from the darkness beyond the hearth's meagre glow.

The woman studied Kiska from the far side of the mantle. 'All right,' she said. 'If you wish to come, fine. But you'll do as I say.'

'Yes.'

'Your name is Kiska, yes?'

'And yours?'

She answered with a teasing smile, the black tattooing at her brow wrinkling. 'Corinn. Now, Kiska: have you ever travelled by Warren?'

Kiska's first impulse was to lie, fearing such a lack would end her chances. She shook her head, frustrated by her inexperience.

Corinn's lips pursed for an instant, making Kiska's heart sink, but then she shrugged. 'Never mind. Just stay close. Lubben, stay to the rear.'

He grunted, impatient.

'But the hounds?' Kiska asked.

Again the smile, daring and spirited. 'We'll just have to move quickly.' She waved a hand. The air shimmered before the hearth, as if hot air billowed from it. Grey streaks appeared, brightening into tatters of purest glimmering silver. These met and fused, creating a floating mirror of mercury that rippled like water.

From Agayla's hints, dropped here and there, Kiska recognized the Warren as that of Thyr, the Path of Light. She'd heard that the Enchantress, the Queen of Dreams, was supposed to be a practitioner of Thyr.

Corinn stepped forward and disappeared into the floating oval of quicksilver as if submerging.

Kiska hesitated, fearful despite her fascination.

'Hurry, lass,' Lubben urged. 'It'll not do to lose her and wander the paths alone forever.'

Spurred by horror at the thought, Kiska jumped through. Whether Lubben followed she had no idea. It was as if she'd

227

leapt into a hall of mirrors. Reflections of herself and Corinn serried off into infinite distances. Hundreds of Corinns turned, reaching out to her. She stood, unable to move, her heart thudding in panic. Which one was real? Which should she respond to?

Like a swimmer broaching a lake, a new Corinn emerged from one image of herself. Kiska extended a hand and sighed in relief as it met flesh.

'Where is Lubben?'

Corinn pulled Kiska on. 'Everyone walks their own path in Thyr. Now stay close.'

They strode on without moving, or so it seemed to Kiska. She couldn't discern any progress at all, yet still Corinn pulled her on. Then, as she studied the passing images of herself, she began to see differences, some slight, others startling. In one she appeared painfully gaunt and wore clothes no better than rags; in another she was maimed, her right arm missing from the elbow. That sent a shudder down through that arm, recalling a wound from a childhood fall. In yet another she wore the dark cloth of a Claw. She almost shouted her amazement.

'What's going on?' she called to Corinn, yanking her to a halt. 'What do all these images mean?'

Corinn turned, irritation darkening the tattoos at her forehead. 'You see images?'

'Yes. Don't you?'

Corinn raised her brows, impressed. 'So. You are a natural. Thyr must suit you.' She urged Kiska on, saying over her shoulder, 'They are just possibilities – phantasms – pay them no mind. That's not why we're here.'

'What is it you see?'

Corinn answered without turning, 'I am walking a stone bridge over emptiness with open blue sky all round.'

Kiska stared at the confusing, shifting silver walls all about her – even above and below. 'Why? Why a bridge over emptiness? How?'

Corinn glanced back with that same mysterious smile. 'I like to think of things that way – it's safer. As to how, well, that would take years.'

Kiska nodded, grimacing. Yes. Years of study and practice. The same dusty mental exercises and meditation Agayla had tried to impose on her long ago, only giving up the day Kiska opened a ceiling window and risked a dangerous third-storey climb rather than sit for hours and, in her own words, try to cross her eyes. After that Agayla had been good on her agreement: providing every other form of instruction, though no longer pressing any arcane training upon her. She'd simply warned her that she'd come to regret the choice later in life.

And almost immediately she did, yet her pride wouldn't allow her to admit it. Her stubborn pride that turned the failure around until she actually boasted of her ignorance! All she felt now was shame at such childish wilfulness. After *this* night she would beg Agayla to forgive her.

Thinking of Agayla, the brushing of her rich embroidered dresses and her thick mane of auburn hair, brought a tingling to Kiska's neck. She slowed, dizzied for a moment, then jerked to a halt as one of the images before her rippled like the surface of a pool. It shifted, darkened into a likeness of a woman sitting at a shoreline, lashed by punishing wind and threatened by low clouds. The woman raised her head and Kiska saw Agayla such as she had never known her: exhausted, haggard, her face drawn and pale, her hair wind-whipped and soaked. Agayla looked up, confused then alarmed. 'Not here, child,' she said, hoarse, distracted.

Kiska lunged forward. 'Agayla!' But the image rippled away and instead Corinn re-emerged. The look she gave Kiska made her feel as if she'd sprouted wings. The filigree of tattooing at her brow seemed to pulse.

229

'What in the name of the Elder Ones do you think you're doing?'

Kiska stammered, 'I thought I saw someone. Someone I know. She's in trouble. I have to go to her!'

Corinn muttered, gestured curtly. All hints of her earlier mischievous smiles had gone. 'I don't sense a thing. Stay with me. This is no place for games.'

Stung, Kiska opened her mouth to explain, but the woman started off without waiting. Kiska hurried after, struggling to stay close.

'We must leave before our goal,' Corinn said over her shoulder. 'Something blocks the way – do you see it?'

Kiska's vision went no further than the image of herself just beyond Corinn. It was as if she walked towards herself, though each step brought her no closer. 'I don't see anything different from before,' Kiska said. But Corinn didn't reply. She had disappeared.

A cry died on Kiska's lips as the reflective silver of the Warren dulled and thickened to an opaque fog. Her training closed her mouth to still any betraying shout, for she recognized where she now stood. It was her third visit to Shadow Realm.

She stood upon a flat plain of dust and wind-scoured dirt. A sky of pallid lead arched overhead. From a great distance rose a low drawn-out moan, the wind or a hound.

In front of her towered a rock outcropping such as she had never seen before. It resembled a jumbled pile of enormous crystalline blades, black and smudged like frozen smoke. She thought of the stones Agayla possessed in her shop, the clusters of quartz and salt crystals. Smoke-quartz! That's what it reminded her of! And it was changing. While she watched, individual blades altered, rotated, disappeared or changed translucence. The entire structure seemed undefined and shifting. She could not even be certain of its size. It was beautiful, seeming to speak to her, and she felt that it must hold the solutions to every mystery she had ever wondered about, all the answers to any questions regarding Agayla. All she had to do was enter and she would know how Agayla fared this very moment. Even where Tayschrenn was right now. Any question at all. The fate of her father. Who would be her lover. Kiska took a step towards it.

Something blocked her way. A hand as hard as stone pushed her back. 'It doesn't do to stare quite so closely,' said a breathless voice.

It was the being from the bridge, Edgewalker. Dazed, Kiska blinked, rubbed her eyes with the heels of her palms. What had happened? Hadn't something . . . ? She could have sworn something odd had occurred. She shrugged but kept her face averted from the crystal outcropping.

Beyond, the sands gave way to bare mounded granite which descended to a lake of smooth water that reflected the dull sky like a mirror. An immense wall of ice reared on the opposite shore; the glacier that earlier had been nothing more than a distant line on the horizon. Now the ice stretched like a vast plain. Lights played over it such as she had seen in the southern night skies: rainbow banners and curtains that flickered, dancing.

Had she moved, or had the ice? 'This is Shadow,' she told the being. It inclined its desiccated head in agreement. 'I shouldn't be here.'

'Yet you do seem most persistent.'

She studied the empty dark sockets where its eyes should have been; had that been a joke? 'And you can send me back again?'

'You may say that is my duty.'

'Before you do – what is it? That thing?' Kiska gestured to the quartz-like heap of crystals.

'That is Shadow House. The heart of Shadow, so to speak.'

'Really? That?' But it's—'

'Alive. Quite so. And very dangerous.'

'Dangerous? But what of – of those who would claim it?'

It shrugged its thin shoulders. 'Occupants of the throne come and go.' It raised a clawed hand to point to the glacier across the lake of melt-water. 'But that. That is the true danger.'

'What is it?'

'It is alien to this realm. It reminds me of the Jaghut, but profoundly alien from them. They, at least, were not so different from you. It is said that long ago the Jaghut inadvertently allowed it into this world when they wrought their ice-magic too strongly.'

'But there is a madman, a murderer, who may be taking the throne. Won't you do something? He doesn't belong here either!'

The creature did not turn away from the glacial cliff. 'True. But this is the more deadly threat. I must remain ready should this break through and reach the House.'

'Break through?'

'It is being resisted. But that could change at any moment. Those facing it weaken even as we speak.'

Kiska fairly wailed: 'But what of Kell— the throne?'

'I am sorry. That is a minor concern given everything at stake this Conjunction.'

'*Minor!*'

Kiska believed she could hear the dried flesh at its neck creak as the head turned to her. 'Yes. In the larger picture. I am sorry. Now, you must go.'

'But wait! I have so many questions. I—'

Opalescent grey closed about Kiska obscuring her vision as surely as smoke. From close by came cries, screams, the clash of arms. She heard a woman shout something – her name?

She hunched, ready for combat, a hand groping at the billowing curtains. 'Corinn?'

'Here.'

Kiska spun, could discern nothing but fog. Was she back in Malaz? But where? She circled, peering uselessly.

'Corinn?' she whispered, louder. Carefully, she drew the curved fighting knife.

'*Quiet*,' a distant voice cautioned.

Had that been Corinn? What kind of game was this? 'Where are you? Show yourself!'

'Right behind you,' came a taunt at Kiska's ear.

She swung: empty vapour churned and curled. Kiska bit down on her panic, clenching her hands so tightly her nails bit into her palms. *Never mind what may or may not be happening: remain calm*. This was a war of nerves and she was losing.

Listen girl, she challenged herself. *Listen. What do you hear?* She strained, attempted to sort through the background of muted shouts and screams to discern nearby hints, scrapes and whisperings. There! A footstep to her right. And either very distant, or somehow muted, a roar of outrage. Lubben?

Again, the scuff of leather on stone. Behind her now, closer. Not waiting for another mocking whisper Kiska launched herself, arms outstretched. Coarse woven cloth brushed her right hand. She clutched at it, pulling it close.

The cloth was loosely woven, dyed grey. A cultist.

A cold blade bit at Kiska's shoulder as the assassin's sleeve brushed her neck. Recognizing the thrust and her opponent's stance, she reacted automatically. She clinched the arm, smashed her elbow into her assailant's throat, then thrust at the chest. Her opponent tumbled to the ground.

Kiska threw herself upon the body, clamped a hand over the mouth. She listened. Satisfied they were alone, or at least giving up trying to detect another's presence, she lowered her face. It was a young woman. Perhaps her blow had broken the spell of disguise, or the fall had done it, but in any case the woman's face was bared and the hood lay flat upon the cobbled street.

A few small bubbles rose and fell on the woman's lips as she struggled to breathe. Her hair and complexion were light, the cheekbones high and thin – refined. Talian perhaps, rich-looking. Kiska gently lifted the dagger from her hand. The nails were clean, manicured, the palm soft. The woman's eyes followed the thin blade as Kiska brought it up between their faces.

'Why?' Kiska whispered.

The woman's breath wheezed shallow and moist. A howl tore through the fog like a scream in Kiska's ear. She couldn't still the flinch of her muscles. The woman smiled at that. The smile bespoke a victory over Kiska, triumph at her betrayal of fear.

Snarling, Kiska pushed herself up and scanned the churning curtains for the hound. Was it coming for her? Perhaps the cultist's mission had been to delay her long enough for it to arrive. Thus the games, the hide and seek. Kiska damned herself for cooperating, hanging about like a fool, reacting rather than taking the initiative. She'd played into her hands.

A low chuffing cough brought her around. There, off in the mist, hung two green eyes. Green – a different one this time. Not that it mattered. Having seen one of them up close, Kiska despaired. It had smashed through a door and chewed armoured men in half. Now the only choice she had left was to be pulled down from behind running, or be struck down fighting. Screaming her rage at the unfairness of it, the naked blade in her hand, she charged the eyes.

At the sixth step, she stumbled. Her leading foot caught on a rise of uneven ground. She rolled forward into an explosion of noise – a deafening firefight of crackling power, shouts in a multitude of languages – smacking her head against a wall. She lay dazed while rippling phosphorescent energies played above her.

*

Stepping out of the House's doorway, the giant stooped to avoid the lintel. Alien, ornamental armour of bronze plates and embossed, tooled leather gleamed at its chest, arms and legs. A gold sash wrapped its inhumanly broad shoulders, and from another at its waist hung two swords. Its face was hidden by a war helm of polished iron gilded in bronze spirals, and bronze-scaled gauntlets covered its hands.

Temper backed away, sparing a quick glance to his rear. Trenech blocked the frail gate, pike-axe levelled. As the apparition stepped down from the porch the stones of the walk sank beneath its feet. Temper heard shouts of dismay from behind him, cut off by searing laughter from Faro.

'See!' the old man shouted, his voice cracking. 'Fools! You have brought out the Jaghut. Greatest of those fallen attempting to master the House. Now see what you face!'

Temper retreated to the gate, but pulled short as Trenech thrust the broad axe-head at him.

'Let me out, blast you!'

Behind Trenech and Faro the cultists fanned out, Pralt and Jasmine among them, rushing the length of low wall.

'Soldier,' Faro called to Temper, 'you entered of your own will.' The phosphorescent flickering of Warren energies danced about his emaciated arms. 'I am sorry, but we cannot allow anyone to leave the grounds. You made your choice.'

What? But he'd only just entered. Well, to the Abyss with them! The walls were low enough to jump. A clash of swords spun Temper around. The Jaghut held its blades ready. They shimmered, light rippling along their four-foot length, and it struck them together again. Over the House thunder erupted.

The grounds heaved and hundreds of desiccated skeletal hands and arms emerged, digging and clawing, as corpses fought to tear free of the dirt. Cyan energies flickered over the walls while the tree limbs twitched and swung. The noise of it all, the roaring and crackling, the terrified screams of the cultists, deafened Temper.

All around the flagged walkway sinewy hands, their flesh dried to leather, grasped at the air. He kicked at the nearest but it snatched his foot and it took all his strength to pull free. They flailed between him and the wall, a malevolent crop that would pull him down. He wondered how his blades would fare against them but the Jaghut was almost upon him. He struck a ready stance though he doubted he'd survive a single blow. Yet, like Surgen Ress, the Jaghut hardly noticed him; its visor was fixed on the gate beyond. Only its legs moved, feet slamming heavily onto the walkway. Then, flashing like liquid light, its blades lashed out. Temper barely managed to react. He blocked, but the second blow's force knocked him from the path like the side-swipe of a battering ram. He rolled, tumbling, and came to rest on the cold loose earth of the grounds.

Face down, he struggled to regain his breath, choking on the dust and dirt. Distantly, through the tumult, he heard heavy steps as the Jaghut strode to the gate. Things squirmed and shifted beneath him like snakes. A voice shouted within his dazed thoughts: *move, man! Move to the wall!*

'Right,' he gasped aloud, spitting out dirt. 'Move.' Swords still clenched in his fists, he crawled like an exhausted swimmer aiming at a too distant shore. He pulled himself over a sea of grasping withered hands and lashing arms – so far the dead seemed more intent upon freeing themselves than attacking him. A new note of urgency entered the fray as anvil-like clanging rang out and a bellow reverberated from the gate.

He dragged himself on. The crude wall rose almost within reach, laughably low, almost useless. Behind it a cultist ran past not even bothering to look down to where he lay. Ahead, whole armoured corpses had clawed their way free. Something caught at Temper's foot. He kicked, but it held on. Temper rolled to his side and peered down to find a skeletal hand wrapped around his ankle. Dread tore out a yell and he swung, slashing the thing repeatedly. Other hands now grasped at him. The sinews parted like dry wood and he yanked his foot free.

The chill of horror still on him, Temper crawled frantically, but beneath him the earth shifted and broke. The musty stench of ages-dead flesh seeped out, then long-nailed fingers pushed through the cracks. At the wall, the freed corpses heaved themselves against the stones, lunging at the cultists beyond. They caught one by the sleeve and yanked him in. Sinking with him wrapped in their bone-thin arms, his screams were cut off as his head sank beneath the earth.

Temper stared, horrified. *Burn help him – he would be next!* He leapt for the wall, but something yanked at his leg and he fell short, his blades just brushing the stones. A corpse held him. Its shattered skull wobbled as he kicked at it. Temper lashed out, smashing its torso and the broken thing fell away.

The hot acid bile of nausea bit at Temper's throat. He'd face any warrior from any land – but this! He pushed himself up and was about to leap over the wall when something rammed him in the side and sent him tumbling farther into the yard.

Lying in the dirt, Temper twisted to face the wall. There stood a Claw dressed in black, a staff at his side. What by Fener's prang was a Claw doing here? Yells and the explosions of Warren energy out beyond the walls answered his question. In a chaotic melee of smoke, mist, Warren-fire and whirling, snapping robes, black fought grey. At the gate, Trenech and Faro battled the Jaghut and no one, wisely, seemed willing to interfere with that titanic duel. Elsewhere at the walls, cultists and Claws fought side-by-side against the dead, who seemed less inclined to defend the walls than to clamber over them.

The Claw who'd struck him pulled back his hood, revealing long black hair and a narrow hatchet-face. Possum. The man looked to have been in a fight himself, his robes torn and bloodied. Possum grinned at Temper the way a starving man might regard a roast ox.

Temper invited him in with a wave. Possum shook his head. He pushed himself up to rush the bastard but fell; another grip like a dog's jaws held his ankle. His foot had already been yanked into the earth.

'Damn you to Hood's Abyss!' he screamed.

'After you!' Possum answered through the bursts of magefire.

Enraged, Temper threw one of his swords at the Claw who knocked it aside with his staff. Laughing, Possum waved, stepped back, and disappeared.

Temper struggled to rise, almost weeping his frustration. He'd nearly made it! If it weren't for that bastard he'd have escaped. With a yell, he reached down into the loose earth and blindly felt about. This wasn't a hand but a vine or root of some kind, its grip like iron. He yanked but it was as taut as a rope.

From down the hillside a particularly fierce exchange of Warren energy caught his attention. There, what looked like the few remaining cultists had gathered in a fighting retreat against the Claws. Trenech and Faro still held the gate against the huge bellowing Jaghut. At the walls Claws had replaced cultists but from their panicked shouts they appeared to be faring no better.

A dry creaking whispered from his rear and he twisted round. There stood one of the yard's stunted trees, its branches reaching for him. *The tree!* The blasted tree had him! Stark horror drove all coherent thought from him. Throwing his second sword out over the wall, he pulled out both fighting gauches and slammed the short heavy blades into the earth.

At the first touch of iron the root jerked and the tree shuddered from bottom to top. Temper thought that he'd bested it, but then the root tightened about his ankle and yanked his leg farther into the earth, up to the knee. He grunted his pain and terror and drove one arm down, cutting and slicing. Now pain flamed in his other leg as it too was drawn into the dirt. Frantic, he slashed with both blades as deeply as he dared reach. Yet no sooner had he severed one root than another wrapped itself around him. Tendrils grasped at his arms. One cheek-guard was pressed against the earth and he knew that at any moment a root would take his neck. From where he lay he could see the tree dark against the sky. He eyed it. It was a scrawny thing, stunted and gnarled, the trunk no thicker than his wrist and barely his height. He grinned, thinking *You look to be in reach you bastard.* With a bellow of rage, he tore his arms out of the earth and lunged.

Kiska may have lay stunned for some time; she did not know. She simply became aware of something wavering at the edge of her vision and a voice familiar and close saying, 'I am very surprised to see you here.' Blinking back tears of pain, Kiska squinted up at Oleg Vikat's furrowed, madness-contorted face. His shade looked remarkably solid here, wherever *here* was. Next to her stood a wall of haphazardly piled granite and limestone blocks – it was against this she'd cracked her head.

'Where are we?' she whispered, wincing and rubbing her skull behind an ear.

Oleg slipped a hand under her arm to lift her up and pointed over the wall. 'The eye of the storm.'

Groaning, Kiska rested her chin on the low wall. They were at the one building in Malaz she'd never dared enter. The old building with its ridiculous name, the Deadhouse. Call it superstition, but she'd never ever seen anyone come or go from the place, using that as her excuse for never taking a closer look. An abandoned building held no interest for her.

They were behind the House, at the rear wall that ran unevenly at more or less waist height. Beyond, in the grounds, rose four major mounds humped like rubbish heaps, steaming as if recently turned. Squat twisted trees, black-limbed, grew here and there apparently without order. In one corner stood a stone cairn of granite plinths piled together like cards and smothered beneath vines that snaked all over the grounds. As for the House, its windows appeared dark and empty, its only rear access – a narrow servant's entrance at the bottom of stairs – choked with weeds.

Nothing moved except the twitching tree branches. From the front she heard the clash of fighting. Layers of fog cloaked the distance, but she could make out corpses lying here and there against the wall. Of Corinn or Lubben she saw nothing. Where were they?

A low hiss from Oleg brought her attention back. He glared over the wall, hunched but tensed, like an arched cat. Seeing nothing, she whispered, 'What is it?'

'Do you not see them?'

'No. Who? Where?' Kiska asked *who*, but from the venom in Oleg's voice she could guess.

'Look between the farthest two mounds. See the vines move?'

Kiska watched and after a moment saw the matting of foliage shake slightly, shift and stretch as if twisting after something. Then they blackened, smoked, and fell away to ash.

Oleg, fists at his chin, moaned. 'Nooo! He's getting away!' He turned to her. 'You were in Shadow. You met the Elder One?'

'Elder?'

Oleg hissed exasperation: 'The one who watches its borders.'

'Oh, yes. I met him.'

'And? What did he say? Where is he? Will he act?'

Kiska groaned inwardly. 'He can't, that is, he won't. I'm sorry.'

Oleg's spirit hands lunged for Kiska's throat but whipped

away at the last instant. She flinched from him. Glaring wildly, he muttered to himself, then rubbed his hands over the wall with quick tentative strokes as if it were hot and burning his fingers.

'Nothing for it,' she heard him whimper. 'I'll see him enslaved for an eternity! It must be mine!' Warren energies crackled and flashed, blinding her. When she looked back Oleg was inside the wall, scrambling across the ground on all fours. Vines snatched at him but also blackened and crumbled to ash.

Soon he neared where the vines shuddered and jerked. Kiska heard a shout – a challenge or warning. Close to Oleg crawled another man, but she had barely seen him when power burst, gold and violet between them, shattering nearby trees and blowing clouds of earth from a mound. The force of the impact shook the wall and hurled Kiska sprawling onto her back, stones and sand pattering down around her. Pushing to her knees, Kiska squinted over the wall, shading her eyes against the glare of power. Oleg knelt, pouring a mauve snake-like flow of energy from his hands onto the back of a man. Despite this punishment, the man crawled onwards towards the House.

Then, so quick and startling did it move, another figure – this one in rags, scarecrow thin with elongated, oddly pro-portioned limbs – sprang like a striking snake from the ravaged mound and wrapped its arms around Oleg's quarry.

Oleg shouted in triumph and broke off the energies he'd been summoning. In the resulting silence Kiska's ears thrummed. The captured man clawed and flailed at the loose earth as he was dragged toward the mound. Now Kiska could see him more clearly: a short Dal Honese, grey haired, his clothing torn and dirt-smeared. Kellanved – or what was left of him – snatched just shy of his goal. He let out a shattering howl as he clutched uselessly at the soil. Kneeling in the broken steaming earth, Oleg cackled victory.

A third figure appeared, causing Kiska to catch her breath.

Dancer! He tottered, cloak gone, a dark shirt hanging in ribbons about him. Blood streaked his torso and arms, dripped to the torn earth. Before Kiska could shout a warning, he snatched Oleg up as if he were a bundle of rags and tossed him onto the writhing figures. Immediately the pale skeletal form released Kellanved and grasped Oleg. They wrestled, Oleg shrieking, the other silent . . . disturbingly so. Dancer stepped in and dragged Kellanved free. Together they staggered the last few steps to the House and fell against its rear wall as Oleg flailed and screamed, tossing up dirt while the creature drew him slowly into its mound.

Oleg disappeared a bit at a time. But he's dead – a spirit – Kiska thought. How could this be? Unless here, on the grounds, no distinction remained between flesh and spirit – here, the House captured any and all that entered.

Presently, Oleg's hoarse pleading ceased. She glanced back to the mound. Now all that moved was the bare settling of earth, slumping a bit to one side. At the back of the House Kellanved and Dancer struggled with a narrow warped door. Dancer pulled it open and lunged through so quickly it was as if he'd been grabbed. Kellanved waited. As if sensing her gaze, he turned towards her. She meant to duck behind the wall, but something drew her, enticed her, to stand. A weary smile passed Kellanved's lips, as if he'd be amused if he yet retained the energy. Kiska felt a summons to step over the wall. He merely lifted his chin and she was compelled to enter. Her foot in its soft leather sandal settled on top of the wall. A jolt from the rock, like a spark of static, jarred her, and she yelped as she tumbled back.

An angry curse sounded from inside the grounds, then something like a giant fist smashed against the wall. Stones stung her back and flames licked over her. She leapt up, slapped at her hair and clothing as a mocking laugh rang out. It finished abruptly as a door slammed shut.

Kiska ran. She wanted to run on forever through the mist, away from such horrors, but her way was blocked by a grey figure. She shrieked, thinking it was Dancer come for her. But the figure flashed past like a wounded animal and collapsed against the wall with a gasp. It lay there, shuddering, weeping. Kiska reached out, feeling a strange compassion but a deep bellow and clash of steel snapped her attention forwards. There, an armoured giant duelled a man armed with a pike-axe who was backed up by a frail-looking elder. The Warren energies that crackled between them had left the earth scorched and smoking.

Laughter, and Kiska looked down to the cultist. He was a young man with pale eyes filled with hopelessness, despite his soft chuckle. He wiped his mouth, leaving a smear of blood across his face.

'It's over,' he said, and winced. 'Won or lost – it's finished.' He let a dagger slip from his blood-slick hand, let his head fall.

Kiska stared. 'Finished?' she echoed.

He nodded, exhausted beyond care. Kiska meant to ask just what exactly was finished, but backed away instead as a dirt-smeared armoured hand appeared from behind the stones. It encircled the youth's neck and dragged him in over the wall. He didn't seem startled at all. Without struggle, he simply disappeared.

The gauntlet appeared again, scrabbling at the wall. Head and shoulders followed, the head hidden within a war helm with faceguards and an articulating neck guard. The creature gasped, its breath ragged and wet, and it babbled to itself. Wild eyes, all whites, blazed from within the darkness of its helm. Kiska stepped back. She'd seen this – or another just like it – at Mock's Hold. Perhaps it had escaped from here in the first place. It rolled over the wall and crashed to the ground with a clatter of armour. Soil fell from it in clumps. So, she thought, it had dragged itself from the grave. But bizarrely, in its other hand, it gripped a shattered tree branch.

As it lay there, chest heaving – heaving? Was it alive? – Kiska tried to decide whether to stab the thing now while it seemed helpless, or to run. While she hesitated it fumbled at the ground, its breath rasping as it dragged itself along. That, she now realized, was the only sound. Silence reigned. Her hearing rang in the absence of conflict and the explosion of Warren magics. She circled around to the front of the House. The pike-man simply faced his giant opponent, and suddenly Kiska recognized him – the drunkard from Coop's inn! But how could that possibly be? Was *everything* insane tonight? The armoured giant's arms hung at its sides. It didn't appear defeated or wounded, just watchful, patient. The old man called, addressing it in a language of fluting musical vowels. After a moment, it responded in kind.

Was that the end of the hostilities for the night? Kiska looked around. The grounds resembled a battlefield of ploughed up corpses – but then it had always had something of that atmosphere. No one else seemed to be about. Clouds of fog still obscured the distance, anonymous as ever. She wondered if it were dawn yet over the town. She felt chill, as if the fog and dark beyond belonged to a typical Malaz Island mid-winter morning, when the fishing boats snapped and moaned with sea-rime.

Down the slope from the gate, shadowy figures flickered in and out of sight. More fighting? The final savage exchanges? But she heard not a sound. Maybe it was just another of the mist's shifting tricks. Nevertheless, she felt exposed just standing there. From out of the fog forms were coming towards her. They looked familiar, and once Kiska was sure who they were, she crossed her arms and grinned, waiting.

Tayschrenn and Hattar climbed the shallow slope out of the fogbank, the bodyguard supporting the mage, who sagged at his side. Was he injured? She saw no wound upon him. He merely appeared pale and haggard and exhausted. He gave a slow shake of his head as he recognized her. Hattar scowled as if a cat he'd tossed into a river had just reappeared.

Kiska tried to hide the immense relief the High Mage's presence instilled in her. She remembered her earlier cockiness – the girl who had followed him to Mock's Hold – what seemed so long ago. She shouted, 'Are you all right? What are you doing here?'

Tayschrenn called out in a weak voice, 'And how did you get here?'

'A friend brought me.'

'Your friend shows poor judgement.'

She ached to tell him all that she'd seen, but if tonight had taught her anything, it was a caginess with information. Coming closer, she noticed an uncomfortable chill emanating from him like an aura of winter. Vapour coiled from his shoulders.

'What's going on back there?'

Tayschrenn hesitated. Then with a sigh he told her, 'Surly had long suspected that renegades from her order had joined the Shadow cult. They're just cleaning up now.'

Kiska snorted. '*Cleaning up?* Why so delicate? They're wiping out the cult. They're rivals, aren't they?'

'Something like that. Old rivals.'

'Well, it's too late now for that anyway.'

It seemed to Kiska that his drained expression became brittle. 'What do you mean?'

'I mean that while the cultists sacrifice themselves to lead the Claws on a useless chase, I saw two men reach the House at the rear. The two Surly claimed dead.'

Tayschrenn winced as if physically pained by her words. He shook his head. 'No. You're mistaken.'

'Mistaken? I saw them!'

The magus swallowed an angry retort, took a slow breath to calm himself. 'Kiska,' he said carefully, emphatically, 'you *must* be mistaken, because both Surly and I have agreed that those two are dead and gone. Do you understand?'

For the third time that night Kiska wanted to object, to say *but*, and for the third time she suspected that remaining silent, resisting the urge, might save her life. She simply nodded at Tayschrenn's assertion, her jaw clamped shut. Hattar echoed the nod, underscoring it as a standing warning.

Tayschrenn waved a hand as if to say that was all behind them now. 'I'm going to see if the Guardian will speak to me, then we'll return to Mock's Hold. You should accompany us.'

Kiska looked about. There was still no sign of Corinn or Lubben. She agreed. She had no idea how else to get out of wherever, or whatever, this was.

Tayschrenn straightened from Hattar's grip and, leaving him behind, continued unsteadily on to the gate. He stopped a respectful distance from the old man and addressed him. Kiska was too far away to hear much. The old man replied curtly. His gaze didn't waver from the armoured giant who stood like a statue of solid bronze just inside the open gate. It no longer attacked, but nor did it give any impression of defeat. Rather, Kiska sensed, it was waiting for something, gathering strength for a new onslaught. A few steps away the guard remained at ready, pike-axe held high. While tall, he barely reached the giant's shoulders. He was almost as broad though, shaped like a blunt spur of stone. A match for the giant so far.

The two men spoke, unlike in appearance yet somehow brethren to Kiska's eye. Was this the end of the encounter then? A civilized exchange over a carpet of bodies, then a warm fire and off to another errand tomorrow? And what of her? Could she return to the usual rounds of spying and petty theft, knowing what she did? Having tasted what could be? As if the island had seemed small and provincial before!

Hattar suddenly stiffened, loosing a galvanizing shout. Kiska caught an instant's glimpse of a tall Shadow cultist behind the guard, who spasmed and toppled to his side without a sound. Killed instantly, it seemed.

The giant launched himself at the gate's threshold. Warren energies erupted in a curtain of carmine and silver flames, shaking the ground and knocking Kiska flat. The giant bellowed, thrust at the barrier while the old man raised his arms, bending all his strength.

Kiska crawled away, one arm raised over her face against the glare of the inferno. As the giant pushed an arm through the warding, Tayschrenn joined the battle. Raw coursing power arced about the hillside in random blasts of lightning. Again Kiska tumbled, straining to raise herself against the hammering pressure. She heard a snarl of desperate rage from Hattar as he ran towards the gate. He disappeared into pure incandescent energy.

Moments later, out of the blinding furnace, came Hattar, dragging Tayschrenn with him. He dumped the mage beside Kiska. One side of the bodyguard's hair was gone, and smoke curled from his cheek and ear. His right arm swung limply, blackened, a livid gash welling blood.

No wound that Kiska saw affected the High Mage. His body and limbs appeared whole, though blood ran from his nose and ears, and pink clouds discoloured his eyes.

'We must take him to be healed,' Hattar shouted at Kiska. He glared like a madman and Kiska was shocked to see despair filling his eyes. 'Help me!'

'But the demon – will it escape?'

'Only he can stop it if it does! Carry him!'

'But—'

'Raise him up!' A sob escaped from Hattar as he fumbled at one of the knives sheathed at his waist.

Kiska swallowed any further objections. She yanked the mage to his feet, his arms to either side of her neck and his weight on her back. With Hattar's help, she clasped his arms and staggered forward, the magus's legs dragging behind them. Hattar pushed her down the slope. She half-stumbled, each step jarring her knees. She fully expected to run headlong into something in the mist. Catching up, Hattar used his one good arm to steady Tayschrenn against her back. They jogged like that for a time, side by side, then Hattar moved up.

'Follow my lead,' he mumbled as he limped forward. Blood dripped like spilt water from his torn arm. Though the weight on her back threatened to topple her, she followed as quickly as possible, drawing strength from Hattar's example.

She almost fell as she stepped onto wet cobbles. Hattar stood to one side, leaning against a dark form in the mist: a brick wall. He pressed his head against it, his eyes shut. In the distance, the fog thinned, shredding into wisps. Kiska recognized where they were now.

'You know the town,' challenged Hattar.

'Yes.'

'The nearest medicer or healer?' He licked his lips, forced his eyes open. He'd had the colour of cured leather earlier this evening, but now his face was as pale as the fog. 'Where?'

Kiska glared about, thinking. They were in the old town, not too distant from the Deadhouse in fact. She thought for a moment longer, then gestured to the left with her chin. 'This way.'

Temper took grim pleasure from the fact that not once did he lose consciousness – not even when the tree whispered to him.

And not many would have blamed him then if he had either, what with the tree promising in its creaking voice how it would send shoots down his throat to feed on his heart blood, or tear at his soul for eternity, growing stronger and taller feeding upon him.

But he'd bested it! He wrenched and broke it asunder! He didn't break. He'd never broken. He was annealed in the fury of the last Talian, Falar, and Seven City campaigns. Dassem himself had picked him from the ranks: for conspicuous pig-headedness, the champion had joked. For more than a decade he'd served in the Sword. But now all were dead and he the last. Ferrule and Dassem were gone. Was this Hood's welcome?

Hands grasped at him, turned him over. A face stared down. A woman, tattooed – Corinn. Her gaze searched his face; he didn't like the way she bit her lip at what she saw.

'How do I look?' he croaked.

She gasped, amazed he was able to speak.

'That bad, huh?'

'Hood himself. Can you stand?'

'Don't know. Haven't recently,' and he tried to laugh but only spat up grit and blood.

Another face appeared: side-long, anxious. Lubben. 'You look like an Imass reject.'

'Help me stand and I'll whip you for that.'

They took his arms, hauled him upright. 'Later,' Lubben rumbled. 'Right now we're on our way out. The Claws and grey-boys are busy chasing each others' asses. We'll just slip out the back, eh?'

Temper saw that the hunchback had retrieved his swords. He didn't answer. He held his jaws tight against the agony of life returning to his legs. Corinn watched as if he were made of glass and might burst into pieces at any moment.

From the gate a shout sounded. Lubben turned, grunted his surprise. A sudden detonation kicked Temper's numb legs out from under him and he fell again. The blast reminded him of Moranth alchemical explosions he'd endured. The ground buckled and heaved and a gust of heated air seared his lungs. He rolled over, righting his helm. Crimson and silver energies thundered and coursed at the gate like an enormous waterfall. Within, the shadowy figure of the Jaghut battled.

Temper turned to Lubben, shouted through the detonations, 'Bad as I think?'

Lubben nodded, grimaced his disgust. 'A grey took down the axe-man. I think the old guy and another fellow bought it too!' He crawled to Temper, took his arm. 'Hood himself is about to arrive. Let's get going!'

Temper took his swords from Lubben, shook him off. 'No. Those two held the gate for a reason. That thing can't be allowed out.'

'Dammit Temper! It's not your fight! Leave it to the Claws.'

Temper laughed. 'They're too clever. They've run off.'

Corinn threw herself down next to them. 'What're you two waiting for? Let's get out of here!'

Temper pointed: 'Look.' A figure, blackened and smoking, crawled from the wash of blinding energies. Temper stood, staggered towards it. After a few steps Lubben came to his side, steadied him. As they closed, the hunchback let out a whistle at the ravaged corpse before them. The raw energies had scoured it. Burnt beyond recognition, its hands were missing, the forearms reduced to white cracked bone.

Temper turned his face away from the smoke and stink of scorched flesh. 'Faro,' he whispered.

Thunder erupted anew from the gate. The curtain of power wavered, rippled like a pool struck by a stone, reformed itself.

'Soldier . . .' hissed a voice from the fleshless jaws.

'Soliel's Mercy!' Lubben choked and staggered away, dry heaving.

'Soldier—'

Temper kneeled at the seared corpse. 'Faro?'

'Step into the gap, soldier,' came a breathless call, as if the ground itself spoke. 'Accept the burden.'

'What of the fires?'

Horribly, the figure raised a blackened and charred forearm, entreating. 'Receive the Guardianship!'

Temper felt wrenched and utterly spent. He rested his hands on his knees. Why did it always fall to him? Hadn't he done enough? 'I accept,' he answered, as if that were the only response he was capable of, as if this alone was what had drawn him to the island in the first place.

He eyed the coursing energies, scratched his chin with the back of one gauntlet. 'What of those flames?' No answer came. He looked down. The corpse lay motionless. Temper sensed that whatever had held Faro together had fled. He felt dread dry his throat. Just what *had* he promised?

Corinn arrived, crouched. 'The old man?' Temper nodded, eyeing the pulsing firestorm; past it, he thought he saw figures retreating into the fog.

'Doesn't matter anymore.'

He felt her hand at his shoulder. 'We have to go. Now.'

'Corinn – could you shield me from those energies?'

'What?'

'Could you cover me?'

Corinn stared, appalled. 'You're mad!'

'Could you!'

Her gaze snapped from him towards the gate, then back again. Temper caught something in her eyes – a glimmer of fight, of spirit – until dread smothered it. She shook her head. 'Forget it.'

He looked to her vest, to where the bridge and flame sigil would have been pinned.

Corinn caught his gaze and flushed instantly. 'Damn you! How dare you!' He watched her, waiting. She sighed, eyed the barrier once more. 'Maybe – for a moment.' He nodded, took a long breath, started for the gate. 'Just one heart-beat!'

Temper continued on. 'Good enough,' he muttered, 'that's probably all I'll have.'

He stopped just outside the wash of energies, shielded his eyes. The indistinct shape of the Jaghut flickered just beyond.

The barrier appeared thinner, less opaque than before. Temper wished he knew how close it was to collapse, but he'd been asked to step into the gap once more, just as he had for Dassem, and couldn't refuse.

Lubben came up alongside. He didn't even turn his head to see what Temper thought of that – his blind side anyway. Temper glanced to Corinn who lifted her arms. She mouthed: *a short time*.

Temper nodded, adjusted his gauntlets, and eased his shoulders. He slowed his breathing and the pounding of his heart. He shouted to Lubben, 'In quick. You low, I'll go high.'

Lubben gave a curt jerk of his head, hefted his axe. Temper straightened his helm.

'Now!' Corinn shouted.

Leaping into the curtain of energies, Temper felt his hair singe and his armour heat as if tossed into a furnace. But he remained unscorched, though the barrier's energy shrilled and churned all around him. The scoured path he walked smoked and hissed beneath his feet. He sensed Lubben by his side.

A bare three steps and he reached the Jaghut. The creature's struggle to escape the House grounds appeared to have been almost as punishing for it as for Faro. The bronze armour smoked at its shoulders and chest. The fine gilding had run, blackening. But the swords shone even more brightly than before, glowing as if immersed in the fiercest fires.

Temper lunged and swung high. One blade caught a shoulder plate, twisted up and rebounded from the helm. Lubben feinted a low swipe then thrust with the killing-spike on the axe-head.

The Jaghut turned, slipped the thrust, cut Lubben down his shoulder and spine. Lubben jerked down and away from Temper's side.

They'd failed their first and best chance. In the following fraction of a heartbeat Temper decided on new tactics. He screamed and lunged in what he hoped appeared to be outright berserk fury. After two exchanges the Jaghut believed it – it yielded ground, waiting for Temper's blind rage to provide an opening. Temper now held the gate's threshold. The barrier of channelled power snapped away like a door slammed shut.

Temper stopped attacking. He was rewarded by a fraction's hesitation from his opponent that betrayed a stumble of rhythm. At that instant Temper felt the glow of a gambit's success along with something more: renewed strength coursing up from the ground through his legs. The leaden weight of exhaustion and pain sloughed from him like a layer of dirt in a cold reviving stream. His fighting calm, the inner peace that had carried him through all the chaos of past battles, settled upon him like an affirmation. He allowed himself a fierce, taut grin.

The Jaghut clashed its blades together, advanced once more. Temper could not see its face, but he imagined its re-evaluation of the duel, and its determination to hack him to pieces for daring to oppose him. The attack rolled against Temper like the slamming waves of a storm. He held the gate, crouching low under the blows like a rock that could not be cracked as the swords rang out. He parried as carefully as he could to spare his own, much lighter, blades. The Jaghut gave him openings but he ignored them, refusing to yield his stance.

Soon Temper realized that here he faced no lethal artistry such as that offered by Surgen or Dassem, swordsmen you could never anticipate because you never lasted long enough to grasp their style. Instead, this was raw power incarnate, like the direct irresistible onslaught of a tidal wave. The Jaghut's blades smashed the stones to either side, ploughed through the earth.

Temper thought it impossible that he could turn such blows. But something gave him the strength, pouring up from the earth to empower him, and he wondered – was this true

Patronage? If so, with whom or what had he entered into service?

The style of the attack changed then, bearing on steadily; the creature had abandoned the quick decisive blow and would grind him down instead. That would take longer, it likely judged, but was more certain. And Temper had to agree with the estimate. He'd already used up the fresh reserve that had come to him like a blessing at the slamming of the gate. He was down to pure blind cussedness and was slowing, tiring. The blades hissed closer and closer. Then stopped.

Temper straightened, startled.

The Jaghut had withdrawn a step. Temper risked a glimpse away. He was alone. Everyone and everything had vanished. Bare, time-rounded hills stretched all around. And the House was no longer a house. A pile of megalithic blocks stood in its place, looking like a tumbled-down cairn. Even the trees and mounds in the yard were gone. The Jaghut stood to one side, helm raised as it gazed to the south-west.

Rainbow lights weaved and shimmered in a clear night sky. A darkened vault of constellations strangely distorted. At the horizon stretched a blue-green glow such as he had once seen at sea, when his ship passed close to the shores of the ice-bound Fenn Mountains. His breath, he noticed, steamed from his helm like smoke and a dire cold bit at his limbs. *Where in Burn's Wisdom was he?*

The Jaghut turned its helm to him and pointed one sword south. 'They've failed,' it said in perfect Talian.

'Who failed?' Temper said, startled to find himself addressed.

The Jaghut spoke as if Temper hadn't responded. 'Never rely upon uncertain allies, human. They will always disappoint you.'

Temper reminded himself not to lower his guard. The game had changed to one perhaps even more perilous; he'd heard enough legends and tales of Jaghuts plying subtle arguments and poisoned gifts. Physically, he felt strong. Whatever power's service he had entered into had found him a vessel sufficient to the task of standing before this being's onslaught. Perhaps the Jaghut knew it too, and that was why he now found himself here. *A change in strategy.* He felt the power of its regard like a giant's hand pushing him back. 'Do you know who I am, human?'

Temper struggled to find his voice: 'No.'

'I am Jhenna. Do you know the name?'

Jhenna? He'd been facing a female all along? 'No.'

'Truly not?' It shook its helmed head. 'How far into ignorance you humans have fallen. I was one of your kind's teachers long ago. We raised you up out of the muck. Did you know that?'

Temper slapped his clenched hands to his sides to warm them. 'No.'

'We were puissant upon the world while your ancestors dressed in hides and squatted in their own filth. We gave you fire! We shielded you from the K'Chain!'

Temper shrugged. He was no scholar, just a soldier.

'What I am saying, human, is name your price.'

'What?'

'What is it you wish? Name anything. Simply stand aside. Nothing in the world of your age lies beyond my reach. Is it rulership you crave? I will carve out a continent-wide kingdom for you. Power? I will instruct you in mysteries entirely for-gotten by the practitioners of your age. Riches? The locations of hoards beyond your imagination are known to me. Immortality? I know arts that will inure your flesh against the passage of time. Stand aside and these or anything you desire can be yours. What do you say?'

Temper snorted his scorn. *Some things never change.* It was as if the old ogre himself stood before him, promising Moon's

Spawn itself. He remembered how the council of nobles of Quon Tali province fared after sealing a deal with Kellanved. They were rounded up and beheaded. And there was a timeless saying for deceit and betrayal: dealing with a Jaghut. He struck a ready stance, tensed his arms to warm them. 'You jammed back in your hole interests me.'

The Jaghut shook its head as if in pity. 'I can see you lack the imagination necessary to grasp the unparalleled opportunity before you. I am disappointed . . . but not surprised.' Temper expected a renewed onslaught after that rejection, yet Jhenna made no move towards him. Instead, she pointed her sword south again. 'Here comes another disappointment.'

Keeping a wary eye on Jhenna, Temper allowed himself one quick glimpse. Someone was slowly approaching up the slope of naked stone, someone wounded or crippled. Temper waited, weapons poised. Jhenna said conversationally, as if to be companionable: 'Have you yet begun to worry about the time here, human? How much of the night has passed? Or has any time passed at all? Has your limited imagination yet begun to fathom that prickly problem?'

In fact he hadn't, but he wasn't about to admit it to Jhenna. What was the fiend getting at? That she could keep him here – wherever here was – forever? Was that possible? Would he have to stand guard here for eternity? Temper reclasped his weapons through his tattered gauntlets. Frost, he saw, feathered the iron links of his sleeves.

Jhenna half-turned away. 'I have brought you to Omtose Phellack. It is the home of my kind. Our Warren, such as you call them. It is us and we are it. This night of Conjunction has allowed me at least this one small boon: to revisit my old home.' The helmed head faced Temper. 'More to the point for you, human, is that time as you know it does not pass here. I could keep you here for an age only to return an instant after we left.'

She shoved her weapons through the sash at her waist, then lifted her helm away and held it negligently. She regarded him through lambent eyes that glittered with inhuman emotion. Tusklike canines thrust up from its wide jaws, but other than this, Temper found her features almost human, simply over-sized: a cliff-like brow ridge, broad cheek bones, a wide sloped forehead. Her leonine mane was matted and greasy. Twists of gold thread and lengths of leather tied off a multitude of small braids – rat-tails, soldiers called them.

'Think more on my offer, human.' She crossed her long arms. 'We have the time.'

The world began to crumble for Temper. Was he doomed to face this monster for centuries? Surely, eventually, he would be defeated or driven insane. Curse Faro to D'rek's pits! He would know how to counter this tactic; why couldn't he have warned him? What was he to do? He was only a soldier. After what seemed its own eternity, Jhenna spoke to someone behind him. 'And what gifts do you bring, skulking wanderer?'

Temper shifted until he could keep both beings in sight at once. He was startled to find that the newcomer was the creature who had rescued him earlier this evening – Edgewalker. The desiccated creature cradled to its chest a long object wrapped in rags. Tendrils of vapour fumed from it.

Just outside the low wall Edgewalker stopped and tossed his burden inside. It rolled free of its rags. Fog burst forth like smoke from burning green leaves. It drifted away, revealing something like a rod that appeared carved from precious gem-stone: crystal shot through with veins of purple, bright blue, and startling verdant green. It foamed before their eyes, dissipating, leaving nothing.

'I bring sign of your failure, Jhenna. The Riders have been repulsed. No release will come from that avenue this Conjunction. The Shadow cultists have withdrawn. And further, I am here to deny you access to Shadow should you attempt that route, while this one blocks your main exit. Your options are falling away quickly. What will you do?'

The giant turned to regard Temper. 'Did you hear that, human? It is all down to you now. Only you stand in my way. Surely you must see the wisdom of accepting my offer. Is it not obvious that I will overcome you?'

Temper raised his swords; he didn't remember lowering them. He addressed Edgewalker: 'This one says she can keep me here forever. Is that true?'

The creature was motionless for a time, until it breathed, 'A half-truth. Yet what is time to you or me? Myself, I can wait. Time is nothing to me.'

Temper let out an angry snort. 'I can't wait. I can't stand here forever! What do you mean? Is it true or isn't it?'

'You are speaking with a Jaghut, human. The Conjunction is like an eclipse between Realms. Even here it passes as we speak. Jhenna's time is still limited.'

The Jaghut woman laughed her scorn. She pointed to the creature. 'There speaks self-interest, human. We are old enemies, he and I, and he knows that if you stand aside, then it is his role to be the next defender of the path. He will have to step into the gap and he dreads being destroyed. He is a coward who wishes to benefit from your sacrifice. Do not needlessly throw away your life. Let him stand where he should – in *your* place.'

Temper attempted to blow on his hands. He risked a glance at Edgewalker. 'Is that true?'

'Again, a Jaghut half-truth. It is true I am here to dispute Jhenna's freedom – to stand in her way as you do. But I would only deny her access to Shadow. All other paths would remain open. Including the way to your world.'

'Imposture!' Jhenna cried. 'Either he stands where you do or he does not! Don't let him get away with such equivocating.'

Temper hunched his shoulders. 'It's not for me to say.'

Jhenna stepped closer and Temper fought an urge to flinch away. He raised his weapons as high as he dared, though the woman had none ready – there were, after all, many kinds of weapons. 'You poor man. I am doing everything I can to spare your life but you are not cooperating.' Her eyes shone like golden lanterns and Temper winced. He fixed his gaze dead-centre on the Jaghut's torso, clenched his teeth and waited.

'Temper, is it?' Jhenna asked, then nodded at his flinch of recognition. 'Why of course! Temper of the Sword!' She spread her arms out wide. 'What a fool I've been. Who else could possibly stand against a Jaghut? But this is wonderful.'

Temper shivered beneath a sudden gust of cold air. He found he couldn't open his hands – they were frozen to the grips of his weapons. His feet were numb and his thoughts felt thick and slow. He blinked against the ice gathering over his lashes, managed, 'What do you mean?'

Jhenna lowered her voice to a whisper: 'I mean that it is wonderful because I know for a fact that Dassem Ultor yet lives.'

Temper jerked upright. '*What?*'

'Yes, it is true. He lives. And I can find him! Surely Fate itself conspired to bring the two of us together – you, his last and truest companion, and I, the one who can bring you to him.'

Grimacing against a cold that numbed his lips and made his teeth ache, Temper whispered, 'You're lying.'

'No. On this matter I need not shade the naked facts at all. He still lives.'

The Jaghut's head now hovered almost within arm's reach of Temper's and he felt a dull alarm.

'Is that not so, Tracer of Edges?' Jhenna called.

'I cannot say whether this man lives or not.'

'Ha! Cannot or will not? Note how spare this one is with his wisdom now, human.'

His thoughts crawled, gelid and viscous as if frozen themselves. Dassem alive? Truly? Why should he throw his life away now?

'My wisdom I limit to one last comment, mortal,' Edgewalker urged in its breathless, spare voice.

'What?' Temper snarled, annoyed by the thing's dry-rustling words.

''Ware the cold, human. 'Ware the ice that grips. The frost that silences.'

Temper heard, distantly, a growl from the Jaghut, followed by an explosion as if the barrier was under assault once more. His head was heavy and his chin had sunk to his breastbone. He opened his eyes to see that a sheath of ice now encased his legs up to his knees, and that his feet had disappeared within a block of jet-black ice that seemed to have grown like a crystal from cracks in the very bedrock itself.

Something within Temper shieked an ancient terror. A firestorm of energies burst to life over him. Instead of burning his flesh and sloughing the metal of his armour, it made his limbs sing, and he snapped his blades up to parry twin blows from Jhenna who bore down upon him relentlessly, her helm rolling on the stones behind. The ice at Temper's legs exploded into vapour that vanished in the crackling energies.

Jhenna roared as she swung again and again, seeking to drive Temper into the ground. But he held, strength flowing up from the rock to meet the naked might hammering against him. On they fought, and on, until the Jaghut lifted one blade to reach out to the curtain of energy. The aura snapped away as if snatched from existence and left a roll of thunder echoing over the hills in its wake. Jhenna stumbled, snarling and spitting, utterly devoid of reason, and Temper was appalled that he had half-listened to the frothing monster before him.

The landscape shimmered, the night sky brightening to a pale slate. From behind the Jaghut the mounds and trees reappeared, and the House frowned down once more on Temper.

Distracted, he was nearly decapitated by a lightning assault. A head swipe caught the top of his helmet. It bit at the iron and snapped his head back, dazzling him with sparks. Stunned, he managed to parry the most deadly thrusts, but he was slowing. The next hit shaved scales from his shoulder. He spasmed as a sweep gashed his right thigh. His defence was crumbling. Had he lasted long enough? Could such a short stand have made any difference at all?

Jhenna twisted away, parrying a hurled weapon: an axe. It struck her upper arm a glancing blow and she bellowed.

In that split-second Temper crouched and managed to gather himself. Jhenna flexed her arm but something else flew at her from over Temper's shoulder: white crackling energy that smashed into her breast-plate. The Jaghut retreated one step, spluttering hoarse curses. She came on again, inexorable like a force of nature. Such power awed Temper. Perhaps it would never tire. Already he was beyond exhaustion. He thought he heard yelling, muffled to his ears after the waterfall thunder of the barrier. The next attack came as an angry flurry, off-balanced and desperate. Temper sloughed the blows, his arms burning with the stabbing agony of fatigue. Shrieking her frustration to the sky, Jhenna drew back her arm to throw a sword, point-first.

Temper knew he was dead. Involuntarily he tensed and caught his breath. But the blade never touched him. Instead Jhenna tottered, then fell to her knees with a clashing of armour.

She sat motionless for a time, blades resting on the ground. 'I am finished, human,' she slurred. 'I have nothing left.' She chuckled, low and throaty. 'Now you will see how the House rewards the treachery of its servants.' Slowly roots gathered, twisting and worming from the soil. They coiled about the

261

Jaghut's legs. She strained against them but the tightening cords dragged her to her side. Fist-thick roots wrapped around her torso. As she was yanked ever deeper into the steaming earth, she offered Temper a mocking smile. 'Careful, human, or this too will be your fate.' The golden eyes held his as if to pull him along even as her head sank beneath the crumbling dirt. Her arms and hands slipped down last, still grasping the smoking swords.

Temper blinked away the sweat running into his eyes. He tried to swallow, but his mouth was stone dry. Sucking cool air into his lungs, he watched as the fog dispersed, revealing no trace of the mangled corpses, torn robes, or scattered weapons. The House stared at him blindly, and now its neighbouring buildings surrounded it again. He stood with fists numb around his sword-grips, gasping, his body twitching with exhaustion. A hand touched his shoulder and he jumped, staggering. He fell like a corpse, back against the low stone wall.

'It's dawn,' Corinn said, steadying him. 'We were trying to tell you . . .' Lubben stood behind her, covering her back as if expecting a last-minute Shadow cultist's attack.

'Dawn?' he croaked. He mouthed the word, uncomprehending. *Dawn*. Corinn fumbled to catch him as he slid onto ground glistening with the morning dew.

CHAPTER SIX

RESOLUTIONS

THE RICH SCENT OF STEWING BROTH TEASED THE TAG-END of Kiska's dreams. She smiled, stretched, then hissed as pain flared from almost every limb. Something touched her shoulder and she flinched awake. A pale, fat man yelped, jerking away.

'What do you want?' she demanded.

Smiling nervously, he pointed under her. 'My apron. You're lying on my apron.'

She recognized him: Coop, tavern-keeper of the Hanged Man Inn. She looked down and saw that she'd been sleeping on a bench cushioned by blankets, a tattered quilt and bundled clothing. 'Sorry.' She moved her arm and the man tugged his apron free.

'Told you she'd wake up,' someone observed from across the room.

Kiska realized she was wearing somebody else's clothes: a thick wool sweater of the kind she hated because it made her look like a child, and a long skirt of layered patched linen. She swung her legs down and rubbed at her eyes. She was in a private dwelling, ground level. Its door appeared to have been smashed from its hinges. Beyond, a sun-washed street lay empty. A boy with dirty bare feet scrubbed at dark stains on the wood floor while nearby a man sat at a table, his kinky black hair in his eyes, sopping up stew with a crust of bread. Coop backed away to the door, bowing his thanks for his apron.

'See you later, Coop,' the man called, waving the sodden crust.

Coop bowed again. Nervous laughter burst from him and he hurried out of the door.

Kiska tried to stand, hissed at the flame of pain from her knee and fell back to the bench. She limped to the table and grasped it to remain standing as her vision blurred and her heart raced. She squeezed her side. The pain there threatened to double her over.

The man jumped up and eased her into a chair. 'Have a care,' he warned – rather late, she thought.

She sat, wincing. 'Thanks. What's the matter with him?'

'Oh, when you arrived last night you gave him something of a fright. I understand you had a bit of a scare yourself.'

She laughed. 'Yes, I—'. She stopped herself, glared about. 'Where are they?'

'Who?'

'Tay – the men I came in with.' She jumped up, groaned as her side knotted. 'Are they gone?'

The man drew her down again with a touch of his hand. 'Relax. I've a message, and there's hot stew over the fireplace. Have some?'

'Who are you? Oh. You're the medicer aren't you? Yeah, I'll have some.'

'Seal's the name. Yours?'

'Kiska.' She plucked at her sweater. 'Why the clothes?'

'Ah, sorry.' Seal shrugged an apology. 'Best I could do. Your old clothes I had to burn.' He leaned to the black pot, ladled out a bowlful.

Burn? Kiska wondered. Did he really have to *burn* them?

'Well, Kiska. Speaking of frights, you gave me an ugly one last night.'

She took the bowl of steaming stew, tore off some bread and started stuffing it into her mouth. She hadn't realized how famished she was. Seal watched her eat, a smile tugging at his mouth. 'Where are they and how are they?' she demanded around a mouthful.

'We've got time – and they'll live. The one, a Seti tribesman I believe, I take especial credit for. The other, well . . . he pretty much took care of himself. I do take credit for you too, however.'

'Me?'

'Yes. Spraining and bruising of the bones of the knee. Sundry mundane cuts and contusions of the flesh. Worst: a bruised kidney and torn musculature. Possibly resulting from a serious impact or blow.'

Kiska grimaced, remembering that. She'd felt as if that table had cut her in half, but she'd run on anyway. Amazing what being scared out of one's wits can do. She swallowed, forced down the food against a rising tide of nausea. 'And?'

'And?'

'What's the message? Where are they?'

Seal sat up straighter. 'Ah! You ask what you should do about the various injuries you have inflicted upon your body? Well, I advise a hearty meal. And if you get sick tonight I suggest a regurgitant. Boiled alder leaves, I understand, works well for that. Also, I advise you take things easy for the next few weeks. Rest; no undue strain. Definitely no fighting or running. Understand?' Kiska stared at the man, noted his drawn face, the sunken eyes circled in shadow and the tremor of his hands at his bowl. He caught her gaze and waved languidly. 'Don't bother to thank me.'

The man was utterly wrecked. He had obviously drawn

upon his Denul Warren to the utmost to accomplish what was needed last night. She suspected she owed him much more than he'd suggested. Pushing the stew around the bowl for a moment, she cleared her throat. 'So, is there really a message or not?'

'Oh, yes,' and he smiled secretly, pleased with himself.

'And? That is?'

He raised a finger. 'Ah! Treatment first. Finish your meal.'

The boy came to her elbow and handed her a ladle of water. Distracted, Kiska took it and swallowed. The water was sweet, fresh and cool, straight from an inland well. She thanked him. He stared at her with big brown eyes full of curiosity.

'That's all, Jonat,' Seal said. The boy returned to his scrubbing. 'My son, Jonat,' he told Kiska.

She nodded, then remembered herself and glared. Stuffing down more of the bread, she said through her mouthful, 'I think I know what the message is.'

Seal smiled simply, watching her eat. 'You were quite a mess last night. You don't remember?'

'No, I don't. I think the message is that they are down at the wharf.'

Seal started, his eyes widening. Then he coughed and laughed at the same time, thumped a fist to his chest and rocked in his chair.

Kiska was already on her feet. She gave him her own smug smile and he waved her away with the back of his hand. 'Well done,' he managed, 'Very well done indeed.'

She limped out onto the Way of the Eel.

The residents of Malaz greeted the dawn like stunned survivors of a typhoon and earthquake combined. Faces peered out at the morning from behind storm-shutters and doors opened barely a crack. Though the sun already shone halfway to midday, and only thin clouds marred the sky's perfect bowl, most of the inhabitants seemed unconvinced that last night's nightmare had come to an end.

Walking down the streets, Kiska found faces spying on her, wary. She realized what a sight she must present, in her oversized sweater and long skirts gathered up in one hand. Seal seemed to have selected the worst mish-mash of garments he could possibly find. Still, she figured she ought to be thankful the man had a few women's things around his place.

At first the stares bothered her. Then she elected not to give a damn. As she met knots of suspicious citizenry – usually huddled near a site of wreckage, or a suspiciously stained circle of cobbles, whispering, comparing stories – she just walked on, or hobbled actually, teeth clenched, cradling her side. They'd stop their whispers to gape openly, then, as she'd passed, start up again. At least they didn't point, she told herself.

Soon she was down at the sea-walk and could see movement on the message cutter's deck and gangway. Figures came and went, stowing gear and supplies. She limped down the stairs to the wharf.

At the dock she recognized most of the workers as local stevedores. A few men on board looked like sailing-hands, inspecting the rigging and handling the dunnage. Hattar, his arm wrapped in white cloth secured across his chest, sat on the roof of the mid-ship quarters, examining himself in a mirror of polished silver balanced on coiled rope. His head shone flushed, as if freshly shaved, and half his face glowed even pinker, blistered and gleaming under a greasy unguent. Beside him sat a bucket and his chin was wet with soap. The idiot was trying to shave himself one-handed.

'Hoy, message cutter!' Kiska called from the dock.

Hattar looked over without a word or nod hello. He banged his fist on the roof, then returned to studying his chin by twisting his mouth side to side; lips that looked strange to Kiska until she realized the man's moustache was gone – he'd lost

267

half of it last night and had now made a clean sweep of it.

After a moment Tayschrenn stepped up from the companionway. He was dressed in loose trousers and a long tunic of deepest cyan. His queue was pulled back, freshly oiled. He looked as if he'd slept a full night on a feather mattress.

'Greetings,' he called up.

'You're leaving.'

'Yes. Soon.'

Kiska nodded – stupidly, she thought. She wet her lips with the tip of her tongue. This was really it. Opportunity about to set sail. Could she let it slip by? 'Take me with you,' she blurted, relieved and terrified by having finally asked what she had been meaning to ask all night.

Tayschrenn stroked a forefinger over his lips. 'Really? Are you formally offering your service?' Kiska gave a tense nod. 'Well, you'll have to talk to my chief of staff here.' He swept an arm to Hattar.

Kiska deflated. She knew Agayla always stressed that she should disguise her emotions, but she couldn't help herself from glancing skyward and allowing her shoulders to fall. She prayed he was leading her on, but dared not risk the challenge. She was sure that if she jumped down onto the ship Hattar would simply toss her overboard – one arm or not.

'What say you, Hattar?' Tayschrenn asked.

The tribesman continued to inspect his chin. 'She has potential,' he allowed. 'But little discipline.'

'Discipline!' Kiska shouted in disbelief.

Hattar froze, his knife held next to his throat. He stared, and even from the dock Kiska felt the icy disapproval of that glare. She swallowed, nodding her apology. 'As I said. Very little discipline.'

'Perhaps schooling,' Tayschrenn suggested. 'Training might sort that out.'

Hattar frowned. 'Perhaps.' He nodded. 'Yes. Perhaps after a few years she might—'

'A few years!'

Hattar jumped up and snapped his arm in a throw. The knife quivered, imbedded in the wood of the dock just before Kiska's feet. 'Perhaps in a few years she'll learn not to interrupt!'

Kiska grimaced. Her damned big mouth! Her impatience! She wanted to apologize, to explain that it was just that this was so important to her. But this time she restrained herself. One more outburst and they'd probably send her packing. She knelt, pulled the knife free and tossed it back to Hattar. He caught it, smiled at the throw. 'Good.' He returned to shaving, glowering at himself in the mirror. She wanted to laugh: he'd probably never seen himself without a moustache. Tayschrenn half-bowed, retreated back inside the cabin.

Kiska leaned against a barrel to cradle her side while the dockhands came and went on the gangway carrying on kegs of water and supplies. She stared at Hattar. Was that a yes or a no? What *was* the decision? More silent treatment? Should she speak? 'Well?'

Hattar glanced up. 'Hmm?'

'Well? What's your answer? I've offered my service. Do you accept?'

Hattar eyed the mirror, scraped the blade over his chin. 'We leave in two bells. With or without you.' He held up the knife. 'Understand?'

'Yes! Oh, yes!' She started up the dock then stopped to point back as if to prevent them from leaving that instant. 'Yes. I'll be here. Absolutely. Thank you. You'll see!' Kiska ran halfway up the steps before a cramp at her side took her breath away and left her gasping, hanging onto the chiselled embrasure to stop from tumbling back down. Slowly girl, she told herself. Don't faint now. Steady. She'd see Agayla first, then head home and break the news to her mother. She'd be glad, wouldn't she?

Yes, she would. Agayla would support her. And she'd send word back. As soon as she could.

She walked the rising slope of Coral Way, the sun warming her neck and cheek. It drained the tension from her, eased the ache of her muscles and the burn of her cuts. She felt more relaxed, more comfortable than she could ever remember. Did this delicious sensation come from the knowledge that very shortly she would be giving her back to the island – perhaps never to return? Kiska savoured the thought.

She brushed past people who dazedly wandered the streets to stare at wreckage left by the battle, at broken windows and smashed shop fronts. They seemed to study each other as if searching for some reassurance, in the face of such proof, that the night had been nothing more than a foolish nightmare.

Kiska found Reach Lane unnaturally deserted. Any other day of the year would have seen it choked with vendors at carts, squatting on outstretched mats or standing with their wares overflowing baskets. Even the mongrel dogs that should have been running underfoot were nowhere to be seen. Terrified by the lingering scents, Kiska supposed. She banged on Agayla's door. The garlands of dried flowers hung limp; their musky pungency surprised Kiska. 'Auntie! Hello! Are you there?'

While Kiska waited an old woman pushed a cart of sweet-breads up the street. This she manoeuvred against one wall, then took her pipe from her mouth to nod.

'Morning,' Kiska responded.

'Thank Burn and the Blessed Lady for it!'

'Yes. Thank them.'

Breathing out smoke she announced, 'I was nearly eaten by one of those fiends.'

'Were you?'

'Oh, yes. But I prayed to Hood himself all night and the demons passed me by.'

'Hood?' Kiska echoed, startled.

'Oh, yes. Hood, I prayed. Ol' Bone-Rattler. Please pass over my poor, thin, worn-out soul. Take my neighbour instead. And sure enough – he took my neighbour.' The old woman cackled and winked.

Kiska laughed uneasily. Oponn deliver her from this crazy island! She banged again on the door while the old woman shooed flies from her sweetbreads. 'Agayla! Open up! It's me, Kiska.' Silence. She pushed on the heavy plank door and it swung open. Surprised, she gazed for a time into the dark shop. Leaning in, she called, 'Agayla?'

'Go on in, lass,' the old woman urged from across the way. 'No one enters there that she don't wish to. Go on.'

Kiska stepped in and closed the door. Just to be careful, she barred it as well. 'Auntie?' No one answered. She edged in between the shelves. In the rear, she found Agayla sitting before a stool, head bowed under a towel. '*Auntie?*'

Agayla raised the towel, peered up blearily. 'Oh, hello, child.'

'Auntie, what are you doing?'

Agayla sat back, pressed the towel to her face. A bowl of water on the stool sent up whisps of aromatic steam. 'I've caught a terrible cold.'

'Oh. Are you all right?'

'Yes, yes. Just tired. Very, very tired.' She raised a hand to Kiska. 'What of you? Safe and sound I see.'

Kiska pulled a chair next to her. 'Yes. Auntie, the most amazing thing has happened. This is the best day of my life—'

'You're leaving Malaz.'

'*Auntie!* How did you know?'

'Only that could possibly make you so happy.'

Kiska gripped her arm. 'Oh, Auntie. It's not that I *want* to leave you. It's just that I have to get off this island. You understand that, don't you?'

She covered Kiska's hand, smiled faintly. 'Yes, child. I under-stand.' Then a coughing fit took her and she held the towel to her mouth.

Kiska watched anxiously; in all the time she had known her, never had she betrayed the slightest illness before. 'You *are* all right, aren't you?'

'Yes, yes. Quite. It's just been a very trying night for me. One of the most trying I have ever known.'

Kiska eyed her critically. 'I thought I saw you—'

'Just a dream, child. A vision on a night of visions.'

'Still, there *was* something . . .'

The same ghost of a smile raised Agayla's lips. 'Mere shadows.'

Kiska didn't believe her, but time was passing. She stood. 'I have to go – I can't wait.'

Agayla used the chair to help herself to her feet. Kiska steadied her arm. 'Yes, yes,' she urged. 'Certainly. Go. Run to your dear mother's. Let her know you're fine.'

'Yes, I will. Thank you, Auntie. Thank you for everything.'

Agayla took her in her arms and hugged her, kissed her brow. 'Send word soon or I swear I will send you a curse.'

'I will.'

'Good. Now run. Don't keep Artan waiting.'

Kiska was halfway down Reach Lane before the thought occurred to her: how on earth did Agayla know that name? She stopped, half a mind to turn around. But time was press-ing and she had a suspicion that saying goodbye to her mother would take much longer than she thought it might.

Though his vision swam and he had to rest at every landing to stave off passing out, Temper climbed Rampart Way up to the Hold. It was madness for him to be about and walking, but there was no way he would miss the morning's excitement at the keep. A crowd already choked the main entrance –

272

tradesmen and citizens in a panic with pleas and complaints for Sub-Fist Pell. Wearing a thick cloak taken from the Hanged Man, Temper bulled his way through. He found Lubben snoring in a chair tilted back against the damp wall, his chest wrapped in dressings under his unlaced jerkin.

'Wake up, you lazy disgrace!'

The hunchback cracked open his eye. Temper was amazed by how red it was. Lubben looked him up and down. He smacked his lips and grimaced at the taste. 'What in Hood's own burial pit are you doing here?'

'Got the day watch.'

'The what? The *day watch*? Gods man, give it a rest! You make me feel old just looking at you. Go on sick call.'

'What, and miss all the entertainment?'

Lubben rolled his eye. 'Well, if you must . . .' he raised a pewter flask to Temper. 'A little fortification for the trial ahead.'

Temper tucked the flask under his shirt. 'Thanks. See you later.'

Lubben shifted his seat, hissed in pain as he flexed his back. 'I suppose so. Can't be helped.'

Before he even got to the barracks Temper was challenged four times. In the Hold there was more general rushing about, more whispering and pale faces than ever before. He chuckled about that as he carefully drew on his hauberk and guard uniform. He might have laughed, but he gritted his teeth as he flexed his stiff arms and stretched his battered back. Guards hurried in and out and Temper was pleased to see most of them alive and well, though none were up to the usual banter. The one face he didn't see was that braggart, Larkin's.

Temper stopped Wess, a young recruit from the plains south of Li Heng. 'Where's Larkin?'

The youth stared, his eyes wide with awe. 'Haven't you heard?'

Temper's stomach tightened. 'Heard what?'

'He's under arrest. Refused to stand his post last night. Defied orders.' Temper's burst of laughter caused Wess to jump. He gaped. 'It's a serious charge.' Temper waved him past. The youth spared him one last quizzical glance before running on.

Chuckling, Temper picked up his spear outside the barracks and headed for the inner stairs. He felt in a better mood than he'd known in a long time. Chase stood at the battlements. Temper never thought he'd be happy to see the green officer, but this morning he was. For once the Claws had kept things entirely to themselves and ignored the local garrison.

Chase turned to him. 'You're late, soldier.' He sounded more distracted than irritated.

'Had a bit of a wrestle with a bottle last night. I lost.' Temper leaned his elbows on a crenel.

'Why am I not surprised?' Chase sneered.

'So,' Temper began, waving down to the inner bailey and the men rushing in and out, 'what's all the commotion?'

'You mean you don't know?'

'No,' Temper drawled, 'can't say as I'm sure.'

'Hood's bones, man! And you're a guard here!' Chase choked back his outrage. He seemed unable to comprehend Temper's lack of concern. He almost walked away, dismissing him as an utter lost cause, but sighed instead. 'While you were blind drunk last night there was an assassination attempt on the visiting official.' He leaned close to lower his voice. 'The fighting was real quick and ugly, so I hear.'

'So you hear? You mean the garrison wasn't roused?'

Chase cleared his throat, uncomfortable. He looked away. 'No. Everything happened upstairs, inside the tower. We didn't hear a sound.'

Temper hid a smile. The fellow was actually disappointed. He scratched his chin. 'What about the night watch?'

Chase stepped up beside him, all disgust and disapproval forgotten. 'That's the thing! I heard it's come out that the entire night watch saw nothing! So there you are.'

Temper blinked, 'Sorry—?'

'The Warrens,' he whispered, confidingly. 'We didn't have a chance.'

'Ahh.' Temper nodded his understanding. 'How unfair of them, hey?'

Chase jerked away. His hazel eyes flashed anger. 'There you go again! Taking the high ground. Always mocking. Well, it's just chance, you know. The Twins of Chance and age. You've just had more luck. So I say to Hood with you! Where were you when the cats caught fire here, eh? You had your nose trapped in a bottle! And you look like you got into a drunken brawl, too!'

He marched off and Temper watched him go. He wasn't sure what to make of all that so he chuckled softly to himself. Ahh, youth! So sure, yet so uncertain. He rested more of his weight onto the crenel, leaned his head against the limestone merlon. He felt as if he'd been dragged by horses across broken rock, which, he reflected, wasn't too far from the truth. But he couldn't keep a satisfied grin from his lips; he'd done it again – stepped into the gap. Held the wall.

All last year he'd done nothing but run. And the suspicion had haunted him: did he still have what it took? Could he still make a stand anymore? Or more importantly, was there anything left worth fighting for? Well, now he knew and felt more comfortable for the knowing. More at ease with himself. He even felt a measure of gratitude for all that had happened.

Corinn especially. He couldn't have done it without her. He'd have to tell her that tonight, and ask if she was leaving now that what she'd come for was over. Maybe he could even tell her that he hoped she wouldn't go, because he suspected he'd be spending a long time on the island. A long while to come at Coop's Hanged Man Inn.

He rubbed his shoulder and flexed his leg, all the time grimacing. At least he was in no danger of falling asleep, what with half his body yammering its pain at him. Down the wall, Mock's Vane stood silent on its pike. Temper eyed it – the damn thing appeared frozen athwart the wind. He turned away from the day's glare to ease into what always got him through the day: watching the sea.

Down below, the bay glimmered calmly. The Strait seemed to be holding its breath. In the shimmering distance a few warships were passing. Closer in, anchored in the bay, merchant caravels and barks rocked gently in the harbour's lee. The message cutter caught Temper's eye. Sails up, it was on its way out of the bay with good speed – even in this relative calm. He'd seen it arrive just before dusk yesterday, and now today towards the noon bell it was again on its way. Message delivered, Temper supposed.

What a night to have lain over! Idly, he speculated on the co-incidence. Could that be Surly or another, on their way back to Unta or beyond? Probably not. Too mundane. Surly and the others would have left already by way of the Warrens. In either case, he bid them all a warm farewell and added the heartfelt wish that none should ever again set foot on the island.

He tossed back a swig from the flask to salute the thought.

EPILOGUE

AT HIS CRIPPLE'S PACE EDGEWALKER STRUGGLED ACROSS THE chamber of slanted walls dark as vitrified night. He followed a path smeared through a finger-bone's thickness of otherwise undisturbed dust. The trail ended at two prone men, motionless as the dust itself. He paused, stared down at them for the longest time as if searching for signs of life.

'What in the Word of the Nameless Ones do you want?' croaked one.

Edgewalker inclined his head in a shallow bow. 'Greetings and welcome, Lord, to Shadow House.'

The one who had spoken sat up. Aside, as if to a third party, he offered the tired flick of two fingers of his left hand. Edgewalker turned to his rear where a twin to the other man now stood with barred blades. As he shifted to study the shape on the floor, it shimmered from sight.

The sitting one giggled. 'My apologies. Old habits. You are?'

'Edgewalker.'

The man nodded thoughtfully. 'Ah yes. I recall the name. You are mentioned . . . here and there.'

The man raised an arm. 'Help me up . . . ah, that is . . . Cotillion.'

The weapons in Cotillion's hands disappeared and Edgewalker saw that in fact they had not been true weapons at all but the shadows of weapons, and that from now on these two might create whatever they wished from the raw stuff at their disposal.

Standing, the man hardly reached Edgwalker's breast. Hunched and grizzled, he gave the appearance of an old man, yet his movements betrayed no hesitancy. He glanced about at the slanted angular dimensions of the chamber and grimaced his distaste. 'No,' he decided. 'Not to my liking at all.' He waved and the chamber blurred, shifting. Edgewalker now found himself standing in a keep's main hall. Stone flags lay beneath his bare feet and a stone hearth flamed at one wall. Above, blackened timbers spanned the darkness. The man cast a sharp eye right and left then nodded, pleased with himself. 'That will do. For the nonce. Now, Cotillion, care to make a turn about the Realm?'

'What of this one?'

'Ah. Edgewalker. You may be our guide.'

'I think not.'

The old man paused, blinking. 'I'm sorry. You said . . . ?'

'I do not take your orders.'

A walking stick poked Edgewalker at his chest. He could not quite recall exactly when it appeared in the old man's hand. 'Perhaps I should summon the Hounds to tear you limb from limb.'

'They would not do so.'

'Truly? Why?'

'Because we are all kin. Slaves to Shadow.'

The old man peered closely at him, raised his brows. 'Ah, I see. You have been taken by Shadow. You are a slave to the House. Very well. I shall allow you your small impertinences.

But remember, while you are slave to Shadow, I *command* Shadow. Remember that.'

Edgewalker said nothing.

The old man leant both his hands on the silver hound's head of his walking stick. He and his companion Cotillion faded from view, like proverbial shadows under gathering moonlight, until they disappeared, eventually, from sight.

Edgewalker turned and limped from the House. Out upon the open plain he struck a direction towards the featureless horizon. Dust-devils dogged his heels. How many times, he wondered, had he heard that very same conceit from a claimant to the Throne? Would they never learn? How long, he wondered, would this one last? Why was it none of the long chain of hopefuls ever bothered to ask why the Throne should be empty in the first place? After all, perhaps there was a reason.

Still, this one's residence should bode new and interesting times for Shadow. He should be thankful to these men, for in the end the one thing their presence might bring to the enduring eternity of the Realm was the potential for change and thus, the continuing possibility of . . . *progression.*

The strange thing looked like nothing the boy or his sister had ever seen or heard of before. Out crabbing during the evening low tide they came across it wedged between limpet-encrusted rocks, half buried in sand. Against his sister's silent urgings to move away, the boy used a stick to prod the pale shape.

'It's a man drowned,' whispered the girl, hushed.

'No,' the boy answered, scornful of his sister's knowledge of fishing, or anything else for that matter. 'It's scaled. It's a fish.'

The girl peered down to where her brother knelt, and the pale shadowed length at his feet. Its glimmer in the fading light reminded her of the glow she sometimes saw at night along the edge of waves. To tease her brother, she asked, 'Oh? What kind of a fish is it then?'

The boy's face puckered with vexation at the silliness of girls' questions. 'I don't know. A big one. It sure stinks like a fish.'

The smell was undeniable. Yet the girl remained uneasy. She thought she saw the glint of an eye, watching them from behind a tangle of seaweed at one end of the body. Hoping to scare her younger brother away from the thing, she whispered, 'It's a corpse. A drowned man. Come away or his ghost will haunt you.'

The boy glared back. 'I'm not afraid.'

The girl did not answer, for behind her brother the pale shape moved. An arm, lustrous in the dark, slipped from under it. The seaweed fell back from a face of angular, knife-like lines holding molten golden eyes.

The girl screamed. The boy shrieked as a cold hand clasped his ankle. Both screamed into the empty twilight while the thing's mouth moved, its message obliterated beneath their combined cries. Then the thing released the boy's ankle.

Sobbing, the boy scrambled away on all fours, his sister tugging upon his tunic, urging him on, as if he were yet held back. Behind them the shape collapsed among the shadows of the rocks.

After sunset a single torch approached the rocks. The incoming tide slapped and splashed among their black, glistening teeth. Torch held high, an old man eased his way through the pools and gaps. His long hair and beard shone white, whipped in the contrary winds. At the shore, a glowing lantern revealed brother and sister, hands clasped together.

Methodically, the old man advanced. He swept the torch before him, down into crevasses between boulders and low over the rising water. He turned back to the children and called, 'Here?'

'Farther out,' the girl answered in a near gasp.

The old man drew a knife from his belt. Its blade was thin,

honed down to a sickle moon. He exchanged torch and knife from hand to hand, then edged farther into the tide. Standing waist-deep in the frigid water he decided that he had gone out quite far enough. He would step up onto the last remaining tall rocks standing like a bastion before the waves, then return to tell his grandchildren that the ghost had fled back to its salty rest.

Sister and brother watched their grandfather pull himself awkwardly up the very tall rocks amid the spray of the gathering tide, then disappear down into their recesses. They waited, silent, neither daring to speak. It seemed to the girl that her grandfather had been gone a very long time when her brother cleared his throat and whispered haltingly, 'Do you think it got him?'

'Shush! Of course not,' the girl soothed. But she wondered, *had it*? And if it had, what would they do? Where could they go? The town? Pyre was a day's walk away. And besides, what help would come from there?

The girl was brought back to herself by her brother's hissed intake of breath, his chill damp hand tightening on her own. She looked up to see the ghost lowering itself down from the boulders. But it was not a haunt because it carried a torch and no ghost would carry one of those, no matter how potent a shade it might be. Watching her grandfather gingerly feel his way from rock to rock, a new, disturbing thought occurred to her: even though their grandfather was safely returned, how could she ever be sure the ghost hadn't got him? For haunts, she had heard from many, were notoriously slippery things, and who could say what had happened out there in the darkness, hidden among the rocks and foam and sea?

When her grandfather stepped up out of the surf, smiling, he teased her brother. The spirit, he said, was long gone back to his home in the sea. The girl knew he was lying. The ghost *had* got him. She saw it in his eyes – something new that had not been there when he left them. Her brother was too young to see. It was there and did not go away even as he told them that sea-spirits might visit the shore from time to time, but that they all must return to the deeps, just as this one had. She nodded but was not fooled. She would keep a close eye on him.

Walking home the old man took no notice of his grandson's tight grasp of his hand, or of his granddaughter's thoughtful face as she trailed behind with the lantern. He saw instead the churning amber eyes of the man from the sea with hair like weeds – the Stormrider. The Rider had spoken to him and to his amazement he had understood. It had spoken a halting Korelan, the language of the isles south of the Cut where the Riders and Korel inhabitants continually warred over the Stormwall – the human-raised barricade that stands between land and sea. His own grandfather had claimed the family had come out of Korel ages ago, and had taught him bits and pieces of the tongue when he'd been a lad, enough to understand the Rider's own crude mouthing of it. It made sense to him that the Riders should simply assume that Korelan was the human tongue.

Lying half-dead in the foam the Rider had asked a question – a single simple question that triggered an avalanche of inquiry in the old man's thoughts.

'Why are you killing us?' the Rider asked, and he had stared, thinking the alien must not understand what he was asking. Us killing *them*? *They* were the demons that cracked ships open and sent men to their doom. But three more times the Rider asked before he'd managed to steel himself sufficiently to reach down close enough to draw his blade across its throat. He would never forget his surprise as the Rider's blood gushed warm and red over his hand.

GLOSSARY

Titles and Groups

First Sword of the Empire: Malazan and T'lan Imass, a title denoting an Imperial Champion

The Sword: self-named bodyguard to Dassem Ultor, First Sword of the Empire

Fist: a military governor of the Malazan Empire

High Fist: a commader of armies within the Malazan Empire

T'lan Imass: ancient, undead army commanded by the Emperor

The Bridgeburners: a legendary elite division of the Malazan 2nd Army

The Crimson Guard: a famous mercenary company opposed to the Malazan Empire

The Claw: the covert organization of the Malazan Empire

The Talon: rumoured Imperial covert organization predating the Claw.

Shadow Cult: worshippers of the Shadow Realm

Peoples and Places

Stormriders, 'Riders': nonhuman inhabitants of Seas of Storms

Sea of Storms: an ocean strait between Malaz Island and the

Korel subcontinent, inhabited by the Stormriders
Y'Ghatan: an ancient city of the Seven City region
Korel: one name for an archipelago and subcontinent south of Quon Tali. Also known as 'Fist'.
Mock's Hold: an old fort overlooking Malaz city
Shadow Hounds: guardians of the Shadow Realm

Sorcery

The Warrens: (Other realms/worlds from which mages draw their power)
Denul: The Path of Healing
D'riss: The Path of the Earth
Hood's Path: The Path of Death
Meanas: The Path of Shadow and illusion
Ruse: The Path of the Sea
Rashan: The Path of Darkness
Serc: The Path of the Sky
Shadow: The Path of Shadow
Thyr: The Path of Light
Telas: The Path of Fire

The Elder Warrens
Kurald Galain: The Elder Warren of Darkness
Kurald Emurlahn: The Elder Warren of Shadow
Omtose Phellack: The Elder Jaghut Warren of Ice

IAN CAMERON ESSLEMONT grew up in Winnipeg, Manitoba. He has studied archaeology and creative writing, has traveled extensively in Southeast Asia, and lived in Thailand and Japan for several years. He now lives in Alaska with his wife and children and is currently working on another novel set in the world of Malaz, a world he cocreated with his friend Steven Erikson.